THE SECOND REVOLUTION

GARY HANSEN

HOLESHOT PRESS.COM

GARY HANSEN

HOLE SHOT PRESS

This book is an original publication of Hole Shot Press holeshotpress.com

www.holeshotpress.com

ISBN: 09793521-1-8
ISBN-13: 978-0-9793521-1-9

To the most dedicated and hard-working salesperson an author could ever have, my mother, Joan Hansen

CHAPTER 1

Jake McKinley jerked awake to the sound of shattering glass. The only light in the pitch-black room came from his digital clock. He forced his eyes to focus on the time— 2:26 a.m. He heard more glass breaking, as if pieces of a broken window were hitting the floor. Jake's chest constricted and he sat up, wide-awake. The noise came from the back of the house—the kitchen or the back porch. Someone was trying to break into his house!

He cursed to himself for procrastinating buying a handgun since moving to Pittsburgh after the divorce. He gritted his teeth in frustration and forced himself to think. His eyes scanned the dark bedroom, seeing nothing. What could he use for a weapon? If only he had a baseball bat or a shovel. He pictured himself bringing an aluminum bat down on an assailant's head. But he didn't have a bat, and the shovel was out back.

He heard steps. Someone was inside! Slowly and quietly, he edged off the mattress, wearing only his boxers. He gingerly put weight on his bare feet, trying not to make a noise. He knelt down then lay flat on the floor and reached under the bed. There had to be something he could use to defend himself. He swept his hands underneath. Whatever was under there, it had been there since the move. His fingers brushed against a few dusty cardboard boxes then some blankets. His heart raced. He moved to the other side, crawling over shoes and clothes. For the first time in his life, Jake regretted not taking up golf. He swept again. More boxes.

Another noise. Kitchen? It sounded like a cabinet door or maybe a drawer. Jake lay still and listened. He could hear his heart pounding. He felt the floor tremor as someone approached the living room from the kitchen. The intruder could be in his bedroom any second. Jake swept his hand frantically under the bed again, up closer to the headboard. His hand found something—a rubber handle. His heart sank when he realized it was only a badminton racquet, practically worthless. He grabbed it anyway—it was all he had.

He backed out from under the bed and stood. He swung the racquet and realized he could at least surprise the guy with it if he hit him in the face. But it would collapse on a good hit. Why couldn't it have been a tennis racket?

He heard a loud sound. Someone had banged into something—probably the kitchen table. Was he back in the kitchen? He could have sworn he'd heard the guy in the living room. Jake tiptoed to his bedroom door. He put his ear against it, listening. He felt, more than heard, someone moving through the house. His heart was pounding.

What did the guy want? If he was looking for a jackpot, he had broken into the wrong house. Jake had nothing of value. Maybe a hundred bucks in cash. Probably less. Valuables? He was thirty-three years old, but he had very few possessions, not since the divorce. Tools? They were mostly in his truck—the one thing of value Jake couldn't afford to replace right now. Hopefully it was just a bum, looking for food.

He wiped his forehead and realized he was sweating. His mind went through the options: confront him, wait, hide. He thought about crawling back under the bed. He remembered all the boxes and wondered if he could fit under there. An image popped into his mind of a couple guys pulling him out by his legs, or worse, shooting him like a defenseless dog. He cringed and decided he would not hide under the bed.

Something occurred to him. The intruder was probably nervous too. Maybe he was hurrying and as panicked as Jake. If only Jake had a pump shotgun. Just the sound of someone chambering a round had to be one of the most intimidating sounds in the world. That would make the guy wet himself and send him diving out the window and running down the street.

In that moment Jake made his decision. He swallowed and wetted his lips and positioned himself behind the bedroom door, clutching the racket, waiting for the right moment. He took two deep breaths.

Jake jerked the door open and let it smash loudly against the wall. He yelled, "Another step and I blow your head off! Get the hell out of my house or you're dead!"

Jake saw the guy in the kitchen with a flashlight. He cast a shadowy silhouette as his body masked the flashlight he was aiming in the drawers. At Jake's voice, the flashlight jerked around and aimed directly into Jake's eyes, blinding him. Jake squinted at the bright light and tried to shield his eyes. He realized immediately the whole plan to scare the intruder had been a stupid idea. The guy could obviously see Jake had only a badminton racket and no gun. Jake was screwed.

Then Jake was hit hard from the other side. There were two of them! Jake was thrown to the ground. He tried to roll away from the man on top of him, aware of the first guy with the flashlight running toward them to help his partner. The attacker clenched his hands around Jake's throat. Jake bucked and grabbed the guy's hands, trying to pry them off. The man released Jake's neck, but used his hands to ram Jake's head to the floor. An explosion went off in Jake's head. All the energy went out of him. He felt nauseous, and his vision went foggy. One of the man's hands released his head. He tried to take advantage, to roll, but his attempt was feeble. His body wasn't following directions anymore. Time seemed to have slowed down. The man was reaching for something. Then Jake felt the cold steel of a barrel pressed to his ear.

"I got him!" the guy yelled.

Jake rolled helplessly onto his side. The gun barrel moved so that it was pointing at his forehead.

The guy with the flashlight approached and shined it directly in Jake's eyes. "Did ya kill him?"

"No, he's not dead."

Jake felt like throwing up. He smelled alcohol and cigarettes on the guy's breath. His head throbbed. He tried to focus, but the light was blinding him.

"Has he got any money on him?"

"No. He's in his underwear." He pointed in Jake's bedroom. "Look around in there. That's where he was sleeping. Find his wallet."

The guy with the flashlight left. But Jake still had a light in his eyes. He realized the guy who'd tackled him, and hit him on the head, wore a headlamp. Jake was aware of his bedroom light coming on and drawers slamming. Jake wanted to fight, but his head was rolling and he had no strength.

The guy's alcohol breath was strong as he bent down by Jake. "How much cash you got in the house?"

Jake couldn't remember how much was in his wallet. He had just hit the ATM a couple days ago. He usually got a hundred, but he had spent some.

"I got his wallet, but it's only got forty bucks." The guy called from the bedroom.

"See what else you can find!"

"I already looked around. This guy's got nothing."

Jake registered the comment. They were right; he had nothing. He felt the gun pressed harder to his forehead.

"What else you got in this place? How about jewels or watches?"

Jake almost laughed. His ex-wife had cleaned him out in the divorce. He had brought everything he owned to Pittsburgh in his pickup.

Jake slurred his response, "You picked the wrong house."

"Look in that other room." The man holding him called out.

Jake realized they were talking about the other bedroom. His business computer was in there on a desk. It was old and not worth much. He used it to pay the bills. But it had all his information on it. He couldn't afford to lose that. Jake groaned inwardly.

"There's a laptop," the guy called.

"Take it!"

Jake pushed up hard, trying to shove the guy off, but the move was feeble and accomplished nothing.

The guy holding Jake laughed mockingly. "You got a gun to your head, bozo. You trying to get shot?"

Jake's head throbbed worse after the exertion. He could smell body odor now and almost retched at the smell of the man.

He felt the barrel pressed even harder into his forehead. Jake was fairly sure the guy would pull the trigger now, and he wasn't all that upset about it. Who cared at this point? He just wished he had a gun of his own and could kill this scumbag before he died.

The guy with the flashlight came out of the second bedroom. He had Jake's laptop under his arm. Jake's financial records were on it, along with all his contacts and all his pictures.

4

"Are we ready? What are you gonna to do with him? You're not gonna kill him, are you?"

"What da ya think? Should I kill ya?" the guy mocked.

Jake looked up, but saw only the blinding light in his eyes. He felt the barrel removed from his forehead, and then before he could react, the gun was swinging at his head again.

* * *

Jake awoke to the worst headache he had ever had. It radiated out from the left side of his head. At first he thought he was blind, but then he saw the green glow from the microwave in the kitchen and realized he was lying on the floor in the darkness. He remembered the attack and listened to see if the thieves were still around. But the house was empty. They were gone.

He crawled, too dizzy to stand, into his bedroom. He felt around on his dresser for his cell phone. He couldn't find it. They had probably taken that too. He bumped something small on the floor just below the dresser with his knee and found the phone with his hand. It took a minute to focus enough to pull it off, but then Jake McKinley dialed 911 for the first time in his life.

CHAPTER 2

While waiting for the police to arrive, Jake pulled on some Levi's and a black Steelers T-shirt. He took some Advil for the pain and made an icepack for his head. By the time the Pittsburgh police department arrived, Jake's head had cleared.

Jake was now sitting on the couch and holding the ice pack on the left side of his head. The cop, who'd introduced himself as Officer Sampson, sat in a folding chair across from him. Jake guessed he was over fifty. He had a whitewalls haircut, and he wore a black uniform with a belt loaded with gadgets. Jake recognized a gun, some handcuffs, a club, a square thing that might be a taser, a radio, and other stuff Jake could not identify. He wondered how cops could sit with all that crap on their belts.

He was about the same size as Jake: six feet and about two hundred pounds. But the policeman seemed bigger. He had an authoritative aura. He kept shooting questions at Jake.

"How come you didn't call us as soon as you heard the broken window? You really couldn't see their faces? You don't remember anything to identify them by? You're lucky they didn't shoot you when you tried to scare them away. That was risky. You need to consider better locks."

Although the questions exposed Jake's reckless behavior during the episode, the officer seemed concerned. He seemed to know Jake was lucky to have escaped as unscathed as he did.

Only a few minutes after the 911 call, four police cars had arrived. Officer Sampson and another officer had searched inside the house while the rest searched the perimeter. After finding nothing,

Sampson had released the three other cars, and then sat down with Jake to do a report on a clipboard. They had been at it for a while.

"How long have you lived here?"

"Five and a half months."

"Where did you live before?"

"Indianapolis."

"What do you do for work?"

"I do remodeling."

Officer Sampson raised an eyebrow. "Like a decorator?"

Jake rolled his eyes. "No. I'm a contractor—like adding new rooms and moving walls, construction stuff."

"Married?"

"Divorced."

"What happened?"

Jake stared at him. "What does that have to do with anything?"

The cop's head went down. "Sorry. Just curious."

Jake pointed at the form. "Are you about done with that?"

Officer Sampson looked up and down his form. "Yeah, that should do it." He stood.

Jake stood as well. He hesitated before asking the next question, but he liked the cop, and thought he could trust him. He pointed at the policeman's belt. "What kind of gun you carry?"

Sampson glanced down at his weapon. "Glock. Why?"

"You like it? I've been thinking about getting something. I wish I'd had something . . ."

Sampson considered this. "You ever shot guns before?"

"Not for quite a few years."

Sampson looked around, although no one else was in the room. "Well, if you're gonna get a gun, you need to go to a range and shoot it and get familiar with it. There are a lot of idiots out there with guns that don't know what they're doing."

Jake pressed. "What about tonight? What if I'd had a gun and used it on those guys?"

Sampson grimaced. "It would be a mess. There would be a homicide team here." He pointed into the kitchen. "There would be an outline of white chalk on the floor where the bodies were. There would be bloodstains in the carpet. There would be yellow tape all over the place. Your gun would be in the back of my car in an evidence bag, and you would be down at the station answering questions from the homicide detectives. You would probably be sleeping in the county jail tonight on a cot."

"Why?" Jake asked. "What about self-defense?"

Sampson held out the palms of his hands. "Well, that has to be established, right? Killing someone, even in self-defense, is a big deal. Probably after a day or so, the homicide boys would satisfy themselves that it really was self-defense. And then you would be free to go."

"What about my gun?"

Sampson smiled. "We'd keep that. You know, for evidence."

That didn't seem right to Jake. "Forever?"

Sampson shrugged. "For a few months at least, until we're sure the case is not gonna go to court."

Officer Sampson tore off a copy of the report and handed it to Jake. "I'm not saying you shouldn't get a gun. But it's not as easy as pulling the trigger and saying it was self-defense. The world isn't that simple anymore. There are lawyers and judges and the media. You know."

Jake understood what the cop was saying.

Realizing Sampson was leaving, Jake glanced back to the rear of the house where the break-in had occurred. "Isn't somebody gonna come over and dust for prints or anything?"

Sampson stopped, turned back, and stared at Jake. Finally, he shook his head. "No."

Jake was flabbergasted. "How do you expect to find these guys?"

Sampson shrugged. "We don't do prints unless someone is killed, or raped, or something substantial. It costs a lot of money."

Jake was confused. "But they threatened to kill me, and assaulted me. Besides, isn't breaking and entering a felony?"

Sampson looked around again. "Sorry."

Jake's neck grew hot. "So you're gonna wait until these guys break into more homes and hurt somebody else before you do anything?"

Sampson held out his hands. "Listen, Mr. McKinley. I know it's frustrating, but let us do our job. If these guys keep doing this, we'll catch them. From what you told me, these guys weren't murderers, they just wanted to rob you. I don't expect them to come back, especially since you put up a fight."

He turned to leave again, then turned back. "And you should definitely go to the hospital and get your head checked. You probably have a concussion."

Jake wasn't about to go to any hospital. He had no insurance, and besides, what could they do for a concussion anyway? He watched the NFL; he'd be fine in a week.

Officer Sampson walked out the front door, down the sidewalk to his car, and drove away.

Jake thought about the cop. Generally, Jake thought cops were jerks. It was like they knew they had the power of the badge. He wasn't sure whether the profession attracted bullies, or created them—probably both. But Sampson wasn't like that. He didn't fit the mold.

* * *

Jake tried to go back to sleep. But after lying in bed for a half-hour staring at the ceiling, he finally gave up. He went into the kitchen in his t-shirt and boxers, retrieved a large glass from the cupboard, and poured himself some orange juice from the refrigerator. He took two more painkillers and thought about the break-in. What was wrong with America when thugs could make a living breaking into homes and robbing people? He had heard that in Saudi Arabia or someplace in the Middle East, they cut off the hands of thieves, and therefore had almost no problems with theft. Yet the United States kept messing around with these idiots. Everybody said the prisons were equipped with revolving doors.

Even if they caught these guys, Jake knew the feeling in his gut that he had been violated would never go away. Of all the things to focus on, Jake kept picturing the guy carrying his laptop under his arm. They would probably end up hawking it for $25 or less. It would cost Jake at least $500 to replace it, and how was he supposed to get back all the lost pictures and information on it?

He guessed the window would cost fifty bucks. But the bigger issue was the hassle. When was he supposed to shop for a new computer and get the window fixed? It wasn't fair, that people could go around destroying property, and he would end up with the repair bill and the effort to get it fixed. Even if they caught the intruders, he knew he would never be reimbursed. Jake could have died from the head trauma, but to them it was only about $40 in cash and a $25 computer.

He carried his drink into the living room and sat on the couch. He thought of his ex-wife Julianne. If they were still married, he would disassemble the window, and she would take it in to get it fixed. She would have shopped for a new computer for him. Julianne hadn't minded running errands during their marriage. But then came the affair with the doctor and his money. Because that's what it had really been about, wasn't it? The money. The doctor was a disgusting loud mouth with a big gut. But he had lots of money. The arguments had started between her and Jake, about his lack of earning potential, about the small old house they were renting in Indianapolis, about the rusty pickup, about the old furniture, about her clothes, blah, blah, blah. Well, he hoped she was happy now. She'd gotten what she wanted. She was a doctor's wife now, and drove a new BMW. She had the new clothes and the furniture. She had the doctor's wallet, which is all she really wanted. Unfortunately for her, every night she had to crawl into bed and sleep next to that fat slob. He pictured her in a fancy nightgown with his hairy arm draped over her, snoring. Jake hoped she liked the money, because she was earning it, the whore.

For the millionth time since the divorce, he considered what he could have done differently. College? Maybe, but Jake had never been good at studying. Besides, his business was just around the corner from making better money. He just needed the economy to recover a little. If she had just been a little more patient. But Jake knew deep down it wouldn't have been enough. Julianne had her eyes up, at status and social prominence, and Jake was never going to take her there, no matter how much money he made. He never could have satisfied her.

He sat in the dark and thought about the police. Sampson seemed like a good cop, but what about dusting for fingerprints? Jake was blown away by that one. The police don't have resources to investigate break-ins and physical attacks? He now remembered a similar story from a friend who'd had his car stolen and stripped. No fingerprints. No investigation. If someone is caught red-handed, they get arrested, otherwise nothing. It was like the car theft rings that operated for years before anybody did anything.

He remembered about ten years back when the president of the United States had increased the budget and added thousands of new policemen. Shortly after, Jake had been pulled over and ticketed by a cop with an attitude for not making a complete stop. Jake remembered arguing adamantly that he had in fact stopped. But the policeman had dared him to fight it, "Who's the judge gonna believe, you or me?"

Jake was not an idiot. Even though ticket quotas were not officially and openly discussed, everyone knew that cities all over America used traffic violation revenue to fund large portions of their communities. It was like another tax. Parking ticket revenue alone probably funded half the beach cities in America. Did Jake believe the police served the public? Sure, when they weren't too busing harassing the law-abiding citizens they were supposed to be serving.

Jake caught himself clenching his fists. Besides, Sampson had not been like that. He had treated Jake fairly.

He decided he had stewed too much about his problems. He found the remote and began channel surfing. For over an hour, he watched what seemed like five minutes of fifty different shows. Every time a commercial came on, he switched the channel. A few minutes after five, he stumbled on a national news program talking about the current president. Jake normally avoided the news at all costs, but nothing else was on.

A male reporter stood in front of the White House. "President Singleton has lashed out against both parties in the House and Senate, accusing them of not caring about the working class. He demanded that they stop their positioning and pass his tax bill. The economy depends on it. As reported over the last week, economists violently disagree on the potential effects of President Singleton's tax bill. They all agree it's a radical departure from the current system."

A lady reporter asked, "This bill was only introduced a week ago. Has anyone broken it down yet?"

The man in front of the White House responded, "That's just it. It's hard to break down. It changes everything. For earners under $100,000, income tax will be eliminated, replaced by a federal sales tax, with food exempted. Cigarettes, alcohol, guns, and ammunition will have punitive sales taxes assessed. Inheritance taxes, which are sometimes referred to as death taxes, will be quadrupled, essentially preventing families from passing wealth to their children. Business taxes will be eliminated. Capital gains taxes will be treated at the same rate as income, and income taxes for the rich will be doubled. Amazingly, Social Security and Medicare taxes would be completely eliminated. Lastly, the bill includes an energy BTU sales tax that would tax fossil fuels to discourage energy consumption to help the environment."

He continued, "Both political parties are split on the bill since some taxes are drastically increased, while others are drastically decreased or eliminated altogether. The Democrats hate the elimination of business taxes, although conservatives have long argued that business taxes always trickle down to consumers. The Republicans hate the death tax, which will kill multi-generation family wealth. They also hate the BTU taxes, which they argue will kill interstate commerce. The Republicans also argue that higher income taxes for the rich will stifle trade. The punitive taxes on cigarettes, alcohol, and guns are not popular with either party, but for different reasons. Both parties are extremely nervous about the elimination of Social Security and Medicare, wondering if normal tax revenue will be enough to cover the expenses."

She interrupted, "Seems pretty theoretical."

He answered, "I think they realize that and are trying to dumb it down a little. Over the past week numerous politicians have brought forth specific citizens, which they have used as examples of how the tax bill would help or hurt. I think we all remember Jason from Ohio, a traveling product rep, who would be severely affected by the gas prices that many have estimated would double. Or William from Idaho, who farms a ranch owned by his family for generations, which he would not be able to pass on to his children."

The TV showed the woman reporter in studio. "How is the bill doing overall? Are the votes close?"

The reporter in front of the White House responded, "It's hard to tell, there are many politicians who say they would endorse it if just a few things could be eliminated, the death tax for instance, or the BTU tax. The business taxes seem to be a stickler for the Democrats."

"Isn't it rare for politicians to be so uncommitted on an issue?"

The White House reporter laughed. "No question. I don't remember ever seeing a bill that was as revolutionary as this one. It seems like everyone, the politicians and the public, are trying to figure out the long-term ramifications of such a drastic change. There are aspects to the bill that people from both sides have been craving for years, different issues obviously; but there are equally huge negative issues on the other side for both. Leaders from both parties have met separately with the president trying to convince him to separate these issues into separate bills, which President Singleton has adamantly refused, saying that we don't have twenty years to modify our system with band aids. We need surgery. And we need it now."

"Does anyone agree with the president on all aspects of the bill?"

"Yes, quite a few. Senator Johnson from North Dakota is probably the most notable. I haven't seen any counts, but the word on the hill is, if the vote took place right now, the president might get thirty percent. However, as I said, the other seventy percent are not opposed, just undecided."

"Just how hard is the president pushing this bill?"

The reporter grimaced and shook his head. "You know, I don't remember ever seeing a president, any president, push so hard on a bill. He has used the bully pulpit five times this week already. He has called out congressmen personally, Senator Rigby from New York for instance. Don't forget, this president was considered a moderate—back when he was the vice president, before President Swenson died and he took over. But since then, in the year he has been president, congressmen in both parties seem somewhat scared of him. I almost get the feeling that his first year was a warm-up for this battle. It's like he was preparing for this fight all along. It's as if he sees this bill as his destiny, his legacy, to permanently fix the economy. And the word on the hill is that he will fight to the death to get it passed."

Jake pressed the power button on the remote, and the room went into darkness.

Holy crap. Jake had heard talk about the new tax bill at work and tidbits on the radio. Everyone was talking about it, but he hadn't paid much attention. Now he wished he had. There was no way he or any other American would be unaffected by this. No income tax for people making less than $100,000? No Social Security tax? No Medicare? The thought of that made him dizzy. Sales tax would go way up, of course, especially gas. Most of the other stuff would not affect him directly, but the elimination of business taxes? Holy crap! What would that do to the economy?

Jake had only attended a semester of college, and had not taken economics since high school, but elimination of business taxes seemed like a huge deal. Intuitively, he assumed that the economy would take off like a rocket. Would the government collect enough tax money to pay the bills? That was the question. Would upping the taxes on the rich make up for everything else? How could he know? How could anyone know? No one could predict all the ramifications of this. It was too big.

There was one very specific thing in the news story that Jake could predict however. The story mentioned that if the president got his way, a big gun tax was coming. And he needed a gun.

CHAPTER 3

Jake adjusted the brim of his black Steelers cap as he entered the large sporting goods store. He had driven straight there after work. As he entered, he glanced up at the trophy mounts of deer, elk, moose, and bear on the walls. Highlands Hunting and Fishing was Jake's idea of the perfect man's store. It had everything. One particular elk on the left side caught his attention. It was larger than the others and mounted alone. He didn't stop to look, however. He walked purposefully back through the aisles, past the camping section, past the cooking stoves and coolers, past the fishing poles, past the huge section of camouflage clothing, past the ammunition, to his final destination, the guns. The gun counter was packed, and Jake had to take a number from a dispenser on the counter. He listened to the other customers' questions while he waited for his turn. Jake wondered if it was always this crowded, or if others were buying now because of the president's threat of new gun taxes. He guessed the potential taxes had something to do with it.

"Number seventy-two!"

Jake walked to the man with a bushy mustache and handed him his number.

"How can I help you?" The man asked from behind a glass counter.

The glass counter was fifty feet long. The shelves were stacked with revolvers, semi auto handguns, scopes, and optics. Behind the counter were the rifles and shotguns. Five additional salesmen were busy showing various guns to customers. Jake took a moment to scan the site before pointing at the semi-automatic pistols.

"I need a gun," Jake said.

"You know what you want?" The guy with the bushy mustache asked.

Jake saw the guy's tag. His name was Larry. "No. Not really."

"What do you want it for? Hunting? Target shooting?"

"Defense," Jake said.

Larry smiled. "Good idea. Have you shot pistols before?"

"Yeah, when I was a kid. Not for a while though."

Larry opened the glass counter with revolvers and pulled a gun out. He flipped the cylinder out and verified it was not loaded, then laid it on a pad on the counter in front of Jake. "This here is a 38 special, made by Ruger. Very popular. Great gun for self-defense in the home. Double action, which means it can be fired without cocking it, but trigger pull is stiff enough that it won't fire by accident."

Jake picked it up. "Can I aim it at one of those deer heads?"

Larry smiled again. "Sure. Deer's already dead, and the gun's not loaded."

Jake laughed at the comment while sighting on the eye of the deer mount. He remembered shooting cans at his Grandpa's ranch years ago. He hadn't been bad for a kid. The gun felt good. The handgrip was extremely comfortable, contoured perfectly for his hand, not like the old revolvers he'd shot on the ranch. He relaxed his aim, and put the gun back on the counter.

"That's nice, but I think I want a semi-auto."

"All right." Larry walked the gun back to its cabinet and then returned. He reached down in the semi-autos and pulled a black gun up. "Let's start with this one." He pulled the slide back to assure it wasn't loaded and then placed the gun on the pad in front of Jake. "This is a Beretta model 92. It's a nine-millimeter. This model was standardized by the army. Very popular." Larry smiled. "You'll like this one."

Jake picked it up and studied both sides of it, flipping it back and forth. He grasped it in his right hand and then took aim at the same deer. He brought his left hand up for support and aimed from a two-hand stance. He lined the sights up on the deer's other eye. Jake liked the feel of the Beretta much better than the revolver. He set it back down on the pad.

"What do you think about 45s?" Jake asked. He knew a 45 had more punch than a nine millimeter.

Larry shrugged. "I sell a lot of 45s, but most people can't shoot them accurately. Forty is the gun of choice for law enforcement nowadays."

Jake had never heard of that caliber before. "What's a forty?"

Larry retrieved three bullets from a counter behind him. He put them in Jake's hand. He pointed to each bullet as he spoke. "The small one is a 9mm. The fat one is a 45. In the old days, law enforcement was split on which caliber to use. There were cases where the 9mm didn't have enough power, but even seasoned officers tended to flinch at the kick of a 45. It was just less accurate. So, in the early nineties, Smith and Wesson developed this medium guy, which they called a 40 S&W. More power than a 9mm, but not enough to scare you like a 45. Now about sixty percent of all law enforcement use the forty."

Jake was intrigued. "What do you have that shoots a forty?"

"Everybody makes a forty."

Jake spotted one on a lower shelf with a shiny silver slide on the top of the black gun. "What's that?"

"That's an FN. They bought Browning."

Jake had heard of Browning. From what he knew, they had a good reputation.

Larry retrieved it. "This is a 40, but it also comes in 9mm, or 45."

Jake took the gun and sighted on the same deer. He liked this one even better than the Beretta. It felt solid. He liked the idea of the 40 S&W caliber.

Jake spent a while looking at other guns, but kept coming back to the FN. They discussed price, and Larry threw in a free plastic clip-on holster. Jake added two boxes of shells.

Larry took the gun and went into a back room. He returned a moment later with the plastic case for the gun. It had two additional magazines inside. He retrieved two pieces of paperwork from a shelf and slid one to Jake with a pen.

"What are these?" Jake fiddled with the pen, hesitating to write his information. He would have felt better if there was no paperwork.

"The one you have is an ATF FORM 4473. It's a federal document that we use for the background check. The store keeps it as a record of the sale." Larry wrote the serial number of the gun on the form. "The other one is a Pennsylvania State Police Record of Sale."

"What happens with the police one?"

"We send it to the state."

Jake reluctantly began by filling in his name and address. "So that's the registration?" Jake asked.

Larry smiled. "Is this your first gun in Pennsylvania?"

Jake nodded.

"Technically, the United States does not require registration of guns. The 4473 is just a record that we sold you this gun on this day. It has to be kept by the storeowner. It's a federal law. It takes a court order for anyone to view the 4473. The police form is state record that a handgun was purchased."

"How is that not registration? What's the difference? The feds and state keep track of every gun sale, but it's not registration?"

Larry smiled and looked around to see who else was listening. "I understand your concern. The 4473 is locally controlled, no copies at federal or state levels. Pennsylvania originally started the police form so they could track new purchases. If no crimes were committed after a period of time, they were supposed to destroy the records." He glanced around again, and lowered his voice slightly. "But the state has not been destroying the records as agreed. So, yeah, the gun community thinks Pennsylvania is trying to pull a fast one and register handguns."

"Most states don't keep records, do they?"

"It depends on the state. The Virginias, for example, don't keep any records at the state level. If you want to see gun registration, go to New York City or Washington D.C., they basically require a license and a list of every gun you own."

Jake didn't really like the idea of registering the gun. He envisioned someday in the future where the government called him to tax his gun, or take it away, but he saw no alternatives. He signed the forms and handed them to Larry.

Larry took the paperwork and called a number from a phone by the register. Larry read them some of Jake's personal information, then hung up. It only took a minute.

"I passed?" "No problem," Larry said, grinning.

He pointed for Jake to swipe his credit card, which Jake did.

Larry put the FN in its plastic case and locked it closed using a small padlock. He advised Jake on some of the laws regarding transporting weapons.

"When can I pick it up?" Jake asked.

Larry tore off the receipt and handed the plastic case and the padlock key to Jake. "You can take it now." Larry held up a copy of the receipt. "Show them this at the front door."

Jake hesitated. "I thought there was a waiting period." Jake had had no idea he would be taking it home right now. He felt giddy.

Larry responded, "Technically, the feds require a waiting period for handguns, part of the Brady Bill. But the bill was not funded, which makes it optional to the states, so many states don't require the waiting period, including Pennsylvania. Good luck with your gun."

Jake took the plastic box from Larry and smiled broadly. Larry returned the smile, gave Jake a thumbs-up, then went to help the next customer. Jake looked down at the box in his hand. He felt more secure already.

* * *

The next day, work dragged on forever. Jake thought of little else besides taking his new gun to a range and shooting it. What if he couldn't hit anything? The thought that he should have gone to a range first, and rented a few different guns, to see which he liked best before purchasing anything seemed clear now, after the fact. But he had been too eager, too impulsive, it being the same day of the break-in and all. Jake felt dumb for letting his own impulsiveness push him into a quick decision on what weapon to buy.

But even so, Jake couldn't bring himself to regret it. He daydreamed of holding the FN in his hand all day as he worked. The lightweight black polymer handle contoured perfectly to his hand, and the shiny slide on top made it look classy as well.

When he finally arrived home and parked his pickup in the driveway, Jake practically ran to the house. Before the break-in, he had never had a crime problem in the six months he had lived in the house. But what if the crooks had returned while he was at work and had stolen the gun? He fumbled with his keys at the front door then entered quickly. He hustled to the bedroom. In the dresser next to his bed, under his socks, he found the FN's plastic case. Relief poured through him.

He removed the case from the drawer and placed it on top of the dresser. He opened it. All thoughts about other weapons were forgotten as he lifted it out of the box, held it in a two-hand grip and aimed at a nail hole on the wall. He thought of the deer's head in the sporting goods store and how fun that had been to aim at. He needed something like that here, in his bedroom. If only he had kept a portrait of his ex-wife. He smiled as he imagined a picture of her with a single hole in her forehead.

He replaced the gun in its case and clicked on the small padlock. Larry had recommended Jake use the padlock whenever he transported the gun in a car. Pennsylvania law did not require the lock, it only specified that handguns were not loaded when inside the car, and the ammo kept in a separate compartment. But in many states if you got caught with a handgun in an unlocked bag, it was considered a concealed weapon, a felony. Larry said gun owners all over America were being prosecuted for this infraction, many not knowing the law, and most of them not even thinking about committing a crime. So he'd suggested Jake always use the padlock just to be safe.

In the house, the padlock was a problem. Jake felt relieved that he didn't currently have kids. If he stored the gun locked, it would take too long searching pockets for a key and fumbling with the lock in the dark before he could use it. Leave the gun unlocked and your kid could sneak in and show it to his buddy, and accidentally shoot somebody. The same dilemma existed for storing the weapon loaded. The gun needed to be loaded to be useful, but useful was also dangerous. Last night, the first night for Jake's new gun in the house, he had split the difference, leaving it unlocked, but not loaded. In the long term, he needed a system to safely make the gun more ready, meaning that he wanted to leave it loaded at night, so he could be ready at a moment's notice.

Jake shed his work shirt and replaced it with a clean black Steelers t-shirt. He took the gun and the two boxes of shells into the kitchen and made himself a tuna sandwich. He began walking toward the office to use his laptop to search the Internet for a local shooting range, but remembered with distaste that it was stolen. He was forced to do it the old fashioned way by letting his fingers do the walking in the yellow pages.

The phone book listed many outdoor ranges, many affiliated with clubs, but he liked the looks of an indoor range, just across the river in Blawnox, by the train tracks. It was called BullsEye Shooters Range, and the ad said it had 16 lanes. Jake had never shot at an indoor range before. His familiarity with indoor ranges came from the movie Lethal Weapon where Mel Gibson and Danny Glover are practicing at a range when Mel Gibson shoots a smiley face on his target. Jake hoped that the range in Blawnox had the same system, where you could attach a target to a string overhead, then push a lever and motor it out to the distance you wanted to shoot, then motor it back after to see how well you shot. Maybe someday he'd be good enough to shoot a smiley face on his target.

Jake took the Highland Park Bridge over the Allegheny, then followed Freeport Road along the tracks. BullsEye Shooters Range was not well marked on the outside, and he drove past it the first time. It wasn't that the building was hard to see; it was impossible to miss. It was a large metal building that used to be part of the steel mills on the Allegheny River. But Jake had not expected the range to be in a steel mill. He parked next to a half dozen other cars near the large metal building. Carrying the FN's plastic case and the two boxes of shells, he entered the building.

A small office area was the first room inside the old steel mill. It felt like a mini gun store. A bearded man in his forties stood behind a glass counter filled with handguns. More guns hung on the wall behind him. Shelves on both sides were stacked with ammunition. Jake heard muffled gunshots in the distance. While Jake looked around, a couple guys walked out a door that led to the ranges. They both carried black duffle bags that Jake assumed held their guns and ammo. They were both laughing at something.

"Can I help you?" The bearded man behind the counter asked.

Jake felt himself blush. "Yeah. I've never been to a range before. Your ad in the yellow pages said you could rent a lane for $12."

The man slid a clipboard over to Jake. "No problem. These here are the rules. Read 'em, then sign down here at the bottom." He motioned at Jake's gun. "Is that new?"

Jake nodded. "Last night. Never shot it."

"You'll love it." He pointed at Jake's two boxes of shells. "I got more ammo if you shoot all yours. I got reloads that we do right here. They'll save you some dough over buying new stuff. Or I got new ammo too, if you prefer that."

Jake nodded and started reading the rules while the man rang up the two other shooters. Most of the rules seemed like common sense. Keep weapons pointed down range. No shooting outside of your lane. No loaded weapons allowed outside the shooting area.

The bearded man returned. "You need eyes and ears?"

Jake understood the words, but not the meaning. "Huh?"

"Do you need safety glasses and ear protection, or did you bring your own?"

Jake shook his head. "I didn't bring any."

The man put a pair of glasses and headphones on the counter, both well worn. "Targets?"

Jake realized he was unprepared. "No. I need some of those too."

The man pointed at a wall where a million different types of targets hung. Among others, Jake noticed large targets with silhouettes of human torsos. They had dots on strategic areas like the heart and the middle of the face. He saw other targets with people's actual faces including one of Osama bin Laden. Jake was overwhelmed by the target choices and relieved when the man pulled a pad of targets from under the counter.

"These are standard pistol targets, and you save money if you buy a pad of twenty."

Jake agreed. "Put it on my bill."

One of the shooters interrupted, "Hey, when are ya gonna get some targets of President Singleton?"

The other shooter laughed out loud.

The bearded man laughed as well. "You're not the first to ask. I think a lot of people are getting nervous about his tax bill."

The shooter mimed shooting a pistol. "Yeah, I'd say. He'll shut down the whole damn economy if he ain't careful."

Jake was having trouble concentrating on the paperwork as they discussed President Singleton's tax bill. People were joking about killing him to prevent him destroying the economy. It made Jake feel like his head had been buried in the sand for the last few weeks. He vowed to get better informed. He forced himself to concentrate on reading the remaining rules while the other shooters paid and left.

He finished, and then signed the form. He pulled his wallet out, but the man waved him off.

"Just leave your drivers license, and we'll settle up when you leave."

Jake handed him his license and returned his wallet to his pocket.

"You're in lane 7. Since it's your first time, I'll send somebody in to show you around." The man pointed toward the door the two guys used earlier. "In there."

The bearded man knocked on the side door as Jake left. Jake opened the range door and walked into a dead space with another door beyond the first, a small transition room. A big sign said, "Ear & eye protection required beyond this point." There was a cartoon poster of someone holding earphones on their head. Jake was glad of the reminder and donned both his glasses and earphones. He opened the second door and immediately felt and heard the loud percussion of gunshots. He was shocked at the intensity, even with the headphones, and could literally feel the repercussions of each shot in his chest. Shell casings ejected from a man's gun shooting in lane 1, hitting his lane barrier, and then rattling to the floor. Jake looked down the shooting lane, which extended for at least a hundred feet.

As he walked toward the higher lane numbers, he couldn't avoid stepping on the empty shells scattered everywhere. A long bench stretched along the wall behind the lanes, obviously where everyone stored their gun cases, ammo, and targets. He found the lane with the number 7 painted above it and placed his things on the bench. He retrieved his key ring, found the small key for the padlock, then knelt down and unlocked the gun case. Then he felt someone touch him.

He jumped at the touch. Turning, he looked up with an undoubtedly shocked expression on his face.

She was smiling with both hands up, and he saw her mouth the words, "Sorry." The sound of her voice was covered by gunshots. Her smile was intoxicating.

She was startling looking, dark black hair, huge green eyes, white teeth, and flawless complexion except for a large dimple on her left cheek—like that model, Cindy Crawford. He guessed she was in her late twenties. Thin, but curvy. She wore a blue tank top over faded jeans. She had another large dimple on her right shoulder. No wedding ring.

She caught him looking her over but didn't seem to mind. She seemed to be checking him out as well. They both stared at each other until it became uncomfortable.

She pointed at herself. "Monica," she mouthed.

He heard part of it between gunshots. He pointed at himself. "Jake."

She smiled. She pointed at his targets and held up a single finger.

He understood. He tore one from the pad and handed it to her. She stepped to the lane cockpit, which had a shelf at stomach level. She pointed to a switch located at shoulder height on the right side, and then flipped it toward them. In response, a target about twenty yards down the lane started motoring closer. When the target reached the cockpit, she stopped it. The paper was peppered with holes, and she reached to remove it. Jake intercepted her. He wanted to do it himself. He inspected where it was attached and found two clips behind a thick metal guard. He used the clips to release the old target. She handed him his new one, and he attached it. She smiled at him to let him know he had done it correctly. He pointed at the switch, and she nodded. He pressed it away from them, and the target raced down the lane. He stopped it about where the other had been.

She pointed to his gun.

He retrieved it from its plastic case and placed it on the shelf in the cockpit.

She clamped both hands over her cheeks in an expression of horror.

He put his palms out and mouthed, "What?"

She laughed, and then pantomimed Jake's actions while he watched. She walked over to the plastic gun case and pretended to remove the gun. She pointed her thumb up and her index finger out, in a classic fake pistol gesture. She then exaggerated her motions of being inattentive by swinging the pistol back and forth so it was aimed at everyone in the range, she then yawned, licked her lips like a moron, and even looked down the barrel and pretended to shoot herself in the eye, finally tossing the gun on the shelf.

He rolled his eyes.

She pointed at herself, communicating for him to watch. She pantomimed again, but this time she checked her surroundings, carefully removed the weapon, which was still just her finger, then exaggerated pointing the weapon down, so as to never point the barrel at anyone else, then carefully placed it on the shelf with the barrel pointing down range. She mouthed, "Okay?"

He put his hands out in surrender and nodded.

She gave him that beautiful smile, then pointed at his ammo. He retrieved one of the boxes. She pointed at the gun and mouthed, "Load it."

He released the magazine from the gun and slowly started to press bullets into the magazine. After he struggled and finally got two in, she smiled and held out her hand. She showed him how to hold the magazine, then in a single motion press the bullet down and back. She did it effortlessly, quickly loading three shells. She handed it back to him. After watching her, he was much better, although not nearly as fast as she was.

She mouthed. "Practice."

He nodded.

She motioned for him to shoot.

He felt himself blush, knowing he was probably going to embarrass himself again. Snapping the magazine into the pistol, he then aimed using a two-hand grip. But when he pulled the trigger, nothing happened. He felt her touch his shoulder. She motioned for him to pull back the slide and chamber a round. He had forgotten. What an idiot. He smiled sheepishly at her. He pulled the slide and released it.

He aimed again, sighting the bull's-eye. He could feel the concussions of gunshots around him, and he tensed slightly at the anticipated recoil. He fired. The gun barked in his hand, fire blasting from the barrel. But the recoil was not painful, or even uncomfortable. If anything, it felt great, powerful. He looked at the target and saw that his shot was ten inches low, and a few inches to the left. He took aim again and this time he knew what to expect. He fired and saw he was much closer, about six inches left and down. He kept firing, until the gun was empty. Most of his shots were low and to the left. He looked back at Monica, and she gave him a thumbs-up signal. He relaxed a little, figuring his shooting wasn't too embarrassing.

He reloaded the magazine, but before he could snap it into the gun, she put her hand on his, telling him to wait. She motioned for him to aim. He aimed the empty gun at the target. She slid next to him in the cockpit. It was tight and he felt the skin-on-skin touch of her arms on his. She smiled shyly at him, and he noticed both of her dimples, the one on her cheek, and the other on her shoulder.

She caught him looking again but, ignoring that, reached out and adjusted the way his left hand wrapped around his right in his two-hand grip. Then she brought the gun down and took it from him.

"Can I try?" she asked.

He nodded, aware that she was going to show him up in a major way. She inserted the magazine and took a single shot, which was very close to the bull's-eye. But she seemed uninterested in her accuracy. She removed the magazine and cleared the round from the chamber so the gun was empty again. She placed the gun on the pad. She brought her right finger in front of Jake like a trigger finger. At the same time, she held her left index finger up, as if signaling step one. She exaggerated pulling her trigger finger back in a long slow stroke, and then she stopped as if she'd hit something. She raised a second finger on her left hand, indicating step two. She pulled the trigger back past the obstacle. Jake thought he understood. She repeated the lesson. Step one, pull trigger back to obstacle. Step two, pull trigger the rest of the way. She motioned for him to shoot.

Jake inserted the magazine, chambered a round, and then held his hands as she had shown him. This time, as he pulled the trigger back, he was aware of its motion. Sure enough, the trigger pulled back until it hit a barrier. Jake pulled past the barrier and the gun fired. His shot was good. Close to the bull's-eye. He turned and smiled at Monica. She smiled back. He fired the remainder of his bullets, now much more aware of the trigger. He was noticeably better. His shots were no longer low and left, but evenly spread around the bull's-eye, although he still had a few wild ones.

She motioned for him to continue. She was obviously done and ready to leave. But she didn't move. Jake stared at her. He had this sudden urge to wrap his arms around her and pull her close. It was like a deja-vu type feeling, as if they were meant for each other. But that was stupid. He didn't know her, and she obviously thought he was a klutz with guns. Finally, after an awkward moment of them staring at each other, and Jake thinking that she looked like she wanted to hug him as well, she waved and slowly turned, then walked away from him, exiting the range.

He stood like a zombie for a few moments, staring at where she had been, asking himself what had just occurred. Had she felt it too? Or had he imagined the whole thing? She was a striking woman, but it was more than that. Maybe it was something in her eyes. It almost felt as if she had put a spell on him or something. He had never felt like that around a woman before, not even his ex-wife. His arm tingled where it had touched hers.

As the feeling subsided, Jake looked around and remembered he was at a gun range, and his new 40 caliber FN was waiting for him. He put up a new target, reloaded the clip, and shot again. His aim improved, and he actually hit the bull's-eye a few times. He kept shooting, getting a better feel for the gun. He had been a pretty good shot when he was a kid on his grandfather's ranch, and it seemed like those skills were returning. He kept shooting until he'd shot both boxes of shells, a hundred rounds, and used all his targets. The last few targets had many bull's-eyes. He decided he would keep the last target and hang it on the empty walls of his room.

As he locked his weapon back in its plastic case and gathered his things, he felt a knot in his stomach thinking about Monica. He was nervous about what he should say to her when he saw her again. Maybe he shouldn't say anything at all. He recalled how well they had communicated in the loud range without really talking. What if it was different between them when they actually talked to each other? He thought about the deja-vu feeling. Had it just been his imagination? But what if she had felt it too? Did he believe in that kind of crap, or was it just the hormones of a lonely divorced guy? The latter seemed more likely.

He had still not decided what to say to her as he exited the range. But when he entered the front office, she was nowhere in sight, just the bearded man at the counter. Jake felt a huge letdown, almost a panic. Was she back in the side room? Should he ask? If he did, what would the bearded man think?

"How did it go?" the man asked.

Even though he was disappointed about Monica, he thought about his shooting and how good it felt to shoot the FN. "Great. I like it."

The bearded man wrote down the lane fee, and the price of the targets on a receipt. "I told you you'd like it. Need anything else?"

Jake shook his head but then remembered he had shot all his bullets and had nothing left for home. What good was a gun with no bullets? "Actually, I better get some more ammo."

The man helped him choose, and Jake bought two more boxes.

He paid. As he picked up his gun and readied to leave, he felt nauseous. He was incredibly disappointed she had not reappeared. He was almost out the door before the bearded man stopped him.

"Wait!" He grabbed a business card tucked under the edge of his clipboard. "Monica said to give this to you."

Jake's pulse quickened. He took the business card, which had a pistol as its logo, and the words Tactical Training printed just below. There was a phone number printed at the bottom.

"She said you might be interested," the man said.

So that was it, huh? She was interested in him, but as a client for his money. Jake felt like an idiot. He thanked the bearded man and walked out to his truck. He crammed the card in his rear pocket. He drove home without really seeing anything. A divorced guy with raging hormones, that was all, and a pretty girl who could see right through him. Was he that pitiful?

When he arrived home, he took the gun back to his bedroom. He removed the padlock, but before he replaced it in the drawer, he opened the case, and lifted the FN out. He held the gun and admired the workmanship. Suddenly, he spun and aimed at the nail hole on the wall. He might not be able to put a bullet in the same hole, but he would be close, within an inch or two, close enough to kill someone if he had to.

CHAPTER 4

When the alarm woke him in the morning, it interrupted a night of dreams of guns and the woman. He couldn't remember anything concrete, just a fog of images—him shooting the FN; her shooting a shotgun; her pantomiming how to safely remove the gun from its case; her shooting a bull's-eye, then blowing smoke from the barrel with a sly look; her smiling at him; him embracing her like he'd wanted to the night before.

After he sat up and his eyes focused, he glanced at the business card on his dresser. She only wanted his money. How could he be so taken by a girl who was just scamming him? He read the words on the card—tactical training, and frowned. What did that involve? He imagined himself with his face painted black, the FN in his hand, learning how to search a hostile house with bad guys inside. He pictured Monica, in her tank top, the dimple on her shoulder, standing next to him, advising him on what to watch for. He imagined her snuggled next to him in the tight cockpit of the shooting range, with her hands on his, showing him how to aim better. He saw her smiling at him after he hit the bull's-eye.

And the decision was made. He would call the number on her card and check into her tactical training class. Depending on the price, maybe he would let her give him a few lessons on how to handle a gun. He would let her show him how to shoot. He wasn't rich, but maybe he could drum up some money for her training. Maybe it was the price to know if there were any possibilities for him and her, or if it had just been his imagination. He'd call her after work and see.

After dressing for work, he flipped on the TV while he made some toast and poured some cereal in a bowl. This time he went straight for the news, surfing until he found something about the president's tax bill.

A male reporter spoke in the studio, with a picture of President Singleton behind him. "We expect a vote from the house later today. It's still hard to predict whether they will give the president what he wants, or if they'll give him a watered-down version. The president made it adamantly clear that he will not compromise. He says this tax bill needs all the elements to retain balance, to avoid stifling the economy or bankrupting the federal government."

"Any movement from the Democrats or Republicans?" The screen widened to show a woman next to the man in the studio.

Jake used the remote to turn up the volume.

"Actually, yes. Senator Godfrey, from Idaho, a staunch Republican, told CNN less than an hour ago, that there are things in this bill that he hates, like the death taxes and the energy taxes, but he said the upside from eliminating business taxes was incredible, a Republican fantasy he called it. He said removing the shackles from business would create an economy where businesses would grow exponentially. It would reverse the trend of businesses bailing out of the states and heading for China. It would create an atmosphere where U.S. exports would grow aggressively, with the chance of actually eliminating the trade deficit. Senator Godfrey says that many of his Republican counterparts are seeing it the way he sees it. He predicted that most Republicans will support the president's plan, even with the liberal baggage in the bill."

"Wow," the woman exclaimed. "Do you believe him?"

Jake realized he had stopped eating. He knew he needed to leave soon, so he began shoveling the cereal into his mouth.

The reporter answered, "Well, we haven't heard any other Republicans say anything even close to as positive as Senator Godfrey. Don't get me wrong, the Republicans love the elimination of business taxes, but they're also worried about the elimination of income tax for everyone but the rich, and the sudden transition to sales taxes. And remember, this tax bill goes directly at the rich, making it very difficult for them to pass their wealth to their children. The Republicans are terrified about that."

"What about the Democrats?" she asked. "Any movement?"

"The Democrats hate the elimination of business taxes as much as the Republicans love it. That's the stickler for them. If that issue were dropped, I think all of them would pile on in a second. But the president has told the Democrats that this tax bill cannot exist without the elimination of business taxes. That's the portion of the bill that will help the economy grow."

"So business taxes are really the biggest issue, then?"

Jake finished his cereal and put his dish in the sink without taking his eyes off the television.

"That's what seems to be shaking out. This president, who ultimately is neither Republican nor Democrat, is basically forcing both parties to compromise in a huge way, by offering something they really want, but asking them to give up something they can't bear to part with."

"Will the elimination of business taxes really do what the president thinks? And make the economy grow aggressively?"

"That's the question, isn't it? Republicans have long argued that business taxes always trickle down to consumers. But the Democrats have a completely different perspective. They don't trust big business. Business taxes, they argue, are one of the few ways to tax the rich, who they argue have the means to avoid whatever tax is thrown at them."

"Does anyone know what percentage of government revenue comes from corporate taxes versus individual taxes? How big of a loss would it be?"

"President Singleton's numbers say that in 2012, corporate taxes only made up 12% of revenue, compared to 81% from individual and payroll taxes."

"That's lower than I would have guessed."

"And that's the crux of President Singleton's tax plan, remove the shackles from business so it can grow, and make up the 12% in other ways."

The woman reporter seemed to be thinking out loud about the ramifications, "So the Democrats basically need to decide if they can live with no business taxes, if they get huge taxes on the rich in trade?"

"Complete elimination of the rich, if you listen to some. This bill doubles their income tax, and attempts to eliminate their ability to pass wealth to their children. It means all millionaires of the future will be self-made. No more inheriting a fortune."

"Wow. That seems like a—"

Jake turned off the TV. He had to get to work. But his mind was reeling.

* * *

When Jake arrived at the construction site, a family room add-on in North Pittsburgh, it seemed everyone was arguing about the president's tax bill. After watching the news, Jake had favored Congress waiting a while before making such a huge decision. Jimmy, an electrician sub-contractor in his fifties, disagreed as he tucked wires into a junction box in the hallway.

"They're gonna vote this afternoon, right?" Jimmy asked.

Jake rested the long two-by-six he was carrying on the floor. "I didn't hear. But that seems kinda fast. Don't they have to debate?"

Jimmy said, "Singleton told them he wants a vote today. He's pushing them hard. He said they've already spent a week debating. I agree. We've had this screwed-up tax system too long."

Jake scratched his forehead with his gloved hand. "Yeah, but this is a big change. Don't you think they should study it more? Run a few models to try to predict—"

"Naw." Jimmy grabbed a metal plate from his belt. He talked while he covered the junction box. "They can't predict everything that's gonna happen. Nobody can. We just need to do it. Singleton can make adjustments after."

Jake felt a knot in his stomach. "Adjustments for what? Whole industries going broke? What if the rich stop remodeling their houses? Where does that leave us?"

Jimmy pointed down the hall to a full-sized bronze statue of Franco Harris reaching down to scoop up a football just inches from the ground. The statue was covered with a tarp to avoid damage during the construction, but all the workers had lifted the tarp and admired it. The statue depicted Franco during the legendary playoff game of 1972 when the Pittsburgh Steelers defeated the Oakland Raiders. The play where Franco scooped up the loose ball and scored a touchdown with time expired was called the Immaculate Reception, the most famous play in NFL history. In the city of Pittsburgh and the surrounding areas of western Pennsylvania, the Immaculate Reception was not just a football event; it signified the most famous event in local history, known by every citizen, old and young.

"I think they have plenty of money," Jimmy said. "I wouldn't worry about these guys."

"Yeah, but what about the inheritance tax? They wouldn't be able to pass anything to their kids? What's going to happen if every family business in America dies at the end of each generation? That can't be good."

Jimmy smiled. "Maybe you and I will get a chance at some of those businesses." I think we could do better than their spoiled kids anyway. That's a plus in my book."

Jake motioned at the window with his arm. "It seems like too big of a change all at once. How can anyone predict all the ramifications?"

"What kind of ramifications?" Jimmy asked. "Rich kids learning to work? More level playing field?"

Jake wasn't sure what to say. "I don't know. Completely eliminating wealth after each generation seems drastic. Some of America's best companies have been run by the same families for years. Is it gonna be better for the government to confiscate those businesses when grandpa dies? I'm not sure. When did the government ever add value?"

"Give it a chance, Jake. Heaven knows we've given the current tax system a chance. Look what that's got us."

"I'm just worried everyone's thinking the grass is greener on the other side of the fence. Don't get me wrong. I like lots of it, especially the elimination of business taxes. That's a no brainier. I'm just worried that we haven't taken time to think everything out. What's the downside?"

Jimmy waved his hand dismissively. "What downside? You worry too much."

Jake picked up the two-by-six and carried it over to the saw, wondering if Jimmy was right.

* * *

Jake and the subs knocked off at four that afternoon. The next day the insulation would be installed, and they had everything ready.

Insulation would take a couple days and would keep everyone away until it was done.

Jake tuned the pickup's radio to the news on the way home. The news was dominated by the forthcoming vote in the House on the tax bill. The word from the House was that debate would be halted in an hour, at 5:00 p.m. eastern, followed immediately by the vote. The commentators reiterated that they could not recall any president pushing harder on any bill than President Singleton had on this bill.

As he drove down the hill toward the West End Bridge over the Ohio, the traffic bunched up. He veered slightly left of the cars in front of him to see what was causing the slowing, maybe an accident. What he saw instead surprised him. It was people, lots of them. They stood in the middle of the road holding signs and approaching the cars from both sides. It looked like some sort of demonstration. Jake groaned at the delay, but he was curious to see what they were demonstrating about.

When Jake's truck neared the demonstrators, a man in a hardhat approached. His sign was colored red and black, emblazoned with a swastika, and read: "Singleton is a Nazi!" He spoke through Jake's open window.

"Don't let President Singleton ruin our country."

Jake was actually happy they were out here about the tax bill. He wondered what they would say. He leaned out the window to talk to the guy. "You think the bill will pass?"

The man in the hardhat walked with Jake's truck as he slowly crept along. "It better not, or God help us all."

"What's so bad about it?"

The guy became more aggressive. "Are you kidding? Completely eliminate business taxes? All those environmental taxes? What'll happen to our Social Security if he bankrupts us?"

As the man finished his statement, Jake's truck reached a larger group of protesters and the hardhat man moved to another car. Jake saw a sign that said: "4X taxes on the rich? Singleton's trying to shift the power base."

From the crowd next to the truck, Jake focused on a clean brunette lady in her thirties. She looked like a soccer mom. Her sign said: "Don't throw the baby out with the bathwater. He's replacing freedom with equality."

He spotted an old man, maybe in his eighties. He was leaning on his sign like a cane. It said: "My children have worked in my laundry business for years, why shouldn't I be able to pass it to them?"

That one bothered Jake. It was a laundry business. What gave the government the authority to seize it? It was his. He should be able to give it to whomever he wanted.

Jake rolled up his window and accelerated after passing through the throng. He thought about the lady's sign about trading freedom for equality. Couldn't they have both? Were the two mutually exclusive? Jake remembered someone else saying that they were opposites, that to grant equality required someone else to give up freedom. Welfare was the biggest example. Take from the rich, and give to the poor. Rob the rich's freedom, and give it to the poor, making them more equal.

But wasn't America based on both, freedom and equality? He had heard someone say that it was a balancing act, and that we must try to do both, without moving too far toward one and killing the other.

Jake thought about where America was right now. If it was out of balance—which way was it leaning? Freedom? No, if he had to say, he would say equality was winning. A previous president had been black. Women were all over the place in politics and business. The media was flooded with vocal minorities. There was constant talk about government programs for every group that could be imagined. And Jake, especially since the divorce, was getting taxed to death to pay for it all. It seemed like the government was like Robin Hood, redistributing the wealth from the workers to the non-workers.

Jake considered President Singleton's tax plan. Would it favor freedom or equality? Eliminating business taxes was definitely a plus for freedom. Eliminating income tax for the poor helped freedom for them. Quadrupling taxes for the rich definitely favored equality. In fact, grossly higher taxes for the rich felt like stealing to Jake. The inheritance taxes were clearly a money grab to help equality at the cost of freedom. The environmental and gun taxes, he couldn't see how they helped equality, but they definitely hurt freedom.

Jake frowned, mulling it all over. He realized he agreed with the soccer mom. President Singleton's tax plan would tip the scales further towards equality in America, but it would be paid for by huge concessions in freedom, especially for the rich.

As Jake drove onto the West End Bridge, he glanced right over the Ohio River as he always did at Heinz Field, the home of the Pittsburgh Steelers. From a distance it looked like there were many cars in the parking lot, and lots of people mulling around. Were they holding signs too? Was there another demonstration by the arena? Jake guessed so.

* * *

During the last few miles of Jake's commute, he forgot all about the president's tax bill. In fact, he turned off the radio and rode in silence. He was thinking about Monica's business card. The plan since this morning had been to call her after work. But now he was nervous. He kept telling himself it was just a routine call, just to ask her about the tactical training, how much it cost, etc. But he couldn't deny he was attracted to her and was afraid it would be evident when he talked to her. He would start mumbling, and she would see right through him.

As he pulled in the driveway, he asked himself if he should wait another day and let some of his hormones dissipate. Then he chided himself for being a chicken. He wasn't some teenage kid. He was a grown man, married and divorced. She was just a woman. How hard was it to call a woman on the phone and ask about her business? How hard was it to have a simple discussion? Besides, the phone would hide him staring at that damn dimple on her shoulder and prevent him from slobbering on her.

He shut off the truck and climbed out. He would call her as soon as he got inside. On second thought, maybe he would eat first. Let her wait. Yeah, he should make her wait a few minutes longer. He wasn't chicken; he was just showing her that he wasn't too anxious.

Inside the house, he removed his work shirt and pulled open the drawer where he kept his t-shirts. He pulled a white Steelers t-shirt off the top. For Jake, it was never a question of what kind of t-shirt he would wear, since every shirt in the drawer had the Pittsburgh Steelers logo. The question was whether to wear black, yellow, white, or gray. Jake had always been a huge Steelers fan, even when he lived in Indianapolis. So after the divorce, when he was feeling hemmed in and needing a new start, the logical place was Pittsburgh. And Jake hadn't regretted it for an instant, except for the break-in, of course.

Pittsburgh had a reputation of being dirty, with black smoke hovering overhead from all the steel refineries. But that was long ago. Although it was still referred to as the Steel City, the massive steel mills had been shut down in the seventies and eighties in a gut-wrenching loss of employment for the entire area. Over a hundred fifty thousand workers had been laid off following the 1981-1982 recession alone. But unlike other cities decimated by the collapse of their industries, Pittsburgh had adapted and evolved, becoming a hub for financial corporations, healthcare, robotics, and many other industries. The steel mills were demolished and replaced with shopping centers, business complexes, and apartments. The skies cleared over Pittsburgh, and the view of the city and its steel bridges over its three rivers became postcard fodder.

After changing his clothes, Jake retrieved the business card from his dresser. He studied it closely, just a logo, the words "Tactical Training," a first name "Monica" and a phone number. No address. No email. No border. No color. Nothing. It was the plainest business card he had ever seen. He flipped it over, and tensed. Why hadn't he looked on the back the night before?

Scrolled across the back in blue ink were two elegant cursive words: "Call Me!" Jake stared at the back of the card and wondered. This message seemed far more personal than an invitation for tactical training. This was more like: Call me and let's get together, or: Call me and let's talk, or: Call me and let's discuss what happened at the shooting range, the feeling I felt, and the feeling I think you felt.

Without thinking, Jake pulled out his cell phone, keyed in the phone number, and pressed send. His hand shook slightly as he heard the phone ringing. He hadn't considered what he would say.

She answered, "Hello?"

Her voice sounded different without the ear protection in the shooting range. It was lower than he remembered, husky. He heard a muffled gun shot in the background.

"Is this Monica?"

"Yes, who is this?"

"This is Jake. . . uh, from the range last night." Silence. He wondered if she remembered him. "Lane 7. You helped me."

More silence before, "I expected you to call last night."

Jake grimaced. "I was going to. I mean, I wanted to. But I never turned the card over. I didn't see your message. So, I thought . . ."

What was he trying to say? What a mumbling idiot he was!

She said in her husky voice, "I was in the mood for ice cream last night. I was hoping you would call."

Jake thought about the wasted opportunity. He pictured himself at a small table, across from her, watching her licking ice cream from a cone.

"What about tonight?" he asked.

"I'm not sure I'm in the mood for ice cream anymore."

Jake smiled and relaxed a little. She was messing with him now. "Oh, and what are you in the mood for tonight?"

"Hmm," she considered, taking her time.

Jake waited. He heard more muffled gunshots in the background. She probably had to work. Maybe he should go shoot the FN again tonight. He thought of her squeezed next to him in the cockpit.

"French fries," she said.

"French fries?"

"Yes. And I know where. Have you eaten yet?" she asked.

"No."

"Then come and pick me up at the range."

"When?" Jake asked.

"Now! While I'm still in the mood."

Jake laughed. Bossy little thing. "Okay," he said. "I'll be there in a half hour."

CHAPTER 5

It was starting to get dark when he drove up to the range. He felt awkward thinking about going inside and asking for her. What would her co-workers think? But when he pulled up to the building, she was outside standing on the curb. He stopped next to her, and she peered in until she recognized his face. She smiled, opened the door, and climbed in, pulling on a seat belt. She was dressed exactly as the night before, except tonight her tank top was green. She had a sweater draped over her arm and a small purse in her hand. When she looked at him, he was again struck by her dark eyes.

"Where are we going?" he asked.

"Take 28 along the river. Head toward downtown."

He turned the truck around and headed back toward the city. They were silent for a while. When he looked over at her, she was staring at him. She smiled, and he thought he saw a slight tremor of her lips and guessed that in her own way she was as nervous as he was.

He tried to break the tension. "Are you still in the mood?"

She smiled wide. "Yeah. I am."

"Are we in a hurry? Do you need to be back?"

She shook her head. "No. They can get along without me."

Jake kept driving. This didn't feel anything like being recruited for tactical training. This felt more like two people that were very excited to meet each other.

She broke the silence. "That wasn't your first time last night, was it?"

He glanced over at her. "No. I used to shoot at my grandfather's ranch when I was a kid. We shot cans off a fence. But it's been a while."

"I could tell. You're not a bad shot. You were just rusty."

"I never shot an automatic before. It was my first time for that."

"They're awesome aren't they?"

"Yeah. I really liked the way it shot. After I got used to it, it seemed very predictable."

Up ahead there was confluence of roads. Jake pointed ahead at the signs. "Where now?"

She pointed to the right. "Get on 279, then we're going to take the Fort Duquesne Bridge."

Jake nodded. He knew the way. This was close to the job site. They were only on the 279 for less than a mile before lanes for the bridge took him left over the river.

"Get off here," she said, pointing.

As they came off the bridge, Jake took the first exit into downtown Pittsburgh. She told him where to turn, and he drove to Point State Park. They found a parking spot near the north end. Jake had never been to the park although he had driven over it many times. Point State Park was situated at the point of Pittsburgh where the three rivers joined, the Allegheny and Monongahela combining to form the Ohio.

They climbed out of the truck and walked to a concession stand. They ordered hot dogs, drinks, and cups filled with French fries.

When they picked up their food, she smiled widely. "These are the best fries ever."

Jake pointed to a table. "Is over there alright?"

She shook her head. "Bring your food. We're going someplace else."

He laughed. "Lead the way."

She led him on a walkway through the trees until they arrived at the riverfront. The view was spectacular. Just northwest across the Allegheny loomed Heinz Field, with a purple sunset behind the stadium. The stadium was very close and lit up. Although Jake had been a hard-core Steelers fan as long as he could remember, he hadn't yet attended a game. He had only lived in Pittsburgh for six months, and the pre-season had just started a few weeks ago. Besides, the Steelers had sold out every home game for over fifteen years, making tickets expensive and almost impossible to get.

"What an incredible view!" he said.

She led him to a bench on the edge of the river. The water was black, and Jake could hear it lapping at the walkway as it slowly moved past them. A hundred yards to their left, a huge water fountain sprayed at the point where the three rivers joined.

Jake admired the whole atmosphere. "Amazing! I think I'm in love."

She sat down on the bench and arranged her food next to her. "Slow down, Poncho, it's only our first date." She patted the seat next to her.

Jake laughed at her joke. What do you say to that? "No, I meant the place. It's way cool here. I'm thinkin' I should bring my other girlfriends here."

She gave him a dirty look.

He sat next to her and placed his food between them. He tried the fries and agreed they were good, just the right amount of salt. He looked over at her and saw her taking a bite of her hotdog. He could see the muscles in her jaw and neck.

She caught him looking. She spoke with her mouth full, "You can't have mine. Eat your own."

Jake smiled and took her advice, unwrapping his hotdog and taking a bite. She seemed to know what he was thinking. And she could communicate with a look, or an expression, or as she had proven the night before, she could pantomime it. He smiled at the memory.

After both hotdogs were gone, they sat back and looked out over the river. They were silent for a while before she spoke.

She gave him a devilish look. "Look, even though we're in love, we need to get a few things straight."

Jake knew she was trying to shock him, but he didn't allow it. He turned to face her on the bench and smiled. He took a long swig of his soda. "I agree. What things?"

She continued. "I mean it's obvious we like looking at each other. We're both practically sitting on our hands to stop from reaching out and touching each other. Neither of us are wearing wedding rings, and we're both adults."

Jake had never met a girl this blunt.

She continued. "You like my favorite French fries. We both like the Steelers. You've just rediscovered guns, which is good. You're obviously obsessed with the thing on my shoulder, which I'm not sure whether you like or hate. I'm guessing like. I'm obsessed with your blondish hair and can't wait to play with it. I like your chin."

She smiled. "Am I making you nervous?"

He opened his mouth, but no words came out.

"No? Good. I've been accused of being too bold. Some guys can't handle that."

Jake had known immediately when she got in the truck tonight she was messing with him, and he felt like he had held his own so far, but she had just raised the stakes.

She continued. "Anyway, before we get engaged, we need to make sure there aren't any skeletons. You're not a pedophile are you?"

Jake laughed. "No, I'm not a pedophile."

"Alcoholic? Drug addict? Compulsive gambler? Physically abusive? Addicted to video games?"

Jake shook his head. "I have an ex-wife." He regretted blurting it out like that.

He could tell it took some of the wind out of her sails because her smile faded and her shoulders slumped.

"Kids?"

"No kids."

"Tell me about it."

He told her about the brief marriage. He told her about the money and the doctor. She asked him questions like how often he still talked to his ex. She asked him if he still loved her.

Jake said, "Sometimes I think about the girl that I married and think I still love her. But then I think about the lies and the person she turned into, and I think the girl I loved probably never existed."

She considered his story. "Well, we're gonna have to slow down a little and make sure you're not rebounding."

"What about you," he asked. "You an alcoholic, a gambler, a drug addict, or worse—a gold digger?"

"If I was a gold digger, I'd go after the same doctor that your wife did."

Jake grimaced. "Ouch."

She touched his hand. "I don't need anybody's money, and I got no addictions, except running my hands through hair like yours.

Actually, that's not true. My father would say I'm addicted to talking too much, and scaring all the good boys away."

"What do you say?"

"I scared 'em off because they weren't right for me. I've been waiting for you. What took you so long?"

Jake laughed again. Monica was different than any girl he had ever been with, especially a first date. Usually, on a first date, they acted reserved and apprehensive, waiting for the man to reveal himself first. Monica seemed to have no reservations, no inhibitions. She immediately kicked the tires, opened the hood, and inspected the engine. She seemed intent on determining how much horsepower it had on the first test drive. He liked her and didn't mind her teasing.

They spent the next hour talking about their past lives. They talked about dreams, parents, pets, cars. She probed into his background, and he surprised himself by asking pretty bold questions himself. It was as if her boldness was rubbing off on him.

He sat across from her on the bench and studied her face as she talked. He liked how the corner of her lip went up as she talked about her time at the University of Pittsburgh. She'd enjoyed the social life but not the books. She'd studied psychology, physical education, and even business but had never settled on anything.

"So you never finished?"

Monica shrugged, and her smile slipped away.

"My mom got sick—cancer. Dad asked me to come home."

Jake tensed. Was her mother dead?

She seemed to read his mind. "She lasted a little over a year, but . . ." she shook her head. "Anyway, by the time it was all over and I could go back, I realized I didn't want to."

Jake said nothing

"That was four years ago." She locked eyes with Jake. "She's in heaven now, waiting for me and my father to join her."

He was surprised at her certainty of an afterlife and her openness to talk about it. There was no doubt she believed her mother was still alive. Jake didn't know.

She changed the subject and talked about her job. It turned out her father owned the shooting range, and Monica had been a popular instructor, so she had essentially backed into the tactical training. Besides guns, her father was also a minister of a Christian church, so she helped her father out there as well.

Jake wasn't sure how he felt about her father being a preacher. He had never been a churchgoer himself. He pictured a small squat man with a round face in a robe pointing a finger at him and shouting, "Sinner!" She still lived with her father, which made Jake even more nervous.

She picked up on his nervousness. She pinched his chin. "Don't worry. He's not that scary. You'll like him."

Jake wasn't so sure.

She got an idea. "What are you doing tomorrow night?"

He shook his head and shrugged. "No plans."

"Then you're coming with us."

"Where? Who?"

"My dad and me. We're going to the club."

"What club?" Jake asked. He pictured them in a church which a bunch of other priests. He was all for spending more time with Monica, but he definitely did not want to rush into meeting a father who was a priest.

"Three Rivers. It's about forty five minutes north of here."

"Never heard of it. What kind of club is it?"

"I wouldn't expect you to have heard of it. It's very exclusive. You have to be invited."

"What kind of club is it?" he asked again. "Religious?"

She smiled. "Why? You afraid of religion?"

He hesitated. "It's not that." He tried to think of the right words. "I don't go to church, so . . ." He looked down and brushed some lint off his jeans. Maybe she was right. He certainly had avoided church in the past. He believed in God, kind of. But he felt like most parts of organized religion were fake. His experience with religion was drama and scare tactics.

"You're afraid," she teased.

"I don't think I'd call it fear. It's more like . . ." How could he put this? "I mean, I believe."

"What do you believe?" she asked, "Tell me."

He had no idea how to verbalize his feelings. He tried for the emergency escape. "I don't think you should talk too much about religion on your first date."

She smiled. "Better reconsider, Poncho, or it'll be our last date." She leaned toward him, waiting for an answer. She wasn't going to let him off the hook.

Jake looked away, at the swirling water. "Well, I believe there's a God."

"Are you a Christian?"

He thought about the story of Christmas, the baby in a manger, the shepherds and wise men, the new star. "Yeah. I believe that stuff."

"Drum roll," she said, pretending to rapidly drum with two imaginary drumsticks. "Time for the big question."

He had no idea where she was going and was a little afraid to find out. "What's the big question?"

She smiled. "The question that separates the believers from the pretenders. Did Jesus rise from the dead after three days in the tomb?"

"What do you mean?"

"I mean do you believe he died on the cross, then after being dead for three days, came back to life and appeared to many, like it says in the New Testament?"

He nodded. "Okay, yeah, I've heard the stories."

"Do you believe it actually happened?" she pressed.

He shrugged. "How can anyone know? I hope it happened."

She smiled again, then reached out and put her arm around his neck. She pulled his head to hers and kissed him passionately on the lips. He felt warmth and tingling through his entire body. Finally, she released him and their lips parted. They were both out of breath. His lips were tingling.

"Sorry," she panted.

He blinked his eyes. "You don't have to apologize for that. That was awesome."

She shook her head. "No, about the religious questions. I pushed you, hard."

After her aggressive affection, Jake thought he could forgive her for anything. "I'm just not used to talking about that stuff."

"Fair enough. I guess I better tell you, Three Rivers Club is not a religious club per se."

Jake finally felt defensive and raised his voice. "Then why the third degree? Why were you asking me all those questions?"

She shrugged. "You brought it up. You're the one who asked if we were going to a religious club. You're the one who was obsessed with religion."

Jake knew she was messing with him big time. "The way you said it, your dad being a priest and all."

"No, I just said you could join us at the club. I didn't say—"

Jake interrupted her. "What kind of club is it?

She smiled like a devil, her eyes sparkling. "It's a private sportsmen's club, a shooting club."

"Guns?" Jake grinned. He felt a flood of relief at avoiding the religious meeting. "We're gonna shoot guns?"

She nodded, smiling. "If you prefer, we can go to a Bible study? I can probably talk my dad into it."

He rolled his eyes at her. "No. Let's definitely go to the gun club. That sounds cool." He looked at her and thought about the kiss. He wanted more, and he considered reaching out and pulling her to him. He noticed she was watching him, reading his thoughts. They were interrupted by a couple walking along the river toward them.

She stood and gathered the remainder of her meal. "Come on. Let's walk down toward the fountain."

Jake followed her lead. After he deposited his trash in a bin by the river, he took a few quick steps and caught up to her. They walked right next to the river. Without thinking, he reached out and took her hand. She kept her eyes pointed ahead, but she was smiling.

* * *

The next morning, Jake woke before his alarm. As he lay in bed, he recalled the night before, the evening in the park, the moving black water, Monica's husky voice, and her eyes. Her eyes were alive. You looked at those eyes and knew something was going on behind them. He recalled the first time he met her at the shooting range and how well she could communicate without talking. He could still picture her recklessly swinging the pretend gun barrel around. He wondered if she was awake yet. He wanted to talk to her, but it was probably too early.

As he thought about getting up and getting ready for work, he suddenly remembered the vote, the president's tax bill. Crazy, the tax bill had been the most important thing on his mind the entire previous day, including the discussions at work, yet the date with Monica had erased it from his consciousness. Had it passed? Jake glanced at his clock and saw it was almost time to get up anyway. A few minutes later he was dressed for work, and turned on the television while he fixed breakfast.

A female reporter stood in front of a hospital. "Although nothing has been said officially, the word is that he died of a bullet wound to the forehead."

Jake was not interested in hearing details of a murder, and was preparing to change the channel, when the reporter made him stop cold.

"If so, then both congressmen who led the house in opposing the president's tax bill yesterday have been murdered during the night, both killed by gunshots to the head."

What? Had he heard correctly? Opposing congressmen murdered, shot in the head? How could that happen? Jake turned up the volume.

The TV screen split, simultaneously showing the female reporter at the hospital, and a male anchor in the studio. The male anchor said, "Do the police have any witnesses, or suspects?"

The woman answered, "The police are not talking to the press yet, so if they have witnesses, I haven't heard. However, Representative Oliver from Ohio was shot on the sidewalk as he was exiting his car. He had just arrived at the condominium where he stays in Washington. He was not alone. So, there were witnesses. Representative Augustine, from Wisconsin, was still in his car when he was shot just as he arrived at his residence last night. Since the two murders were performed simultaneously, there are interesting implications.

It means that after the vote, somebody targeted two key representatives and sent professional hit men to their homes to murder them. It means that this entity probably already knew where they lived. It means they had information and were organized. It probably means it wasn't just a deranged person who watched the vote on TV, then got angry and killed them. This feels like professional hits, where they had teams ready, or at least at their disposal when the vote failed."

The male anchor said, "We haven't heard from President Singleton yet, but this looks bad for him, doesn't it? I mean two congressmen who opposed his tax plan are killed by professional hit men, hit men that had inside information about where the victims lived. We need to let the police investigate, but it seems the primary suspects have to be powerful organizations that supported the president's tax bill. I hate to say it, but won't some people suspect President Singleton himself of ordering the hits? He has to be a suspect."

Jake realized he had stopped eating. He was just staring with his mouth hanging open. He considered President Singleton. He pictured him holding his arm to the square as he took the oath a year before, after President Swenson died. He was clean cut and good looking. He was an independent, neither Republican nor Democrat, and relatively unknown when he was chosen as Swenson's vice-president. Did he have the connections to have people murdered? Was he that type of guy? If so, it was certainly something Jake had never suspected of him. He couldn't remember ever considering the man sinister or evil, not any more than any other politician. But the circumstantial evidence pointed to him. It seemed the president, or his friends, had just murdered two of his opponents.

CHAPTER 6

Jake was still trying to wrap his mind around the two murders when he arrived at work. The radio had not provided much more information than the television, just more speculation about who did it. The guy on the radio didn't think the president was involved. He thought it was big business, corrupt organizations that wanted the elimination of business taxes. According to the reporter, the president had boatloads of money pouring in ever since the bill was announced. The bill now had more corporate sponsors than anyone could keep track of. It was the reporter's opinion that one of these businesses had killed the two congressmen.

Jake figured the reporter didn't know much more than he did, so his theory was only that—a theory. He hoped the guy was right, because he didn't want to think about the president killing people. He remembered all the stories during Bill Clinton's two terms, about how anyone who crossed the Clintons had seemed to die suddenly, but like most other Americans, Jake had only considered that a conspiracy theory.

When he arrived at the job site, the insulation guys were already there. He unlocked the house and let them in. The lead guy, Rick, had already been to the house a few days before to inspect the project, and to make sure they brought enough insulation, so once they were inside, he set the crew to work.

Hours later, Jake stood in the great room and marveled. The first day of insulation was always a strange day. A framed construction site was mostly open, and acoustically had an airy feel about it. You could see between the rooms. Then adding fiberglass insulation to a few walls, and even piling the material in the middle of the room, changed the feel of the place. The cushy material absorbed all the sounds and the place became like a recording studio, dead, no echo at all. That feeling was only temporary though, because in a few days, when the sheetrock went up and covered the insulation, the acoustics would revert back to normal.

Jake was considering this when he saw William Henry Campbell III enter the room. Being the owner of the home, he was ultimately Jake's boss. He was over seventy and walked with a cane. Jake wasn't sure why he carried it though, since he didn't limp and seemed to carry it more than use it. He had gray hair, a well-groomed goatee, and bifocals. Today he was dressed in an elegant, gray pin-stripe suit.

Jake liked him. The old man, his wife, and their housekeeper had all moved out for the construction. They had rented a place nearby. Jake never saw the women, but William came by daily to check on the construction.

"How's it going, Jake?" he asked.

"Can't complain."

"How long will these guys take?"

Jake noticed that the old man's voice sounded funny with no echo in the room. "They're quick. Today or tomorrow."

"You used them before?"

This particular job was Jake's first since moving to Pittsburgh, so he had never used any of his subs before. He thought William knew that as well. "No. But everyone I talked to says they do great work."

William nodded. He poked a wall of insulation with his cane. "The room already feels smaller."

Jake knew it was normal for a room to feel smaller when the studs were filled with insulation. Technically, the room was actually six inches smaller in every direction. The muffled acoustics also contributed to the perception of a smaller room. "It'll look bigger again when the sheetrock goes up next week."

The old man glanced around the room as if picturing how it would look with the sheetrock. "What did you think about the news this morning?" he asked.

Jake shook his head. "Unbelievable." He motioned to the old man. "Who do you think did it?"

William poked some discarded insulation on the floor with his cane. "I think that's obvious."

"Obvious? Who?"

William looked away. "Singleton had them killed."

Jake stared at the old man as he poked the wall again. He had just called the president a murderer. "What about big business?" Jake asked. "The guy on the radio thought it was them."

"Could be." The old man scratched his chin. "But I don't think so. Well, maybe Singleton hired 'em to. But this is Singleton's baby."

"What makes you think the president did it?"

William raised his voice. "Cause he's not accustomed to being told no. He doesn't like to lose. And this tax bill, everybody knows he wanted it bad."

Jake laughed. "But that's not really proof."

William came back immediately, tapping Jake's leg with his cane. "Oh, there will never be any proof. That's for sure. Don't be surprised if they find the killers dead in an alley someplace. They'll clean up. Don't be holding your breath waiting for proof."

Jake was starting to feel like the old man had a few conspiracy theories of his own. "Has the president said anything yet?"

William pointed out the window with his cane. "You didn't hear his press conference this morning?"

Jake shook his head. "No. When?"

William looked at his watch. "About eight thirty. You were probably already here."

"What'd he say?"

"Oh, he gave a great speech. He held on to both sides of the podium and spoke with authority." William pantomimed holding a podium with his chest puffed out. "He consoled the poor families. He spoke out against gun violence. He swore he would leave no stone unturned in a hunt for the killers. He promised to bring them to justice. He hinted that if big business did it, then he would hunt down every executive involved, and make sure they get the death penalty. He practically volunteered to kill them himself. He reminded me of O.J. Simpson."

Jake laughed at the reference to O.J. He remembered how almost everyone had believed O.J. was guilty, yet O.J. kept promising he would track down the killers. Jake would have liked to have seen the president's speech himself. He wanted to stare into the man's eyes and judge if he thought he was lying. He didn't want to believe the president had done it, but it had to be considered.

"Do you think anyone will actually investigate Singleton?" Jake asked.

William gave him a sour look. "No way. It'd be political suicide. They might ask him a few polite questions, just to say they did, but there won't be any real investigating. The president's people will be all over this investigation like ants. The FBI, or whoever is in charge of the investigation, is going to act like a bunch of puppets, led around like dogs on leashes. And nobody is going to let dogs into the White House to sniff around."

Jake thought about that. Was the president that untouchable? Wasn't there usually somebody who broke ranks and squealed?

"You got any guns?" William asked.

Jake was caught off guard by the question. "Actually, I just bought one a couple days ago. Why?"

"You know this president doesn't like guns. His tax bill went after guns and ammo. And his speech today, he hinted that gun crime had gone on too long, and that he was going to do something about it."

"What could he do?"

"I don't know. What kind of gun did you get?"

"A handgun, semi-auto, forty."

"Is that your only one?"

"Yeah."

William considered this. "I got a bad feeling about Singleton. He had two guys killed last night, and it's almost like he wants to use that as an excuse to keep us peasants from having guns. I don't like it."

Jake thought about the break-in at his house the other night, and his conversation with the policeman. The policeman had seemed to favor citizens owning guns, as long as they got some training and didn't act like idiots. It was different than some of the stuff he heard on TV from politicians. The way they talked, they were smart enough to make decisions about guns, but Jake wasn't. Jake hated the double standard.

"At least the tax bill didn't pass."

William pointed the cane at him. "Oh, it's not over. That's why those two were killed. The president will regroup, and there will be another vote. Remember, those two were the biggest opposition. They had lots of votes lined up behind them. Without them to lead, the other votes are going to evaporate. I bet if they voted right now, the tax bill would pass by a landslide."

Jake shook his head. "But some of the other congressmen probably suspect the president in the killings, right? They're not going to vote for his bill until this all gets cleared up, are they?"

William smiled an evil smile. "If you were sitting behind one of those two congressmen that just got gunned down, how fast would you want to stand up in their place?"

Jake realized that others probably felt exposed no matter who ordered the killings. He wondered if any others were in danger. A thought struck him. What if some of the others had already been threatened?

"They should delay any votes until this gets straightened out," Jake said.

William smiled. "If the president killed two congressmen to get his tax bill passed, you think he's gonna put it on hold? Not likely."

Jake felt a chill run up his back. He hoped William was wrong about Singleton. Everyone knew the United States political system didn't preclude the people from electing a knucklehead. They had proven that more than once. But a rogue president? Jake had a feeling the system wasn't set up to deal with that.

* * *

The afternoon dragged on forever. Jake was not busy. He basically just kept an eye on the insulation guys as they worked. His thoughts ping-ponged between the killings in Washington and the evening ahead with Monica and her father at the gun club.

He still felt nervous about her father being a preacher. How would that feel to have him looking at Jake every time he and Monica were around? How would it feel, to have a preacher as a father-in-law? Jake thought of his ex-father-in-law. He had been a nice guy. He had liked Jake and had actually apologized for his daughter's behavior when the marriage broke up. How would Jake deal with a preacher?

And why was he thinking about marriage already? He had only met her two nights ago. How could she talk about them ending up together so boldly, so soon? Why hadn't he recoiled at her words? Was he under her spell? Or was there such a thing as fate? Logic told him that even considering marriage this soon was reckless. But some weird part of him was completely comfortable thinking about marrying her, thinking they were meant for each other, and that fate had brought them together. A non-logical part of Jake wanted to believe that. Hopefully, it wasn't hormones.

Jake had a feeling that this evening would answer some of his questions, meeting her father and seeing the two of them interact. He had a feeling that Monica would act differently. He would be surprised if the words engagement, fate, or marriage even came up.

* * *

Jake picked up Monica at the range again. She had worked there until six. She was waiting for him on the curb just like the night before. This time she wore a black V-neck blouse over her jeans. She looked different, more elegant. She slid in next to him on the truck's bench seat, and kissed him briefly on the lips.

"Hi," she said.

He hadn't been expecting the kiss, but he liked it. He smiled. "Hi, yourself."

She told him to drive to the 279, then head north. A dozen miles north of Pittsburgh, they merged onto the 79. Several miles later she told him to exit and head east. They traveled for a while on a small highway before she had him turn north again.

During the trip, they talked about the news and the murdered congressmen. Jake was surprised when she agreed with William, that Singleton had probably been responsible for the killings.

They passed through a small town called Mars. From Mars, they went a few miles north, and then she led him through a series of turns that seemed to take him in a northeast direction. The terrain was very green with private roads leading into the trees on both sides of the road. Just when Jake was hopelessly lost, she had him turn onto a small road on the left. A hundred feet up the road they came on a wrought-iron gate with an electronic keypad. Jake stopped at the keypad and opened his window.

"What's the combination?" he asked her.

She gave him an evil smile. "We're in love, but that doesn't mean I trust you yet." She then leaned over him. He had to let go of the steering wheel as her body pushed over him. He had an urge to wrap his hands around her waist, but he resisted. She reached out and punched in a code. The gate began to roll open.

He laughed as she sat back down next to him. "So we can kiss and hold hands on our first date, but I don't get the code to the club? Do we have to be married before I get it?"

She grinned and held up two fingers. "Two babies, then you get the code."

Jake had no response to that. He knew she was kidding but was still shocked by her response. He looked at her face and saw a vision of her holding a baby in her arms, his baby. She was beaming as she cuddled the baby. Jake felt weird thinking about them married and having kids already, but the image of her holding his baby felt right, like it was supposed to be.

When the gate opened, he drove for a half-mile down a dark heavily forested road before the trees opened into a clearing. In the center was a spectacular lodge made of logs. Half a dozen other cars were parked in front. Jake parked on the end of the row.

"Wow!" he said. "This place is amazing."

She smiled at him. "Wait until you see inside."

Jake grabbed his gun and his two boxes of shells from behind the seat as they got out of the truck. She held his other hand, leading him up the stairs and across the huge porch to the front door. Jake could already see an elegant sitting room through the glass windows. When they walked in, he stopped and looked up at the spacious cathedral ceiling supported by a huge log running the length of the building. He had not worked with logs before, and wondered how they had supported it. At the end of the sitting room was an impressive rock fireplace stretching at least twenty feet up the chimney out of the lodge. The rockwork was incredible and had to be astronomically expensive.

She pulled him along to keep him moving toward the back. In contrast to the airy open space on the right, Jake saw that the left of the lodge was enclosed, with a stairway leading up to what he guessed were bedrooms or meeting rooms. The first floor on the left was probably the kitchen, or offices. There were also stairs that went down, meaning there was also a basement. A fifteen-foot wall separated the sitting room in the front from a huge dining space in the back.

The dining area was spectacular, with a dozen large round tables scattered through the vast space. But Jake's eyes were drawn to the windows. The back of the building was a wall of windows twenty feet high. There was an incredible view out over a massive rear deck with more tables, then out into the forest, where Jake saw areas lit by bright lights. Outside to the right, Jake saw a professional-looking trap and skeet area, where several men were shooting. To the left was a pistol range, and down the middle was a rifle range that stretched a few hundred yards into the distance.

"He's over there," Monica said, and started dragging Jake to a table in the corner by the window.

There were three men at the table. All looked to be in their fifties. On the left sat a gray haired man in an expensive-looking, khaki, long-sleeve shirt with a green shooting pad on the right shoulder. In the middle was a tall, muscular man with a chiseled face, wearing an olive, short-sleeve shirt with a Remington logo on it. On the right, a small squat man with thin hair combed over a balding head, wearing a white shirt and tie. Jake knew at once the small man wearing the white shirt and tie was the preacher. The three men were obviously in an animated conversation, because the gray-haired man was waving his arms.

As they approached, the three looked up. They cooled their conversation. Surprisingly, it was not the small man in the white shirt who stood to receive them, but the large man in the middle with the chiseled face.

"So this is him?" he asked Monica with a deep resonating voice. "The one that fate has brought you?"

Jake couldn't believe he'd actually said fate, and that Monica had talked to her father about that. Jake was still confused about why the middle guy was talking to him. Jake looked down at the man in the white shirt as if he would suddenly stand and confess it had been a joke, and that he was Monica's father. But the large man walked around the table to meet them and reached for Jake's hand.

"Hi, I'm Monica's dad, Clive Lombardi. Nice to meet you." His handshake was firm and powerful.

Jake was speechless. This guy didn't look like any preacher he had ever seen. And the last name, Lombardi, like the Green Bay Packers famous coach. Jake realized he had never learned Monica's last name.

"I'm Jake."

The man looked down at Monica. "You're right, he's a handsome one."

Jake's jaw fell open, and he looked down at Monica. Now Jake knew where she had learned to speak so openly about personal things.

"Sit down," Clive said, motioning to two chairs at the table. "We were just waiting to order some food."

His face became serious. "Did either of you hear the news this afternoon?"

Jake shook his head. "Not this afternoon. Are you talking about the president's press conference this morning?"

All three men shook their heads.

Clive spoke. "Late in the afternoon, the president signed an executive order, temporarily suspending all handgun sales in America. Additionally, over the next two weeks, all handguns already owned by citizens are to be temporarily surrendered to local authorities."

Jake looked at Clive like he was crazy. "Can he do that?"

He furrowed his brow and shook his head. "Technically, no. But he just did."

Jake retorted. "What do you mean, technically, no? How could he do it, if he isn't supposed to be able to?"

Clive gave a knowing look to the two men he had been sitting with. All three had seemed tense, their jaws clenched. Clive motioned to the small man in the white shirt, who Jake had mistaken for Monica's father. "This is Arnie Johnson. He's the head of the NRA for Eastern Pennsylvania." He motioned to the gray-haired man in the shooting jacket. "And this is Ben Jamison. He was a two-term congressman from district four, the area just north of Pittsburgh."

Jake quickly shook hands with each man, then asked incredulously, "How could he do this?" Jake thought about his FN. He had only owned it for three days. The thought of surrendering it to politicians made him want to vomit. It was his, how could they take it?

The NRA man in the white shirt, Arnie Johnson, spoke. "There are a million issues with this. First of all, the Second Amendment prevents governments—state and federal—from prohibiting gun ownership. The Supreme Court has held up the amendment multiple times recently, including in 2008 when it struck down Washington D.C.'s law prohibiting handgun ownership." He snorted his displeasure. "So, the Constitution is clear. The second issue is that in the United States, laws are created and modified in the legislative branch, meaning that laws are supposed to be written by Congress. The president is in the executive branch; he's not supposed to write laws. But years ago they invented this thing called executive order. It's basically a way for the president to bypass the legislative branch and write his own laws."

"Aren't there limitations?" Jake asked.

Ben Jamison ,the ex-congressman, spoke up. He shook his head angrily. "No. There should be, but there's not currently any document defining what is allowed in an executive order. Technically, the president is not supposed to be creating laws with executive orders, rather providing details on how to execute laws."

Clive interrupted. "Executive orders have been overturned in the past by the Supreme Court. Harry Truman had one repealed because the court ruled that he had created a law."

"So what makes Singleton think he can use this to take guns away?" Jake asked.

Arnie explained, "Singleton's text in this order is sneaky. He references current gun laws, and his wording for temporarily suspending sales and temporarily checking-in handguns is written as if he is providing temporary crisis details on how to execute the law, not create law, even though we all know that he is creating law, and he intends it to be permanent, not temporary." Arnie's cheeks were red.

Monica's brow knit as she spoke. "But won't the Supreme Court just throw it out?"

Ben answered, "That's the question of the day. And how fast can they react, since the president wants to collect all the guns in the next two weeks? Can we get a ruling fast enough?"

Clive interjected, "And to make it worse, the Supremes are not in session. The official session for hearing cases does not begin until the first Monday in October."

Arnie added with frustration, "Besides, there has to be a ruling at a lower court first, because the Supreme Court generally only looks at appeals. So, that takes even more time."

Jake glanced at Monica, then argued, "But they've done it much faster in the past, haven't they? If the president's order is supposed to happen in two weeks. . ."

Arnie nodded. "The fastest I've ever seen it go down was after the 2000 election, Bush verses Gore, when there were multiple court cases challenging the election results in Florida. All the rulings worked their way up through the courts. When the Supreme Court made their ruling, it had all happened in five days."

Clive spoke up, "Keep in mind also that the 2008 ruling to allow handguns in Washington was five to four. And remember, Singleton himself appointed a new judge since he took over as president. There is no guarantee on what ruling we'd get."

Jake noticed a lady approach. She was pretty woman wearing a camouflage polo shirt and khaki shorts. "Are you ready to order?" she asked.

"I need to go," Arnie said, as he stood.

Ben also stood and took a last drink from his glass. "I'll go, too." He shook Clive's hand. "I'll let you discuss this with your daughter and her friend."

Clive stood with his guests. "Okay, let's talk again tomorrow. I'll brief these guys during dinner on what we discussed."

Jake and Monica stood and shook both men's hands before they left. He watched them walk away and out of the dining room. The waitress in camo waited patiently.

After they sat back down, Clive spoke to the waitress. "What's on the menu tonight?"

She told them the two choices for the evening were fried chicken and country fried steak. Monica and Jake both wanted the steak. Clive ordered the chicken. They ordered salads as well. She told them it would only be a few minutes.

When she was gone, Clive continued the conversation, although the tension seemed to have dissipated. "So, the bottom line is that both the NRA and our representatives are investigating what can be done to overrule this executive order. We have no answers yet."

Monica said. "Can't we just ignore it? I mean, it's not valid, right?"

Jake nodded.

Clive shrugged. "It really depends on the rest of the government. If they ignore the president, then nothing will come of it. But if the government machinery starts moving, if the Attorney General starts wheels rolling, then we can't just ignore it. If they order gun sales to stop and we keep selling, we could be arrested."

Jake scowled. "So, let me get this straight. The president writes a law he has no authority to write on an issue that obviously contradicts the Second Amendment. Everyone knows it shouldn't be done. But the bogus law goes into effect because the Supreme Court is on vacation?"

Clive arched his eyebrows and nodded. "I think you hit the nail on the head."

"Can't we do anything?" Monica asked.

"Give us a day to strategize," Clive said. "There has to be something that can be done."

The table went silent for a moment. Clive changed the subject. He shifted in his chair toward Jake. "Let's lighten things a bit. Jake, tell me about yourself."

Jake felt Monica grab his hand under the table. Jake glanced at her, then began. He told Clive about the construction business and the home he was remodeling in Pittsburgh.

"Monica told me about your unfortunate divorce. Sorry. I hear far too many of those stories nowadays."

Jake didn't know what to say.

"I don't mean anything about you personally. It's just that divorce and infidelity is a plague that is poisoning this country. It's killing our society. You've been through it. Do you agree?"

Jake shifted in his chair. "I wouldn't recommend it to anyone."

"So, that's what brought you to Pittsburgh? Clean start?"

Jake nodded. "I've always liked Pittsburgh."

"Steelers fan I hear?"

Jake glanced at Monica. He was starting to wonder if anything he would tell the man would be new, or if Monica had already told him everything. "Yeah. I like the Steelers." Jake tried to steer the conversation someplace else. "Hey, I have a question. Is this your lodge? Do you own it?"

Clive and Monica both smiled, as if they both knew Jake wanted to change the conversation.

The camo-clad waitress returned with salads and drinks, and placed them in front of them.

"Thanks, Julie," Monica said.

"Your food will be here in a second."

Clive answered the question. "No. I don't own this place. It's a club. There are many partners." He winked at Jake. "A few Steelers, and even a few Pirates, if you're a baseball fan too."

Jake looked around, suddenly more interested in the club's clientele. There were only three other tables with people, and he didn't recognize anyone. He wondered if any of the men shooting tonight were Steelers.

Clive seemed to read his mind. "I don't think there's anyone here tonight. But if you come here enough, you'll see a couple of the guys from the 70s Super Bowl teams."

"Really? They still live around here?"

Clive ate some salad before responding. "Some of them moved away from Pittsburgh, but they still stop by when they're in town."

Jake shook his head in amazement as he scanned the room again.

They ate for a while before Clive spoke again. "Monica tells me you're a good shot."

Jake rolled his eyes at her. "She's wrong. I've only shot two boxes of shells in ten years, and she had to help me with the trigger because I was pulling low and to the left."

Her father laughed. "Well, she said you have good form, and you don't flinch. She says you have potential."

She pointed her fork at him. "I've seen worse. Trust me. You wouldn't believe some of the idiots we see come in the range."

He smiled at her. "Gee, what a nice compliment, Monica."

She rolled her eyes, but she was smiling, too.

"Well," Clive said, "after dinner, we'll take you out back and let you shoot a few other weapons. It'll be fun."

Julie appeared with the three hot plates. The country-fried steak looked mouth-watering covered with gravy, and steamed vegetables on the side. The discussion slowed for a while as they ate. Clive admitted he had inherited a membership to the club from his father, and that he would never be able to afford to buy-in today on a minister's salary. The club also gave him a break on the dues, because he handled stocking the ammunition inventory and keeping the weapons maintained, facilitated by his ownership of the range in town.

As they were finishing the meal, Jake watched Monica. Like the night before eating fries at the Point, she was a fast eater. He smiled as she took a large mouth full of steak, which seemed too big to fit in her mouth. A large fork full of vegetables quickly followed it. Jake watched the dimple on her cheek move as she chewed, and wondered why the fascination with her dimples. When he looked up at her father, he saw that Clive had been watching Jake watch his daughter.

"You've only known her for 48 hours?" Clive asked. "What do you think?"

Jake knew what the preacher wanted to know, but he didn't really want to go there. "I think she's the fastest eater I've ever met, woman or man."

She elbowed him but continued eating.

Clive laughed. "I've told her to slow down her whole life, but she won't listen."

"Does it ever give her gas?" Jake asked, and then regretted it.

She elbowed him again, harder this time.

"Ouch!" Jake rubbed his ribs. "That hurt." When the pain subsided, he took another bite of his steak. He hoped the reverend had decided not to answer his question. They ate silently for a while.

"Over the years, Monica has met some nice men. But she always told me they weren't the one. She always told me she would know when she met him."

Jake glanced down at her and saw that she had stopped eating and was watching him.

"And?" Jake prompted. He felt her hand on his under the table.

"Do you believe in divine destiny, Jake?" Clive asked.

Jake thought about the feeling he had when he first saw Monica at the shooting range, like he had just met someone he had known for a long time. Even then, Jake had wondered if it was just hormones. He looked at Monica's father and realized that Clive had transformed—he finally seemed like a preacher. When he was talking to the NRA man about the murders in Washington, he had been a politician. Now, there was something different, a sensitivity, an ability to see inside others. It seemed to Jake as if Clive could read his thoughts.

"I've never had any destiny feelings before," Jake said, not sure how he was going to finish. "I mean. I guess others had it, but I never did."

"So, you believe other people can know things?"

Jake shrugged. "I guess, others maybe."

"What if I told you I get those feelings, Jake? What if I told you I sometimes know things, when I meet people? Sometimes I meet somebody, and I know things about them that they don't know about themselves. Would you believe me?"

Jake's mind was telling him that this was very weird, but his heart felt different, relaxed, comfortable. "I don't know. I guess I don't know you well enough. As a preacher, you probably can see stuff. . ." Jake didn't know how to finish.

Clive nodded. He seemed satisfied with the response and continued eating.

Jake felt relieved, but a little disappointed that Clive didn't say what he could see when he looked at Jake.

Jake looked back at Monica. While looking at her, almost like a vision, he saw them married. He imagined her in a white wedding dress, and him pulling her into an embrace. He saw Clive looking on with approval. He saw her on a hospital bed, with a huge stomach, pushing a baby, their baby, out into his waiting hands. He felt a kind of happiness and intimacy he had never felt before. He saw himself from behind, all of them, Jake, Monica, and three boys, all holding hands, walking on grass, in a park.

When the vision cleared, Jake noticed Monica was smiling at him. "You just saw something, didn't you?" she asked, "What was it?"

Jake couldn't tell her. It was way too personal, too intimate. He had seen her naked, giving birth to his child. He looked away from her. "Ah, nothing. I was just thinking." He took a drink of his water.

Monica smiled at him, as if she already knew. Could she read his mind? Sometimes it seemed like it.

* * *

After the meal, Monica and Jake took a walk outside the lodge. The night air was cool, and made Jake appreciate the warmth of Monica's hand in his. He felt no discomfort or awkwardness being in her presence, even after the weird discussion at the table. This surprised him. He felt like he should feel embarrassed, and should want to run and be alone to think. But just the opposite—he wanted to be near her, hold her, and talk to her. In fact, the thought of being separated tonight, when he took her home, was something he was already dreading.

He hadn't felt overly weird around the preacher either, which was also surprising. Jake laughed to himself. Both Monica and her father talked different than anyone he'd ever met. They seemed sure about things like life after death and spiritual understandings. Jake had no experience with stuff like that, and last week he would have said those things were nonsense. His mind kept throwing danger signals:

"You've only known her for two days. She could be putting on an act. She and her father are religious fanatics. You're obviously rebounding from your divorce. She must be desperate to latch onto you."

Jake listened to his brain talking, but not seriously. It was like he had two brains now, a nervous one and a calm one. And right now it felt okay to trust the calm one.

They walked past the trap and skeet area to the rifle range. The rifle range had a dozen lanes, with small tables for guns and gear. There were long dikes of dirt ten feet high on both sides of the range. There were targets at various distances. Two other men were already shooting guns that looked like deer rifles. They had wood-grained stocks and scopes. The guns were very loud, and Monica released Jake's hand to retrieve headphones for both of them for the noise.

Jake looked around. "Didn't your father say he would join us?" His voice sounded muffled and strange while wearing the ear protection.

She pointed to the lodge. "He's getting a gun."

She led him to one of the tables on the left side, away from the two other shooters. She motioned for Jake to leave his gun on the table, then led him over to a small kiosk where she extracted a large target from a bin at the base. She walked behind the dirt mound that isolated them from the lanes. Jake followed her and they walked parallel to the shooting lanes, with the dike protecting them from bullets. After they had walked the distance of a football field, the ground dipped a few feet and there was a perpendicular aisle on the right, heading across the shooting lanes. Jake saw that it was basically a trench that kept the person low enough to not get killed as bullets zinged overhead.

He followed Monica into the large trench. There was a target overhead for each lane. Each was counter weighted so they could easily be lowered to replace the target. She walked to the second target and pulled it down, removing four clips from the corners and the old target with a million holes, and replaced it with the new one. After she pivoted the new target back up into the air, they returned to the shooting area.

Clive was waiting at the small table, and he had a gun that Jake recognized as an assault weapon. It was black, had an adjustable rear stock, a pistol grip behind the trigger, a muzzle break on the end of the barrel, and a latch under the barrel to add a bayonet. Jake felt excited. He had never shot an assault weapon before.

"Is that legal?" Jake asked.

Clive was loading rifle shells into a magazine and glanced up. "Sure, as long as you live in a free state. You can't own one in New York, Jersey, Massachusetts, or California."

Monica spoke up. "It's an AR-15. It's semi-auto."

Jake nodded. He knew the difference between semi- and full-auto. A full-auto was like a machine gun, you pulled the trigger and the gun kept shooting. Semi meant you got one shot for every trigger pull.

Clive finished loading the shells in the magazine, then rammed the magazine into the gun in an aggressive motion. He pulled and released a handle above the stock to chamber a round, then handed the gun to Jake. Jake couldn't control the smile on his face. He walked in front of the table and brought the gun to his shoulder. The sites on the AR were a small circle on the rear, which you looked through to center a small post on the barrel. Jake found the target. He had a hard time keeping the gun steady on a target a hundred yards away. It was like it was moving.

He felt Monica click something on the left side of the gun. He broke his aim and looked at her.

"Safety," she said.

He nodded, knowing that she had released the safety and the gun was ready to shoot. He aimed again and waited for his aim to stabilize. He had a feeling the gun was going to kick like a mule, so he tensed and pulled the trigger.

The gun fired and bucked. It was incredibly loud even with the headphones. But the recoil was nothing, surprisingly light, not much more than a .22. He felt the gun move when he fired it, but the kick had been absorbed somehow by the stock. It felt way cool to fire a weapon so powerful without feeling any discomfort.

He looked at Monica and Clive. "Awesome!"

"You missed," Clive said, pointing at the target. "Try again."

Jake took aim again. This time he didn't flinch. The gun bucked.

"Got it!" Clive said.

Jake shot again and again, maybe ten shots. Clive called out hits and misses. Monica interrupted him, and led him back to the table. She helped him prop the gun on his elbow on the table, to stabilize it. It helped a lot. His aim was far more stable. He fired again.

"Six inches low," Clive called out. He was now watching the target through a spotting scope mounted on a tripod.

Jake was more than happy to be only six inches low at a hundred yards. Actually, he was amazed. He shot again.

"Four inches."

He kept shooting. The gun seemed to hold a million bullets. Finally, he pulled the trigger and nothing happened.

"You're out," Monica said.

Jake stood, smiling from ear to ear. He handed the AR to Clive. "What a gun! That was amazing."

"Nice, huh?" Clive said.

The two other shooters in the range seemed to be done. They were packing up their stuff. No one was shooting, so Jake took off the ear protection. Monica and Clive did likewise.

"I used to wonder what the big deal was," Jake said, "why the attraction to assault weapons. No wonder. It's light and way easy to shoot." He looked down at the target. "And pretty accurate." He looked at Monica. "Isn't it?"

She nodded. "You did great for your first time. Of course, with my teaching, you'll get a lot better."

He smiled at her. "What's the discount on tactical training if we're dating?"

She first looked at Clive, and then they both smiled in response. "I think we can arrange something."

They spent another forty-five minutes at the rifle range. Clive left them alone to shoot while he returned to the lodge. Monica helped Jake with everything, his positioning, his hold, his trigger pull, and his breathing. They replaced the target multiple times. By the end, he was shooting far better, most of his shots grouped within a few inches at a hundred yards, which Jake thought was unbelievable. Monica kept hugging him and slapping him on the back. When Jake finished, he held up the gun and admired it. Since they were alone in the range, they both removed their headphones.

Jake handed the gun to her. "How much is one of these?"

* * *

The drive home was quiet. At first Monica had snuggled into him, and Jake put his arm around her. After a while she lay down and put her head on his lap. Jake's right hand alternated between playing with her hair and gently stroking her back through her blouse. He wondered how things could change so fast. Only 48 hours before, he had been alone, still angry about the divorce. If someone would have asked him about a new relationship, he would have said he wasn't ready. But then he'd met Monica. How could he say it? It was like she reached into his black cloud, snatched him, and took him into another world. He hadn't really compared her to his ex. It was like that relationship had never happened. It was like this was Jake's first time being in love. It didn't make sense, but that's how it felt.

She rolled over onto her back so her face looked up at him, her head still on his lap. He used his fingers to comb her black hair out of her eyes and tuck it over her ears. In the dim cab of his pickup her eyes were black pools looking up at him. He wondered what she was thinking. Of him, obviously. She was considering him. Two days before, Jake had never seen this woman. Now it was like she was a part of him. He couldn't imagine ever being apart from her again. The thought of sleeping alone in his bed tonight, it was wrong.

"What are you thinking?" she asked.

He glanced down at her black eyes. "I'm thinking you should stay at my house tonight."

She shook her head. "Can't"

His lifted his hand and broke the touch. He felt extreme disappointment and emptiness at the thought of not snuggling next to her. "Can't tonight? Your father?"

"Can't ever," she said. "Not till after we're married."

He looked down at her. Her eyes were boring into his, making sure he understood what she was saying.

"Serious?" he asked. "Your father? Is it because he's a priest?"

She shook her head. "It's not my father; it's me. Not until we're married."

Jake was a little blown away. Did this mean she was a virgin? He had no idea anyone really waited nowadays. Well, maybe the ugly ones. But Monica was beautiful, sexy, and so alive, so confident. How could she be innocent at the same time?

She sat up in the seat next to him and held his hand. "How does that make you feel?" she asked.

"I don't know," he answered truthfully.

"Did you and your wife wait until you were married?"

He snorted a laugh. "No. Hell no."

"Why not?" she asked.

Jake glanced down at her. She wasn't judging him; she just wanted to understand his state of mind.

"Never entered our minds, I guess." He glanced down at her for a second before returning his eyes to the road. "I'm not sure I ever met anyone who waited until they were married."

"What do you think about it?"

"I didn't think anybody waited anymore. Do all the people, you know, in your church, do they all wait?"

She shrugged. "Not all. Some."

"Then why you?"

"I don't care what everyone else in the church does. I don't care what everyone else in the world does. The Bible is clear on it. I know what God wants me to do, and I'm going to do what he wants. Anything else would be wrong."

Jake considered himself. Divorced. Slept with his ex and a few others before he was married. Not even close to being a virgin. How could she ever want him?

"What about me?" he said.

"What do you mean?" she asked.

"How could you even consider . . ." What was he trying to say? "How could you think that after waiting like you have, that some guy like me . . ."

She shook her head. "To be honest, I always thought I would meet a guy that had waited like me. But then I met you, Jake. And what I was waiting for seems unimportant now."

Jake interrupted. "But how can you wait, yet not expect—"

"I did expect, Jake. I expected to meet somebody just like me. But I didn't. I met you. And it's like my heart has been made okay with your past. All I can see is you. I can forgive you, as long as I get all of you now."

Jake had no words for that. She may have just forgiven him for everything he had ever done, but it wasn't that easy. He hadn't even forgiven himself for all the stuff he'd done in his life. How could he ever live up to that? She might not hold it against him that he wasn't a virgin, but all of a sudden, he felt dirty because of it, and a little bit unworthy of her.

As he saw the signs for downtown Pittsburgh, he welcomed a change of subject, "I don't know where you live. Where do you want me to take you?"

She snuggled into him. "I'm not far from the range. Head that way." She motioned to the left.

They rode in silence for a while.

"You're freaked out," she said.

"A little," he admitted.

She wrapped her arm around his neck and kissed his cheek. "Don't be."

From the range, she had him drive up the slope about ten blocks, then over a couple streets to a small row house in the middle of the block. It looked identical to all the other houses on the street. Like his home, it was a remnant of the steel towns from fifty years ago.

She hugged him tight and whispered in his ear. "I had a wonderful time tonight."

He hugged her back, but was already feeling depressed at their imminent separation. "Me, too."

She released the hug, then kissed him hard on the lips. Her lips were wet and soft and passionate. His hands found her back and pulled her body tight to his. The kiss lasted a long time, but she finally ended it.

"Bye," she said.

He was breathing heavily. "I don't want to let you go."

She smiled. "I don't want you to."

But she slithered out of his hands and slid across the seat to the passenger-side door. She picked up one of his hands and kissed it. She opened the door and ran up the walk to her house. She went in without looking back.

He felt like he was in a daze on the drive back home, like an out-of-body experience. He had only known this girl for two days, and he was already thinking marriage. He couldn't tell anyone, his friends or the guys he worked with. They would think he was nuts. But right now, it felt right. It felt way right. It felt too right, like he was a zombie, like she had hypnotized him, like she was leading him around by the nose. But when he thought about being with her, and remembered the vision of her having his baby, it felt like it was supposed to be. Was that a glimpse into his future destiny, him and her with three boys?

He was startled to find out he was parked in his driveway with the engine running. How long had he been there? He had driven the whole way home in a trance. He laughed at himself and shut off the engine. He gathered his things, including his gun, and headed into the house.

CHAPTER 7

When Jake arrived at work the next morning, the insulation guys were waiting for him again. He let them in, and they went right at it. They said they would be done in a few hours, and they needed to be at another job by noon. He was impressed at how fast they worked.

Jake kept himself busy, cleaning up and moving things away from the walls. Since it was Friday, with insulation due to be finished, a sheet rock crew was scheduled for the next morning. The panels of sheet rock would be delivered that afternoon. He needed to be ready.

As promised, the crew finished installing insulation before lunch. They packed up and were gone, leaving Jake alone. As he finished sweeping up, William Henry Campbell III came in the door. He looked up at the ceiling and poked the insulation with his cane. Jake continued cleaning and let the owner check the work in all the rooms. After five minutes, Jake felt the cane tap him on the shoulder. Jake turned and leaned on the broom.

They spoke about the house for a while. William was curious about the next phase, sheet rocking, and Jake answered his questions.

He spoke to Jake without looking at him. "So what are you going to do about your new gun?"

It was a question Jake had been mulling all morning regarding the president's executive order. He pictured himself handing the gun to some men at a table who checked it off their list then turned and placed it on a pile of guns the size of a house. The pile contained shotguns, hunting rifles, and many black guns like the AR-15 they let him shoot the night before at the range.

"How do you think it's going to go down?" Jake asked.

William rubbed the handle of his cane on his chin. "That's what everyone is wondering. They haven't said yet. Half of Pittsburgh is probably out digging holes in the woods, burying their handguns under a tree or a rock."

Jake laughed at the image. "I assume you got a few guns. What are you going to do?"

"They don't know about mine. They were purchased years ago—before the paperwork."

Jake felt jealous. If only he'd bought his years before, or even when he lived in Indianapolis, or bought a used one from somebody with no paperwork. His gun was only a few days old. His papers were probably on the top of the pile.

"What would you do, if you were me?" Jake asked.

"It depends," William said. "It depends on what everyone else does. Let's say they tell everyone to bring their guns to the police station and turn them in. And let's say most people do. They just check them off their lists, and then come after the few who don't comply. Not much chance for you in that scenario, other than blasting them when they come up to your front door."

Jake imagined himself shooting at cops in his front yard. He grimaced. He didn't think it would come to that.

William continued, "But if they call for people to turn them in, and nobody does, then what? Are they going to go to a million doors, especially when a third of them are loony enough to start shooting?"

Jake had wondered about the logistics himself. Even with the executive order, it seemed like an impossible effort to try to confiscate that many guns when owners didn't want to surrender them. He agreed with the old man; it really depended on the sheep. If they all resisted, there was no way. But if they all went in the pen, then the few remaining outside the corral would be easy pickings.

"It also depends on the cops," William said. He pointed his cane in the general direction of the city. "Probably some city's police departments are going to see themselves as Nazis and aggressively go after every gun until they get everyone on the list. But in other cities, the chief might not really believe in the whole deal, or maybe he's afraid of getting shot. Let's say he sets up a table for people to bring them in, but only a few show up. My guess is that some cities will go get them, and others won't; that and how the citizens respond will determine what happens."

Jake figured William was right. Individual and group dynamics would play a large part in the success of the president's goal. He thought of a few cities across the country and wondered what might happen. Maybe Indianapolis would conform, and Chicago—they already had stiff gun laws. But there might be uprisings in cities like Cleveland or Detroit. What about out west? What about the rednecks in Wyoming, Idaho, or New Mexico? Jake had a feeling there might be some high noon shootouts out there.

"What about here in Pittsburgh?" Jake asked.

"Hard to tell. I don't really care for our police commissioner. I didn't vote for him. The wife and I have met him at a couple social events. He seems like an arrogant prick, full of himself. The real question is, will he have the stomach for this task, or will he floor the accelerator and declare war on his own people? I'd give him fifty/fifty."

Jake didn't know the commissioner, didn't really remember ever seeing his picture on television or in the papers. He wouldn't recognize him if he saw him walking down the street. Jake considered the people of Pittsburgh. Were they the rebellious type? He thought not. Maybe things would have been different back in the steel mill days; those guys were tougher. He imagined a large mob of steel workers in hard hats, waving their guns in the air and daring anyone to try to take them away.

But twenty-first-century Pittsburgh was different. The steel workers were gone or absorbed into the woodwork. Modern Pittsburgh was made up of office workers. It felt like a town that was more likely to conform. He pictured men wearing ties lining up in straight lines to turn in their guns as ordered. Jake hoped he was wrong. But as the old man said, group dynamics would play a critical role in the way things would go.

"You could tell them you sold it." He waved his cane at the window for emphasis. "Hell knows there would be plenty of buyers."

Jake had already considered lying. It would be almost impossible for the police to dispute. But Jake was not a liar. He would feel very uncomfortable doing it, even for a good reason. He was pretty sure he was a bad liar anyway, and they would be able to see right through him. It occurred to Jake that he needed to find somebody to trade guns with. Then, when they asked him to return his FN, he could legitimately tell the truth and say he sold it and no longer had physical possession. He wouldn't need to lie. If they asked who he sold it to, he had no legal mandate to answer, did he?

Better yet, if the citizens organized themselves for a big event, a big trade, out in the country someplace. They could potentially trade guns with each other without even knowing the person they were trading with. Then everyone could say with a straight face that they no longer owned the gun they purchased with paperwork. That would change the whole dynamic, wouldn't it? Then the police wouldn't know who had what. Much harder to confiscate anything.

"I just wish I knew how it was going down," Jake answered. "Hopefully, they'll announce something soon. I need to figure out what options I have."

William III looked skeptical. He stared at Jake in a disapproving way. "Life doesn't always give you time to think. Sometimes you need to make your decisions in advance, before you know how things are going to work out."

Jake didn't know it then, but William couldn't have been more right.

* * *

That night Monica and Jake met downtown, bordering the University of Pittsburgh. Jake had trouble finding a parking spot and had to walk several blocks up Forbes Avenue to Primanti Brothers. Monica was waiting for him out front. She waved enthusiastically, then ran the last few steps and jumped on him, wrapping her legs around him. She was wearing khaki shorts. Jake had never seen her in shorts before. He decided he liked her legs. She wore another tank top, which made Jake wonder how many she had. He wore his usual jeans and Steelers t-shirt.

She kissed him briefly on the lips and smiled. "You're here!"

He laughed. Of course he was here. There was never any question. After discovering Jake had never eaten at Primanti's in his six months in Pittsburgh, Monica had insisted. She called the food a staple of native Pittsburghers. Jake had heard of the Primanti Brothers chain, since there were at least of dozen of the restaurants scattered throughout Pittsburgh. But he had never gotten around to eating at any of them.

Monica released him and slid back to the sidewalk. She grabbed his hand and dragged him to the front door of the small establishment. The Oakland Primanti Brothers looked like a small sports bar, with its neon signs for Samuel Adams and Coors Light. The front facade was constructed of dark wood with modest moldings and numerous windows arched at the tops. A green fabric awning sheltered the front of the store.

A man exiting held the door for them, and Monica whisked them inside. The aroma of grilled onions and steak greeted them. The tables were packed close together with a balcony overhead holding more tables up top. The place was bustling and crowded, and Jake wondered if they would be able to find a seat. Since they were next to the University of Pittsburgh, there were plenty of students, but Jake also saw a few families and quite a few nicely dressed men and women wearing ties and skirts.

Monica pulled them into line at an ordering desk, just behind an older couple in their seventies. Jake looked up at the menu on the wall behind the counter. Among more standard sandwiches, he saw kielbasa, capicola, imported sardine, and ragin' Cajun chicken.

"What's kielbasa?" he asked Monica.

She was looking at the menu as well. "Sausage, spicy!" She turned and looked at him questioningly. "You want that?"

He shook his head. "No, what are you getting?"

She pointed. "My favorite, Pitts-Burgher Cheese Steak."

"Sounds good. I'll have one, too."

She pointed to a couple cleaning up their stuff and leaving, and Jake took the hint to leave the line and go grab their seats. He used some napkins to clean a few greasy spots from the previous customers. He sat down and waited.

"Here's our drinks," she said a few minutes later, depositing two Cokes on the table. She tossed two straws in front of him and returned to wait for the sandwiches.

Jake noticed they had been lucky; the line now stretched to the door. Two guys walked by with their sandwiches on a tray and made a big deal at staring at the empty table Jake was saving. Jake glanced at the counter and saw Monica just getting their order on a tray. When she arrived, she slid his sandwich in front of him.

Jake stared at his sandwich, then up at Monica. He had no idea what to do. The sandwich was huge. And the French fries were inside the sandwich! The fries and a bunch of coleslaw were hanging out the sides. The sandwich had to be four or five inches thick with all that stuff in it. How was he supposed to eat it? No way would it fit in his mouth.

Monica took a dangling fry and ate it, then gathered her sandwich in both hands and took a large bite of the mass. Slaw and fries fell on her plate, and a few bounced onto the table. Jake now understood why the surface was so messy from the previous customers. He copied Monica and took a bite from his. He had to admit the crazy mixture tasted good. The bread was white and soft, and Jake could tell he only had a few more maneuvers left before it fell apart. Monica held hers together far longer than Jake, who only got a half dozen bites before he dumped the whole sandwich in a pile on his plate. Soon they were both eating the slaw, fries, and steak with forks. They laughed as they talked about the weird sandwich.

Jake looked around at the crowd and wondered how many of them were gun owners. Was there a look? He wondered how many of them had handguns, and how many intended to turn them in over the next week or so. Everyone was smiling and laughing. If these people were concerned about gun confiscation, they weren't showing it. He looked at a bearded guy, sitting alone and wearing a worn beer t-shirt. The man looked gruff and nasty. Jake couldn't imagine the guy voluntarily surrendering his guns. Of course, Jake didn't even know if the guy had a gun.

"What are you thinking?" Monica said.

Jake looked around. "I'm wondering how many of them have handguns."

"No way to know. Definitely less than the people out in the country."

"How do you know that?" Jake asked.

"Common knowledge. Haven't you ever seen the blue and red election maps? The cities are blue and the rest of the country is red."

"But does that apply to gun ownership as well?"

She nodded. "Not a hundred percent, but for the most part."

"How do you know?" Jake asked.

"Guns and gun owners are my business. I've seen reports of gun ownership in Pennsylvania before, the percentages are definitely higher outside Pittsburgh and Philly."

"What about the inner city, the gangs?"

Monica smirked. "That's different. I thought we were talking about legal owners. Anyway, the Pittsburgh media and political atmosphere is mostly anti-guns. I'd say Pittsburgh might even have lower gun ownership than most other cities."

Jake motioned around. "How are the few going to react to confiscation?"

Monica glanced around. "Pittsburgh might be easier than most."

Jake looked down at the pile of food on his tray. He took a fry from the pile and ate it. "What a crazy sandwich."

Monica took a swig of her drink before responding. "The Primantis started out serving truckers. They invented the slaw and fry sandwich in the 30s." She winked at him. "Now, ya're really from da Burg."

Jake raised his eyebrows. "I'm a true Yinzer?"

She scoffed and responded with a lazy Scot-Irish accent. "Yinzer? Never. Don't jag me. Yinz gotta be bawn in da Burgh, and speak da proper Pittsburghese. Yinz daddy ha'da work in the mills."

Jake was amazed. The accent was so thick he barely understood. He looked at her and realized it wasn't just the words or the brogue; it was the culture. She was different. It scared him a little, like he would never be like her or completely understand her. But as he stared at her dark green eyes, her smile, and that damn dimple on her cheek, he felt the pull—her pulling him into her world, and him wanting to be pulled. He felt like he was falling.

She pushed her plate aside, obviously done. "Let's redd up."

He looked at her confused. "What?" He wondered if she was joking about guns.

She stood with a napkin in her hand "Redd up," she repeated forcefully. She passed the napkin to him. "Tidy up. Clean up. Geez. Yinz think I wanna hang with these Yinzers all da night." She motioned at the other people in the restaurant.

Jake laughed and took a last drink from his Coke and then started wiping up the mess around his plate.

When they were back outside, she put her arms around his neck and pulled his face to hers. "Never thought you would fall for a Yinzer, did ya?"

He smiled, and they kissed. It was a flavorful kiss. It tasked like cheese steak and slaw.

* * *

After dinner, they drove to Jake's place. Since Monica had never been there before, Jake showed her around.

"It feels like a bachelor pad," she said. "It needs a woman's touch."

"What would you change if it were yours?"

"Everything, except that Super Bowl poster in the office. I'd keep that."

The poster she referred to showed Hines Ward and James Harrison holding up the Lombardi Trophy after the Steelers' sixth Super Bowl victory.

He pointed to the sofa. "What do you want to do? You want to stay a while?"

She took his offer, and they moved over and sat on the couch.

She looked around again. "This place isn't bad, maybe a couple real pictures. Maybe some furniture that matched."

"Bedroom?"

"No thanks," she said, smiling.

He rolled his eyes. "That's not what I meant. What would you change?"

"It could use a real bed spread. But I got that stuff."

Jake smiled. She was already thinking about what it would be like when they merged their possessions.

"I'm hot," she said, and took off her sweater.

He admired her curves in her navy tank.

"It's okay if you want to rub my neck," she said. She pulled her hair to the side to expose the back of her neck.

He laughed at her boldness and scooted close to her. He reached up with both hands, massaging her shoulders, then working them toward the middle until he could run both thumbs up the base of her neck.

She groaned in satisfaction.

He worked his hands higher and massaged into her hairline. She subtly moved her head back and forth to allow better access. After a few minutes of that, he returned his hands to her shoulders and kneaded them and her upper arms. Her arms were firm and strong. He stopped massaging for a minute, and ran his finger over the dimple on her shoulder.

She watched him.

He pulled her face toward him and kissed her cheek. Her skin was creamy soft, and her eyes were black and glistening.

"What does it taste like?"

"Cheese steak and slaw," he lied.

She pulled back. "Do I need to brush my teeth?"

"Let's see." He kissed her aggressively on the mouth. He could, in fact, still taste the sandwich. But he didn't mind. She hungrily responded, and the kiss lasted a while.

When they finally came up for air, she looked over her shoulder at the bedroom. She pulled herself away from him, got up and closed the door, before returning to the couch.

"What was that all about?" he asked.

"I'm not going back in there again."

"Too dirty?" he asked.

"No, too dangerous. I'm pretty sure we can't trust ourselves if we go in there."

"What do you want to do, then?" Jake wasn't sure what to do. She had communicated pretty clearly that home runs were against the rules. He wondered what was okay.

In answer to his thoughts, she reached up and ran her hands through his hair. "We can't really do any of the stuff we want." She looked around, then pointed to the TV. "Maybe we should turn that on. Do you want to see what's on?"

He was happy to settle for just being with her tonight. He had had no other expectations. He grabbed the remote and hit the power button. While it was powering up, she snuggled up to him. The TV came up on a news channel, and a man and two women were talking about the president's executive order. Jake figured a movie would be more appropriate, and he held up the remote to change the channel.

"Leave it here," Monica said.

He sat back on the couch and put his feet up on the coffee table. She did the same, and he put his arm around her. He wasn't that interested in watching TV at the moment, but decided if he had to watch, he liked doing it with her body touching his.

The TV showed a split screen with three windows. On the left was an anchorwoman wearing a white blouse, in the middle a man in a gray suit, and on the right a woman wearing a bright red blouse.

The woman in white asked, "But Congressman, Chicago has already collected 25,000 handguns. How can you say it won't work?"

The man responded, "In a city the size of Chicago, there are probably over a million handguns, 25,000 is a drop in the bucket."

The woman in red spoke up. "But it's only the first day. They still have two weeks, and tomorrow and Sunday are projected to be the biggest days. Obviously the numbers will get way higher."

The man was shaking his head. "Don't count on it. The first people to forfeit guns are obviously people who didn't want them, the people who inherited a gun after their parents or spouse died. Those guns have probably been sitting in drawers for years, and they didn't know what to do with them. Haven't you seen the people they've been interviewing? It's mostly old ladies. I haven't seen a single middle-aged man interviewed who actually wanted to keep his gun, but agreed to turn it in."

The commentator in white asked, "What do you predict the rest of the gun owners are going to do? The middle-aged men, as you described them. Will they ignore the president's executive order?"

He responded, "They're waiting. The scared ones are procrastinating, waiting to see what happens over the next few days. The brave ones are burying their guns in the back yard, or hiding them in the attic, or selling them to their cousins so Chicago loses track of them. The cavalier ones are probably cleaning and loading them and waiting on the front porch, ready to defend them. The criminals, however, the ones the president accused of killing my fellow congressmen, those along with all the other thugs in this country that use guns for crime, including the gangs, which account for way over half of the gun crime, they will not be driving downtown. They will not be surrendering their guns in Chicago. The only guns the president is collecting are the guns from law abiding citizens."

The lady in red spoke up. "The congressman is wrong and doesn't give the people of this country enough credit. I believe most Americans are honorable and will heed the president's order even if they disagree. Don't forget that this is only a temporary measure. These people will eventually get their guns back after the murderers are—"

The man interrupted. "You don't believe that any more than I do."

"Yes, I do. Most Americans are honest, and even if they—"

He interrupted her again. "Nobody in this nation believes this gun grab is temporary. Go do a survey. And nobody is expecting the gangs and the criminals to turn in their guns. This is a permanent confiscation of guns from law-abiding citizens."

She responded, "You're selling Americans short."

He countered, "You're selling them down the road."

The commentator broke in. "We need to stop now. I'd like to thank both Congressman Williams from Wyoming and Samantha Jepson from the Brady Commission for their time. Before we go to break, let me remind you that here in Pittsburgh, all precincts will begin taking guns starting at 9:00 a.m. tomorrow morning."

The picture was replaced by a bar scene, and a frosty bottle of beer slid down the bar toward the viewer. Jake didn't want to watch the commercial and killed the TV.

They sat in silence for a long awkward moment.

"Are you going to turn in your new gun in tomorrow morning?" she asked.

"No chance in hell!" Jake said a little too loudly.

"What about later in the week?"

Jake ran his hands over his face. "I don't know," he said. "The congressman is right. This is a permanent gun grab, and everybody knows it." He looked at her. "What about you and your father?"

"I haven't talked to him. I haven't had the chance. I can't imagine he would even . . ." She shook her head.

They talked for an hour about how the gun confiscations might play out. They talked about options. They talked about potential ways to circumvent the process. If you had an older gun, without paperwork, you had a chance. But new guns with paperwork, like Jake's, would be almost impossible to keep without having a felony warrant against you. Jake knew he only had a day or two to do something before someone came to his house to get it.

After a while, they stretched out on the couch and snuggled. They did lots of kissing and massaging. Jake was into it, and wanted more, but even while they were making out, the gun confiscation issue was competing for part of his brain. What was going to happen, and was there any way he could keep his new FN? A few minutes before eleven, they extracted themselves, and Jake drove her home. He did need to work a few hours in the morning, even if it was Saturday.

CHAPTER 8

In the morning, Jake was eating a toasted waffle when he heard someone knocking loudly on his front door. He looked at the clock, 7:10 a.m. Who would be knocking at this hour? He pictured Monica in some long pajama pants. He swallowed and walked to the door with a smile on his face. When he opened the door, the smile vanished. There were two policemen from the Pittsburgh Police Department. He had not seen these two before. One was a big and heavy white guy, the other a skinny black guy. The fat one held a clipboard in his hand. Jake wondered if they had caught the thugs that had broken into his house.

The fat one read from the clipboard. "I'm officer Dickson, and this is officer Emory. Are you Jake McKinley?"

"You caught 'em?" Jake asked.

"Who?" Dickson asked.

"The guys that broke in here."

The officer looked confused. "When?"

Jake's shoulders slouched and the energy drained out of him. He was getting a bad feeling about this visit. "Monday."

"Sorry. We're not here about that."

Jake had guessed as much. "If you're not here for that . . ."

Dickson looked at his clipboard. "We understand you recently purchased an FN FNS-40 in 40 Smith and Wesson caliber."

Jake said nothing. They were here to confiscate his gun. They didn't give a damn about the scumbags that broke into his house. They were here to take the FN. His new FN, the one he had bought with his own money. It occurred to Jake that the handgun was his favorite possession in the world at the moment.

Dickson looked at his clipboard. "Looks like you just bought it at Highlands Hunting and Fishing on Monday . . ." He looked up from the clipboard. "Was that the same day as your break-in?"

Jake looked at his face. The fat cop was grinning.

"Yeah, that afternoon, after work."

Dickson nodded. "Well, the reason we're here . . ."

Jake already knew why they were here. This was way sooner than he had projected. He had been sure he would have a few days. He tried to think quickly. Was there some way to get out of this? He had just admitted he bought the gun. Of course they had the paperwork, so denying it would be a waste of time. This wasn't supposed to happen so fast. He needed time to think about his response. There were really only a couple directions he could take. Why had he opened the damn door?

"Jake, as you know, the president has issued an executive order requiring that all handguns be turned in to authorities as a temporary measure—"

Jake interrupted, "Bullshit. It's not temporary, and you know it."

Officer Dickson looked up. "The president has assured us this is only temporary, until the murderers are apprehended."

Jake could have sworn the cop had just winked at him. Jake felt his neck getting hot. "Yeah, right. It was probably the president's hit men that killed those guys."

The cop's expression changed, and the skinny black officer beside him perked up for the first time since they arrived.

"Did you just accuse the president of the United States of murder, Mr. McKinley?"

Jake sighed loudly. They were now officially in la la land. "No. I did not accuse anyone of anything, especially the president. I was just repeating speculation from national news."

Jake made a spot decision that he was not going to forfeit his gun. No way, no how.

Dickson seemed to realize they were at the same junction in the conversation. He glanced at his watch, and then back down at his clipboard. "Can you go get your FN FNS-40, and we'll give you a receipt for it?"

"No," Jake answered matter-of-factly.

Dickson looked appraisingly at him. "No? You are refusing to honor a directive from the president of the United States and the Pittsburgh Police Department?"

Jake shook his head. "No, I'm not refusing anything. The gun isn't here."

"Where is it?"

"Friend's house," Jake lied.

Dickson pushed forward to enter the house. "Can we come in and look around?"

Jake panicked, putting his arm up to block them. "No, you can't come in."

The cop reached down and pulled a printout from his clipboard. He held it up to Jake. "This here is a signed search warrant for us to enter." He smirked at Jake. "You can't stop us."

This couldn't be happening. Jake tried to get in front of Dickson who was now pushing past him. "Wait, let me read that."

Dickson handed it to the other officer who had approached the door. "Here, Officer Emory will go over it with you while I search your house." Dickson then pushed past him.

Emory took Jake's arm and led him inside. He motioned to the couch "Why don't you sit over here, Mr. McKinley, while you read it."

Jake saw Dickson head straight for his bedroom. He felt the energy drain out of him. He had lost, and he knew it. He sat on the couch and tried to read the warrant Emory was holding out to him, but his mind was mush. It was just a bunch of words with a blue ink signature at the bottom. Jake heard drawers from the bedroom. It wouldn't be long.

"What have we here?" Dickson yelled from the bedroom.

Jake pinched the bridge of his nose. He felt so violated. In his own house. Why hadn't he taken action? He recalled the jokes about burying guns in the back yard. If only he would have done the same. He should have followed William's advice to decide before the confrontation. They had no right.

Dickson came out of the bedroom with the FN's plastic box cupped under one arm. "That didn't take long."

He filled out a form and put the gun's model and serial number on it. When he was done, he held the form out to Jake. "Okay, here's your claim sheet. Don't lose it." This time he definitely winked at

Jake. "As soon as the killers are caught, and the president says you can have it back, you bring this in."

Jake stood and snatched the form from Dickson. "This is completely illegal."

Dickson pointed to the warrant Officer Emory was holding. "No, it isn't, Mr. McKinley. It was signed by a judge this morning."

"Just because your corrupt judges signed it, doesn't make it legal. This is a violation of the Second Amendment."

Dickson shrugged. "Get a lawyer. Maybe you're right."

The two officers headed for the door. But Dickson stopped before he left. "Oh, and Mr. McKinley—I'm going to go back to the office, and I'm going to discuss your little lie, and decide with Officer Emory here whether you should be charged with obstructing justice and interfering with an investigation." They walked out and closed the door behind them.

Jake put his head in his hands. He felt light headed, with no energy. His stomach felt like it had a rock in it. He felt ashamed for lying and embarrassed for getting caught in the lie. He felt weak for letting them walk over him like that. He felt debased by the entire episode. The search warrant was unexpected. They must have had a pile of them, all signed and ready, for every visit. Made sense now that you thought about it. But how had they done it so quickly?

He walked in the bathroom. He looked at himself in the mirror. What a wimp. When he woke this morning, America was still a free country. Now? They had just pushed him aside, searched his house, and taken his ability to defend himself. And they had done it with attitude. Jake didn't feel free. His stomach was clenched in a painful knot. He glanced at the toilet. He didn't throw up the waffles and orange juice, but he was sure it would have made him feel better if he did.

Jake had never felt so humiliated in his life. Except maybe when his ex had told him she was leaving him for the fat doctor.

* * *

After a few minutes of wandering aimlessly around the house, Jake retrieved his cell phone from the kitchen counter where he had left it the night before. He needed to call Monica and warn her. Why had no one called him? But the screen was dark and the battery dead.

He carried it quickly into the bedroom and connected the charger. After a slow boot cycle and reconnection, it showed numerous missed calls and texts. He didn't take time to check them, he just called Monica. He had to lean over the dresser to prevent pulling the cord out.

She answered immediately. "Jake, where were you? I tried to—"

He cut her off. "I know."

"Did they get—"

"Yes. They were just here."

She moaned, "Oh, I was afraid of that. I tried to warn you."

"What about you guys?"

She sounded like she was in a car. "They cleaned out the range, early this morning."

Jake grimaced and squeezed the bridge of his nose.

"Where are you now?"

She spoke away from the phone, to someone else. "What?"

He definitely heard car noise and a truck passing in the other direction. He heard a man's voice, probably Clive's.

"Jake, are you still working this morning?"

Jake looked his watch. The sheetrock crew would be waiting for him. "Uh, I was planning on it. Why, do you need me?"

"No. We can manage. Call me when you're done."

"Are you guys okay?" Jake had the sense that she wanted him over there, wherever they were going.

"We're fine, Jake. I gotta go. I can't talk now. Call me as soon as you're done."

"Okay."

She hung up without saying goodbye.

* * *

When Jake arrived at the site, three guys from the sheetrock crew were already there waiting for him to unlock the doors and let them in. The lead guy, Pete, was angry and complained that they had been waiting for almost an hour. When Jake explained why he was late, Pete's demeanor changed.

"Uh, would you mind if I ran home real quick?" Pete said. "I got a couple handguns in the house. I need to move 'em." He then asked if anyone else on his crew needed to make any quick trips, and both other guys left as well.

Jake went inside and looked around. He wished someone would have tipped him off this morning. It would have been nice to know the game, and been able to move the gun someplace else. But where would he have moved it? He hesitated and tugged back some insulation between two studs and looked inside. He wished he still had the FN to stuff in there. Then the sheetrock guys could seal it inside. Maybe that's what they were planning for their own guns.

Jake grabbed a broom and started sweeping. As he swept, William Henry Campbell III walked in. Jake looked at his watch. Usually he didn't see the owner until mid-day.

"You see the news this morning?" William asked.

"No," Jake answered.

"The Pittsburgh cops started going house to house."

Jake groaned. "I know. They got mine." He proceeded to tell William the entire episode.

"I was afraid of that. That's why I hurried over. You just bought yours. It was probably on the top of the list."

Jake said, "What about my money? How can they just take something of mine without, you know . . ."

"They killed two cops this morning over in New Homestead. Shot one dead right at a guy's front door."

Jake pictured a gun owner standing over a dead cop on his porch. That had to be expected. There would certainly be more. What were they thinking? "How did it end? Did the cops kill him?"

"It's not over. It was still on the news when I came over. They surrounded the house after the first cop got shot. The other cop got shot in the back by somebody else from a distance, like a sniper. Looks like somebody decided loving his neighbor like the Bible says meant killing the cops harassing him."

Jake's mouth dropped open. "So, you're saying the cops have this house surrounded and a neighbor starts taking shots at the cops?"

William nodded, "We saw the second cop get shot on TV. There were news helicopters circling around with cameras. The guy was hiding behind a police car holding a long gun, probably a shotgun. We saw the cop thrown against the car, then slump down. He left a smear of blood on the car when he went down."

Jake couldn't believe it. "It was on TV? Did they catch the second shooter, the sniper?"

William shook his head. "They hadn't when I left. It's crazy up there. If this keeps up, there's gonna be blood running down the streets all around Pittsburgh."

"Any news outside of Pittsburgh?" Jake asked.

"Oh, yeah. This crap is happening all over. In Boston the cops opened up on a house where a guy brandished a gun, and in the process, the guy, his wife, and a baby were killed. An entire family wiped out by police bullets. In New Orleans, this whole apartment building got together to defend the place. They had guys on the roof, and when the cops arrived, they started shooting at each other. Two or three cops got shot before they retreated. One of the guys on the roof got shot as well."

Jake suddenly wondered why he was standing here in William's house while all this was going down. This sounded like a national riot. He wanted to see for himself what was going on. Why wasn't he helping Monica? That's where he should be.

He dropped the broom he was holding on the floor. "I think I'm gonna go," Jake said.

William took a moment before answering. "I need you to help me with something first."

"What?"

"Follow me," he said, pointing down the hallway.

Jake looked impatiently at his watch, then walked after the man, who Jake noticed was walking quickly and not using his cane. William led them downstairs to a dark storage room where he went inside and turned on the light. The room was built with floor to ceiling shelves stuffed with plastic storage containers. William knew exactly what he was looking for. He pointed to a container on a high shelf marked, "Figurines 3."

"Get that one down," he commanded.

Jake retrieved it and set it carefully down on the floor. William took off the plastic lid, and placed it on the floor next to the container. The container was stuffed with items wrapped in newspaper. William delicately took many of the items out and set them on the lid until he found the one he was looking for. This one looked no different, except Jake noticed it was wrapped in the sports section with large pictures of the Steelers. William handed it to Jake, and he felt through the paper the large "L" frame of a pistol.

William carefully replaced the other items in the container, then snapped on the lid. "Put that container back where you got it." He pointed at the high shelf.

Jake did as he was told. When he turned back around, William had unwrapped the item. He held a worn, black, metal semi-automatic pistol with brown wood handgrips.

"What is that?" Jake asked.

William held it carefully like it was worth a million dollars. "It's a collector's item."

"What is it?"

"I got it from an old friend, a World War II vet. He's dead now." He pointed to a small insignia, barely visible, stamped above the trigger.

"Is that a bird?" Jake asked.

"Eagle," William answered. "The Nazis stamped it on all their guns."

Jake recoiled. "That's a Nazi gun?"

William nodded appreciatively. "Browning Hi-Power, 1935, the granddaddy of all modern 9mm handguns. The first hi-capacity magazine. One of the best handguns of all time. Fought on both sides of World War II."

"Both sides?" Jake asked.

William stroked the gun. "When the Nazis invaded Belgium, they took over the Fabrique Nationale factory and started producing guns for themselves." He smiled at Jake. "You know what they call Fabrique Nationale today, don't you?"

Jake shook his head.

"What are the initials?"

Jake shook his head. "Initials? You mean, F . . ." Jake looked at William with dawning comprehension.

William nodded.

"FN?" Jake said. "You mean my FN was made by this company?"

William nodded. He held up the Hi-Power. "This is its granddaddy."

Jake reached for it. "Can I?"

William handed it to him. Jake took it carefully, then held it in a two-hand grip and aimed at a bracket on the shelf at the end of the room. The metal gun felt more solid than his FN, but it was still very comfortable. The sites weren't as easy to see as the modern dot sights on his FN, and the handle wasn't as contoured, but this Browning still felt wonderful in his hand.

"How does it shoot?" Jake asked.

"Better than all the modern knock-offs in my opinion," William responded.

Jake looked at William, surprised. "Better than the new FN?"

"Better than all of them—FNs, Glocks, Sigs, everything. Best 9mm ever invented. John Browning was a genius."

Jake wasn't sure it was the best ever, especially after almost a hundred years of gun makers making improvements. But listening to William laud it, it must still be a spectacular weapon, and what a collectors' treasure being from the Second World War, and the Nazi marks. He held it out to William.

William held his palms out. "No. It's yours."

Jake couldn't believe it. "What? I can't—"

William nodded. "Yes, you can. You've done fine work on this place. And besides, it will be safe at your house now that the cops have already raided you. Consider it part of your bonus."

"Part?" Jake squinted at William.

William pointed to another plastic container on the floor, under the shelves. It was long, and Jake could see it was full of rolls of Christmas wrapping.

"Pull that out," William ordered.

Jake handed the Browning to William, then bent over and pulled out the container. It was far too heavy to only contain wrapping paper. William handed the Browning back to Jake, removed the plastic lid, and dug underneath the rolls, pulling a hard plastic gun case out. It was long, like a rifle. Jake was dying to see what was inside. William opened the case and retrieved an assault weapon that looked similar to the one Monica had let him shoot at the range a few nights ago.

"An AR-15?" Jake asked excitedly. Was William really going to give this to him?

"No, this is an M16," William corrected.

"What's the difference?" Jake asked.

William pointed to a small lever on the left side. "The AR only has two positions: safe, and fire. The M16 has four positions: safe, semi, auto, and burst."

Jake was blown away. "You mean this is full-auto, a machine gun?"

William nodded. "Absolutely, just like the military uses. I recommend you stick with semi or burst though. Full-auto just wastes bullets."

Jake stared into William's eyes. "Where'd you get this? These things are way illegal, aren't they?"

"Not if you have a permit from ATF," William answered.

"And you have one?"

"Not exactly," William smiled.

"What does that mean?"

"It means you're asking too damn many questions," William answered. "Here." He handed the M16 to Jake.

Jake took the weapon. Aside from the small switch, it looked identical to the AR-15 he shot at the club last week. He aimed it at the same shelf, and sighted through the round sight on the M16. While he was aiming, William replaced the wrapping paper, and then slid the plastic container back under the shelf where it came from.

"Put it back in its case." William pointed at the case for the M16. "You don't want anybody to see you toting that thing around, especially today."

Jake placed the gun carefully in the plastic case, closed it, and snapped the latches closed. "You're not giving this to me, are you?"

William stood and tapped the plastic case with his cane. "Already did."

"Why?" Jake asked. "A full-auto without paperwork has gotta be worth a lot of money."

"I got plenty," William answered. "Besides, my wife and kids don't like guns. So, if I drop dead someday, they're just gonna sell it. And trying to unload a full-auto, without paperwork, might result in my family getting put in jail. I was starting to worry who I was going to give it to, and you're the guy."

"What should I do with it?"

"Hide it. You may need it someday."

Jake snorted. "Need a full-auto, what for?"

William tapped Jake hard on the shoulder with his cane. "Jake, we got a civil war outside in the streets of Pittsburgh today. Same across the country. It might blow over. But it might get worse."

Jake hadn't thought of it that way. What if these confrontations escalated? How would he defend himself? If the government went nuts and came after the people, what would he do? He thought about how he felt when that cop Dickson confiscated his FN. The humiliation. The helplessness. They shouldn't have been able to do that. It was in the Constitution. It specifically prohibited what they did.

"You think it'll get worse?" Jake asked.

William considered the question. "Yeah, I do."

* * *

Jake had intended to go directly to meet Monica, but the M16 had changed that. Instead, he headed back to the house. He drove below the speed limit and meticulously obeyed all traffic laws, even signaling five seconds before changing lanes. He watched his mirrors and studied every vehicle behind him. He felt like the gun was a nuclear weapon and that everyone on the road knew he was smuggling something valuable.

When he arrived at home, he looked up and down the street and made sure nobody was watching. He wiped his sweaty palms on his pants while he waited for a car to drive past and turn the corner before he carried the new guns in the house. He had the browning pistol stuffed in his pants. But the plastic rifle case was long and unmistakable. As he carried it in the house, he resisted glancing around to see if neighbors were watching him from their windows. He tried to calm himself. Even if they saw he had a gun, they had no way of knowing what specific gun was in the case. Surely they wouldn't suspect a full-auto M16.

When he was in the house, he set the case on the floor and began a search for a good hiding place. The cops had started in the bedroom, so that was out. He glanced around the living room. No place big enough. He looked at the couch, then walked over and tipped it up, looking underneath. He decided immediately he couldn't modify it to hide the gun, not without removing frame pieces and springs and making it unfit for a seat.

He went from room to room. Nothing was great. He finally settled on the office closet, stuffed with all his storage boxes. He knew it wasn't ideal and decided sometime in the next week or so, he would bring some sheetrock home and seal it into the wall between two studs, then repaint the room.

He walked back outside to the truck and retrieved four boxes of ammunition for each gun, which William had insisted he take. When he was back in the house, he opened one of the boxes of 9mm, and loaded thirteen into the clip of the browning Hi-Power. To be safe, he did not chamber a round. He then stuffed the gun back into his pants. He realized he needed to get some sort of holster to conceal the pistol. He couldn't really walk around forever with a gun stuffed down his pants.

He then headed for Monica's. He called her from his truck to see where exactly she was, at the range, or at home. She surprised him by saying she was at her father's church. She gave him directions and told him to not be obvious, but to park a block away and she would let him in a rear door.

After parking and walking casually down the sidewalk, he realized that for the first time in his life, he was carrying a loaded concealed weapon, which was surely a felony in Pennsylvania. However, the thought that it was a gun without paperwork, one the authorities knew nothing about, felt liberating.

He approached the rear of the church, wondering how loud he should knock, when the rear door suddenly opened. Monica reached for his hand and pulled him inside. After closing the door, she kissed him hard on the mouth, and then held him in a tight embrace.

"I'm glad you came," she whispered.

"Sorry it took so long."

"I was worried about you. I tried to call you a bunch of times."

Jake looked sheepish. "My phone was dead." He held it up.

She looked at it. "Of all the nights—"

"I know," he said, shaking his head.

She changed the subject. "You sounded bad on the phone this morning."

"This morning sucked," he agreed.

She took his hand and led him up some stairs. They entered a small office with a desk on one wall and a couch on the other. She led him through the office into a narrow hallway, up a few more stairs, then around a corner and they emerged onto the podium of the chapel. He looked down at the benches where the congregation sat.

Jake looked over the space. It was not what he had imagined. He expected a modern building, but this was old, fifty or a hundred years. It had a high ceiling and a stained glass window over the entryway. The lights were off, so the chapel was lit up by the sun shining though the stained glass. There were dust particles in the beams of colored light. The glass design was of Jesus holding a lamb.

As he gauged his surroundings, Monica's father entered from a door next to the organ. He smiled broadly and reached to embrace Jake. Jake put out his hand, but Clive pulled him into a hug, patting him on the back.

"Thanks for coming, Jake." Clive released him and pointed to some boxes on the floor. "Get one of those and follow me." He then grabbed a box himself and disappeared into the door next to the organ.

Jake's box was heavier than he expected. He guessed there were many handguns inside. He carried it through the door and found himself in a small mechanical closet. He saw Clive's feet just before they disappeared, ascending a spiral staircase. Jake followed.

The stairs were small and Jake had to concentrate while carrying the heavy box. As he climbed higher and higher, he felt confused that he had not arrived yet, sensing that he had climbed at least a story and a half, maybe two. Where did the stairs lead?

Finally, he emerged on a platform behind the vertical pipes of the organ. Jake could see far down to the benches below. Clive had set his box on the floor and climbed up on the railing.

Clive pointed at Jake's box. "Open that, and start handing me guns."

Jake set his box on top of Clive's, opened the flaps, and saw many handguns, some semi-autos, and some revolvers. He handed them one-by-one up to Clive who tucked each into recessed areas behind the organ's pipes. Jake knew he was doing something very illegal, but he felt no guilt. It was the president who should feel guilty. The Second Amendment should have guaranteed their right. But everything was scrambled. Jake actually felt good to be doing something to protect the reverend's guns.

Jake wondered where the guns came from, since Monica had said the range had been raided in the early morning. "Are these guns from your house?"

Clive glanced at Jake. "A few, but most of these are from the club."

"Did they take everything from the range?" Jake asked. He couldn't believe the Lombardis had lost that many guns. It could have been fifty or sixty. It was their business. It wasn't right.

Clive nodded. "I think they hit all the gun stores simultaneously after midnight. They grabbed our guns, then got our paperwork for all the people we sold guns to."

That explained how the cops had lists of all the guns purchased recently.

Clive continued. "As soon as we were done at the range, we headed straight out to the club and got these."

Jake had just finished unloading the first box, when Monica arrived with a third box. Jake helped her set her box down. "I'll go get another box."

She called out to him as he descended. "There's only one more."

After they had hidden all the guns, Jake wiped his forehead and pointed at the pipes. "So that's all the guns from the club?"

Clive wiped sweat off his own forehead and shook his head. "We left about a fourth of them for the cops. It would be way too suspicious if there weren't any there when they arrived."

"Is there paperwork on these?" Jake asked.

Clive grimaced at the question, then climbed down next to Jake. "We didn't have time to sort through all that yet. I guessed on most of them. We left mostly new guns at the club."

Jake pointed up at the hiding place again. "That seems like a pretty good place. Nobody would think of looking up there."

Clive shook his head. "I'm not so sure. They know I'm a preacher. If a judge gives them a warrant for the church, they might just tear this place down looking for guns."

"How could they justify a warrant for the church?" Monica argued. "They took over fifty guns from the range. They already got our guns."

Her father put his arm around her. "Obviously not, baby. Besides, when they start going through our paperwork from the range, it's going to lead them to the club."

She was on the verge of tears. "The range is where we made our living. What gives them the right to confiscate fifty guns?"

He pulled her into a full embrace. "They had no right. No right."

After Clive released her, he turned to Jake. "Monica told me they took your gun."

Jake nodded. "Yeah."

"That's too bad," Clive said. He looked back up at the pipes. "Maybe, I should get you—"

Jake interrupted, "No need." He pulled the Browning out of his pants. "My employer gave me this one this morning."

Clive appraised it. "An old Hi-Power. Nice."

Jake pointed at the Nazi insignia. "Check this out."

"What is it?" Monica asked

"Nazi," Clive said. "I always wanted one of those."

She looked at her father. "Nazi? Browning Hi-Powers are Nazi?"

Clive told her the same story William told Jake that morning, about the FN factory in Belgium during World War II. She then took the gun from Jake and studied the logo. She finally returned it to him.

"I like Hi-Powers," she said. "They're one of my favorites."

Jake thought about telling them about the full-auto M16, but he decided the time wasn't right. The three of them carried the empty boxes down the spiral staircase. Monica closed the door next to the organ.

Clive pointed at Monica. "Why don't you go with Jake? I need to go see some people in the community. We need to talk about what's happening."

Monica reached out and took Jake's hand.

Clive continued. "But be careful out there, you two. Today is not a good day to be out in the streets."

CHAPTER 9

Jake and Monica had discussed going to her home or his. But Jake wanted a deli, or bar, someplace with lots of TVs, where they could watch the local news, and at the same time get a sense of how others were feeling. Monica knew just the place. It wasn't far from the church.

When they entered, Jake looked at the walls peppered with big TVs showing a variety of local and national news, and a concerned crowd, and knew Monica had picked the right place. Monica led him to a table with an excellent view of multiple big screens.

Jake inhaled the food smells, glanced at the table next him where he saw a man with a steak sandwich, and a woman taking a bite of pastrami, and decided he was starving.

The closest TV showed a reporter crouching behind a car, while in the distance it looked like five Pittsburgh police cars were parked haphazardly around a small home. Police officers leaned over their cars with guns aimed at the house.

Monica pointed at the screen. "That's Allentown. Only a couple miles from here."

Jake looked around to assure himself they were safe. He didn't see anyone that looked dangerous in the sports bar. He recalled that some bullets traveled a couple miles in the air, but decided the building would protect them from stray bullets from the scene on TV.

A waitress in a number 12 Steelers jersey came by and handed them some menus.

Jake pointed at the TV. "How long has this been going on?"

She looked up to see which one he was pointing at. "Oh, that one's new. Maybe five or ten minutes." She pointed at the menus. "You want me to give you some time?"

Jake looked at Monica. "I'll have one of those steak sandwiches." He pointed at a plate on the table next to them. "You need more time?"

Monica looked at the table next to them as well. "Make it two. And two Cokes and some fries."

The waitress nodded and walked away. Jake noticed the back of her jersey had "Bradshaw" over the number 12.

"Those morons are sending a guy up there!" A guy at the bar shouted loudly, pointing at the screen.

Jake saw a policeman, obviously wearing a bulletproof vest, walking toward the house, talking in a bullhorn as he walked. Jake wished they would turn up the sound on this particular TV so he could hear it over the others.

Suddenly, dirt and bits of grass were propelled out of the ground under the man's feet and the man danced back and forth, and then ran back to his car.

"He's shootin' at 'em!" somebody yelled.

There were screams and shouting in the café as the crowd watched the gun fight. Jake saw the police firing at the house, their shoulders and hands bucking at their guns' recoil. He saw one policeman waving his arms violently for everyone to stop firing, but it took at least ten seconds for them all to stop. Jake wondered if this was going to be another case where innocent women and children were killed in the gunfire. How could it not be with that many cops firing into the house?

The police waited while the dust settled. Then Jake saw the same officer with the bullhorn saying something toward the house.

"Turn up the sound!" yelled a guy from two tables down.

". . . told them to come out with their hands up." The woman reporter said. It was way louder now as the TV had obviously been turned up. She kept narrating. "We haven't heard anything from the house after all that shooting."

"They're probably all dead," said the man at the next table with the steak sandwich.

Jake agreed. How could this be worth it? How many people were going to die across the country as the government tried to disarm everyone? If all this was happening in Pittsburgh, what about other cities? What about the big cities like New York, LA, and Chicago? What about the rougher cities like Detroit, Philadelphia, and Cleveland? This was just Pittsburgh.

"He's going up again!" a voice over by the bar yelled.

Jake saw the same guy with the vest and bullhorn walk slowly toward the house, talking through the bullhorn all the while. This time they could hear parts of what was said. ". . . shoot . . . check if . . . wounded . . . don't shoot . . . take it easy . . . unarmed . . ."

Suddenly, the dust and grass exploded at the officer's feet again, and again he danced around and ran back to his car. The bar erupted again with screams and yells. Jake heard some cheers from the crowd. The police opened fire on the house again.

This was it. This was the classic siege about defending your guns against confiscation by an evil government. This homeowner was unwilling to kill a cop to defend his guns, but he was willing to fire some warning shots. But Jake was afraid it would not end well. How could it?

A woman screamed, "He's trying to kill that policeman."

Another man yelled loudly at her. "No, he's not. He's shooting into the ground at his feet."

Another finished, "If he wanted to kill him, he'd be dead. He's just warning them to stay away from his house."

The same policeman was waving his arms for another cease-fire. But then, everything changed. In quick succession, three officers still firing at the house were dropped. Bam, bam, bam. Jake turned his head away when he saw a pink mist behind the third officer's head as he was shot. Screams erupted from the café.

Something had happened in the house? The man was aiming now. To hell with the warning shots, he had just killed three cops. What had turned him?

The TV cut to studio. The news anchor took a moment to get his bearings. "Uh . . . welcome back. Uh, let's see. Uh, some of you have been watching this scene in Allentown. And in the last few moments it looked like two or three policeman have been shot. Hopefully they are all okay."

"Yeah, right," a guy yelled from the bar. "Did you see all the blood?"

"Shut up!" another guy yelled.

The guy in studio touched his ear. "Wait a minute. Uh, there have been some developments in that scene in Allentown. We're going to transfer you back to Lisa Simmons." The TV switched back and showed Lisa hiding behind a TV news van.

"Just in the last few seconds, we saw someone waving what looks like a white towel. It's on the end of some kind of pole, a broom or something." The camera showed the white towel waving just inside a broken front window.

Someone at the bar pointed at the TV. "He's surrendering."

"Throw out your weapons," the officer with the bullhorn ordered. The sound was very clear now, as if the camera crew had aimed a microphone at the house.

A voice came from the house. "She's shot! She needs help!"

Now Jake knew what had changed in the house. Someone had been shot. Jake felt Monica's hand clamping down on his. It was cutting off his circulation. He winced and pulled his hand free, wrapping his arm around her instead. She pressed her hand to her mouth, watching with horror as the scene unfolded.

"Throw out your weapons!"

Jake saw a deer rifle with a scope fly out the window and clank onto the porch. A moment later, he saw the white towel waving. "I'm coming out."

The front door opened, and the flag came out first, then a skinny, bearded man in a black t-shirt came out with his hands high, the left holding the white towel on a broom. Three officers ran toward him.

"She's on the floor. She's dying. You pricks shot her!" He was crying.

The police roughly pushed him down on the porch and cuffed him.

"She didn't need to—" His voice was interrupted as the cops shoved his face into the porch.

"Why are they being so rough with him?" demanded a lady at the next table.

"He just shot three cops!"

"Yeah, but he was just defending himself."

"Yeah. He didn't shoot them until they shot his wife!"

Jake felt Monica reach over and take his hand again. He looked at her. She looked like she was about ready to cry. "They just kept firing at the house," Monica said. "What did they expect to happen?"

"Yeah, I know."

Amazingly, the waitress arrived with their sandwiches, fries, and drinks. Jake wasn't sure if he could eat now. The waitress set their food in front of them, left some utensils, and then asked if there was anything else they needed. Jake said everything was fine.

Jake focused on another TV to the right. The screen carried the Fox News logo. A graphic on the screen showed 126 civilians dead and 63 police officers dead.

Jake pointed at the screen. "Is that today?"

The guy at the table next to him said, "Holy crap. How many are gonna die by the end of the week?"

A woman at the same table asked, "Can't they just stop this?"

"Agreed," Jake responded. "Even an idiot can see that this is not working."

The guy at the other table pointed to a TV at the left. "The news said that Atlanta already stopped. The mayor called the whole thing off."

Jake said, "Yeah, but Atlanta is in the South. They're not a bunch of liberals."

The guy at the next table responded, "It'd take guts to speak out against the president of the United States. Hopefully, President Singleton doesn't send his killers down to Atlanta to murder the mayor."

The lady at that table asked her husband, "Do you really believe that the president had those congressmen killed?"

He looked at her like she was crazy. "Of course! Don't you?"

Jake looked back at the center TV, which now showed two police officers carrying a stretcher into the house. The skinny man in the black shirt was nowhere to be seen.

The anchorwoman said, "Police have reported a single occupant left in the house. Our news crew just heard on the police scanner she is reported to be critically wounded."

Jake still didn't feel like digging into his steak sandwich, but he took a fry and ate it. Generally he would dip his fries in ketchup, but today ketchup seemed out of the question. He noticed that Monica had actually taken a bite from her sandwich.

The center TV switched back to studio. The man addressed the camera. "We're going to move now from Allentown to a different situation up north. Barry Goodman is at the scene."

The camera focused on a trim bald man with a microphone, standing in front of a large home in a nice neighborhood. "This is Barry Goodman. We're in the Garfield area north of Penn Avenue. As you can see, we have a situation here where it seems like gun owners are massing against the police."

Jake saw police officers carrying gun cases out of the house. But the police had to push their way through a crowd of hecklers. The people were obviously screaming at the policemen.

The news anchor continued. "As you can see, this crowd is making it tough for the police officers to do their jobs."

Jake saw a guy in a windbreaker reach up and knock the cap off a police officer.

"That's where we need to be!" some guy yelled from the bar.

Jake looked at Monica. "Makes you feel like we should be out doing something, doesn't it?"

The TV showed another officer walking out of the house with his arms full of gun cases. Just then, a tomato hit him right in the face, splattering red down his uniform. He stumbled and dropped the guns.

The bar erupted in cheers and laughter.

The lady at the table next to them said, "Why are they cheering at those people doing that to the police?"

The man next to her said incredulously, "Are you nuts? They're stealing his guns. Ya wanna give them a medal?"

"They're just doing their jobs," she argued. "They should be treated with respect."

Jake inserted, "Yeah, they're just doing their job, but today their job is to deny people their constitutional rights."

The man smiled at Jake and gave him a thumbs-up.

Jake looked down and decided he was ready to eat his steak sandwich. He took a bite. He noticed that Monica had eaten almost half of hers.

"What kind of people is your dad meeting with? Is it possible his people can stop this thing?"

Monica took a drink from her Coke. "He knows a lot of people, including some people high up in the Pittsburgh Police Department. But I don't know if any of them can stop this."

Jake looked at the national news on the TV on the right and saw policemen throwing what looked like smoke bombs into a house. A moment later a fat man in a ball cap and muscle shirt ran out with his hands up, followed by a woman carrying a baby, and a little girl in tow rubbing her eyes.

Jake pointed at the TV. "Smoke bombs? Are you kidding?"

The guy at the table next to him said, "They should've just leveled the house."

When Jake looked back at the center TV, he saw that the rowdy crowd was now pushing the policemen back and forth as they tried to pass through. The officer who'd caught the tomato in the face was wiping himself off with a towel. The camera panned the crowd and Jake noticed three signs that he hadn't seen before. The first had an American flag at the top and underneath it said, "Welcome to America. Land of the Free." The next one had a big title across the top that said, "Constitutional Amendments." Underneath the heading were listed the first five amendments, with the 2nd Amendment crossed out in big red X's. The third sign had a swastika at the top, and underneath it said, "First the Nazis Took the Guns, Then They Turned on the Gas."

Jake cringed. He pointed at the TV. "Look at the sign with the swastika."

Monica looked back at him and cringed as well. "How much longer do you want to stay in here?"

Jake saw her sandwich was almost gone. His was not even half eaten. "Why? You wanna go?"

She nodded. "Yeah. Finish eating so we can get out of here. This is scary."

Jake realized that this was freaking her out a little bit. He was also affected by the chaos, but if not for her, he would have never considered leaving. He felt like what was happening out there in the streets was important, historic. And whether it was comfortable to watch or not, he needed to watch it. In fact, a part of him felt guilty for just sitting and watching it, and not being out there. As William had said that morning, there was a revolution going on in America. How could Jake feel satisfied watching it on TV?

He started eating faster. As he scanned the televisions, he saw one show a pile of handguns at least ten feet tall on a concrete floor in some city. Jake guessed there were several thousand guns in the pile. Another screen showed officers marching a dozen men out of an apartment building with their wrists bound by plastic zip ties. Jake wondered if there were enough jail cells in the country to house all the people being arrested today.

The center screen was back in studio. "We're going to transfer you down to New Homestead for another story just developing."

The camera focused on a pretty woman reporter in a green blouse talking to a clean-cut man in a white t-shirt. "Hi, this is Gloria Garcia. I'm here with Richard." She held the microphone toward him, prompting him to continue.

"Jones," he finished.

"According to Richard, he was fired from the Pittsburgh Police Department this morning." She pointed the microphone at him. "Is that true?"

"Yeah, that's right."

"Can you tell us what happened?" she asked.

"Well, me and my partner got a list from my sergeant of, you know, gun owners. And we started going down the list. We'd go to a home, and take the guy's gun, you know, for the president's confiscation order. And we did about three of those, and then me and my partner, we said, this isn't right. So we called in, and said we didn't want to do any more. And my sergeant, he said we didn't have any choice."

"Then what happened?" she prompted.

"Well, me and my partner talked about it for a while. And we both agreed it was wrong, what they were making us do. So I called my sergeant again, and told him we weren't doing it. He told me right over the radio that we were both fired."

"So, what did you do?"

"Well he told us to come in and turn in our badges, so we drove back to the station. And they took our stuff, and told us we were fired. So I just came home. I've been watching the news. And I'm glad I'm not still out there doing it. It's wrong."

"So, there you go. Confiscate or you're fired, this morning at the Pittsburgh Police Department. This is Gloria Garcia."

The camera returned to studio. "Thanks, Gloria."

Jake glanced at the TV on the right and saw that Fox News had updated the national death statistics. The graphic showed 153 civilians and 71 police officers dead. Jake grimaced and rubbed both of his eyes with the palms of his hands.

"Let's go," Monica said pulling on his arm.

Jake looked at the table, to see if there was a bill. There wasn't. "We need the bill."

Monica stood and walked over to the bar. The bartender spoke to her. She pointed at the table. The bartender glanced at Jake and nodded.

Monica returned and took a drink of her Coke, but she didn't sit back down. The waitress in the Bradshaw jersey brought a bill very quickly.

She looked at Monica. "I wish I could go, too. This is giving me the creeps."

Monica handed a twenty and a five to the waitress. "Keep it. I'm sorry you have to stay, but I gotta get out of here."

Monica practically dragged Jake out of the café.

When they arrived outside, Monica turned her face up to the sun, closed her eyes, and soaked in the rays for a moment. Jake looked around, wondering if there were any confiscations going on near there. He saw no police cars. Monica finally brought her face down. She looked at him. Monica had always been so spunky, so positive. Now, she looked drained, depressed.

"Where do you want to go?" he asked.

"Bermuda," she answered. She gave him a slight smile. "But I'll settle for your place, if you promise not to turn on the TV.

* * *

The first hour at his house was spent just holding her. She snuggled up next to him on the couch with her head on his lap. He was running his fingers through her hair. It seemed to help her relax.

For the past few days, Monica had been the most assertive and confident woman Jake had ever seen, but she had obviously reached the end of her rope. They talked for a while, discussing the issues and guessing what would happen over the next few days. They talked about the long term and the false promise of the government returning the confiscated handguns. As they talked, Monica's depression was slowly replaced by anger. Late in the afternoon, she asked Jake if he wanted to turn on the TV, to see if anything else had happened. Jake was relieved. He had felt a growing awareness that history was happening all around him, and whether it was good or bad, he was missing it.

When he turned it on, he searched through the news channels until he found Fox News, the one with the death statistics. It had only been two and a half hours since they left the café, but the stats had grown astronomically. The graphic now showed 417 civilians and 165 police officers dead.

* * *

Later that evening they drove to Monica's house. Clive had called them and told them to hurry home. He had news.

Jake and Monica sat on the couch and listened while Clive told them about his conversations. He told them that most of the people he had talked to that day had violently disagreed with what was going on in the Pittsburgh streets. Some of them had relayed news from other metropolitan areas as well. Other cities besides Atlanta had halted the confiscations. Out west, many cities, including Salt Lake City, Phoenix, Boise, Kansas City, St. Louis, and the whole states of Wyoming and Montana had refused to confiscate at all.

President Singleton was not happy. Rumor had it that he had been on the phone with their mayors and governors and had threatened to send the National Guard to those cities to force them to comply.

In the meantime, there were a couple more suspicious deaths reported. Amazingly, the mayor of Atlanta, the first state to openly rebel against the president's order, had been killed in a car accident on the way home that afternoon in a hit-and-run. Supposedly a car had bumped the mayor's car into oncoming traffic at high speed, and the mayor and his son were killed instantly. The driver of the cement truck that hit them was also critically wounded, making it impossible to get a description of the hit-and-run vehicle.

Jake couldn't believe the Atlanta mayor had been murdered. At least, that's what he considered it. They had just been joking about that in the bar.

Clive went on. It wasn't just Atlanta's mayor who'd mysteriously died. Back in Washington, a Senator Banister from Wisconsin, who had spoken out loudly over the past few days against the president's lack of authority to create laws with executive orders, had been killed walking to the Capitol Building. The news reported it as a mugging, saying he had died of knife wounds and his wallet was missing. The murder had occurred only two blocks from the U.S. Capitol Building.

Both deaths were incredibly suspicious since they represented two more vocal opponents to President Singleton. Skeptics argued that even though foul play might be involved, it didn't necessarily mean President Singleton had ordered the executions—it could easily be explained by independent radicals working on their own.

"I think we have a rogue president on our hands," Clive said.

Something had been bothering Jake all day. "At what point will this executive order get challenged by the Supreme Court? Can't they rush it through, like during the Gore/Bush election? Can the Supreme Court rule on this before it's over, this week?"

Clive nodded. "We talked about that today. You remember Ben Jamison, the two-term congressman that you met at the club the other night?"

Jake and Monica nodded.

"I asked him about that. Today is the first day of real confiscations. So these lawsuits will hopefully be filed in the next day or two. Ben Jamison is hopeful the Supreme Court could have a case to rule on by the end of the week."

"That's way too late!" Jake retorted. "Have you seen the death count on Fox News? It will be in the thousands by the end of the week."

"That's what we're afraid of. I agree. It'll be too late."

Monica spoke up, "This feels like it was planned this way. It's like President Singleton's strategy was for this to happen too fast for anyone to question. How can anyone possibly stop this?"

Clive looked around as if he were afraid someone was listening. "I can't stress enough the sensitivity of what I am about to tell you."

Jake and Monica glanced at each other.

Clive continued, "There are some key people across the country who agree with Monica, that this whole thing was planned such that it was too fast to be stopped. The prevailing opinion is that President Singleton knows that bureaucracy can't react fast enough to stop it. However, he is assuming that bureaucracy is the only way to stop it."

"And you think there's another way?" Monica leaned forward, her voice low and serious.

Clive smiled. "Yes, I've talked to numerous people across the country today, and if these murders of the president's opposition are any indication, then the president actually has a plan to repress politicians from reacting."

Jake inserted, "Yeah, by killing them."

Monica put her hand on Jake's. "Do you really believe the president is having all these people killed? But there's no evidence . . ."

Jake realized this was the same conversation he had had with William a few days ago. He recalled what William had said and repeated it to Monica. "You're right. There is no evidence. And there may never be any. But yeah, I absolutely believe the president is having all these people killed. If we wait for evidence though, it will be too late."

Monica's father nodded in agreement. "I have mixed emotions about this. My whole life I've believed in the 'innocent until proven guilty' thing. But we all know that theory is not foolproof, it allows a percentage of guilty people to go free. Now we have a case where an important person, actually the most powerful person in the world, may be one of the guilty ones to go free under that policy. We can't afford that. I'd argue that the president of the United States needs to be bound to a higher law. He can't be untouchable."

Monica said, "What if we're wrong?"

Clive looked at her sympathetically. "I feel the same. But what if we're right? The safeguards in our Constitution are the ability for Congress to impeach the president, and the Senate to remove him from office. But many have worried about how effective that would be if our representatives were corrupt. In this case, not only have some of them become corrupt, but the ones who speak out end up dead. What kind of a safeguard is that going to be for this situation?"

Jake had had enough theory. "So what non-bureaucratic options are being discussed?"

Clive looked around nervously again. "Okay, let me stress again how sensitive this is."

Jake nodded impatiently.

"The confiscated guns are being stored in a warehouse across the street from police headquarters on Western Avenue."

"Is that downtown?" Jake asked.

"Kind of. It's across the river, a couple of blocks northwest of Heinz Field."

"I've never been there," Jake said.

Monica smiled and patted Jake's hand. "That's a good thing."

Jake motioned to continue. "Then what?"

Clive said, "So while the guns are being stored in the warehouse, where are the police?"

"They're guarding the guns," Jake said.

Monica shook her head. "Wrong! They're all over the city confiscating more guns. There are probably only a few guards and a bunch of accountants logging in all the guns in the warehouse."

Clive nodded. "Yes. That's the theory. They're not expecting a frontal attack. They expect us to act like law-abiding citizens."

"Which we were, before they started taking our guns away," Jake blurted.

Monica looked at her father. "So who is organizing this attack?"

Clive smiled. "That's still being discussed. However, almost everyone believes it's doable. Nobody has stepped up yet to lead the charge. We talked today about how to spread the word without causing a leak. Another question is the timing. When?"

"That's easy," Jake said smiling.

Clive looked questioningly at him. "When?"

"Monday night," Jake said. "Two nights from now. It's perfect."

"Why? What's going on Monday night?"

"The Steelers. They're having a pre-season night game at Heinz Field. We could have 65,000 people storm the police station right after the game." Jake smiled devilishly. "And they're playing the Raiders. Maybe their thug fans will join us."

Clive looked back and forth between Jake and Monica, smiling broadly. "I like it! The timing is perfect. The game and the crowds would be the perfect distraction."

Jake's face became more serious. "What about other cities? When are they going to move?"

Clive shook his head. "I don't know. I didn't hear any dates. I think they're probably still planning."

Monica added, "Even if they did have dates, they wouldn't be talking about it."

"She's right. Specifics are being held close to the vest at this point," Clive said. He sat up as if the conversation was over. He clapped his hands together. "Well, unless there's something else, I have some calls to make." He stood and slapped Jake on the back. "I need to make some suggestions to our local people about timing. I think they may like Jake's suggestion."

CHAPTER 10

The next morning was Sunday. No work. Jake knew Monica and her father had church. He guessed it was possible church would be cancelled due to the unrest, but he guessed not. He decided to call her in the afternoon when she was done.

Jake wondered whether plans were progressing for their revolution. He was confident his idea of attacking Monday night would be adopted. It only made sense. He was now thinking of it as the Pittsburgh Revolution, and wondered if others would call it that as well.

Since the night before, he had worried about communication. How could they possibly find thousands of willing participants throughout the city, and recruit them for an attack Monday night, without someone leaking the plans to the Pittsburgh police department? It seemed like an impossible task. He hoped the reverend and his buddies had some strategy to accomplish it.

Jake was just getting ready to turn on the TV and catch up on the news when Monica called with a request. Jake resisted at first, but Monica begged. After she hung up, Jake jumped in the shower to ready himself to meet her at her father's church.

* * *

Jake felt apprehensive as he parked on the street in front of the old red-brick building. The front looked far more imposing than the rear entrance where he had met Monica the day before. The large stained glass of Jesus holding the lamb towered over the large front doors. A steep pointed roof three stories high arched down on both sides.

He saw many others, including couples, families, and some old people, climbing the stairs to the front door, and walking from both directions toward the building. He glanced at his watch and noted it was 9:55 a.m.

He hustled across the street and followed a couple with young kids through the front doors. He expected to enter directly into the large chapel, but this church had a small lobby area immediately inside with other doors leading into the chapel. A teenage boy smiled at him at the door and handed him a single folded sheet program. He looked around in the crowded lobby, but did not see either Monica or her father. He followed the crowd into the chapel and glanced up at the high ceiling. He heard organ music. He glanced up at the pipes and thought about the guns he had helped Clive stuff behind them.

The crowd carried him up the center aisle between the rows of benches on both sides. Jake guessed the church might hold two hundred people and noted it was mostly full. This surprised him. From what he heard, church attendance was down in the United States. He wondered if the riots and gun confiscations had made any difference.

In answer to his question, he heard a man behind him say, "Of course he'll talk about it. He owns that gun range over in Blawnox."

Jake looked at the podium for Monica's father, but he saw only a couple more of the teenage boys handing out programs. Monica was nowhere to be seen. He was starting to wonder if he should just find a seat when he felt her take his arm.

He was shocked to see her wearing a dress. It was an olive green sleeveless that draped down to her knees. She wore matching heels. The look was sophisticated and classy. He stared at her, taking in the view from head to foot. He'd met this girl in a gun range and hadn't ever considered her in a dress or heels.

She led him through the throng. As they approached the front, most were already seated, and he saw people watching them. He realized they were watching because he was with her, the preacher's daughter. He reached up and straightened his tie.

Monica led him to the front row. Jake finally saw Monica's father over on the far aisle shaking hands with a family. He patted the back of a small boy who was no more than seven or eight years old. Jake glanced behind him at the crowd and wondered if Monica and her father knew most of these people.

He was still looking when he felt a strong hand clamp on his shoulder. He turned to see Monica's father's chiseled face smiling at him.

Reverend Clive Lombardi shook Jake's hand vigorously. "Hi, Jake. Glad you came! Monica says you haven't been to church for a while."

Jake nodded.

"Well, this isn't just any Sunday. You can feel the electricity in the air today. They want a sermon on guns I'm afraid."

"Are you going to give it to them?" Monica asked.

He smiled at his daughter. "It'll come up. But I haven't decided exactly what to say yet. I'll wait and see what the Lord tells me."

Jake's eyebrows came up at that. He looked back at the congregation. How could anyone even consider speaking to a large audience like that without knowing exactly what you wanted to say? As he studied the crowd, they hushed and began to sit down. Jake turned around and saw the reverend approaching the podium. The reverend didn't say anything. He just smiled. The organ music tapered off until the chapel was almost completely silent. Jake and Monica sat.

"Welcome," he said. "I see a few new faces out there today, and some I haven't seen for a while. We're happy you've decided to join us, whatever your reasons. I hope you leave more enlightened that when you arrived, and that you will gain the answers to any questions you may be pondering. Let's start out positive, and sing Count your Many Blessings, which is number twenty-three in your song books."

A lady appeared next to the podium to lead the music. Monica pulled a songbook out from under the bench and turned it to the song. She pointed at the first verse.

Jake shook his head. He never sang, not even in the shower.

The song began. Jake watched Monica sing. The crowd sang enthusiastically. Even with the other voices, he could make out her singing next to him. She had a pretty singing voice, much different than the husky way she talked. The song talked about focusing on the things the Lord had blessed you with even when you were discouraged. Jake looked around at the crowd holding up their books and singing. It was a lively, positive song that he'd never heard before, not that he knew many church hymns. When it ended, the reverend appeared at the podium again.

He bowed his head. "Let us pray."

Jake saw everyone's heads go down, so he followed, looking at his lap. Monica took his hand.

The reverend prayed as if he were talking to someone. He didn't use any scripted words or phrases like Jake had heard in the past. He didn't raise his voice or use any theatrics. Just a humble conversation, as if he were talking to a man next to him that he respected. He did a lot of thanking. He thanked God for the church building itself. He thanked him for the congregation. He thanked God that they lived in America, a free country. He asked for a few things, too: that the sick would be comforted, and that those who'd lost jobs would find work. He prayed that he might deliver an inspired message. When he ended the prayer, he said, "Amen." The congregation repeated "Amen," out loud.

The reverend looked up and smiled. "We don't do this every week, but I felt today would be a good day to pass the bread and wine. Agreed?"

There were some murmurs of confirmation from the crowd, and Jake saw many heads nod in agreement. Reverend Lombardi motioned to a side door, and about a dozen of the teenage boys entered. Each carried a large round tray, which held lots of mini cups filled with wine and a pile of broken bread in the middle. The boys moved down the center aisle and sent the trays down each row. When the tray was offered to Monica, she took a piece of bread, ate it, then took one of the mini cups and drank the wine. She then offered the tray to Jake. He didn't know if he should, but proceeded to eat and drink as Monica had. As the trays were passed, the reverend read scriptures from the New Testament about when Jesus did the same, passing bread and wine to the apostles. It took a few minutes to send trays down all the aisles, but soon the young boys and the trays disappeared through the side doors where they had come from.

The reverend looked appraisingly at the congregation, and Jake sensed they were ready to hear what he had to say.

"As I pointed out when we began, I see a few new faces out there. I also see a few faces I haven't seen for a while. This, I am to assume, is related to what's happening out in the streets of Pittsburgh and across our nation. Since you came to hear what I have to say on the subject, I feel obliged to address it. I will try to temper my personal feelings and focus on what I feel the Lord would say if he were here. Sound good?"

Jake saw heads nodding all around him in the congregation.

"A little over two hundred years ago, this country was in conflict. The pilgrims had immigrated to America seeking freedoms, which included the right to worship without persecution and the right to own property. By the mid-1700s, many had reached the conclusion that moving to America, by itself, had not achieved their goal. The long arm of government stretched across the ocean and still sometimes caused discomfort. One of the primary complaints of the settlers was their lack of say in how they were governed. An example is the colonists' resistance to taxation without representation. In 1773 colonists revolted and dumped a shipload of tea into Boston harbor primarily because they had no say in the new taxes levied against them. Notable is that the tea tax they were rebelling against was only about two percent. The bigger issue was taxation without representation."

Jake looked around to see if others were as surprised as he to learn the Boston Tea Party had been over a tax of only a few percent.

"Within a few years, the colonists had given up on being governed by the Brits and had started creating the framework of a new government. They met together often and discussed how a proper government should operate. They prayed to God and pleaded for his inspiration. Recently in the 1990s, Constitution scholars went back and researched influences on our founding fathers. They studied over 15,000 writings, and they found the book most often sited was the Bible." Clive held up his Bible. "Thirty-four percent of all quotations came from this." He replaced the book on the podium.

"Fifty of the fifty-five signers of the Declaration were Christians. When the Declaration of Independence was finalized, it included the phrases "Nature's God," "created equal," "endowed by their creator," and "with a firm reliance on the protection of divine Providence." Some of you may be asking why we are talking about politics at church." Clive raised his voice to a powerful level. "I believe that the United States government was set up with the help of God, and it is the closest government in the world to how God would have men govern themselves.

Jake felt goose bumps on his arms and felt Monica's hand squeeze his tighter. They exchanged smiles. Her eyes sparkled.

Clive's voice returned to a normal level. "The founders relied on the Bible for concepts such as human nature, that humans are both good, created in the image of God, and bad, subject to sin. They needed a government that would handle both extremes. They were very nervous about men gaining too much power and then exerting unrighteous dominion over others.

On this subject, Thomas Jefferson said, 'In questions of power, then, let not more be heard of confidence in man, but bind him down from mischief by the chains of the Constitution.'

This fear of entrusting man with too much power led them to create the three tiers of power in the Constitution. The executive power of the president would be limited by lack of legislative power, which was to be held by Congress. Congress would be limited by the veto power of the president. Both would lack the judicial power held by the courts. If a president wanted to wage war, he would need Congress to fund it. This separation of powers was integral in the creation of our Constitution."

Clive motioned around him. "When I see things going on in our government, like what's happening out in the streets of Pittsburgh today, I like to put on my Constitutional glasses, to view them through that filter." He pretended to don a pair of glasses, then took a moment, scanning back and forth across the congregation. "And see how it looks from that perspective.

"For example, let's look at executive orders. If the president uses executive orders to legislate new laws, that would be an example of him subverting legislative power from Congress, and might be considered a gross perversion of the Constitution."

Clive looked around to see if he had any dissenters. There were none.

"If all is not right, if men have broken from the Constitution, we must ask ourselves, what can be done? There are safety valves in the Constitution itself that allow for removal, if necessary, of a scoundrel politician. That should be the first alternative. There are judges to throw out bad laws. That could also be an option. But let us be sure of something. We are not sheep. This government is ours, and it is meant to serve our best interests. And if it has grown into something it shouldn't be, and shucked off the rules of the Constitution it was based on, then it is our responsibility to rein it back in."

He looked down at his notes. "I'd like to quote John Hancock, signer of the Declaration of Independence, who said, 'Resistance to tyranny becomes the Christian and social duty of each individual. Continue steadfast and, with a proper sense of your dependence on God, nobly defend those rights which heaven gave, and no man ought to take from us.'"

He looked up. "And George Washington, who said, 'Of all the dispositions and habits which lead to political prosperity, religion and morality are indispensable supports. In vain would that man claim the tribute of patriotism who should labor to subvert these great pillars of human happiness. The federal government can never be in danger of degenerating into a monarchy, an oligarchy, an aristocracy, or any other despotic or oppressive form so long as there shall remain any virtue in the body of the people.'"

Clive had the complete attention of the congregation. "Do you hear what these two patriots are telling us from the grave? My interpretation is that as Christians, we can not sit idly by if the Constitution is being denigrated. We have an obligation to stop it."

Clive let that sink in.

Jake looked around. He wasn't sure about others, but this was not the kind of sermon he had expected. Clive had not yet opened the Bible, yet this felt very much like a religious challenge.

"Now regarding the specifics of what is happening in Pittsburgh and across our proud country, let me read two quotes from our founding fathers on the subject.

First, Samuel Adams, 'And that the said Constitution be never construed to authorize Congress to infringe the just liberty of the Press, or the rights of Conscience; or to prevent the people of the United States, who are peaceable citizens, from keeping their own arms.'

Finally, Thomas Jefferson, 'The greatest danger to American freedom is a government that ignores the Constitution. What country can preserve its liberties if their rulers are not warned from time to time that their people preserve the spirit of resistance? Let them take arms.'"

* * *

Monica and Jake went to the Lombardi's after church. Jake was still buzzing from the sermon, which was unlike any religious sermon he had ever heard. They fixed themselves sandwiches while they waited for her father to arrive. Clive had needed to meet with some people after church. Jake was anxious to know if there were concrete plans for the Pittsburgh Revolution. They ate quietly while they waited. Jake thought they were both somewhat apprehensive to hear what Monica's father had to say.

When the food was finished and cleaned up, they sat on the couch and turned on the TV. Both wanted updates on the gun confiscations. What had happened while they were isolated in church for a few hours? Jake wanted to see the death statistics, so they tuned to Fox News. The graphic now showed 873 civilians and 287 police officers dead.

Jake pointed at the screen. "That's almost double from last night."

Monica shook her head. "Aren't they learning anything?"

"Who?" Jake asked. "The police, or the people?"

"Either."

A news reporter wearing a red baseball cap was standing on the sidewalk in a neighborhood, with yellow tape stretched behind him. There were police cars in the street, but the officers were moving without urgency. One officer was talking to two women, one of whom was pointing down the street. Whatever action had occurred here was over. They were in investigation mode. St. Louis, Missouri was written at the bottom of the screen.

The reporter said, "They've already removed all the wounded, and the people they arrested."

A voice was heard from the studio. "How many dead?"

The reporter tipped his hat. "We're hearing eleven. Five police, and six from this neighborhood."

"Are all the wounded expected to survive? Could there be more fatalities?"

The reporter shook his head. "We have no information on that. Maybe the hospital could provide an update later."

Jake looked at Monica. "Eleven dead?"

She shrugged.

The studio reporter asked, "So, this was basically a whole neighborhood against the police?"

"That's what it looks like." He pointed at a brick house behind him. "We understand the police went to that house first. When the police tried to enter, a gunfight erupted. Both of those policemen were killed. Other police arrived, but the neighbors got involved. We talked to one lady who said the police were being shot at from three or four different houses. So, it looks like there was a wild-west shootout right here in St. Louis."

The screen split to show both reporters. The studio reporter said, "Wow. Four houses firing on multiple police cars? It's a miracle there are only eleven dead."

The guy with the hat said, "We'll have to cross our fingers on the wounded. I haven't been able to get a count on how many were removed before we arrived. Hopefully, the injuries weren't bad."

Jake wondered how a gunshot injury could be considered mild.

The studio reporter said, "Does it seem like these confrontations are changing from yesterday? I mean when the confiscations began yesterday morning, the public was caught off guard at first. But now they know the police are coming. Are we seeing that in some of these incidents?"

The reporter looked behind at the neighborhood, then back. "I guess you could say that. I'm not sure the neighbors would have gotten involved yesterday, but when they heard gun shots today, they guessed what it was about and decided to jump in."

"Is that an indication that things are getting progressively worse?"

He tipped his hat while he considered the question. "Maybe. But on the other hand, I've heard more stories about policeman searching homes and not finding the guns, so the other side of the public knowing what's going on is the opportunity to move or hide the weapons. The net result of that is fewer confrontations. So, maybe the two issues added together make it a wash. What do the national statistics tell you?"

Jake changed the channel. For the next hour, they watched stories from Baltimore, Nashville, Los Angeles, Minneapolis, Detroit, and Chicago, as well as Pittsburgh. At one point Jake had to stretch his arms because he realized he had been tense for the entire time.

They both decided to take a break and shutoff the television for a while. They got drinks and went out in the front yard. They held hands and walked down the sidewalk. They heard the sounds of news coming from almost every house. After an hour or so, they returned to the house. Inside, Monica came to Jake and embraced him, content to be held with her head on his chest. After a while she looked up at him. He kissed her gently, communicating that he was here for her. They stood in the kitchen holding each other for a few minutes. And even though Jake loved the intimacy, he felt the draw of national news. He glanced at the TV, and Monica released him. A moment later they were back on the couch in front of the tube.

It took Jake a moment to make sense of what he saw—a huge crowd in confrontation with helmeted police in riot gear. Jake watched in shock as a policeman beat a downed man with a baton before a half-dozen men tackled him. Haze filled the air from what looked like burning buildings, burning cars, and smoldering items on the ground that could be smoke bombs. The scene could have been from Beirut, or Damascus, or Gaza, or Baghdad, but it wasn't. The ticker at the bottom of the screen read, Philadelphia.

Jake's jaw dropped and he turned to Monica, whose face showed the same expression of shock. "That's Pennsylvania!"

They watched as the riot continued. It seemed as if the police were retreating. The camera angles were amazing, as if they were set up in advance in strategic locations. Monica turned up the volume.

A woman reporter's voice could be heard, ". . . turned in the last few minutes. But the crowd is definitely growing in size. The police are so outnumbered." The camera panned the crowd, which filled the streets as far as you could see in all directions. "As you can see, these officers have been pushed back to police headquarters."

Another camera angle showed the crowd pushing quickly at a huge block of police guarding the front door of the police department. Guns were fired. It looked like the police had fired first, but the reaction was immediate from the armed crowd. Light and smoke could be seen simultaneously from a thousand places in the crowd as the police and crowd fired on each other. Bodies fell everywhere. But there were so many rioters, the police didn't have a chance. The crowd pushed forward, and like a herd of buffalo, split the police and stormed into the building, tromping over dead bodies in the process.

"Our goal is to avoid that," Clive's voice boomed from behind the couch.

He walked around to the front of the couch, pointing at the TV. "How many people do you think just got shot?"

Jake closed his eyes and remembered the scene of bodies falling. It was like counting jellybeans in a jar. "A couple hundred, at least."

Clive grabbed the remote and hit the power button. The TV blinked off and went silent.

"I'd say more like three of four hundred," Clive said.

Monica looked thoughtful. "Some of them were probably just ducking, to avoid getting shot."

Her father seemed to consider. "Okay, but two hundred minimum, probably closer to three. We need to avoid shooting, if we can. We don't want that to happen in Pittsburgh."

"What's our plan?" Jake asked.

Clive led them toward the small kitchen. "Come over here to the table." He held out a chair for Monica.

He waited until they were seated to begin. "Jake, everybody liked your idea. We're doing it tomorrow night after the game."

"How can we organize it so quickly?" Monica asked.

Her father put his hand on hers. "We wanted to keep it simple. But we also wanted everyone on the same plan." He looked back and forth between the two of them "So, we have a key word tomorrow night. Everyone you tell needs to memorize it." He hesitated to make his point.

Jake and Monica said nothing.

"The key word is 'PIRATE.'"

"Pirate?" Monica said.

"Yes, listen closely, and I'll explain. It's an acronym. Each letter stands for something."

He held up his index finger. "'P' stands for Pass the word, but only tell sure sympathizers. Don't tell anyone you think might leak it to the police."

"When?" Jake asked.

"Now!" Clive said. "Tonight. Tomorrow. Pass the word."

He held up two fingers "'I.' Immediately after the game. Keep in mind it takes a while to get out of the stadium. We expect the crowd to max out at police headquarters about 30 or 40 minutes after the game. That's when the action should start."

"What if people are there early?" Jake asked.

"Don't do anything. Peaceful assembling. Wait for the starting gun."

"Starting gun?" Monica asked.

"You'll know," Clive assured her. "Tell them to wait for the sign."

Monica looked like she wanted to ask more, but Clive held his hand out. "'R.' Restrain, don't shoot. We know most are going to have guns, but we want to minimize the killing in Pittsburgh. We want everyone to bring zip ties. When the police are overwhelmed and overpowered, zip their hands behind their backs. Zip their feet together. No hog-tying. Restrain."

"But what if they shoot?" Monica asked.

"Tell your people we want to minimize shooting. If they have to shoot, so be it. But tell them to stop shooting as soon as possible. Restrain, don't shoot. We are not going to execute police officers. Show compassion."

Jake wondered how many other cities in the United States were being led by reverends, how many other cities were being counseled to show compassion. Not many, probably.

"What's next?" Clive prompted.

"A," Monica said.

"Allow access on East, Western Ave. Don't park there. Don't block it. Leave it open, all the way to the warehouse. Leave it open for our vehicle. Clear space when we arrive."

"What vehicle?" Jake asked

"Not important," Clive responded. "That's not part of the message we're telling everyone."

"Can't you tell us?" Monica asked.

"Not important," Clive said again. "Just pass the word to allow access."

Monica didn't seem too happy, but she kept quiet.

"T," Jake prompted.

"'T' stands for take. Take all the confiscated guns. Take the computers. Take all the paperwork. Take the guns, radios, and keys off the police you restrain. Once we get in, take anything the police could use to confiscate more weapons, any records of what they've already confiscated. Clean 'em out."

Jake liked this plan. "What if we can't get inside?"

"Taken care of," Clive assured them. "As long as they allow access from the east on Western Ave."

Jake really liked this plan.

"Last letter is 'E,'" Monica prompted with a smile.

"For evacuate. Vamoose when we're done. Tell everyone to leave. No hanging around and celebrating. When we get the goods, clear out. I want that place to be a ghost town five minutes after we get the guns."

"What if somebody leaks?" Monica asked.

Clive pointed at the TV. "These things are happening all around the country. They'll be expecting us no matter what. Our strength is our numbers. We need to completely overwhelm them, like we just watched in Philly."

"Only without the two hundred dead guys," Monica said.

Clive brought the palms of his hands together in a posture of prayer. "Yes, with minimal deaths." He looked heavenward. "Lord, please help us to minimize the killing."

* * *

Jake went home and made some calls. He didn't have a big network since he had only lived in Pittsburgh for less than a year. There were a couple guys he was iffy about, like his finishing guy. He figured he was the right sort, but had no basis for his feeling. He didn't recall hearing him ever mention guns, good or bad. So he called him and talked about the house, and updated him about when he might be needed after painting. During the conversation, he asked him about what he thought about the stuff on the news.

"I wish somebody would put a bullet in the president's head."

Jake thought he might be the right sort after all, so he told him all about PIRATE, and advised him to pass the word. He was more than willing, and said he would call at least ten guys.

Jake called his concrete guy. He called his plumber. He didn't feel right about the insulation guys or the electrician, so he skipped them.

His last call was to Pete, the sheetrock supervisor.

"Hello."

"Hi, it's Jake."

"Oh, hi. Hey, sorry again about your gun Saturday morning. Thanks to you, I was able to do something with mine before they came by." Pete sounded appreciative.

Jake wondered what "do something" meant, but he didn't ask. "Did they come by?"

"Yeah, but not till this morning. They had the paperwork and everything. I told 'em I didn't have the gun anymore. They came in and searched for a while, but it wasn't there."

"Did they tear the house up?"

"Naw. I think the cops that came by my place weren't that into it. They went through all the bedroom drawers, and all the obvious places, but they didn't trash the place or anything. I got the feeling they were just going through the motions. They probably had enough ugly confrontations on Saturday to learn their lesson."

Jake decided he should get to the point. "The reason I'm calling is, if something were to go down in the Burgh, would you guys want to be a part of it?"

Pete's response was immediate. "Absolutely. You mean like's happening around the country?"

Jake smiled. "What about your guys? You wanna call them?"

"I'll call 'em, but I don't need to. I can tell you already what side they're on."

Jake gave Pete the details and explained PIRATE to him. He could tell Pete was taking notes.

"Who you going with?" Pete asked.

Jake shook his head, even though nobody could see him. "I was just gonna go alone."

Pete argued, "That's crazy. Why don't you come with us? I'll take my cargo van. We'll go as team. Then we can help you get back if you get shot."

Jake had not considered that possibility. He imagined himself trying to drive home with a tourniquet on his arm. Why not? "That sounds like a good plan."

The phone went quiet for a while. Jake finally broke the silence. "You still want to work in the morning?"

Pete took a moment, contemplating. "Sure, but we should probably knock off early."

Jake agreed. "Let's work the morning and see how it goes. If we need to leave, that's not a problem."

They ended the call. That was it for Jake. He had called everyone he knew. Then on a whim, although it was almost ten, Jake walked next door and knocked on his neighbor's door. The solid door was open, and he could see through the screen that they were watching TV. The TV showed rioting in Dallas.

Jake knocked louder, and Johnny Moore jumped up, holding a long-neck beer in his hand. He held the screen open. "Is that you, Jake?"

Jake stayed outside. "Yeah."

"It's kinda late. You need something?"

"What do you think about all this crap?" Jake asked, pointing at the TV.

"I think a lot of cops are getting shot tonight and that might be a good thing." Johnny answered, motioning at the TV with his beer. That told Jake where Johnny stood on the issue. But Jake wondered if they really wanted types like Johnny tomorrow night, then decided, who was he to judge?

"Have you heard about PIRATE yet?" Jake asked.

"Pirate?" Johnny asked. "You mean the Pirates, baseball?"

"Can I come in?"

Johnny motioned inside with the beer. "Sure, Jake. What about the Pirates?"

Jake went inside and told Johnny and his wife about the plan. Johnny had a hard time remembering the meaning of the acronym, so Jake wrote it out on a piece of paper and made him promise to destroy the paper after he told his friends. He reminded Johnny to only tell people that he was sure about. Johnny waved him off as if he worried too much. Then Jake left. Johnny slapped him on the back on the way out and thanked him over and over for the message. Jake hoped he'd done the right thing. He wondered how many Johnny's would be in the crowd the next night.

Having run out of people to tell, Jake watched the news for a while. There had been rioting in many other big cities, including New York City, Washington D.C., Boston, Cleveland, and Chicago. But even watching footage of other cities couldn't hold his attention, so he shut it off.

He knew he should sleep, but his mind wouldn't stop. Scenes of the next evening kept flashing through his mind. One troubling vision was of him firing into a crowd of policemen. It disgusted him. But if bullets were flying at him, if there was an element of self-defense, that was different. Another scene was of the police overpowering the rioters, and Jake running away in a mass exodus from the station, with bullets flying overhead.

Jake realized he was clenching his fists. Adrenaline coursed through him just thinking about it. He felt pent up—in need of something to focus his energy on.

He retrieved the M16 from the closet. He took it out of the plastic case and hefted its weight. He quickly aimed at a nail hole on the wall and imagined shooting it. He tried to remember how loud the rifle had been at the club a few nights before. He imagined the recoil. He kept his eye on the sites and whipped the gun back and forth quickly, pretending to acquire other targets and kill them. He did. He killed them all.

After a while, he sat on the couch and admired the weapon. His intuition was to clean it. He had no idea how long since William had shot it or cleaned it. The M16 smelled of gun chemicals—a good sign. Jake wished he could fire up his computer and go to YouTube. There would certainly be videos on how to tear down the gun for cleaning. But the laptop was still gone. Jake inspected the M16. There was no obvious way to take it apart. Besides, even if he figured out how to open it, he was afraid of parts and springs falling out of it, which he would have no idea how to replace. Better to take his chances that William had cleaned it. Jake placed the M16 on the coffee table and inspected the Browning Hi-Power. Same risks—same conclusion.

When he finally went to bed, he slept fitfully. He kept dreaming of all the bodies dropping in Philadelphia. Sometimes he was in the crowd, and the bodies were dropping all around him. There was no place to step without stepping on somebody. Finally he moved forward anyway, stepping on fallen comrades. Some were dead, but others weren't. They kept moving when he stepped on them.

CHAPTER 11

In the morning, Jake took a long, hot shower. He watched the news while he ate some cereal. Lost in the rioting of the night before, evidently President Singleton had addressed the nation. Jake watched with interest as the news commentators critiqued the message.

A dark-haired commentator with a bright blue tie said, "Listen to what he says about the rioting in America the last few days."

The screen was filled with the president. "What's happening across the country today is completely unacceptable. We have these pockets of people who are basically saying they refuse to be governed by their elected representatives. They refuse to act civilized and abide by rules created by a democracy, a majority who by far oppose violence and seek peace."

The camera returned to the studio. The man with the blue tie asked, "What is he saying here?"

A blonde woman with short hair said, "First of all, he's trying to spin it like it's a small minority rioting. We know that's not true. Look at the numbers in Philadelphia. Try to count the people in Dallas. I heard somebody speculate there were 100,000 people in the streets in Philadelphia. How can the president refer to them as a pocket? It must be a pretty big pocket."

A black man argued. "I think 100,000 is grossly exaggerated. But even if it's true, the population in Philadelphia and its surrounding area is over six million. That means, according to my math, the thugs are fewer than two percent. I agree with the president. I've always felt that at least five percent of the population was a bunch of radicals and non-conformists. I think the president is right on the money."

The man in the blue tie asked, "What about his comments referring to these pockets of people not wanting to be governed, and not abiding by the rules established by a democracy?"

The blonde answered. "Again, the spin. This gun confiscation wasn't created by any democratic process; President Singleton bypassed Congress with his executive order. He wrote new law, which he's not supposed to do, and negated the Second Amendment in the process. And he wasn't elected to boot. He took over when the previous president died. Not to mention the fact that everyone who tries to speak out against him shows up dead. What kind of democracy is that?"

"Wait a minute," the black man said. "Executive orders have been used by presidents for hundreds of years. There is nothing undemocratic about it. And the Second Amendment says nothing about handguns and assault weapons. The NRA and its cronies keep trying to tell us that the Second Amendment guaranteed rights that the founders never dreamed of."

The man with the blue tie said. "Let's play another segment. Here the president talks about the murders. Let's listen."

The screen was filled with the president. "My office was notified yesterday of the tragic deaths of Atlanta's great mayor, John Dixon, and Senator Banister of Wisconsin." The president hesitated and wiped his eyes. His fingers came away wet. "I have met both men in person and, although Senator Banister and I didn't always see eye to eye, we had talked many times over the last few months, and I considered him a personal friend."

Jake considered the president's show of emotion. Was it fake? Could he manufacture tears on demand in front of millions of people? Jake was confused. It seemed real. He was used to giving people the benefit of the doubt. And if he gave President Singleton the same leeway, he would have to say they were legitimate tears.

"Did he order the murders?" the man in the blue tie asked.

The black man answered first. "Absolutely not. I can't believe you would even ask the question. It should be treason for anyone to suggest it. It's obvious the president has positive feelings for both men, especially the congressman. There is not a shred of evidence that the president had anything to do with either death. I can't believe that anyone dares speak the allegation out loud. What has happened in this country—have we completely lost all respect for the office?"

The blonde took her turn. "How many circumstances does it take? Everyone that speaks out against this man ends up dead. I have to admit I was moved by those tears. If he's lying, he's good. Actually, better than good. He's scary good. Look, tears or not, the whole country knows one of two things. Either the president is having these guys killed, or some powerful group that follows the president is murdering them. These are not random. Why didn't the president address that possibility? No one in America thinks these deaths were accidents as the president is saying."

Jake shut off the TV. Scary good. That's how he saw it. Scary good.

* * *

Pete and his sheetrock crew all arrived at the Campbell house a half-hour late. Jake wondered if they had slept as poorly as he had. Before they got busy, they cornered him in the house.

Pete asked. "What kind of vehicle are we," he used his fingers to show the universal quote sign, "allowing access for?"

Jake shrugged. "I have no idea. I asked, but they wouldn't tell me."

Pete pointed to the tallest guy on their team, the one other white guy who tended to do the bulk of the ceiling work. "Trent thinks it's a tank."

Trent pointed toward the city. "It makes sense, don't it?"

One of the other crew members, a Hispanic man with a ridiculously oversized mustache and muscles to match, whistled derisively. "Where they gonna get a tank, man?"

Pete clapped him on the shoulder. "This is America, Miguel. We got everything, as long as you know the right people."

They all laughed at that.

Jake asked Trent and Miguel, "Did the police get any of your guns?"

Both men shook their heads.

Miguel said, "I got a few friends with guns, but not much paperwork, if you understand?"

Jake laughed at the joke, but also realized it was indicative of the situation across America, the more shady the gun ownership, the less likely the gun would be confiscated.

Finally they got to work. The crew busied themselves hanging the panels. The drywall screwdrivers sounded like high-pitched vacuum cleaners.

Jake hoped he would see William Henry Campbell III. He wanted to appraise the old man about PIRATE, but there were no signs of the owner during the morning.

At twelve o'clock on the dot, the sheetrock crew stopped working and started cleaning up. By quarter after they were walking out the door.

"See ya later, Jake." Pete called out.

Miguel shaped his hand like a pistol and fired at Jake. Jake fired back.

Trent waved.

Jake was sweeping up and putting some tools away when the owner walked through the door.

"What's today, a holiday? Do these guys ever put in a full day?" William reached his cane toward a panel hung on the wall, but pulled it back without poking it.

Jake had wanted to tell William about tonight, but now wasn't sure he should.

"Are they all going to the Steelers game?" William asked.

Jake wondered if William knew. "Uh, I don't think so."

"What about the Pirates? Are they playing this afternoon?"

Jake knew the Pirates were out of town. "No."

William reached his cane for another panel, but didn't touch it. "What are you doing tonight, Jake?" He turned and looked pointedly at Jake.

"Uh, well I—" Should he just tell him? "Has anyone told you, um, about what's happening in Pittsburgh? You know like the other cities?"

William pointed his cane at Jake. "Are you going tonight, Jake?"

"So, you know?"

William nodded. "Of course I know. I've lived here my whole life. People were calling me all night. They wouldn't leave me alone." He looked appraisingly at Jake. "You think it'll work?"

Jake nodded. "Yeah, I think it's a good plan. You?"

William turned and inspected the walls. He didn't look at Jake as he answered. "Better than most. Most riots are just a bunch of hotheads. This plan gives them a unified set of goals. It's the best they could hope for when you invite half the city."

"Do you think somebody will squeal?"

William smirked. "Of course. How can you have everyone in the city calling each other, and not?"

Jake thought about the police ready and waiting at the warehouse. Hundreds of officers stacked ten deep all around the building. That would change everything. How could they possibly break through? He thought of the gunfight in Philadelphia and all the bodies dropping. What a mess.

"You still think it's a good plan, if the cops are ready?" Jake asked.

"If they're prepared, more people are gonna die. That's for sure. But if ten thousand people show up, and they're determined, they'll get through."

Jake agreed, but was it worth it? How many people needed to die across the country to protect the Second Amendment? Was there another way? A peaceful way?

William seemed to read Jake's thoughts. "You know what Thomas Jefferson said?"

"No, what?"

William leaned on his cane with both hands and gazed upward. "'The tree of liberty must be refreshed from time to time with the blood of patriots and tyrants.'"

"Really?" Jake asked. "He said that?"

"Jefferson thought an occasional rebellion was a good thing. He said it reminded the leaders that the people 'preserved the spirit of resistance.' He thought it was good for people, too. They needed to be ready at all times to defend their liberties."

It made sense to Jake. A neighbor in Indianapolis used to say that America needed an invasion, here on our soil, something to stir the people up to defend themselves. To remind them how much they had. The guy thought September 11, 2001 had been a small taste of that. "Look at what it had done for patriotism," he said. But for the neighbor, it had not been enough. Americans had already forgotten. He wanted a full invasion. He thought Americans had become spoiled and lazy. They expected freedom for free. They were willing to surrender it, to avoid conflict.

Jake thought about the conflicts going on in America this week. Was it possible they were a good thing? The country was not unanimous by any means. Many Americans, maybe half, thought ridding the country of handguns was a good thing. Many Americans thought the days referred to by Jefferson, where the citizens could rise up and throw off an evil government, were over. It was time to submit to this huge government they had created. It was too big to stop. Jake felt that. He also understood Jefferson's philosophy. He remembered how he felt when the police came in his house and confiscated his FN. That had not been right. That was over the top. He hadn't bought it to commit crimes. He bought it to defend himself. Who were they to tell him he couldn't defend himself?

William was watching Jake. "You're feeling it now, aren't you?"

"What do you mean?"

"Pittsburgh is a low-key place. We quietly go to work and make an honest living. It's become a professional place, white collar. The only times Pittsburgh lets it hair down and yells is when the Steelers play. The fighting spirit is buried, deep. But da Burgh is awakening. You'll see it tonight, Jake. You'll see it in their eyes. The people of Pittsburgh are going to try to take back some of what's been stolen. We'll see what they are made of. I can already see it in your eyes, Jake."

"Well, I hope it goes well tonight," Jake said. "Heaven knows it could go very wrong. You saw the death tallies on Fox News didn't you? It was still growing yesterday afternoon."

"All the channels are running it now," William said. "The numbers are over a thousand this morning. According to the news, the total Americans killed in Afghanistan and Iraq is about 5000. At this rate, more will die here in a week than in ten years of war in the middle east."

Jake tried to gauge that. How could anyone justify that? "You think the president will call it off?"

"Common sense would say, 'Absolutely.'" William shook his head. "But I'm not predicting common sense. Not from this president."

"What about the media?"

"Common sense from the media? One reporter was saying that he expects things to drop off drastically today and tomorrow. And he went on and on about how low crime was going to be after the confiscations."

Jake's voice rose until he was almost yelling. "But they're not taking guns from criminals. They're taking them from law-abiding citizens!"

William smiled at him. "I know that, and you know that. But that's not what these media types are saying. They're telling the people that we're going to be living in the Garden of Eden after this is over."

The reality that the American public was being so grossly misled, and that they were dumb enough to believe it, was incredibly frustrating. Jake felt like grabbing someone by the ears and trying to scream some sense into them. But he knew that wouldn't work. When it came to emotionally charged issues like this one, people believed what they wanted to believe, and no amount of logic could persuade them otherwise. The louder you yelled, the more entrenched each side became in their belief. They just labeled you as a radical and ignored your arguments. Raising taxes on the rich was like that. Abortion was like that. Gay marriage was like that. Capital punishment was like that. Confiscating guns was definitely like that.

"Has anyone ever tried a temporary confiscation like this one before?"

William pointed his cane at Jake. "Nobody believes this is temporary, including you."

Jake knew he was right, even though the media kept reminding everyone that this was only temporary. "You think the president might call it off?"

William waved his finger back and forth. "No way. This chaos of confiscating, and the rioting, is covering up the killings."

Jake had never thought about it that way, that this was a diversion to cover up an even bigger issue. "The dead congressmen?"

"It's more than congressmen now. You heard about the senator? And the reporter?"

Jake had heard about the senator from Wisconsin being stabbed. "What reporter?"

William answered. "Last night, in Virginia, a columnist for the Wall Street Journal, who was vocally calling for the executive order to be put on hold while an investigation is launched to determine how or if President Singleton is involved with all these murders, was killed, two shots to the head. Professional execution, just like the congressmen. No prints. No clues."

Jake felt a cold chill. He knew William already considered the president a killer. Now this just strengthened his resolve. "So, what does the president say about that?"

William waved his hand dismissively. "Same old garbage. 'I won't rest until they're found. They must be brought to justice. This strengthens our resolve to temporarily remove handguns from the riffraff.'"

Jake said nothing as he thought about it.

William continued, "It's always the tyrants that want to disarm everyone. It's the power-hungry egomaniacs, like Hitler and Stalin. It's never about the guns, it's always about power."

William put his cane under his arm and used his hands to shield his eyes like blinders. "I know it's hard, but ignore the guns. Ignore all the chaos. Ignore the morons in the media. Think about the targeted killings in Washington. Think about how it all affects the president's tax bill. Think about what happens after his bill passes. What comes next? Think about the endgame."

Jake had no idea what the president's tax bill meant. Who did? It was too complicated. But the targeted killings, they added up to less opposition for this president. That seemed obvious.

William looked at his watch. "Well, good luck tonight. I wish you the best, Jake, you and all the other rebels. I wish I were younger, and I'd be with you. It's a righteous cause, Jake. Don't forget that when you're out there."

* * *

When Jake pulled into his driveway, Monica was sitting on the step. His heart sped up, and he grinned as he slammed the truck door.

"What are you doing here?" he asked.

She stood and ran to him. Jake was surprised to see tears in her eyes. She almost tackled him in a hug.

"What's the matter?"

She didn't say anything, she just held him.

He tried to pull away, so he could see her face. "What's with the tears?" He wiped her wet cheek with his thumb.

She shivered and pointed. "Inside."

He put his arm around her and led her up the stairs. When they were in the house, she went and sat on the couch, wiping her eyes.

Jake began to feel nervous. "What happened? Your dad?"

She shook her head. "No."

"Then what? Someone else I don't know?"

She patted the cushion next her.

He didn't feel like sitting, but did anyway. She immediately embraced him and sobbed some more.

Jake thumbed her cheek again. "What? Can you tell me?"

"You," she choked.

Jake was taken back. This was about him? "What about me, baby?"

She didn't look at him. Her head was buried in his chest. "We never should have got involved with each other."

Jake jerked at that, and pushed her to arm's length. How could she even consider? He was starting to buy into the whole destiny thing. He had been imagining himself with her, having babies, growing old. "What? What do you mean?"

She looked into his eyes and sobbed a response. "What if you get killed tonight?" Her head went back down.

Then he understood. His body relaxed and he actually laughed a little before he stopped himself. He didn't want to hurt her feelings. "Is that all? You were worried about me?"

She glared at him, wiping tears from her face. "Stop laughing at me. I'm serious."

Jake remembered her and her father's abilities to see stuff, that extra sensory perception. Was it possible she had a vision about him? Him getting shot? He held her chin with his hand so he could watch her eyes. "Did you see something about me tonight?"

She shook her head.

"Your father?"

She shook her head again.

He relaxed anew. No visions. Just emotions. He embraced her. "Don't worry. I'll be fine."

She sobbed, "What if—"

"I'll be fine," he coaxed. "Nothing's going to happen."

He held her for a while, waiting for the pot to stop boiling. Eventually it did. She released him and wiped her eyes. He went in the kitchen and brought her a box of tissues. She wiped her eyes and blew her nose, not a honking blow, but a small petite blow. He smiled at her.

He tried to break the ice. "I thought you had a meeting tonight with your father about the secret vehicle thing."

"I blew it off," she responded, flipping her hand. "Dad said he'd cover for me." She chose her words carefully. "Is there any way for me to convince you to sit tonight out?"

Jake held her eyes for a minute before looking away. She thought he was a klutz, inexperienced. He knew he had limitations, but he was planning accordingly. No gung-ho stuff. Just find someone who acted like they knew what to do and follow suit.

"Look, Monica, I know you're worried about me. I get that. But I'm not gonna do anything crazy. They need bodies tonight." He wasn't sure how to articulate how he felt. "Tonight is something I feel strongly about. You weren't there when those cops took my gun. It was just so—that kind of thing shouldn't happen in America."

She stood, then reached out and took his hand. "I know I wasn't there, but they took our guns, too. I know how it feels. I know how you feel." She hesitated before continuing. "But what if something happens? I'm not sure I could deal . . ."

"I'm not going to let anything happen," He said, too loudly.

Her head went down.

"Besides, they need me. What would happen if not enough people showed up? It would be a disaster. They would become stronger. They need us to stop them now."

Her shoulders drooped. She probably felt the same way he did. She glanced away, then finally smiled at him. Jake could tell it hurt.

"Okay," she said. "If you're going, how can I help you get ready?"

Jake recalled the night before when he wanted to clean the guns, but didn't know how. "Can you help me clean my gun?"

She nodded. "The Browning? Sure."

Jake realized he hadn't told her about the M16 yet.

"I got another one," he said. "A rifle."

Monica looked at him confused. "What kind of rifle? Where did you get it?"

Jake pointed to the office. "I got it yesterday. An M16, full-auto," he added.

Her jaw dropped. "M16? Where the hell did you get one of those?"

Jake shook his head. "I meant to tell you yesterday, when we were hiding your guns. But things got hectic." He remembered her question and added. "I got it from a friend. It was a gift."

She looked at him expectantly.

Jake realized she wanted to know who. "The guy wanted to stay anonymous."

Her eye brows raised. "Your boss, the same guy that gave you that Nazi Hi-Power?"

Jake nodded.

She let it go. "Okay, bring 'em both out. Let me see 'em."

A moment later, Jake had the M16 and the Browning on the coffee table. Monica picked up the M16 and pressed what had looked like a rivet just behind the trigger, and the gun pivoted open. She pressed another and the top and bottom pieces separated.

Jake had her show him where she had pressed. She explained that all ARs and M16s were made up of upper and lower assemblies. Most parts were interchangeable, although the full-auto M16 had a few unique pieces in both upper and lower assemblies. She inspected the lower unit and messed with the trigger. She showed Jake indications that the lower was clean. She then took the upper and removed the bolt assembly. She held the bolt out to Jake.

"Touch it."

Jake did.

"Feel the oil?"

He nodded.

"It's been cleaned since it was last used," she said.

He was amazed how knowledgeable she was with the gun. She acted as if she had taken apart assault weapons her whole life, which she probably had. She reassembled the gun and set it on the coffee table.

She glanced at him. "Did he tell you when he last shot it?"

"I didn't ask."

"Did he tell you anything else about it? Is it reliable? Sighted in? Any problems? Has he shot it full-auto recently?"

Jake held out his hands and shrugged. "I didn't think to ask any questions."

She shook her head. "Taking a gun into battle without testing it on the range first is crazy."

Jake's head drooped. He didn't know what to say.

"On the other hand, it's clean and seems well maintained." She wiped a fingerprint off the side. "I guess it's probably okay." She smirked.

Jake agreed. "I wish we had time to shoot it first."

Monica put the M16 on the coffee table and picked up the pistol. Next, she disassembled the Hi-Power and inspected it. It was also clean and oiled, so she reassembled it.

She turned to Jake. "Get your bullets."

Jake returned a moment later with the ammo for both guns. He assumed that whatever she was going to do would not include firing inside the house or outside in the Pittsburgh neighborhood.

She pointed at the two thirty-round magazines in the M16's plastic case. Jake held them out to her, but she only took one.

"You load that one." She began pressing shells into hers.

Jake did the same with his. "Why are we loading them?"

"I'll show you."

She finished before Jake. She picked up the M16 off the coffee table and inserted the full magazine until it clicked. Jake tensed and now began to wonder if she would fire it in the house, after all. She raised his tension even more when she pulled the t-handle back, released it, and chambered a round. But instead of firing, she pulled the handle again. This resulted in the gun ejecting the chambered round on to the carpet, and chambering a second round. She continued ejecting rounds until there were three shells on the floor.

"Give me yours," she said.

Jake realized he had stopped loading his magazine in order to watch her. "I'm not done."

"It doesn't need to be full." She held her hand out to him expectantly.

Jake gave it to her, and watched her remove hers, and insert his. Then she ejected another three rounds from that magazine. When she was done, she removed the magazine and ejected the chambered round. She then started retrieving the ammunition from the floor.

"What was that—"

She interrupted. "It's not as good as shooting the gun, but we just verified that we can chamber and eject shells from both magazines."

Jake understood. No jams. That was good.

They repeated the same test with the Hi-Power.

She found a nylon strap in the M16 case and attached it so he could carry the rifle on his shoulder. Jake hadn't thought about that.

"You're not going alone are you?" she asked.

Jake told her about the sheet rockers and their cargo van.

"I assume you're not going to the Steelers game?"

He shook his head. There were two reasons for not attending the Steelers game: first, he had no tickets, second, and more important, you couldn't smuggle a gun in and out of the stadium, which meant logistical issues of retrieving guns from your car after the game. Besides, the sheet rockers weren't going to the game either.

"Are you going to eat something?" she asked.

It was time, but Jake's stomach was upset. Some people ate when they were nervous, but Jake was the opposite. "I don't really feel like—"

"You need to eat something, even if it's just a snack." She walked toward the kitchen. "What about some bread, a sandwich?"

"Maybe just toast and jam."

"Okay, show me where everything is, and I'll toast it while you get dressed. I want to see what you're wearing."

Jake showed her where he kept the bread and butter, then went in the bedroom. He donned his black Steelers jersey to help blend in with the people exiting the stadium. His jersey was number 55 and had Porter stitched across the back. Joey Porter was one of Jake's favorite Steelers and was the passion of the team when they won it all in 2005. He wore a pair of dark green cargo pants with pockets on the outsides of his knees. Black would have been better, but they would do. The tennis shoes were black, and they would help if he needed to run. He finished with a black Steelers cap.

When he returned to the kitchen, the toast was buttered on a plate with the open jam next to it. Monica looked him over. "That's a nice jersey. Don't mess it up."

Jake thought about making a joke about the jam being a bigger risk of soiling the jersey than the riot, but decided not to. He took a piece of toast and spread some jam on it. Monica did the same.

They ate in silence for a moment.

"What time are you meeting?" she asked.

The game would run from seven until nine-thirty. If Clive's estimate of thirty minutes staging time was accurate, the action would begin at about ten o'clock. "We're meeting in a parking lot at nine."

She considered that.

"What about you?" Jake asked. "What are you doing?"

She shrugged. "I won't know until dad tells me. They'll probably decide at the meeting."

Jake thought there was a good chance Clive would plan something to keep her out of harm's way, but he didn't say anything.

After they finished eating, and put their dishes in the sink, Jake caught her looking at her watch. It was after eight.

"Need to go?"

She looked apprehensive. "I probably should."

"I'm glad you came."

She came to him then, and they kissed. It was an urgent kiss, and her arms pulled him tight. When they broke off, she put her head on his chest. "Be careful."

"I will."

He walked her out to her car, and she drove away.

He only had a few minutes before he needed to leave as well. He paced around for a while, knowing he was just making himself more nervous, but not knowing what else to do. He put the rifle back in its case and placed it on the coffee table. He sat on the couch for a minute. He looked at his watch for the umpteenth time.

Out of nowhere he decided to pray. The thought didn't come easily to him, since he had not prayed since he was a small child. He wasn't sure exactly what the proper steps were. He knelt down on the floor between the couch and the coffee table. He looked up at the ceiling.

"Uh, God, I'm sorry I haven't prayed for a long time. And, uh, sorry I haven't gone to church for a while. I'm grateful for meeting Monica and her father. It felt good to be in church with them, and to hear them pray." He felt like he was babbling.

"Uh, tonight, as we go out into this situation, please help us to minimize the killing. And please help make sure Monica is safe, that she doesn't get hurt. Help me to use my head and not do anything stupid. Please help the crowd that they can show compassion, like the reverend says." Jake hesitated, realizing he didn't know what else to say, and didn't know how to finish.

"That's all, God." He stood, then remembered. "Amen," he added.

As Jake gathered his weapons, he realized he wasn't much for feelings. But he had to admit he felt better after the prayer. He got in his truck and drove to the parking lot where he and the sheetrock crew had agreed to meet.

* * *

In the back of the cargo van, Jake couldn't really see where they were going. But Pete told them he had studied the map. He said the best way would normally be to take the West End Bridge across the Ohio, but he was afraid that would get jammed up. So he decided to drive a couple miles farther to cross at the McKees Bridge. The sun had set just before eight, and it was now after nine, so it was dark.

Trent was sitting shotgun in the front next to Pete. Miguel and Jake were sitting on opposite sides of the floor in the back. Pete had obviously removed all his tools and equipment from the van because the rear space was empty, although there was sheetrock dust all over. Monica would be disappointed to see Jake had already soiled the Porter jersey.

Miguel handed Jake a small can. "Here. Put this on."

"What is it?" Jake asked.

"Shoe polish. Wipe it on your face."

Jake had already noticed the others' faces, and he was happy to follow their lead. He decided to apply the polish in vertical stripes down his face rather than just rub it on, but he had no mirror to see how it looked.

"Get your guns ready," Pete called.

Trent unbuckled and joined Miguel and Jake in the rear. Trent unzipped a soft gun case and removed an old lever-action rifle.

"Hey, John Wayne," Miguel said.

Trent smiled. "It was my dad's."

Miguel laughed. "Those are for shooting Indians, aren't they?"

Jake noticed Miguel had no rifle, only a revolver. "Is that all you got?"

Miguel held it up. "All I need. A riot like that, it's all close combat. Targets are all less than ten feet. Handgun's better."

"That's why I got a shotgun," Pete said while still driving.

That being said, Jake still felt better with both. He unsnapped his plastic case and pulled out the M16. Both Trent and Miguel stared at it.

"Jake's got an AR-15," Trent called out to Pete.

Pete turned his head and glanced at the gun before returning his eyes to the road.

Jake decided there was no need to correct them. Full-auto was a big deal, and the fewer who knew about it, the better.

When they crossed the bridge, Pete avoided the main highway and instead took California south along the tracks. They used the bridge at Columbus to cross in to the neighborhoods. Pete swore at the traffic jam on the bridge. There were a million cars doing the same thing, and they inched along for a while. The neighborhood was full of one-way streets, and the van followed most of the cars to Manhattan Street.

"Is the game over?" Trent asked. "Pete, turn on the radio."

It was almost nine thirty when Pete found the channel. On the first play after the two-minute warning, the Steelers handed off the ball. They were up by three, and if they made a first down, they could kneel it a couple of times and let the clock run out. The next play they handed it off again, and the play went up the middle for seven yards. Game over. Just a matter of waiting for the clock to run out.

As Pete drove south on Manhattan, he started complaining there was no place to park. Trent went back up and sat in the front. Up ahead, at North Avenue, there was a "Do Not Enter" sign on Manhattan, and the traffic split. Pete swore and turned left on Hamlin Street. Jake leaned forward between the seats. There were no spaces, but when they crossed Fulton the problem solved itself.

"Cheese and crackers!" Pete said. "Now what?"

"Just leave it, like everybody else," Trent responded

In front of them, a sea of abandoned cars filled the street. There was no way through. People had just turned off their cars and left them. Pete pulled the van behind a Honda and did the same.

"Well, I guess this must be our stop." Pete shut off the engine. "Hand me my shotgun, would ya?"

When they exited the van, they were still five blocks from where they needed to be. Jake shouldered the M16 and looked around at the other people on the street. He had never seen so many guns in his life. The crowd was mostly made up of men, but Jake saw a few women as well. One woman wore a pink number seven Rothlesburger jersey and carried a Teflon black deer rifle with scope. The pink jersey was going to stand out pretty bad.

Most of the crowd was walking toward Fontella Street, but Pete suggested they go back to Fulton, which was guaranteed to be less crowded.

"Hijole" Miguel said. "Half the people're probably stuck in traffic."

Jake agreed. "Hopefully, they make it." What if enough didn't show? It would mean more bullets aimed at him.

Pete was feeding shotgun shells into his gun as they started walking. They fell in with streams of other people, most wearing Steelers jerseys or shirts. They walked directly behind a guy with an assault weapon over his shoulder, only his had a nasty-looking bayonet attached to the end of it—a perfect, but terrifying, weapon for close combat. Jake told himself that if he lived through this, he would like to add a bayonet to his arsenal.

CHAPTER 12

The crowd swelled as they approached Western, and the walking slowed due to others slowing in front of them. On the corner of Page and Fulton, an old black woman and a half-dozen small children stood on the porch of their house and watched them walk past. In the poor light, Jake couldn't tell whether the old lady approved or disapproved of a mob of people toting guns past her house.

A huge crowd coming north from Heinz Field met them at the corner of Western. Jake's group turned left at a rundown car repair shop called Mellor's Service and merged with the stadium crowd. Police headquarters was now visible at the end of the block. Jake guessed there were five thousand people on Western between him and the station. Many in the crowd had stopped, deciding they were close enough. But Pete led them through the throng, getting them closer to the action. Jake tried to look over the crowd, to judge how many police were there. Had the police been alerted? But from this far back, he couldn't differentiate the police from the visitors. All he saw were guys like him.

Jake and the people around him jerked at a loud sound. It was a voice over a bullhorn. "Folks. Listen up. Not sure what you heard was going to happen tonight, but you heard wrong. Please evacuate the area. Go back to your cars. Go home."

The crowd yelled a thousand responses at the same time. It came out like the response to a bad sports call.

"Give our guns back!"

"I want my Glock!"

"Ram it pigs!"

Pete and Trent kept weaving them forward through the crowd. Miguel and Jake followed. The crowd was tighter now, and Jake felt people brushing by him on both sides. He felt especially nervous whenever anyone jostled the M16, and he was glad he hadn't chambered rounds in either of his guns. As he moved through the crowd, he couldn't help but rub past other people's rifles and handguns, and he wondered how many of them had taken the same precautions he had, or if they were only an anxious trigger finger away from going off.

The bullhorn went off again. "Pittsburghers, please move back. Having this many weapons in this tight of space is inherently dangerous. Please go back to your cars. We don't want any accidents here tonight."

The crowd reacted the same, yelling back at the voice. The clearest response Jake heard was, "Open the doors!"

Jake felt the energy in the crowd rise after each volley of words and wondered if the police knew the effect of their pleadings. Pete and Trent were walking too fast, and Jake and Miguel had a hard time keeping up. Then suddenly the crowd squeezed in and they were separated. Jake saw Trent's head briefly, then he and Miguel were alone in the mob.

Miguel shrugged. "We're better off."

Jake wondered how they would find each other after. He glanced at his watch and saw it was 9:55. Only about five minutes to Clive's surprise vehicle coming at them down Western Ave., assuming the traffic would allow them through, which Jake thought was impossible.

Jake jumped at a loud gunshot to his right, and the entire crowd flinched away from it in a wave. Miguel was pressed into him. He looked in the direction of the sound but saw nothing other than the crowd jostling around. Men were yelling, and Jake saw gun barrels come up all around him.

"We're gonna get shot by our own people," Jake said.

Miguel nodded, his eyes wide. "This is crazy."

The potential for accidental shootings and panic was enormous. Jake was sure he had never been in such a precarious situation. He was fairly sure the single gunshot had been accidental. He wondered if someone was hurt. He was amazed the shot hadn't caused a chain reaction shoot-out, with all the panicked people mulling around.

"Look at the roof!" Miguel yelled.

Jake saw a half-dozen police officers moving into position on the roof of police headquarters and spreading out along the roofline. All around Jake, gun barrels came up and took aim at the roofline. The angle was extremely dangerous. A missed shot up at the roof would soar right over downtown Pittsburgh.

"Should I shoot?" a guy next to Miguel asked.

Jake cringed and spoke. "No. Remember the plan. Wait for the starting gun. Restrain. Don't shoot."

The guy looked at Jake. His eyes looked like they were about ready to pop out of his head.

"Wait for the sign," Jake repeated calmly, although his own heart was racing.

"You'll know when," Miguel added.

The guy's gun came down. Jake heard others repeating the advice to wait for the sign. The message rippled through the crowd. More barrels came down.

Jake could finally see the officer with the bullhorn. He wore a riot helmet and was standing in front of the warehouse across the street from headquarters. He must have been standing on something, because his head was a few feet higher than everyone else's.

The bullhorn blasted, "People, please backup." He pointed where the gunshot had gone off a moment before. "Can we clear a space over there and make sure everyone is okay?"

Jake thought the guy was baby talking them, trying to calm down the crowd. Nothing threatening. No ultimatums or warnings of arrest. He was good.

A guy behind Jake yelled, "Stand aside and let us get our guns! That's the best way to avoid anyone getting shot."

The bullhorn waited a few seconds before responding. "Sorry, folks. You know I can't do that. We are under direct order of the president of the United States."

Another guy yelled. "You're puppets of a dictator that should be shot!"

The bullhorn said nothing.

It occurred to Jake that maybe Clive's plan should have included a spokesman, to alleviate the slurs from the crowd. Miguel was pushed into Jake as the crowd pressed them from behind. He looked up and saw that the police on the roof of headquarters were now down in sniper shooting positions. If anything happened, they could fire down with impunity on a crowd of sitting ducks.

Suddenly, over the crowd noise, they heard a diesel engine approaching. Jake looked east down Western Ave., but saw nothing over the crowd.

Someone yelled. "Clear access!"

The chant was relayed in various forms.

"Clear the street!"

"Make way!"

"Get back!"

The police officer with the bullhorn cocked his head left at what was coming. He spoke without the bullhorn to other officers behind him.

"Now it begins," Miguel said.

The roar of the diesel engine increased as it approached. The whole crowd craned their necks trying to see what was coming. Then Jake saw it. A huge, yellow front loader roared down the street toward them, black smoke pouring from its pipes. It was the type you might see at a gravel pit, loading dump trucks. The tires were larger than a man. The crowd just east of headquarters parted like the Red Sea, squeezing into the parking lots on both sides of Western Ave.

"Whoa, what did they do to that thing?" Miguel asked, his mouth hanging open in an incredulous smile.

It was obvious as it rumbled closer that the front loader had been radically modified. Steel plates had been welded over the four faces of the cab and over both sides of the engine. There were small eye gaps in the plates so the driver could see.

"I guess Trent was right. It is a friggin' tank," Miguel laughed.

Jake whipped his head back around to police headquarters to see their reaction to this new development. He turned just in time to see the police snipers on the roof repositioning themselves, the barrels of their rifles aiming at the loader. A moment later they began firing on it. The air was filled with gunshots, and sparks could be seen as bullets ricocheted off the metal plates.

In reaction, guns came up all around Jake and Miguel, and a hail of bullets sprayed the snipers on the roofline. Miguel, too, lifted his revolver and began to fire. The loudness from gunshots was deafening. Jake pulled the M16 off his shoulder and chambered a round, but he didn't aim and left the safety on. He was afraid of stray bullets flying over the city. He was sure many of them would land in downtown Pittsburgh, and he could only hope they would hit concrete or metal and not families going home from the game. Besides the cops weren't firing on Jake and Miguel yet.

Jake saw one officer slump on the roof, his gun falling to the street below. Then another. Many of the officers on the roof ducked out of sight to avoid getting shot.

Just when Jake thought the front loader would drive into the crowd and kill them all, it slowed and veered to Jake's left, toward the warehouse. It halted as three rows of officers in helmets moved in front of it, creating a barrier in front of the warehouse. Bullets were still zinging off the metal.

Jake heard a loud voice from the front loader, like a PA. "Bind them, and get 'em out of the way."

The crowd needed no further instructions. They surged at the officers. Men came from all directions to engage the cops. The police were dressed in riot gear, holding clear shields in front of them, but they were hopelessly outnumbered. Men grabbed the tops of the shields and pulled them down. The police resisted, trying to stay in a tight formation, but a dozen rioters to each policeman overwhelmed them one by one and wrestled them down to the ground. A few gunshots were heard, but not many. Jake guessed the officers on the roof were reluctant to fire into the crowd of officers wrestling with rioters.

With the frontlines of the crowd moving forward at the police, then dragging the bodies east, the crowd in front of Jake eased forward. Soon he and Miguel would be in the fray.

Barrels came up around them again. The roof snipers could be seen repositioning to aim directly down into the rioters.

Miguel pointed up at them. "Watch out!"

Then bullets were flying down on them from the roofline. The crowd returned fire. The noise was deafening. A man just in front of Jake was hit and fell hard onto the ground in front of him. He was wearing a Lynn Swan number eighty-eight jersey. Jake felt something wet on his face. Rifles all around lobbed bullets back at the roof. Jake looked down at the man, wondering if he should help him, but he saw the top of his head was missing. He was dead, and Jake knew what he had felt hit his face. Jake felt anger and wanted to spray the roof with the full-auto M16, but there were already plenty of people firing at the roofline, and the cops were retreating back from the edge of the roof. Besides, any second he and Miguel would be needed to engage the police blocking the front loader. He slung the M16 back onto his shoulder.

Miguel had emptied his revolver and was reloading. Jake pointed at where he thought he and Miguel were needed. "Get ready."

"Stand aside!" The voice from the front loader blared.

The rioters dragged the last few policemen out of the way. Only a small crowd separated Jake from the action. The diesel engine roared, sending black smoke out the stacks, and then surged forward at the warehouse. Both police and rioters scattered as the huge bucket on the front loader tore into the brick wall. A cloud of dust belched out of the hole as the bucket disappeared inside the building. The driver stopped, backed up, and hit it again, just to the right of the first impact, and substantially widened the hole. He backed up again, pivoted, then roared away, back east on Western Ave., where he came from. The crowd cheered and parted again to let him through.

Jake and Miguel rushed forward and soon found themselves on the front lines as they climbed through the rubble into the warehouse. It was hard to see in the dust. Jake covered his nose and moved farther inside. He caught sight of an officer running away from them to his left, and he and Miguel gave chase. The officer stopped and went for a handgun in his holster, but Jake grabbed his hands and Miguel wrestled him to the ground. Jake got the pistol out of his hands and pushed it away on the floor. Jake felt others helping from behind. They rolled the cop face down, grabbing his hands, and Miguel zip-tied his hands together behind him. Somebody else zipped his feet together. The captured man said nothing.

Jake didn't remember his heart ever pumping so hard. Miguel gave him a hand and helped him up.

"Where's his gun?" Miguel asked.

Jake pointed to it on the floor. Miguel picked it up and pocketed it. The other guys were going through the officer's pockets.

"Take everything," Jake told them.

"The guns are over here!" someone yelled.

Jake and Miguel moved toward the sound. They passed into a different bay of the warehouse and saw rows of large metal baskets with handguns stacked neatly inside. Jake joined a crowd of rioters at a basket. He picked up the first gun he saw, which was a black revolver. Like the other guns in the basket, it had an orange tag zip-tied to the trigger with the name, address, and phone number of the person it had been confiscated from. This gun belonged to someone named Frank Sessions. Jake looked at the row of baskets, which held thousands of guns. Where was his FN?

"Just take what you can carry!" someone said. "Find the owner later."

Jake decided that was good advice, so he grabbed three more, so that he had two in each hand. Miguel did the same. They headed back for the opening, and fell in line behind others working their way out. Someone had opened a garage door, which became the exit for those carrying confiscated guns back out. Jake and Miguel exited back into the night. As they left the building, they saw a crowd of police officers standing back in defeat, their backs to police headquarters. Two-dozen rioters held them at gunpoint in case they decided to engage again, but their defeat was evident.

Jake looked back at where the hole had been torn in the building and saw the crowd pushing and shoving to get inside. Jake and Miguel turned west, the way they had come, and weaved through the crowd, back toward the corner. Finding Pete and Trent in the crowd would be impossible. They would meet them back at the van.

After hiking five blocks back to the van, Jake and Miguel waited for the other two to show up. As they waited, they laid out the guns they'd taken back from the police. Jake and Miguel each had four from the bins, and Miguel had the one he'd taken from the cop.

Miguel held the cop gun out. "You want it? You took it from him."

"What is it?" Jake asked.

"Glock." He read the side of the gun. "Uh, 9mm."

Sure Jake wanted it. It was probably worth five hundred bucks or so. But he said, "You're the one who brought it out. You keep it."

"You sure?" Miguel said.

Jake really wanted it. It would be a great souvenir from the riot, but he said. "You don't have a semi-auto, do you?"

Miguel shook his head.

Jake held up his Hi-Power. "I already have one. You keep it."

Miguel smiled, obviously happy, and set it next to him on the grass.

As they waited, other rioters returned to their cars, however nobody could leave because they were all blocked in. After a while, things started to get sketchy. Engines revved and horns honked.

When Trent and Pete finally arrived, Trent was limping badly. Pete had dried blood on his face.

Miguel and Jake stood.

"What happened?" Miguel asked.

Both men smiled in spite of their injuries.

"We gave 'em hell, that's what," Pete said.

Jake pointed at Trent's bad leg. "And that?"

Trent waved it off. "That's nothing. I think I got stepped on."

"We were right up there," Pete said. "Tackling those cops in riot gear, the ones blocking the loader."

"I had one down on the ground," Trent said. "And the crowd was jumping over us, and one landed on my knee. It popped."

"Probably an ACL, or MCL, or something," Pete said.

Jake pointed at Pete's head. "What's that blood?"

Pete felt in his hair above his forehead, as if he had forgotten about it. "I don't know. When we were wrestling the cops. This guy tried to grab my hair, and I felt a burning. Then I forgot about it until after."

"Some kinda cut, probably," Miguel said. "We'll need to look at it in the light."

Pete pointed at Jake. "What about you? What's all that blood on your face?"

Jake's hand also went to his face. He had forgotten. He rubbed off a couple pieces he found there.

"It's not mine," Jake said.

"Whatta ya mean?" Trent asked.

"A guy got shot right in front of me," Jake answered.

Pete pointed at Jake's face, "And that?"

"Is the guy's brains," Miguel answered.

The comment took the levity out of the conversation. Jake remembered watching the guy collapse in front of him and feeling the wetness on his face. He remembered the number eighty-eight jersey.

"Did you know him?" Pete asked.

Jake shook his head.

A horn blared for a couple seconds. "Move it!"

Jake and the others looked up in time to see a bearded guy in a pickup. He revved the engine, and his truck lurched forward and hit the car in front of him in a loud crash of metal, moving the car forward a few feet. He backed up and used the space to drive up onto someone's lawn to get around two other cars, then squealed his tires and headed down Fontella.

"Idiots like that give rioters a bad name," Trent said.

Other drivers used the space created by the crazy bearded guy to get their cars out, and gradually the street started to clear, although some cars remained in the middle of the road.

Miguel and Jake gathered their guns to put in the van.

"You guys got some?" Pete asked. "Let me see." He took the black revolver from Jake and read the tag under a street light. "Frank Sessions."

"Cool," Pete said. "By the time Trent and I got in there, all the guns were gone. Did you get your FN back?"

Jake shook his head. "Not yet."

"We got to help destroy their computers, though." Trent said.

Pete held up his shotgun. "This is the perfect weapon for blowing computers to bits."

Jake smiled as he pictured Pete blowing a bunch of small holes into a computer.

After they loaded in the van, they had to wait another fifteen minutes until enough space cleared to get away. They passed the recovered guns around and admired them while they waited. The street cleared behind the van first, so they backed up Hamlin and drove north on Fontella. Pete worked his way northwest, and they merged onto the 65th Infantry Division Highway going north, but it was crowded most of the way and took forever. They crossed back over the river on McKees.

"I'm hungry," Trent said. "I got the munchies."

Miguel raised his hand. "Me, too."

Jake rubbed his hands on his face and thought about the guy in the Swan jersey. He didn't really feel like eating.

"Let's drive for a while," Pete said. "Get farther away. Then we'll hit a drive-thru." He glanced back at Jake. "Sound good, Jake?"

Jake nodded, although he probably wouldn't get anything.

Ten minutes later the van got in line at a drive-thru at some generic late-night hamburger joint. All of them ordered combos with cheeseburgers and fries except Jake, who just got a chocolate shake. When they pulled up to get the food, the kid asked about their painted faces.

"Were you guys at the Steelers game?" he asked

Pete looked over at Trent before responding. "Yeah, man. Go Steelers."

When Jake got home he tried to call Monica, but she didn't answer. He left a message that he was back and okay, and would call her tomorrow. He couldn't wait to get in the shower and wash the dead guy's blood off him. He trusted Clive had kept Monica out of harm, so he didn't worry about her. When he slid under the covers he was worried he might not sleep, but he slept like a log.

CHAPTER 13

Jake awoke to his cell phone ringing at exactly six thirty. It was Monica.

"Hello."

"I'm outside. Come and let me in."

Jake laughed. He pulled on some sweats, turned on some lights, and unlocked the door. She came in and immediately hugged him tightly. He held her as well.

She smiled up at him. "I was so glad to hear your message last night. No close calls?"

He thought about the police snipers firing down into them, and the guy wearing the Swan jersey getting shot right in front of him.

She saw his hesitation. "What?"

How could he put it in perspective to not freak her out? "Well there was definitely some shooting."

"Did you shoot?"

He shook his head. "Not a round." He thought about Miguel, standing right next to him, empting his revolver at the roofline.

"What about you?" Jake asked

She scoffed. "Nothing. I was in a high-rise downtown with binoculars and a radio. Dad had me monitoring the crowd and signaling when to send in the loader."

Just as Jake had guessed. "Where was your father?"

"In the front loader, next to the driver. It was his voice on the PA."

Jake was surprised by that. He had not recognized the voice. "No problems?"

She shrugged. "They took a lot of rounds, but the armor held."

Jake asked a question that had occurred to him the night before. "Why didn't the tires blow out, with all the rounds hitting them?"

"Solid rubber, flat proof. They specifically looked for a loader with that kind of tires."

She hugged him again. "I was worried about you."

"I told you not to." But Jake thought again about the guy in front of him. He wondered how long it would take for the news to figure out how many had been killed. They probably knew by know. He was curious to know the number.

She released him, then pulled him by the hand to the couch. "Tell me the details. What did you see?"

Jake started from the beginning. He told her about the ride in the van, the traffic, how they parked. She was nervous when he told her about the police snipers on the roof.

"Did they hit anyone near you?"

Jake couldn't keep it from her any longer. "Yeah. They got a guy in front of me."

"How bad?"

Jake shrugged. "He's dead."

She sat up. "What? How do you know? Did you check his pulse or something?"

Jake shook his head. "He got shot in the head."

Monica considered this. "How far away from you was he?"

Jake looked out the window. The sun had just risen, and it was getting lighter. "Right in front of me." He didn't want to tell her about the splatter. Some things were better left untold.

"Were you scared? Did they get any others around you?"

Jake shook his head. "As soon as they started firing on us, everybody around started shooting up at them. They retreated so we couldn't see them anymore."

Jake then told her about storming the warehouse and getting the guns.

Her eyes lit up. "Can I see them?"

Jake took her in the kitchen where the four guns were sitting on the table. As she picked them up and inspected them, Jake was relieved she hadn't freaked out too bad about the guy next to him getting killed, but he suspected it wasn't over. She might bring it up again.

"What are you going to do with them?" she asked.

Jake looked at the clock on the microwave. "I'll call them later, when they wake up, and tell them to come and get 'em."

She looked around in the house. "You sure you want them to come here?"

He shrugged. "I could tell them to meet me at the job site. That would probably be easier anyway."

She agreed. She asked questions about the sheet rockers, and Jake answered them. They discussed Clive's plan and how well it had been executed. Ultimately, the plan had been executed exactly as planned, even though the police had been tipped off. During a lull in the conversation, Jake suggested Monica join him for a cold cereal breakfast. She agreed.

When they were done eating, Monica looked at her watch. "What time are you going to work?"

"In a few."

"What are you doing tonight?" she asked.

Jake shrugged. He had no plans. "Nothing."

She winked at him. "Call me."

She gave him a peck, then left. He watched her go.

When she was gone, he changed clothes for work. Then he made four phone calls to the names on all four tags of the guns he had brought home the night before. One guy didn't answer, and Jake didn't leave a message, but the other three were ecstatic. Jake explained that he would take the guns to work, and they could come and get them from him anytime during the day after nine.

He then turned on the news and watched highlights of the attack. He didn't remember seeing any cameras the night before, but evidently they were there. They had close-up footage of the police officer with the bullhorn. They had multiple camera angles of the front loader demolishing the front of the warehouse. They showed incredible footage of the rioters tackling the policemen and moving them out of the way of the front loader. They even had footage of rioters exiting the warehouse with tagged guns.

But the coverage was biased. There was no mention of the effort taken to bind, but not kill the policeman. There was no footage of the cops on the building shooting rioters below. They repeatedly played a clip of a rioter punching a bound policeman in the face. There was no summary of how the guns were retrieved with almost

GARY HANSEN

no police killings. Instead, the coverage made it sound like a reckless disregard for the law. Jake finally turned it off. It gave him a bad taste in his mouth.

When he arrived at the job site a few minutes before nine, a man in an old rusted Chevy pickup was waiting for him. It turned out to be Frank Sessions, the owner of the black revolver Jake had grabbed first the night before. Jake guessed Frank was in his eighties. He was thin and bent over, and Jake wondered how much longer he would last. But he shook Jake's hand with vigor and thanked Jake over and over for returning his gun.

"You guys really did 'em last night," he said. "Wished I could'a been there." He turned the gun over in his hands. "Thank you so much. My dad bought this when I was little boy. It's a Smith and Wesson model 27, the first ever .357 magnum handgun. He gave it to me when I turned eighteen. I thought I'd lost it forever."

Jake asked, "If the gun's that old, how did they know you had it? There shouldn't have been any paperwork."

Frank laughed. "Just a few months ago my wife took it to the pawn shop, and I had to go buy it back."

Jake cringed. "Ouch! So, it was off the grid for all those years . . ."

"Yeah, tell me about it. Good thing I didn't have the gun, or I probably would've killed her."

Jake laughed. "Well, at least it's recovered now."

Frank looked up, confused. "The gun, or the marriage?"

Jake mumbled, "Uh, I was talking about the gun."

Frank smiled. "Yes, the gun is recovered. Not sure about the marriage."

Jake had no response for that one.

Frank took out his wallet. "Let me give you something."

Jake held up his hands. "No. I don't want your money. I'm just glad you got your gun back."

The old man looked frustrated. "You risked your life. The least I can do is give you enough to buy a pizza."

Jake shook his head. "I don't want your money, Frank."

Frank shrugged and tossed two twenties on the street. He turned and walked away. "Your call."

Jake bent over and picked up the twenties and put them in his wallet. He called out to the old man, "Hide it better this time. They might come after you again."

156

Frank climbed in his truck, started it, and called out the window, "Don't worry, I've got the perfect place. There's no way they're gonna get it twice."

Jake watched Frank drive away, and smiled.

Jake unlocked the front door and went inside. Pete and his crew arrived a few minutes later. Trent limped in wearing a sophisticated knee brace over the top of his pants. It looked like the type worn by football linemen.

"You didn't go to the doctor?" Jake asked.

Trent scoffed. "I told you, it's been messed up before. My wife's gonna make an appointment. She'll let me know."

Miguel pointed at Pete. "He went."

Pete parted his hair for Jake. "Six stiches."

Jake wondered if the hospitals were looking for injuries from the night before. "Did they ask how you did it?"

"Sure."

"And?"

"I told them I got it fighting with the police."

"Really?

Pete smirked. "'Course not. I made up a story about scraping my head in the van." He touched another spot on his scalp. "I've actually done that before."

"Did they buy it?" Jake asked.

"Hope so."

Trent interrupted. "We should be more concerned about being seen on TV, did you see the coverage?"

Jake recalled the crisp videos he had seen that morning. "Did you see any of our faces?"

Trent pointed at Jake. "No, but I saw a rear view of a guy wearing a number fifty-five Porter jersey with an assault weapon climbing over the rubble into the warehouse."

Jake groaned. "Really?"

"Really," Trent said. "I recognized you, even without the jersey."

Pete inserted. "I wouldn't worry about that. I'd worry more about the video we haven't seen yet. Hopefully, they don't have good face shots of any of us."

"How could they not?" Trent said.

Miguel waved his arms. "There were thousands there last night, man. They don't got time to try to identify everybody. Besides, even if they did, Jake could say he was there to help the police."

All of them looked at each other. Trent laughed first. "I'm not sure that dog would hunt."

"Besides, we had face paint." Miguel argued.

Jake thought about that. He had been surprised, when he arrived home the night before and looked in the mirror, how much the vertical stripes had changed his appearance. Maybe it would be enough. Besides, he was new in the Burgh. Even if they had a clear view of his face, who would know him?

Pete looked at his watch. "I need to make a living. Let's get to work."

A few minutes later the chatter was replaced by the high pitched whine of the drywall screwdrivers.

It wasn't until afternoon that Jake saw the owner. Pete's team had finished paneling the great room and had moved to other rooms. Jake was inspecting the cut around an outlet when he saw the old man enter. William Henry III was poking the sheetrock with his cane.

"You guys started a little late today, didn't you?"

Jake wondered how William knew, had he come by before they arrived? "Yeah. Sorry, we've been a little distracted lately."

William smiled. "I saw the news. I assume you guys were all there?"

Jake held out his hands. "I admit nothing."

William nodded. "If I were part of a riot that stole thousands of guns, and shot a few cops, I wouldn't admit it either." But he smiled broadly.

Jake said nothing.

William used his cane to trace a seam in the sheetrock. He didn't look at Jake. "But if I was part of the Pittsburgh Revolution last night, I'd take pride in how smoothly it went off."

Jake reacted at that. "That's not how the media is painting it. They made it sound like a bunch of armed hooligans came in and shot every policeman they saw. They definitely made the police the good guys, and the crowd, the criminals."

William looked at Jake. "What'd you expect? Did you expect the media to compliment the rioters?"

Jake shrugged. "I guess I expected a balanced view. When was the last time you saw coverage of rioters tying up policeman, and not killing them?"

"Never. But the media is the media. They always emphasize the blood. It's about headlines." He looked back at the sheetrock and touched another seam with his cane. He spoke without looking back, "Besides, they're scared. Reporters are getting killed for speaking out against the president."

Jake pointed to his boss. "You seemed to figure out what really happened."

He began walking around the large room. Jake followed.

William spoke while inspecting the drywall. "It was obvious. They have pictures of policemen being tied up. Who does that? No stats were released on killed policemen; must mean the numbers were too low to report." He looked Jake in the eye. "Like I told you yesterday, a riot with a plan was an advantage. It seems the whole 'restrain, don't shoot' thing worked."

"Yeah. For a riot, it was well organized. Without the plan, there definitely would have been a lot more killing. Lots of dead cops."

Williams said, "Whoever organized this had a brain."

The conversation went silent for a while. Jake was counting unused panels of drywall when he heard William's voice.

"This is not over, you know?"

Jake frowned. "What do you mean?"

"Singleton. He's not going to stand by while you guys undo everything he's done."

Jake asked, "So what's next?"

William pointed out the window. "America just stood up to a bully. The bully is going to hit back. Expect it." William looked like he was going to walk out of the room, then hesitated.

"How?" Jake asked.

"I don't know, but expect something, and soon."

What William was saying made a lot of sense and Jake felt perturbed that he hadn't thought of it himself. He remembered Monica asking if he had any plans tonight, and him thinking he didn't have any the whole week. Under the circumstances, that was pretty short sighted.

He wanted to pick William's brain before he escaped. "What should we be doing? You know, to prepare?"

"America needs to pull its head out. This fight is going escalate. It'll get ugly, and we'll see if the people have the guts to do what it takes to finish."

"Finish what?" Jake asked.

William stared into Jake's eyes. "Revolution," he said. "We've crossed the threshold. There are only two options left: surrender to Singleton, or revolt."

"Revolution?" Jake asked, flabbergasted.

William nodded. "Over half of the population wants this guy to stop killing people that disagree with him. Now we need to see if they have the stomach to do what it takes and take their country back." He stared at Jake to make sure his point was taken.

"Why are you looking at me?"

William shrugged. "Because I'm too old, and I don't have the contacts. It's going to take organization at the national level. We need somebody connected. Don't you know anybody?" William didn't wait for an answer, he just walked away.

*　*　*

By the time the sheet rockers decided to knock off for the day, Jake was exhausted. Being out so late the night before had taken something out of him, and by the way Pete's crew was dragging as they left, they were feeling it as well.

Jake went home, showered, and changed. Although he was tired physically, his mind wouldn't settle. He couldn't get his mind off the police possibly identifying him with their cameras, or what William had suggested about them headed for a revolution.

His mind was still buzzing when he arrived at Monica's house. When she opened the door, it was obvious she and her father were watching television coverage of the previous night. Monica waved Jake in through the screen door. Clive turned off the television. Jake noticed Clive stare at the blank screen as if he were adding up something, or trying to get his facts straight.

"Are they still making us out like a bunch of thugs?" Jake asked.

Clive looked at Jake blankly, as if he just realized he had entered the room. "Huh?"

"Is it still slanted?" Jake asked.

Monica touched her father on the shoulder. "Daddy?"

Clive broke his trance. He stood and shook Jake's hand vigorously. "Hey, Jake. How was work?"

"Okay, Mr. Lombardi, uh, I mean, Reverend."

160

Clive slapped Jake on the back. "Clive, Jake! No mister or reverend. It's Clive."

Jake pointed at the TV. "So is the coverage still bad?"

Clive looked at the television as if he had never seen it before. "What? Bad? No. The word is getting out, Jake. They couldn't bury it forever. This coverage we just watched didn't talk about the numbers, but KDKA broadcast the numbers a few minutes ago. It's just a matter of time, Jake. The message will get out."

"What numbers?" Jake asked.

"The dead. Seventeen total, only five of them were police. The police shot twelve rioters. That's it!" Clive smiled.

Jake's jaw dropped. "Seventeen? That's it?"

Clive rubbed his hands together. "Yeah, that's it. Nothing compared to Philadelphia. There were definitely over a hundred in Philly."

The plan had actually worked. Who would've thought they could overwhelm the police with so few casualties. He looked at the reverend with admiration.

Monica added, "And the bias is getting better too. KDKA criticized the police for opening fire on the crowd from the roof of police headquarters."

Jake pointed at the TV even though it was off. "Yeah, that's who shot the guy standing in front of me."

Clive grimaced. "Monica told me about that. I'm sorry you had to see that so close."

Jake put his head down, remembering scrubbing his face in the shower the night before.

Clive said, "And you're sure he died?"

Jake nodded. "His head—"

Monica said to her father, "I told you."

Clive shrugged. "Sorry, I just wanted to be sure. He was obviously one of the seventeen. With such a small number, over the next few days the news should get full bios on all of them.

Jake wasn't sure he wanted to know any more about the man.

Monica said, "I can't believe you were that close to the killing, what if. . ." She shook her head and put her hand over her mouth.

Clive placed his hand on her shoulder. "Monica, the Lord protected Jake. Nothing was going to happen to him."

Monica came over and hugged Jake. She held on, and he hugged her back.

"I'm fine, Monica. Your father's right. There were guns going off all around me, but I never really felt in danger."

"How is that possible?" Monica asked.

"I don't know," Jake said. "The most danger I ever felt was at the beginning when the crowd was restless. I was afraid I was gonna get shot by accident. That's when I was the most nervous."

Clive sat on the couch and pointed to the seat across from him. Jake and Monica sat together.

"Tell us about it, Jake. Where were you when it went down?"

Jake told Clive the entire story.

"It was a great plan, Reverend. Without it, there would have been a lot more people shot." Jake finished, "You saved a lot of lives, Reverend."

Jake expected to be reprimanded for referring to him as reverend, but he seemed not to have noticed. Instead, he seemed emotional. He wiped his eyes at the feedback that many people were still alive because of him.

Monica got up and hugged her father. "I told you so, daddy."

Jake thought about the conversation he had just had with William. He spoke after Monica released her father. "What's next, Reverend?"

Clive wiped a tear from his eye. "What do you mean?"

"I mean, how do you expect President Singleton to react? And what's our plan to counter it?"

Clive pointed expectantly at Jake. "Continue."

Jake rubbed his hands together. "I mean, Pittsburgh takes back its guns. Philly takes back its guns. Atlanta, Dallas refused to confiscate them in the first place. How does President Singleton react?"

Clive glanced over at his daughter. "Well, that's the question, isn't it? He's going to react. It's not his nature to take defeat. Obviously, the mayor of Atlanta is already dead." He looked Jake in the eye. "What would you do if you were him?"

Jake said, "I'd recant the confiscation order."

"I said if you were him,. Remember, he's a narcissist."

Jake reconsidered. He pictured President Singleton in front of the microphones, denying that he had anything to do with the killings, but explaining his rationale for confiscating all handguns. "I guess he ups the ante."

Clive prompted, "How?"

"He sends the National Guard in, maybe the Army. More force, right?"

Clive nodded. "You're probably right. So how long does he wait?"

"Why are you asking me all these questions? I'm just a guy. What do you think? Your people?"

Clive smiled. "I just wanted to see how much of it you had figured out." He looked at Monica. "What he says is closer than you think."

"What?" Jake asked. "Do you know something?"

Clive smiled. "I had Singleton doing the same thing, reacting. And I expected it fast. The tide is turning, and he needs to get the momentum back. I pictured him with the wagons circled in the Oval Office."

"What do you know?" Jake said.

Clive looked around and lowered his voice. We don't have anybody in the White House. Singleton cleaned house after he took over. But we have sources in the Pentagon. When the White House reached out to them, we started hearing stuff."

Monica was obviously hearing this for the first time, because she sat up. "Like what?"

"Like a call for troops like Jake said."

"And?" Jake asked

"The president is preparing to declare martial law to supersede local laws. He wants the National Guard and the Army deployed immediately, with the Marines on standby. The focus will be on the cities that rioted, like Pittsburgh."

"Did you talk to this guy?" Jake asked. "From the Pentagon?"

Clive shook his head. "No, not personally. But someone in my network did. It's legit."

"How soon?" Jake asked.

Clive shook his head again. "We don't know that yet. They're still finalizing the plan."

"What exactly is martial law?" Monica asked. "We hear about it, but . . ."

Clive nodded. "It's when the military takes charge. It's usually imposed temporarily, in places where the local authorities have been overwhelmed. We haven't seen it in the U.S. very much, it's more common in Asia, or the Middle East."

"But it's been used here before, right?" Jake asked.

Clive shrugged. "Sure. In the nineties during the Rodney King riots, they sent the National Guard into LA. I remember the military trucks heading up the freeway. I saw it on TV."

Jake was just a baby when that happened, but he had heard about it. "That was local. What about nationwide?"

Clive shrugged. "Not sure."

"What about World War II?" Monica said. She pulled out her smart phone and started searching. A moment later she described what she found. "According to this, there have been a few instances, including New Orleans after Katrina, but most of those are local and about humanitarian aid. Looks like the last big one was after Pearl Harbor."

"How long did it last?" Jake asked.

Monica was still scrolling on her phone. "Hey, listen to this. According to Wikipedia, after the Civil War, Congress passed the Posse Comitatus Act, which forbids military involvement in domestic law enforcement without congressional approval."

"So Singleton can't declare martial law without Congress," Jake said.

Monica was still reading. "Hang on, it's a little messy. It looks like lawyers are debating whether a 2012 bill might have given the president more power."

Clive snapped his fingers. "Ah, a loophole, how convenient."

Jake pointed at Clive. "What is your Pentagon source saying? Is it on, or are they waiting for approval?"

Clive showed his palms. "The word I got is that it's a done deal. There will be martial law, and troops, the only questions are about timing and logistics."

Monica pocketed her phone. "So much for Congress."

Jake imagined lines of National Guard vehicles driving down the freeway and crossing the bridges into Pittsburgh. "So, what do we expect to happen?"

Clive looked at the ceiling. "It isn't pretty, is it? Everything comes to a standstill. They don't necessarily get back all the guns the rioters stole, but they make a strong show, and they blast any moron stupid enough to challenge them. The president saves face."

"So how does it end?" Jake asked. "They can't stay here forever. And like you said, they're not going to get all the guns, so what's next?"

Monica added "Remember, this guy is an ego-maniac. Why did he issue the handgun ban to start with? Was it ever temporary, as he told us?"

Jake responded, "No way."

Clive nodded, "I don't think it was ever about handguns? That was just the first step."

Jake hadn't thought about that. "What do you mean?"

Clive shrugged. "If it's about power, then he can't afford for us to have any guns. And when is a better time to disarm us than when we're under martial law?"

Jake summarized. "So you're saying that this is going to be a continuous fight until this president takes everything he wants from Americans? You're talking years of civil war until he has every pocket knife in a vault in Washington."

Clive nodded. "Maybe not years. Maybe the president is thinking months."

Jake considered what that scenario would do to America. It would demoralize the people. It would glorify the power of the government. They could do anything they wanted to after that. Was that the endgame William had referred to? How could they just stand by and let this happen?

Jake asked, "If that's the play then how do we stop it? We can't allow that to happen."

Monica prompted, "Our Constitution has a provision for this. You get rid of the rogue president. Impeach him."

Jake got impatient. "That's not going to work. He's killing them faster than they can impeach him, and the congressmen are too scared, they're lining up behind Singleton to protect themselves."

Clive gave him a thumbs-up. "I think you're on to something here, Jake. We can't wait for the lawyers in Washington to solve this problem. They don't have the stomach for it."

"Are you saying what I think you're saying?" Jake asked.

Clive looked at his daughter again briefly. "Jake, I believe this president has started a fight he has no intention of losing. I think he won't stop until he has taken all our guns, and our will to fight back."

Jake said, "And are we going to do anything about it? Or, are we gonna sit back and let it happen?"

Clive nodded. "I don't see an alternative."

"I heard a quote the other day," Jake said "From Thomas Jefferson. It said something like a revolution was needed every now and then."

Clive smiled. "I know that one. 'The tree of liberty must be refreshed from time to time with the blood of patriots and tyrants.'"

"That's it."

Jake thought over Jefferson's words. How could they assemble a new government like America over two hundred years before, yet be thinking that sometime in the future they were going to need another revolution, or many revolutions, to keep the Republic heading in the right direction? It made you wonder how many critical American revolutions had already been missed. He thought about the implications of what Clive was suggesting. He was basically saying that we couldn't wait for Congress to impeach the president. They'd been neutralized.

"What about an assassination?" Monica asked

Jake hadn't considered that, but it seemed easier than a revolution.

Clive shook his head. "If only it were that easy. Singleton's not stupid. We'll probably never see him in public where someone could focus cross-hairs on him. He knows what we want, and he won't give us the opportunity."

No one spoke for a minute.

"How soon?" Jake asked, breaking the silence.

"How soon will the troops arrive?" Clive asked. "I don't have a crystal ball, Jake. Do you?"

"No. How soon before we start the revolution?"

Clive shook his head. "I don't know. We're talking organization at the national level."

"We already agree we'll never have peace again with this president," Jake said. "And we already agreed the trucks are gonna roll into Pittsburgh. You think we can mount a better revolution after we're under martial law, or before?"

Clive looked at Monica and pointed his index finger at his forehead. "This boy you found isn't stupid."

Monica smiled. "I told you."

Jake looked at her. "I wish it wasn't necessary. I mean, I liked him at first. Even up to a few weeks ago. His tax plan had possibilities. I was thinking, finally we had a president with vision, who wasn't afraid to go after something controversial. But then . . ."

Clive said, "Yeah, I know. I think we all felt that way, before he started to go overboard—and before people started dying."

Monica said, "Are we sure President Singleton is killing these people? I mean, it's possible somebody else is doing it, right?"

Clive said, "That's where things get tough. We don't have time to gather evidence right now. What we're seeing is everyone who stands up to him, or speaks out against him, is killed. The witnesses are dying too fast for anyone to figure out what's happening."

Jake said, "He's moving faster than the bureaucracy. Congress should call for an investigation, and put all this chaos on hold until they find out what's going on. But they're afraid to do what they're supposed to do, or they'll get killed."

Monica said, "Look, I think he's guilty, and I'm ready to see him taken out. But is there any way to quickly figure out if he's really guilty before we kill him?"

Clive put his hand on hers. "I wish there was, baby. I wish there was. Unfortunately, he's covered his tracks too well. And there are too many others involved in the conspiracy, and they're moving too fast. Like Jake says, they're moving faster than the bureaucracy that's supposed to be watching them."

"Is it okay that we take matters into our own hands?" Monica asked.

Jake nodded. "Yes, the only question is when."

The three of them looked at each other without speaking.

"How do we proceed?" Monica asked.

Jake looked at Clive.

Clive knew. "I need to meet with our people again, now. Like Jake says, we can't wait until the troops arrive. We have to put together something fast." Clive stood, then looked back at Jake and Monica. "I'll let you know later."

* * *

Monica and Jake moved into the kitchen after Clive left. Jake sliced the cheese while Monica made grilled cheese sandwiches.

"Even if we throw him out," Monica said, "This is not going to go away. Half the people in the country hate guns. They're going to look at this like we threw out a good president."

The same thought had been bothering Jake. "But what's the choice? We stand by, while this president disarms us, because half the people support him?"

"No," she said, shaking her head. "Neither of us believes that. We have to defend our rights. But what happens after the president is removed? Then what?"

Jake thought about that, the negative reaction, the negative media. He thought about the next election and the mud that would be slung around. Why couldn't the other half see the disarming for what it was? "Have you ever tried talking to some of these people? The ones who want all guns taken away?"

"Of course. I'm in the gun business. They have good intentions by the way. They argue that if all the guns are gone, violent crime will be substantially reduced."

Jake cut a grilled cheese in half and pointed the knife for emphasis. "We both know that isn't true. If you take the guns from the good guys, you make the problem worse, not better."

Monica smiled at him. "If you're going to point a knife at me, you should at least use a sharp one."

Jake continued. "You know what I mean."

Monica shrugged. "Nobody is looking at the whole issue, they're only looking at it from their own perspective."

"Are we looking at the whole view?"

Monica shrugged. "A little. Maybe. Some people on our side want the guns to defend themselves. Some want them for hunting. The real fanatics, like us, think we need guns to keep the government in check. Even half the gun owners can't get their minds around that one. Nobody wants to think about that."

"But they need to think about it!" Jake said, too loudly. "They're thinking about it now, comfortable or not. How can we hope to get on the same page, if we're not talking about the same stuff?"

Monica put her hand on his. "People don't work that way. People compartmentalize. They don't think about things they are uncomfortable with. We eat meat without thinking about the killing and blood. We wear leather shoes without thinking about skinning the animal. We live in a free society without thinking about the killing and war necessary to establish that freedom, and to defend it."

"To compartmentalize is bad, isn't it?" Jake took his hand from under hers and ran it down her arm.

She smiled before answering his question. "Compartmentalizing can be good or bad. I'm more than happy to be isolated from whoever kills and skins the meat I eat."

Jake was confused. "So are you compartmentalizing, or not?"

Monica chose her words carefully. "I am compartmentalizing, to a degree. I put some of that ugly stuff out of my mind."

"But you know it's happening," Jake argued.

"Yes."

"Then you're not totally compartmentalizing it. You know there's an ugly side to it. Like with the wars in the Middle East. You know that people have died in Afghanistan and other places to maintain our freedom here."

"Yes, I know that."

"Then you're not like them. They compartmentalize everything. If somebody has to die in Afghanistan, then it has to stop. Bring the troops home. There's no good reason to kill anyone. If a cow has to die, then we all gotta eat carrots the rest of our lives."

She shook her head. "No, I'm not like that."

When she was done grilling, they finished eating at the table.

Jake wanted to finish the conversation. "You were saying about people . . ."

She nodded. "You're right. Some people can't live with themselves if somebody has to die for freedom. They can't rectify that. They would give up freedom to avoid the killings if they had to."

"They haven't considered how bad it could be, if we lost our freedom."

"No," she said. "They've compartmentalized that too."

Jake shook his head. "How can you not think about what it would be like to lose freedom? How can we get them to listen? The other side."

Monica shook her head. "They won't. There's no way to make anyone listen. Their brain is programmed to not hear. Think about abortion. No progress for decades. Took a war to abolish slavery. If people don't want to hear, they won't."

Jake remembered what his friend in Indianapolis had said about America. How it would take a war, here, on American soil, to get most people to realize what they had, and what it would take to retain it. Had America gone that far? Were heads stuck in the sand that deep, that the only way to make people realize they need to fight for something was to lose it?

* * *

It was almost nine o'clock when Clive came back. He caught them in a somewhat awkward condition, making out on the couch.

They were jerked out of their embrace by the loud voice. "I leave you two alone for a few hours . . ."

Monica bounced off Jake to stand next to the couch. She hurriedly crossed her arms and slouched into a semblance of casualness, but her face was beet red. Jake just sat on the couch, too stunned by her quick reaction to move or do anything.

Clive was smiling down at them.

"Daddy?" Monica said. "We were just talking."

Jake sat up and ran his fingers through his hair. "Sorry, Reverend."

Clive looked down at the couch where they had been a moment before. "Talking, huh?" He looked at Jake and nodded. "Looked like quite a conversation you were having."

Jake couldn't stop from smiling.

Monica looked uncomfortable, but her father cut the teasing; he obviously had other things to talk about.

Clive eased himself onto the other couch. He motioned for Monica to sit next to Jake. "We need to talk."

Jake sat up straight. "What did you find out?"

"Have you been watching TV?" Clive asked.

Jake and Monica both shook their heads. Jake wanted to kick himself. Something important happened again, and he had missed it.

Clive pointed at the television. "This evening the president arrived on the White House lawn in a helicopter. As he was waving and walking toward the White House, a gun was fired at him. You can hear the shot on the video. The president ducked and was immediately surrounded by Secret Service, who escorted him into the White House. The news crews were out there, so they got it on camera, and they've been broadcasting it ever since."

"Did they catch the shooter?" Monica asked.

"They shot him," Clive said. "He's dead."

Jake felt disappointment. It could have been over. Now it would be worse.

Clive continued. "So President Singleton is holed up in the White House, and they got the Secret Service on high alert. They're swarming the place."

Jake motioned outside. "So does that kill our plan?"

"It was part of our plan," Clive said, "at least, part of somebody's plan."

Jake asked, "So, the plan was to snipe him."

Clive responded, "That or to get him to stay put. We want him in the White House."

"Then?" Jake asked.

"So we can bring the troops in. We didn't want him leaving to Camp David or some other secure site."

"Bring what troops in?" Jake asked.

"The people. Us." He held his hands wide, as if he were encompassing a huge crowd. "The plan is the same as before. We overwhelm them with numbers. They're not equipped for that. It's our only advantage. But we needed him in one place, preferably in the White House. Someplace we can get close to and surround."

"And this guy that shot at him, that got killed?"

"It was done to make him dig in. Stay put."

"Did he know he was going to die?" Monica asked.

Clive nodded. "They. More than one guy, seven to be exact. They knew. They gave their lives to fire a wild shot, to force him to dig in. To give us time to get there."

"Seven guys were killed?" Monica asked. She covered her mouth.

"Seven of our guys," Clive corrected. "Plus three Secret Service. There was a gunfight at the White House fence to get the shooter into position to take the shot."

Jake registered the significance of Clive's words. "To give us time to get there? You mean, this is happening now? We're going now?"

Clive nodded. "Turned out others were already thinking the same way you were, Jake. To attack Singleton before he can control us with his troops."

Jake stood. "When do we leave?"

Clive stood as well. "Our people are preparing to leave now."

"What time? I need to go get my stuff."

Clive glanced quickly at Monica, then back to Jake. "Jake, you've only just recently got a gun, and I thought that, uh . . ."

"I want to go," Jake said. "Don't you need a bunch of people?"

Clive hesitated. "Yes, we do. We need as many qualified and able men as we can get. But it's not like last night. We're targeting people with military or law enforcement experience, or shooters with combat training, or something like it." He looked at Monica for support.

Monica looked at Jake. She reached out and took his hand. "Maybe he's right, Jake. Maybe . . ."

"Maybe what?" Jake asked. "Maybe, I should stay home and watch it on TV?"

The reverend stepped forward and put his hand on Jake's shoulder. "Jake, listen. I understand your enthusiasm. We all feel it. But we expect the president to defend himself. At the very least, we will be fighting against the Secret Service, very highly trained forces. When they get wind of all the people coming into the city, they'll become even more entrenched, probably call in the National Guard or the Army. We can't have a bunch of— "

"Untrained idiots," Jake finished.

Clive shook his head. "That's not what I said."

"How many people are you sending?" Jake asked.

Clive looked around. "Uh, from Pittsburgh, we're targeting twenty-five thousand."

"That's it?" Jake asked.

Clive responded. "From Pittsburgh, yeah. But all the cities around here are sending people."

"How many?"

Clive looked frustrated. He checked his watch. "Okay, this can't take too long." He walked over to the table and opened a folder. He motioned for Jake and Monica to sit around him. He unfolded a map of the eastern United States. Someone had drawn three circles around Washington D.C. Clive pointed at the innermost circle.

"This circle is just under three hundred miles radius from Washington. It's being referred to as 'Scene One.'" He pointed to some of the cities inside the circle. "The biggest populations are here: New York, Washington itself, Philadelphia, Baltimore, Richmond, the whole state of New Jersey, Raleigh, and of course, Pittsburgh."

Monica looked up. "What's the total population of the inner circle, approximately?"

Clive shrugged. "I'm sure there are people that know that off the top of their head, but our guess is around fifty million. The New York metropolitan area alone is almost twenty."

Jake felt goose bumps on his neck. He found that his hands were clenching. "So how many people are we sending, from Scene One?"

Clive found a piece of paper where he had taken notes. "We're targeting one percent, plus or minus, for each area." He looked at Jake. "So, figure about a half a million for Scene One."

"When?" Monica asked.

Clive looked around, then spoke softly, "We want them in the city by morning, before rush hour."

Jake and Monica stood and looked at the map. Jake tried to imagine a half a million people swarming into Washington through the night. He thought of the traffic. He remembered Washington had entertained million man marches before, just not with guns. "Do they all just drive to the White House and meet there?"

Clive shook his head. He pulled out another map, this one of Washington D.C. "We have eight generals leading up the Scene One advance. They're stationed around these points." He pointed to eight dots on his map. They made a tight circle, about two to four miles radius around the White House. "We're sending the volunteers to one of the eight areas."

"And Pittsburgh?" Monica asked.

Clive put his finger on a dot labeled #3, on the left side. "These bridges over the Potomac are big problems. They funnel all the traffic going in and out of the city to the suburbs. Pittsburgh and most of West Virginia have been assigned responsibility for three bridges: Key, Theodore Roosevelt, and Arlington."

Jake felt more goose bumps. He had to be there. He needed to be there. "And we're supposed to what, guard them?"

Clive said, "We secure them, leave a contingent which can be relieved by Scene Two personnel when they arrive, then advance on the White House from that location." He drew a line between the dot and the White House. "We need to strike and control this whole area. The other cities will do the same, creating a spoke-like attack from all directions simultaneously."

Monica pointed back at the map with the circles. "You said Scene Two would replace us?"

"Follow us, is a better way of saying it," Clive said. "We expect Scene Two to be arriving throughout the day tomorrow, then Scene Three by tomorrow night and throughout the night."

"How many people," Jake asked, "total?"

Clive shrugged. "Almost two hundred million people live east of the Mississippi. If we get one percent, that's two million."

"What about the people out west?" Monica asked.

Clive nodded. "We'd love to have them. Politically, the west is much better positioned than us on guns. Some of those states like Montana, Utah, Idaho, Arizona, and places in Texas, they've got lots of guns, and they want to keep 'em. I'd give anything to have them with us, but they're too far away. It'll take too long for them to get here."

"So they don't know about it?" Monica asked.

"Sure, they've been told, some of them. And we can probably expect a few private jets to arrive stocked to the hilt with guns and cowboys, but overall, it won't be many."

Jake changed the subject. "Clive, I want to go."

Clive looked at him, considering.

Jake argued, "You need all the people you can get, and this is important. We can't lose. If President Singleton wins . . ." Jake shook his head with disgust.

"What about me?" Monica asked. "I have all the qualifications you talked about."

The reverend looked at his daughter. He looked shocked. He looked like he might cry. "No, Monica. Your mother would—"

"Mom's dead," she said. "This is not about her. This is about keeping America free."

Clive shook his head. "No, Monica. Please." He reached for her hands, but she pulled them away. "Monica?"

Jake knew she was a better shot than he. She knew guns infinitely better, and she certainly would know how to handle tactical situations better. But over the past few days, since the confiscations began, Monica had not seemed to have the stomach for it. There was her inability to watch coverage on TV, and her reaction to bullets being shot at the rioters. Not that her feelings weren't understandable, but she seemed squeamish about what needed to be done.

"I don't want you to go," Jake said to Monica.

She looked at him as if he had slapped her. "Oh? And, why not?" Her voice cracked as she started crying. "What good is it if I stay, and you go get killed?" She looked at her father. "What if you both get killed? You think I want to be here in Pittsburgh all by myself?"

Jake thought about what she was saying. It made sense from a logical perspective. But his feelings said something completely different. His feelings told him he and Clive should go, and she should stay. Not that Jake was a person who did things based on feelings.

He took her hand. "What does your heart tell you?" he asked.

She looked at him with tears running down her cheeks. "What?"

"Look inside your heart. What is it saying?"

She looked back and forth between her father and Jake.

Clive nodded. "Do it. Do what Jake is telling you. The Lord has always spoken to you before. What's he telling you now?"

She put her head down and shook it back and forth. "I don't want to. I don't want to know."

Jake knew what was in her heart. He didn't know how he knew, but he did. He didn't know if it was God telling him. What difference did it make? He just knew. "Trust your heart, Monica. What does it say?"

She looked up shuddering and responded, "He says I need to stay." She glared at Jake. "And, you need to go. But I don't like it. I hate it!"

She ran to Jake and pulled him into a tight embrace. Jake could feel her wet tears on his neck. Her whole body shuddered. But Jake knew it was the right decision. She didn't belong in D.C.

Clive interrupted their hug. "Jake, if you're going. You need to get ready. We're leaving soon."

Jake extracted himself from Monica and looked at the reverend.

Clive continued. "You need to get the right clothes, something black, a small backpack for provisions, and your rifle."

Jake nodded.

Clive looked at him with admiration. "An M16. Monica told me. Where on earth did you get one of those?"

Jake smiled. "A good friend."

Clive gave him a sly smile. "Well, well. Full-auto. He must be a good friend. You know on full-auto you can empty a thirty-round clip in less than four seconds. Guess we better get you lots of ammo."

Jake said. "Let me run home. I'll get some black clothes and stuff, and the rifle. I can be back in," he checked his watch, "about a half hour, maybe forty minutes. Is that soon enough?"

Clive nodded.

"I'm going with him," Monica said.

* * *

Monica snuggled against him as he drove back to the house. Neither spoke. They were both dreading the imminent separation. Jake wondered in amazement at how fast his life had changed. He was part of something now. Even though they were not yet married, he felt closer to her than he ever had with his ex-wife. Jake had never really believed in soul mates, but it occurred to him now that, maybe, it was his destiny to meet Monica, and be with her, and that the other marriage had just been a detour.

And with the realization that he was part of something special, he wondered about the mission he had been so anxious to join. What if something did happen to him? What would happen to her? He had seen the racking sobs and tears earlier in the evening. He dreaded the thought of living the remainder of his life without her. It was common sense that she would feel the same. He decided at that moment that he would be more careful, less reckless on this mission. He didn't know what that meant, but felt the time would come when he would.

Jake pulled in his driveway and shut off the truck. Monica let go of him and slid out the passenger door. They joined hands again as they walked up to the front porch.

Inside, Jake shut the blinds, and then dug the M16 out of the closet. He handed the gun case to Monica while he went in his room and changed. He put on some black jeans and his lace up work boots. He deliberated between a long-sleeve black t-shirt and the Joey Porter Steelers jersey, sticking with the t-shirt, which had less color. He threw the jersey on the bed as a spare, in case he was in Washington for more than a day. And on that note, he tossed spare socks and underwear on the bed as well. He found a black baseball cap, Steelers of course, and threw it on the pile. He came out of the bedroom and saw Monica with the M16 in her hands, inspecting it.

He walked past her into the spare bedroom. He dug into some boxes against the wall, finally finding an old backpack loaded with spare tools. The design included lots of small pockets. He dumped the tools in a pile in the middle of the floor. The pack was old, but it was black and would hold a few things, including his spare clothes. He walked past Monica, back into the bedroom, and stuffed the clothes in the pack. On a whim, he rummaged in a drawer and found one of those strap-on LED headlamps. He flipped the switch, and the light illuminated, confirming the batteries were still good. He put it in the pack along with a small pocketknife he found in the same drawer. Finally, he carried the loaded pack into the living room and dropped it on the couch next to Monica.

"Where's your Hi-Power?"

He pulled up his shirt and pulled it out of his pants. He held it out to her.

She grimaced again, and took it. "You don't have a holster yet?

He shrugged. "I haven't had the chance."

She turned the weapon over in her hands. "When we get back to the house, I have one that should work for you. You can't march around Washington very long with a gun stuffed down your pants."

He remembered something and hustled back into the spare bedroom. He rummaged through the same box he found the backpack in, and retrieved a small holster for a drill. He brought it back in the living room where Monica was waiting. He held it out for her to see. "This'll work for a holster, if you can't find yours."

She rolled her eyes. "Whatever."

Food occurred to him. "Did your dad say anything about provisions?"

"You were there. He didn't say anything. I'm guessing they have something planned, but I'd still take as much as you can fit in your pack. You know, snacks and stuff."

Jake went in the kitchen and started rummaging around. He didn't have much. Some crackers, a handful of candy bars, licorice, but luckily, he had about a dozen energy bars. He liked them at work, for those hours between meals. He retrieved four full water bottles from the cabinet as well. He put all the items in a plastic grocery bag and stuffed the whole bag in the backpack.

"Are you ready?" she asked.

He nodded. They locked the house, climbed in the truck, and headed into the night.

* * *

When they got back to Monica's, she found him a proper holster. It was made of black fabric, and she threaded it onto his belt. It had a small pocket on the front for a spare magazine. It was slightly large for the Browning, but it would be sufficient. Much better than Jake's drill holster. She also added some goodies from the kitchen, including a few packages of beef jerky. Jake could feel the tension building between them. He was sure they only had a few more moments before he needed to leave. Neither spoke.

They were both standing in the kitchen when Reverend Lombardi walked in the room. He looked nothing like a preacher. He was dressed in full black SWAT gear. He carried an AR-15 over his shoulder. He carried a black backpack in his hand and wore a black baseball cap. No stripes, patches, logos, Steelers or otherwise, anywhere on him. Jake admired his appearance and wondered if he was in over his head.

Clive set his stuff on the table and retreated to the back room. When he returned, he was carrying a heavy green military box of ammunition. He clanked it on the table and opened it exposing the ammunition inside. He pointed to Jake and Monica. "There are more than five hundred rounds of .223 in there. Load his clips with that, and see how much more he can carry in his pack."

Jake said. "My magazines are already loaded, from last night."

"How many do you have?" Clive asked.

"Two."

Clive walked into the back again, returning a moment later. "Here's another."

The new magazine was black plastic with a square pattern on the side. It looked very robust.

"It'll work in my gun?"

"AR, M16, M4, they're all the same. Try it if you're nervous."

Monica loaded it for him. She was much faster. When she finished, she opened the M16 gun case, picked up the weapon, slammed the magazine in, pulled back on the bolt, and chambered a round. She cycled it a few more times, as they had done the night before, ejecting shells onto the carpet with each motion. She nodded satisfaction, removed the magazine, ejected the chambered round, and returned the gun to its case. "No problem," she stated. She gathered the ejected rounds off the floor and loaded them back into the magazine.

Jake put all three in the backpack and tested the weight. It was heavy.

Clive pointed at the green metal box of ammunition. "Take that, too. You may need it."

Jake closed the lid on the ammo and set it on the floor next to his pack. The three of them stood, looking at each other.

"Are you driving?" Monica asked her father.

"No. We're getting picked up in a few minutes." He motioned to Monica and Jake. "Time to say goodbye."

Jake's stomach was in a knot. He looked at Monica, and she came into his arms. He felt the wet of her tears on his shoulder again. He had a sudden urge that he needed to do something for her, flowers, a gift, something, anything. He loved her. What could he do to communicate how much he cared before he left? But he had nothing. He was going, and he had nothing for the most import person in his life. Someday, after he got back. He looked down at her, and an idea popped into his head. It was crazy. It was rushed. But it felt right, and there was no time to waste.

He released her, and knelt down in front of her. He held her hands. "Monica?"

She looked down at him. "Yes."

"I know it's kind of last minute, but, uh." He noticed Clive was smiling at him. "What I mean to say is, uh, do you want to be my wife? Do you want to get married?"

She smiled broadly and wiped a tear away. "Are you proposing? Now?"

He nodded. "Yeah. I'm proposing. If you'll have me, I'll try to take good care of you." He glanced at Clive and saw Clive had an approving look on his face.

She bent over and kissed him. "Yes. I'll marry you, Jake McKinley. Yes." She looked at her father, then back at Jake. "When?"

Her father spoke. "Well, I am a priest."

Both Jake and Monica looked at Clive in surprise.

Clive looked at his watch. "I can do it right now, if you want. But we need to hurry."

Monica bobbed her head up and down. Jake tried to assimilate what Clive had just said.

"Jake," Clive asked. "Do you want to marry her right now?"

Jake stood. He considered. No cakes? No reception? No ring? He guessed some of that could come later. It was just the three of them.

"Okay," Jake said. "Let's do it."

And so they did. Clive stepped forward, wearing his SWAT getup. Monica and Jake faced each other. Monica wiped a tear from her face. Clive began.

"Please hold hands," he said.

Jake reached out and took both of Monica's hands in his.

"We are gathered here, in the presence of God, to join Jake and Monica, a couple that is most dear to me personally, in holy matrimony, to bond them together as one until a last breath is taken." He hesitated, then spoke again. "Normally, I would ask someone to give up the bride, but I guess that's me. And, yes, I give my daughter freely to this young man." Clive returned to his formal voice. "Jake, do you take Monica to be your wedded wife, to be a part of you for the rest of your life? Do you promise to love her, to honor her, and cherish her, and be loyal to her, in sickness and in health, in good times and bad, for as long as you both shall live?"

Jake thought of the vision he had of her, of their family. He definitely wanted to be with her forever. "Yes, I do."

Clive turned to his daughter. "Monica, we've both wondered when this day would come. For the record, I'm glad you waited for this guy. He's the right one. If only your mother," Clive's voice cracked, "were here to see—"

"Go ahead, Daddy."

Clive wiped his eyes, and regained his composure. "Dear Monica, my wonderful daughter, do you take Jake to be your wedded husband, to be a part of you for the rest of your life? Do you promise to love him, to honor him, and cherish him, and be loyal to him, in sickness and in health, in good times and bad, for as long as you both shall live?"

"Yes," she said.

Clive hesitated then continued, "As an ordained minister in the state of Pennsylvania, I pronounce you, Jake McKinley, and you,

Monica Lombardi, as one couple, bound together as husband and wife, sealed together as one, for as long as you both shall live."

A car pulled into the driveway, and its headlights added light to the room.

Clive rushed the last words. "Jake, kiss the bride, then we gotta go."

Jake took his new wife and pulled her to him. She reached around his neck. Her eyes were glistening. When their lips met, he felt sparks. It was a hungry kiss, a rough kiss. Neither wanted it to end. He couldn't believe she was his forever. How could he be so lucky? How did she pick him?

"We gotta go, Jake," Clive urged.

Jake tried to release the kiss, but Monica held on. Jake's lips hurt, but he didn't care. She held tight for another moment. Finally, they both released. When he looked down at her and saw her lips were red and swollen. Too much passion behind the dam. He smiled and shook his head.

"What?" she said.

"It's just that . . . I can't believe it."

Clive had already gathered his pack and gun. Jake knew he needed to do the same. He looked around, then shouldered his pack and grabbed the gun case.

"Don't forget that." Clive pointed at the metal box of ammo.

Jake grabbed the heavy can. He stopped and looked at Monica again before he left. She looked apprehensive, but happier than before. The impromptu wedding had been a good idea. Actually, it had been a great idea. He hadn't felt this good for a long time, maybe ever.

"Hurry back," she said.

He nodded. "I will."

He followed Clive out the door.

"I'll be waiting, Jake," she said softly.

CHAPTER 14

Jake sat in the cramped back seat of the Chevy Suburban as it drove down the Pennsylvania Turnpike. The inside was dark and quiet. Clive was in the front passenger seat next to Jordan, the driver. There were three guys in the second seat, then Jake and another guy in the small rear seat, for a total of seven. They had been on the road now for over an hour since leaving Pittsburgh. They had departed the city on the Lincoln Parkway before getting on the turnpike. Jake had seen other SUVs and vans on both the parkway and the turnpike, and he wondered if they too, were full of . . . what should he call them, soldiers? Freedom fighters? Terrorists? Rioters? Assassins?

They were all awake, but no one spoke. They all stared vacantly out the windows at the passing darkness. There were three rifle cases stacked between Jake and the other guy in the back so Jake couldn't see him unless he sat up. His name was Mario. Jake had been briefly introduced to all of them when they loaded up. Mario had not been happy Jake was joining them, probably due to the cramped rear seat. Mario was smaller than the three guys in the second seat, which is why he and Jake had been seated together.

Jake was fairly sure all the other guys were ex-soldiers. They were in great shape. They all looked experienced, and their black combat clothes looked worn, but it was more than that. It was the way they moved and spoke. Jake wasn't an expert on how soldiers acted, but he guessed they moved like these guys. Jake was fairly sure he didn't look like a soldier, and he wondered if he could overcome their apprehension about him being here. They probably thought the rookie might get them killed.

The three guys in the second seat had not acknowledged him. The guy on the left was the thinnest of the three, and black. His name was Noah. The guy in the middle was older than the rest, probably in his forties. His name was Mason. He had a soldier haircut like Mario. The guy on the right was the scariest. He was built like a tank and had long black hair. He wore a well-worn Steelers jersey with the number '43', and the name Polamalu on it. His name was Troy, just like the jersey. But in spite of the long black hair, he looked nothing like the football player. His hair was straight. He was huge. Unlike the real guy, who looked like a kitten and spoke in a whisper, this Troy looked like a savage and spoke harshly in a deep baritone voice.

Jake wondered if it had been a good idea for him to come. The decision had been based on passion, more than common sense. Sure, they needed sheer numbers in the cause, but as Clive said, they really needed seasoned veterans, not a bunch of trigger-happy idiots. He thought about Monica at home, waiting. They would be together now if Jake hadn't insisted on coming. He felt sure that if he told the driver to pull over and let him out, Clive and the others wouldn't argue. The guys in the car would probably feel relieved. Then Monica could come and get him, and they could spend the night together as husband and wife, a mini honeymoon with his new bride.

The thought made him sick. It kept lurking in the back of his mind like a loud ticking odometer clicking miles over and over, and a little devil on his shoulder whispering, "You're getting farther away, Jake. Go back. She's waiting for you, Jake. They don't need you. You'll just be in the way. You're probably just gonna get yourself killed anyway. These guys will do better without you. They know what they're doing. You don't. What if President Singleton is innocent after all? This whole trip is a folly. She's probably waiting, in a sexy nightgown. It's your honeymoon, Jake, how could you leave her?"

He wished the men were talking in the car. It would help get his mind under control. They could talk about anything, the Steelers, the Pirates, the president, what they would find in D.C., how the contestants were doing on American Idol, what they were wearing on the red carpet for the Oscars, the cost of eggs, the weather in Nepal, it didn't matter. He needed to talk about something, anything to shut up that devil in his head.

"We're coming up on Somerset," Jordan said. "There's a service plaza coming up, a rest stop. Does anybody need to stretch their legs?"

"I do," Mario said.

The three guys in the second seat sat up.

"Yeah," Noah said.

Clive turned around in his seat and looked at them, then back at Jordan. "These guys are dressed like a SWAT team. They'd stand out like a bomb squad." He asked them, "Can you hang on another hour, until we get off the toll road?"

No one said anything. The tension in the SUV rose. Mario rearranged himself. Jake did the same. Jake rested his head against the gun cases between them. He closed his eyes and tried to sleep. He wondered what they would encounter in the morning. Would the police or the FBI be waiting for them? Jake had never fired his M16. Would tomorrow be his first day? What if it jammed?

He opened his eyes and stared out the window. Trying to sleep was absurd. There was no way to sleep now, and he wondered if it would be possible later. How could any of them function tomorrow with no sleep? As if in answer to his question, he heard the deep breaths of sleep from Mario next to him. Jake guessed that when you were in combat you learned to rest when you had the opportunity.

* * *

An hour later, they were standing in the shadows outside a remote convenience store just north of the Pennsylvania/Maryland border while Jordan gassed up the SUV. Mario stood smoking a cigarette next to Jake. Jake watched the orange glow brighten as Mario took a long drag. Mario reached in his pocket and retrieved the pack and held it out to Jake.

Jake shook his head. "No, thanks. I don't smoke."

"Good time to start," Mario said, holding the pack under Jake's nose.

Jake laughed. "Yeah, probably, but no thanks."

Mario returned the pack to his pocket "You get any sleep?" He pointed at the Suburban.

Jake shook his head. "No way, I'm too wound up."

Mario took another drag, then tossed the butt on the ground and smashed it. "I didn't think so. You gotta learn to sleep when you get the opportunity, especially before a mission. Otherwise, you're no good." He tapped the side of his head with his forefinger.

"What's the trick?" Jake asked.

"Everybody has their own way," Mario said. "But basically, you need to hypnotize yourself." He held his hands up next to his cheeks, closed his eyes, and tilted his head back. "You gotta force yourself to relax." He took a couple deep breaths. "Then you gotta picture yourself someplace calm." His voice became low and monotone. "My place is this cave along the beach." He didn't speak for a while. "I gotta walk along the sand to get there." He sniffed. "I can smell the ocean. I can feel the sand between my toes."

Jake wanted to ask him some questions, like if the place was real or if he had invented the place in his mind, but he didn't want to disturb him.

"When I finally get there, the cave is almost hidden by some vines. They're hanging from above. When I touch them, they're wet. You gotta add as much sensory stuff as you can. It makes it more real." He used his hand to sweep something aside. "I move the vines and go inside. They're waiting for me.

"There's two of them. They smile at me. They're wearing those flowered dresses, you know, they're called . . ." He snapped his fingers. "I can't remember what they're called. They wear them in Hawaii sometimes. They tie them around them. It doesn't matter, you know what I'm talking about."

Jake did. They were called sarongs or sulus. His ex-wife had been into them. Jake decided his sleep fantasy would not include a sarong. It wouldn't help to think about his ex-wife while he tried to relax.

Mario continued, "They take my hands, and lead me to this low table. It's like real soft and padded, like a bed. They lay me down on it, on my back. One, she starts massaging my face, the other my feet." Mario shakes his head "I feel like I might melt. I can hear the waves. I can smell—"

"You guys ready to go?" Clive asked.

Jake jumped. He was still with Mario in the cave.

"Yeah, we're ready," Mario said, talking normally, completely out of the dream.

Jake nodded. "Sure."

"What time are we trying to get there?" Mario asked.

"We want to be in place before the sun comes up," Clive said.

Jake looked at his watch and saw it was 2:15 a.m. He guessed they still had a few more hours until they arrived at their destination. They should have no problems getting there in time, barring a traffic problem.

"Do they know we're coming?" Mario asked.

"I haven't heard," Clive responded.

Mario scoffed, "How can they not? They listen to everybody's calls. They read our emails, Facebook. They got satellites aimed at us. They definitely count the cars on the roads. They know. They'll be waiting, you'll see."

Jake found it amazing that Mario could be so relaxed in a dream, only a moment before, and yet be completely paranoid they were walking into an ambush.

"I hope not," Clive answered.

Mario climbed in the back still mumbling. "In a couple hours, you'll be saying Mario was right."

Jake followed Mario into the back seat and re-positioned the three rifles between them.

After Noah, Mason, and Troy climbed in, Jordan started the engine, and they headed out. As they pulled onto the street, Jake saw a white cargo van at the pumps with some guys piling out of it. They looked like a SWAT team. He felt pretty sure they were on the same errand.

A few minutes later they crossed the border into Maryland and passed through a small town called Hancock. As they settled in on the Dwight Eisenhower Highway, Jake tried out Mario's self-hypnosis advice. He laid his head against the rifle cases and closed his eyes. He imagined himself walking down a beach. He saw the cave up ahead with the hanging vines. He tried to smell, but he instead smelled the inside of the Suburban, and the hint of tobacco from Mario. It reminded him of the bright orange glow of Mario's cigarette back at the gas station. Jake shook his head in frustration and tried to get back to the beach. He was almost to the cave. He was happy to feel the wet sand between his toes. Maybe this was working. He reached forward with his hand and swept the vines aside to enter the cave. His ex-wife had one of those flowered dresses on. She was standing above the fat doctor lying on his back. She was massaging his shoulders. They both shouted at him to leave, that this cave was taken.

Jake's eyes came open. He would need a different fantasy if this was going to work.

* * *

An hour later Jake's neck was stiff, and he realized he had actually slept for a few moments. He heard Clive speaking on his cell phone.

"We're only a few minutes away from your position," Clive said into the phone

"Are we there?" Mario asked.

"No, guys. We're just making a quick stop," Clive answered. He pointed to another black SUV parked next to an isolated sports park that looked like it was used for soccer games. In the headlights, he could see some goals lined up across the large grass field.

They pulled up behind the other SUV and turned off their lights. Someone walked back along the sidewalk, and Clive rolled down his window to talk to him. The guy leaned in and handed something to Clive.

"Okay. Here it is. It has 256-bit encryption on receive and transmit."

Jake couldn't see the device the guy was giving to Clive, but he assumed it was an encrypted cell phone or radio.

"You need to key in your code whenever you turn it on, and then every five minutes you need to key it in again because it times out. All the codes are different. Yours is 1776. Can you remember that?"

"Yes," Clive answered.

"The general says, 'Don't be chatty.' The battery should do eight to ten hours, depending on how much you transmit. AC and DC chargers are in the bag. The radio is only good for line of sight unless somebody gets a repeater up. But don't count on it. If that happens, go to channel 2. Last, if this gets in enemy hands, don't give them the password. Give them 2000. It will self-destruct the encryption circuitry. One more thing— total radio silence until 5:15 a.m. Questions?"

Clive shook his head. The man walked back to his vehicle. Clive motioned for Jordan to leave, and they did.

Clive turned to talk to them. "Any of you guys used one of these before?" He held the radio up.

The older guy, Mason, nodded. "Yeah. I think so, in Iraq." He held out his hand. "Can I see it?"

Clive handed it to him.

"Yeah, I used the same model, 256 bit. But I never heard of the self-destruct thing. I wonder how they did that." He handed it back to Clive. "Let me know if you need help."

"Just stay close," Clive said.

"Where are we?" Mario asked.

"Leesburg," Jordan responded, "Maryland. We're only forty-five minutes away on the parkways, but we're going to exit and do surface streets the rest of the way. It should take us a little over an hour. We're right where we want to be."

Jake checked his watch, 3:40 a.m. They should be to the bridges by 5:00. Radio silence until 5:15, then the fireworks.

CHAPTER 15

The last hour had been the longest of Jake's life. The apprehension in the Suburban had been palpable, an hour of slow driving through Falls Church and Arlington city streets, from stoplight to stoplight. They had gotten close a few minutes before, earlier than desired, so Clive had them turn and drive west for a while, then circle back. The closer they got, the more vans and SUVs Jake saw on the streets. Now it seemed like they were in a convoy stacked ten deep in both lanes at every stoplight. The numbers gave Jake a reassuring feeling.

"What time is it?" Mario asked.

"Ten after five," Clive responded.

"How far away are we?" Mario asked.

Clive had briefed them a few minutes ago regarding their path. The Pittsburgh contingent would drive onto the Theodore Roosevelt Bridge and just park. The goal was to completely block the bridge in both directions. The West Virginians would do the same on the Arlington Bridge, and other groups from Western Pennsylvania would block the Key Bridge. The West Virginians would also park cars in front of all the northern exits and entrances to Fort Myers and the Arlington Cemetery, just off the Arlington Bridge. Fort Myers wasn't exactly a combat center like it once was. It mostly housed the Army diplomats and employees in Washington, including the Army band. But the color guards and other troops did have real guns, assuming they had some real bullets to substitute for the blanks they usually fired at ceremonies.

"We're only a couple miles away," Clive said. "As soon as we hear the radio, we'll jump on Arlington Boulevard and move out onto the bridge."

Then, two minutes early according to Jake's watch, the radio came to life.

"Hello visitors. Parking is very limited this morning, so please hurry to your parking spots." The voice was cheerful and casual, and could have easily been attributed to a company picnic or a kid's baseball tournament.

"That's it!" Mario said.

All the vans and SUVs in the street came to life, lurching to higher speeds. Vans and pickups parked along the street started moving.

Clive pointed to a line of vehicles veering right onto 15th street, "Go there." He was looking at a map app on his iPad.

The light turned red, but the Suburban didn't even slow, running the light and following a line of vans in front of them. Fifteenth Street wound to the right, then came left again.

Clive navigated from the iPad. "Okay, 15th is now 14th. Don't take this next street on the right, our turn is up a little farther." A few of the cars in front took the turn, but the Suburban stayed on 14th as instructed. "Okay, right up here." He pointed. "Okay take the 'Do not Enter.' Go up it backwards."

As Jordan went up the exit backwards into oncoming traffic, a car swerved to their left to avoid them.

"Stay on the right side!" Clive ordered. "Give 'em room."

Jake steadied the guns next him as the SUV drove up the ramp onto Arlington Blvd. There were more cars here, but the Suburban hugged the right shoulder, and the oncoming traffic avoided them on their left, honking as they passed and flicking their lights. Jake looked back and saw a line of vans and SUVs that had followed them backwards up the ramp.

"Watch it!" Jordan yelled as he slammed the brakes and let a car veer past. He then accelerated back to speed.

Arlington rounded to the right, and they could see a bridge ahead.

"There! Take it!" Clive ordered, pointing to the left.

Jordan swerved in front of an oncoming car, leaving it no choice but to swerve and pass on their right side. Jake stiffened and felt a slight impact as the car had obviously touched them on the way past. They swerved onto a ramp exiting the bridge and followed it under the main bridge lanes, passing terrified drivers along the way, then up around and onto the bridge. Jake's arms were locked against the seat in front of him. He glanced behind and saw there were now many vans and SUVs following. As they merged onto the three-lane bridge, they stayed left and let the cars, horns blaring, go past on the right.

"Okay, wait for a gap in the traffic. Up there!" Clive pointed ahead. "Then swerve across, and stop!" He waited for several cars to pass. "You see it, after that one?"

"Ah, yeah." Jordan responded.

"Now!" Clive ordered.

The Suburban veered in front of the oncoming cars. He headed to the far right median and slammed on his brakes. The Suburban screeched to a halt in tire smoke. The oncoming cars slammed on their brakes as well.

"He's going to hit us!" Noah yelled.

The oncoming car had waited too long to brake. They saw tire smoke and heard the squeal, but he was coming too fast.

"Brace!" Clive yelled.

Jake braced, but he had already been braced for the whole time they were driving backwards up the ramps. When the car plowed into them, he felt the seat belt bite into his shoulder, and he saw the air bags blow in the front of the Suburban. His body jerked forward, then rebounded back. He smelled a chemical odor from the airbags.

"Open the doors! Get out!" Mason yelled. Noah opened the left door, but Troy's right door was blocked by the center median. Noah jumped out and Mason followed, then Troy slid his bulk across the seat and got out as well. Mario and Jake followed. Noah opened the driver's door, and they all looked in. Jordan didn't look good. He had a bloody nose from the airbag and looked dazed. Clive looked okay, but concerned.

"Who's gonna pay for this?" Jordan slurred. He pointed to the scrunched up hood and the mist wafting out.

Jake heard more impacts in front of them and looked up to see another car slam into the car in front of him. Jake looked across the median to the other lanes and saw that they were stopped as well, although their task had been easier—just stop and let the cars pile up behind, no oncoming traffic.

The Theodore Roosevelt Bridge was now completely blocked in both directions.

CHAPTER 16

They opened the back of the Suburban and grabbed their stuff. Jake put his backpack on, then took the M16 out of its case and shouldered it. He rammed one magazine in and chambered a round. He verified the safety was on. He found the heavy box of ammunition and placed it on the ground by his feet. Cars all around them were doing the same. He saw hundreds of rifles, many of them black assault weapons, slung over shoulders. Jake heard the radio.

"Visitors, there is still some parking available on the north side of Fort Myers. Anyone in the area that needs a parking spot should consider Rhodes Street."

Jake laughed at the casual radio announcement and its meaning. He imagined vans darting onto the overpass in reaction to block traffic exiting Fort Myers. He wondered where the radio announcer was positioned to see everything.

"If you planned on passing over the bridges into the city this morning, I'm sorry to tell you that traffic is terrible on all three of the north bridges. Unless you are walking, I would consider another way."

"Holy crap!" Mario said. "All three are blocked already." He yelled, "Way to go, Pittsburgh!"

Jake heard a few cheers, and he saw numerous fists in the air.

As he looked ahead, he saw the Washington Monument, and a hint of light behind it, signaling that sun-up would begin in less than an hour. Just to their right across the bridge was the Lincoln Memorial, which was larger than Jake remembered. Westbound civilians were now exiting their cars and looking around. Jake couldn't imagine what they might think, looking at lines of vehicles facing the wrong direction and men climbing out of them with guns. One lady screamed and ran away back through the cars.

Clive spoke to them while they finished packing. "Jordan's still dazed from the crash. He says his head hurts. I told him to stay with the car. I think he might have a mild concussion. If he's feeling better when the second wave comes, he can join them, but we need to go."

They said nothing. The guys kept assembling their stuff. Mario was applying black paint from a stick, like a small glue stick. Noah had an assault weapon with a large diameter tube under it, a grenade launcher? Troy, the guy with the long black hair, was mounting a nasty looking serrated knife to the end of his AR, like a bayonet. Jake shuddered while imagining a screaming Troy charging into a crowd and aggressively sticking people with the bayonet. He was glad Troy was on their side.

The radio blared. "Sorry to tell you this, but parking is now full on the north side of Fort Myers. Traffic on the bridges is jammed, but that's still the best place to go for our tour of the city today."

Jake loved the sarcasm of the radio messages, and how they communicated to the masses exactly what to do. He felt sure that not everyone had radios like Clive did. In fact, most probably didn't. But a few informed people passing the word would go a long way.

"Let's go!" Clive said.

Jake picked up the heavy ammo box, and they fell in behind Clive. They all climbed over the median and joined a mass of volunteers walking toward the city. As they marched, they walked in and out of the illumination from poles mounted along the rails of the bridge.

Two black guys in a pickup from the city climbed over the median. "You guys here to get Singleton? Take the guns back?"

Jake didn't want to stop and hold up the line so he walked past them. He heard Noah address them from behind, "Damn right!"

The men started walking along with them, keeping pace "Can we join you all?"

"If you don't mind getting shot at," someone farther back said.

One of them answered, "Man, we get shot at all the time. This is D.C., man."

The other asked, "Can you borrow us a couple of your guns?"

Jake laughed as he walked ahead. He noticed that many of the people caught on the bridge while attempting to leave the city just stood by their cars and stared at them. Some looked angry, and some just curious. Jake caught the eye of a young man in a suit and tie. He was smiling. He gave Jake a thumbs-up.

When they approached the east shore where the bridge ended, Jake transferred the heavy ammo box to his left hand. Their lanes rounded right onto Constitution Avenue; the opposite lanes however, were now jammed by cars trying to leave the city.

Clive yelled to a group working their way through the stopped cars on the other side of the divider, "I need about thirty of you guys to position yourselves on this ramp." He pointed where the ramp joined the bridge from the left. "Keep it secured. Watch for attacks. Keep an eye out for other rebels working their way south from Key Bridge. Don't shoot them. Got it?"

A group of men took positions on the ramp. As he looked behind him, back over the Roosevelt Bridge, Jake saw a continuous mass of men following them on both sides of the median, most with rifles on their shoulders, a few carrying only handguns. Volunteers were moving vehicles forward. Pickups drove past, loaded with guys holding rifles, and another that looked like it was full of ammo boxes. Behind it was one of those off-road side-by-side units, a black Polaris with two seats. The driver stopped when he saw Clive. He looked to be almost sixty, with a buzz cut. He was wearing fatigues. A kid in his twenties sat next to him, wearing a headset with a microphone. The old man definitely looked military. The kid looked like a video gamer.

"Reverend Lombardi, good job! You guys were one of the first on the west bound bridge, weren't you?"

Clive patted the man's back. "The first. We actually got in a head-on with a car coming the other direction."

The man winced and gave him a once over. "You look okay."

Clive nodded. "Everybody but one—concussion, probably. He stayed with the car."

People were piling up behind them, so Jake and the others walked ahead.

Mario spoke to Jake. "I bet that's the general."

Jake looked at him. "You think?"

"Sure. And that kid is the radio announcer. You see the radio he had on his lap?"

They joined with the eastbound lines and walked down the ramp toward Constitution Avenue. The area around the ramps was mostly green lawn and trees. Up on their left was a funky angular building with a roof that looked like a sail, very modern.

"What's that?" Jake asked.

"How should I know?" Mario responded.

Mason said, "The U.S. Institute of Peace."

Jake considered that. He wondered what they did there, and who worked there.

"I have a feeling they're gonna be closed today," Mario said. "In fact, everybody in Washington that sits around spending my tax money, talking about how to be peaceful, can have the day off."

They heard an engine behind them and stood aside as the general and the geeky kid drove by.

When Clive caught up to them, Mario asked. "Was that the general?"

Clive nodded. "He's from West Virginia. General Bowen, U.S. Army, retired."

Jake heard gunshots. They sounded like they were a half-mile away or so, northeast of them. It was hard to tell. All the men hesitated. Hair stood up on Jake's back. Rifles came up, and Jake saw many pull back on the bolts of their weapons and chamber rounds. Jake took his rifle off his shoulder but left the safety on. He hadn't seen anything yet.

Then gunshots could be heard much closer and louder. They sounded like they were coming from the trees just up ahead, between the funky Peace building and the Lincoln Memorial on their right. He saw a guy go down a few steps in front of him, and men just in front of him started firing their weapons wildly into the trees.

"Who's shooting at us?" someone asked.

Before the question could be answered, the entire area erupted in gunfire. Jake saw sparks fly at the barricade as bullets ricocheted off the vehicles. He saw fire from the barrels of guns in the same area. People all around him opened fire. The sound was deafening. Jake pulled the M16 off his shoulder and aimed in the direction of the barricade. His peep sight registered policemen behind a car, and he pulled the trigger. Nothing! Damn safety! He flicked it off, re-aimed, and fired.

He kept firing as fast as he could acquire new targets. He saw multiple targets drop, but he had no idea whether they were his shots or someone else's. Just when he started to feel invincible, like they were shooting ducks in a pond, a guy on Jake's right went down. Then another. Then the M16 was empty, out of ammo.

Jake felt someone dragging him by the back of his shirt toward the lane barrier on the right side. Jake was pushed down behind it. It was Mario.

"Get down!" Mario screamed over the gunfire.

Jake saw the bright muzzle flashes from guns in the trees ahead of them. They were police and soldiers. Jake dug through his pack and exchanged magazines. He then lifted his M16 and aimed over the barrier through the peep sight. He found a policeman in his sights. He was leaning over the hood of his car. He could see the muzzle flash from the policeman's gun. Jake didn't hesitate. He pulled the trigger. The man was thrown back, his weapon flying.

Jake was a killer now, of a policeman, no less. But he felt no remorse. Not yet. No time. Bullets were flying over his head from both sides. Men were dropping all around him. The police were taking a large toll on the rebels on the exposed ramp. Jake aimed again and found another target, a soldier in camo. He pulled the trigger and watched him drop. Two shots, two dead. Jake saw the numbers of muzzle flashes below and guessed there were hundreds of guns down there. If only they had more firepower. And then he remembered the M16. It would waste bullets, he knew. But it would make a few guys down there hesitate—and maybe run for cover. Jake turned the gun sideways, moved the selector to full, and then aimed to the right of the group. When he pulled the trigger, he swept the gun left along the line of muzzle flashes.

The M16 bucked fast, unloaded the remaining bullets in a few seconds, spitting fire out of the barrel in a continuous flame. He had no way of knowing whether any of the bullets had found their mark, but it seemed the muzzle flashes below had slowed slightly. Maybe he had gotten a few, or maybe they were just distracted. Who knew?

Jake ducked behind the barrier. He felt in his pack for another magazine. With his head down, he looked behind where they had been standing a moment before, and saw men down all over the place, blood, screaming, and frantic convulsions of agony. He saw infinite others replacing them. Men were running forward, no thought for safety, draping themselves over fallen comrades and firing as fast as they could.

Jake saw Mario's face in his. He pointed at Jake's gun in amazement. Mario helped Jake eject the empty magazine as gunfire continued unabated above them, then helped Jake jam the new one home. Then they both peeked over the abatement. Mario pointed to an area thick with muzzle flash. Jake aimed and pulled the trigger again, keeping the barrel pointed in the general area where Mario had pointed. Again flames burst from the barrel. Before Jake ducked below the barrier, he saw that almost all the muzzle flashes in the small area had ceased. The M16 had done some serious damage.

Grabbing in the backpack for another magazine, Jake felt concrete dust scatter just above his head as a bullet hit right where his head had been a moment before. Jake pressed his face to the ground and tasted dust. His heart raced. That was close. They knew where he was now. Mario helped him replace the magazine, then held out the two empty magazines, and pointed at the heavy can of ammunition. The message was clear, "One of us load, while the other shoots."

Jake held the M16 out to Mario, and Mario took it with a devilish smile. Jake pulled the green box close to him and opened it while Mario turned to send another volley of bullets at the barricade. Jake only had two bullets loaded before he heard the machine gun fire of the M16. A moment later Mario dropped next to him. All three of Jake's magazines were empty now, so Mario ejected the last from the M16 and started loading it. He was much faster than Jake, just as Monica had been.

Jake knew enough about the military from documentaries and movies to know that the enemy focused on machine guns, so taking a break to reload was a good thing, at least for them. It could prolong their lives. Jake looked back at the other men firing and saw so many men down he couldn't count them. But infinite new replacements surged forward.

Mario finished loading his magazine and handed it to Jake. He took Jake's partially loaded one from him. Jake rammed the full one home. He turned and peeked over the barrier. There was a dense area of muzzle flash over to the left. He saw one barrel of almost continuous fire, obviously another full-auto. He aimed and unloaded the entire magazine into the area. Jake saw chaos where he had fired, and saw two men try to get up to run before taking bullets from other shooters. Mario was waiting and replaced the magazine without Jake dropping below the wall. Jake found another hot spot and lit it up. He felt vulnerable after and dropped below the wall. He heard bullets hit the concrete, and dust fell down on him from above. Mario was still loading the third magazine. So, Jake started loading an empty.

The man firing over the barrier next to Mario and Jake went limp, then slumped next to them, the top of his head missing. Jake felt sick, but he couldn't move his gaze from the man's remaining glazed eye. Mario grabbed Jake's face and aimed it at his. Mario pointed at his own eye and wagged his finger back and forth. The meaning was clear, "Don't look."

Jake began re-loading the magazine, but he was shaking. He needed to calm down. His fingers were weak. Mario finished loading his and inserted it in the M16. He moved to peek over the rail, but Jake held him down. Jake remembered the shots at his position. They needed to move, even if only a few feet. He wagged his finger at Mario, and pointed down the row. Mario nodded his understanding. They gathered their packs, and the box of ammo, and crawled down the barrier. It was very crowded, and they had to move over a couple of dead men. When Mario found a spot he liked, they dropped their stuff, and Jake opened the ammunition box and continued loading. He heard a volley of shots from Mario, but Mario stopped mid-magazine, then emptied the remainder in a different spot. He ducked back down. When Jake was done loading his magazine, he took another turn with the M16.

When he peeked over the barrier, he quickly scanned for an active area to fire on, again looking for concentrated muzzle fire, but it seemed to Jake that they were making some progress. There were far fewer, and they were not as concentrated. Jake picked two spots as Mario had. He put half of the magazine into the first area, then the other half to the second, and then he dropped below.

Suddenly, while he and Mario were both below the wall re-loading magazines, Jake heard the gunfire dissipate to only a few scattered shots, and arms started pumping in the air, and cheering. Jake felt the celebration, more than heard, since he was almost deaf from the noise of gunfire over the last few minutes.

Then he saw Clive waving his arms. Clive's lips were moving, but there was only the sound of gunfire.

Jake ejected the empty magazine and stuffed it in his pack, replacing it with a full one. He looked behind him and saw hundreds of men with their rifles pointed, seemingly, at him. It was a miracle he hadn't been killed by friendly fire. He looked around. Many men were down, some writhing in pain. The gunfire on Constitution stopped.

"I need twenty men," an authoritative man yelled, "to go down there and make sure it's secure." He pointed at the abandoned roadblock.

At least thirty guys rushed him, many with rifles in the air.

The authoritative guy nodded. "Okay, all of you go." He yelled so they all could hear, "If anyone is alive, let me know so we can question them."

The thirty headed quickly down the ramp to where the assault had occurred. When they got close, they approached in crouched positions, rifles ready. Jake saw no movement on the other side of the barricade.

When the volunteers were only a few feet away from the barrier, a policeman reared from behind a car and shot one of them. He was dispatched less than a second later, by probably a dozen shots. The guns quieted again. The volunteers on the avenue climbed over the barrier and began cleanup. No further shots were fired, and soon the volunteers brought out a half-dozen police and a few National Guardsmen with their hands in the air. Jake saw these men put on the ground cuffed with zip ties.

Jake and Mario continued loading magazines while they waited. Just when they were finishing, two men approached. They held out a spare magazine each.

"Here. We got these from a guy from our team from Johnstown." One pointed solemnly over his shoulder. "He didn't make it."

The other guy pointed at Jake's gun. "Looks like you could use a few more for your full-auto."

The other one nodded. "That thing was awesome." He pointed at Jake. "I saw you take out the machine gun down there." He cocked his head. "I wasn't sure how we were gonna crack that nut."

They all turned and looked when they heard gunfire again. It was a single shot behind the police cars, but no one panicked. It must have been someone hiding. "Clear!" a voice yelled.

Jake looked around for Clive. The reverend had disappeared. Jake stood and walked through the large crowd of men, many of whom were looking down at the fallen. Jake looked down as well at a continuous carpet of bodies. Many were obviously dead, but many were not. Both the dead and injured were often accompanied by someone crouching, cradling, or crying over them. This is where Jake finally found Clive. Clive was kneeling next to a young man with a beard. Clive was talking to him. The words were soothing.

"You did good. You don't need to worry. Your loved ones who passed before you, they'll be waiting."

The man's eyes were glassy and focused in the air. "Will . . . my brother be there?" He coughed blood up onto his beard.

Clive kept the lullaby going. "He'll be there, your brother. He'll come and take you home."

Suddenly the man tensed in pain, the spasm lasting a couple seconds, then he completely relaxed and his eyes lost their focus. Clive held him for a moment longer, then gently closed the man's eyelids and laid his head on the ground. Clive stood and brushed himself off. Only then did he look up and see Jake.

"Oh, thank the Lord you're okay." He looked around. "Heaven knows we lost enough."

Clive took a step forward and embraced him in a bear hug. "I never should have let you come," Clive said, patting Jake's back.

"You should be glad you did," Mario said, interrupting the hug. He pointed at the fallen. "There would have been a lot more of them, if it wasn't for Jake and his gun."

Clive released him from the hug, but held him at arm's length by his shoulders. He looked at Jake appraisingly. "The M16?" He glanced at Mario.

Mario pointed down at the barrier. "Yeah! And they had a full-auto, too. Jake took 'em out."

Clive smiled at Jake. "Well, well. Who would have thought, a construction guy no less. Any close calls?"

Jake looked quickly at Mario before answering, "Uh, yeah. Using a full-auto kinda draws attention. We had to hide behind the barrier and change positions."

Clive took this in. "Well, remember that whenever you go full-auto." He looked at Mario. "Sounds like you two worked well as a team."

Mario nodded. "He's way too slow reloading the mags. I'm probably gonna need to stay with him and baby-sit him," Mario said in jest.

Jake looked around, "Where are the other guys?"

Clive shook his head sadly. "We lost Mason, right at the start. He took one in the head."

Jake thought about the guy next to him who had died like that. Hopefully Mason hadn't suffered.

Jake felt a huge pit in his stomach. "Did he have family?"

Clive shook his head.

"What about the others?" Mario asked.

"Noah and Troy went down with the cleanup crew." Clive pointed down at the barricade.

"Let's join 'em," Mario said.

* * *

They gathered their gear, and began moving down the ramp again. Jake noticed a half-dozen men wearing black shirts with red crosses on white patches. They were scattered around checking on all the down men. Jake was relieved someone had thought to bring medics, but there weren't nearly enough, they needed way more.

Eventually the ramp joined the street. They marched past the Peace Institute, and walked through a large intersection onto Constitution Ave. Looking east, the sun was just peeking its head over the eastern horizon behind the Washington Monument. They had officially entered the National Mall. Jake was back in Washington for the first time since he was a boy.

The barrier was just on the other side of the intersection. It was a vehicle barrier of a dozen police cars and two Humvees. Looking to the right toward the Lincoln Memorial, they could see they were being joined by another large group of rebels. It had to be the West Virginians who had just crossed the Potomac on the Arlington Bridge.

When Jake and the others reached the barrier, they climbed over some bullet-riddled police cars to the other side. There were bodies of police officers lying in odd positions. Empty shell casings were everywhere. Three rebels had an injured policemen propped up against a Humvee.

"Then why were you shooting at us?" A rebel in a hard hat yelled at the injured man.

Jake couldn't hear the answer.

201

GARY HANSEN

"Everybody has a choice," another guy yelled. "You fought for a president you didn't believe in, and now you're dying."

Another yelled. "If you're gonna die for something, you should at least die fighting for the right cause."

"What happened?" the guy in the hard hat asked.

One of the men reached up to the policeman's neck and felt for a pulse. After a moment he stood. "Geez, he just died."

The three rebels moved on, but Jake stopped and looked at the dead man. He wore dark navy pants and a light blue short sleeve shirt. A large patch decorated his left shoulder with an insignia of the Capital that said "Metropolitan Police, Washington, D.C." The officer was maybe thirty. He had curly black hair and a round baby face. Jake noticed he wore a wedding band on his left hand. Maybe had a few kids. From what Jake had deciphered from the yelling, the officer had confessed with his dying breath that he didn't really agree with President Singleton. He was just doing his job as a police officer.

Jake looked at all the dead bodies scattered behind the barricade. How many of them didn't believe in what they were doing, but were just doing their jobs? Half? Jake wondered if he could kill people just because it was his job. Could he kill them if he knew he was fighting for the wrong side? He remembered the Pittsburgh policeman on television who had called his supervisor and said he refused to confiscate guns anymore because it wasn't right. How many people had enough guts to lose a job over refusing to do something they considered unethical? Not many, Jake thought. Here was a guy, probably a good guy, who was killing people for his job, even though he didn't believe in it. He was probably more typical.

There were a lot of sheep out there in America that did what they were told. It was all part of the political correctness culture. Don't buck the system. That all worked when your leader was good and competent. But what if he wasn't? What if your leader was an evil egomaniac? Does everyone follow him off the cliff like lemmings? Isn't that what happened to the Nazis? People all over the world were still scratching their heads wondering how the Germans had been hoodwinked into helping Hitler exterminate the Jews. But ultimately, you didn't need to be evil, you just had to be committed to doing what you were told whether you liked it or not.

"You coming?" Mario asked. He wagged his finger again at Jake. "Don't look at 'em. It's easier that way."

CHAPTER 17

They heard gunfire ahead again, loud and close. Simultaneously, Clive's radio went off. The radio voice was calm and cheerful.

"Group three volunteers, there are more free fireworks on Constitution Avenue, back at 19th Street, just past the Board of Governors for the Federal Reserve. For best viewing, we recommend some of you spread out into the beautiful gardens between Constitution and the Reflecting Pool."

The calm line scattered in all directions. Jake saw the long black hair of Troy in the chaos and followed him through the trees on their right. Troy moved fast, his hair dangling over the Steelers jersey, and Jake almost lost him. He wanted to ditch the heavy ammo box but resisted. Troy darted over a diagonal road that led back toward the Lincoln Memorial then through some more trees into a grassy area. Troy didn't take them out in the open grass but hugged the tree line on the left.

Jake looked out at the grassy area and realized where they were. Even with the rising sun, lights illuminated a long sidewalk, which gently curved through the middle of the manicured grass. A black wall covered with names ran along the north side of the wall. It was the Vietnam Veterans Memorial. Jake saw more rebels running through the trees on the other side of the memorial.

Troy hustled them past the memorial wall and stopped under a large tree. He peered through the brush back at Constitution Avenue. As soon as they stopped, others joined them from behind. Jake glanced back and saw thousands of men running toward them from behind in the semi-dark. Thousands more came from the south, probably across the Arlington Bridge. No sign of Clive, or Mario, or Noah. In the chaos, the team had been separated.

They rounded the trees, and gunfire erupted. Everyone hit the ground or dove for cover, although many dropped due to being shot. The shooting came from another barricade, larger than the first. It was set up at 19th Street and extended out into the grass to the large pond. This second barricade completely blocked the rebels passing through to the White House on the north side of the pond, creating a funnel. This time there were more Humvees, maybe a dozen, plus more Metropolitan Police cars in between. Behind the barricade were two large green military trucks, troop transport, probably National Guard. Jake found himself prone on the ground next to Troy, behind a large tree.

A guy on Jake's right, just past the tree, lifted his head for a better view and took a bullet to the head. Another man in coveralls was shot ten feet farther away. They were way too exposed, and this second barrier offered better protection to the other side. Jake wanted to retreat, but he didn't dare leave the protection of the trees. And where were Mario and Clive? Were they as exposed as Jake?

"Give me your full auto!" Troy yelled into his ear.

Jake held out the weapon, happy to relinquish it.

Troy aimed it around the tree, then let loose, dumping the entire magazine into a concentrated area of gunfire. Sparks flew from ricocheting bullets. Troy held out the empty magazine to Jake, a signal to give him a replacement. Jake dug into his pack and found another, trading Troy. Troy unloaded another volley into a different spot. This time Jake had a replacement magazine ready for Troy. Jake saw more men hit around them. He knew he needed to start reloading the magazines from the ammo box, but he was busy just exchanging loaded mags with Troy. Finally all five mags were empty, including the two new gifted ones, Jake shook his head at Troy, letting him know that they were done for a while. Jake clawed at the ammo box, opening the lid, and started loading shells one by one, knowing each breath might be his last.

Troy set the M16 aside and returned to his own gun, the one with the bayonet on the end. It had the distinctive look of an AK-47 with the small tube above the barrel for its piston cycling mechanism. Jake saw that Troy could shoot it fast, but it was not full auto. Jake finished loading the first magazine, and started on number two. Troy had emptied the magazine from his AK and replaced it with another. Jake wished the two weapons used the same ammo so he and Troy could share magazines, but unfortunately that was one of the downsides of a quickly assembled militia from the neighborhood. Everyone brought what they had. There was no time to coordinate or assign people together based on common weapons.

The barricade, meanwhile, was still firing as fast as ever. It was as if the rebels had made no impact on it. Jake saw the fire-breathing barrels of at least three full-auto guns in the barricade. They had much better protection this time. The rebels couldn't do any damage shooting up at them while lying prone in the grass.

Jake finished loading the second magazine and stacked it on top of the first. He had just started on the third when Troy switched guns again, going back to the M16. He quickly emptied both of the magazines Jake had just loaded. Jake saw another prone man on his left jerk, then go stiff. It was only a matter of time for him and Troy.

Then he felt someone climbing over his back.

"Stay down!"

It was Noah. The quiet black man didn't bother trying to make a place for himself. He just lay prone over Jake's lower back and buttocks. Jake looked over his shoulder and saw Noah pull a huge army-green bullet, slightly smaller than a can of shaving cream out of his pack. He yanked the tube of his grenade launcher forward, exposing a cavity, and rammed the grenade inside. He closed the tube and aimed. The barricade looked about a football field away. Noah's gun rocked as he fired, but Jake heard nothing with all the gunfire around him. Jake didn't know where Noah had aimed until he saw an explosion of fire over by the troop carriers, behind the front row of Humvees. All shooting from that side of the barricade stopped. They were probably all dead.

Noah opened the tube, and the large empty shell dropped out. He loaded another grenade and aimed over to the left of his first shot. The grenade went long, past the barricade, and Noah cursed. He hurriedly dumped the empty and loaded another. This time his aim was true, and a fireball erupted from the other side. With the barricade somewhat disabled, men all around them rose and charged.

Troy, Noah, and Jake let them go. Noah rolled off Jake. Jake sat up and watched the combat at the barrier. The numbers heavily favored the rebels who climbed en masse over the Humvees and squad cars. Jake saw many rebels fall, but it was only a small percentage compared to the numbers who made it. They heard sporadic gunfire between the combatants, but it was over in a short time. A few minutes later, Jake watched them march five men out with their hands up.

Next to Jake, a rebel soldier felt for the pulse of a downed comrade. The injured man was not moving and was lying in an awkward position. The rebel removed his hand and crossed himself with it.

Two other rebels were trying to comfort a soldier who was rocking back and forth in agony, clutching himself. His eyes were wide, his teeth gritted. One man held his head and the other his arm. Even in the morning light, Jake could see the man was covered with blood. One of the medics ran up from the ranks with his bag. He was the first medic Jake had seen at the second barrier. He wondered if the rest were still back at the first barrier. The medic knelt next to the man, moving the man's hands aside for a better look. After a glance, he grimaced. He shook his head to the two helpers and moved on to another victim. It was only a moment later that the man stopped struggling and fell unconscious, or dead.

Jake could still hear gunfire, but it was farther away in other parts of the city. It was hard to believe that these skirmishes were probably happening all the around the White House. Jake had to remind himself that they were only one of eight attack points. He wondered if the other groups had had as much success as they'd had, defeating two barricades. He looked around at the fallen, and wondered if all eight points were experiencing the same casualties as they were. Maybe their group was winning these battles at too high of a cost.

The crowd at the second barrier made room as General Bowen drove up in the Polaris side-by-side. He jumped out of the vehicle and hurried over to where the five men were being questioned. He obviously wanted to hear what they had to say.

Jake looked at Noah. He had single-handedly turned a suicidal mission completely around to their advantage. He obviously knew what he was doing. It wasn't the first time he had fired grenades, that was for sure. His movements were practiced. His confidence with the weapon was obvious. Jake also knew that, like the M16, just possessing a grenade launcher and live grenades had to be a felony in the United States.

"Where did you get that?" Jake asked.

Noah smirked at him. "Where did you get the M16?"

Jake realized he'd asked a stupid question, but he was still curious. "Are there lots of them, you know, in America?"

Noah shook his head. "The launcher itself isn't the hard part. You can get those. It's the grenades themselves. They count every one in the good old U.S. They're cataloged and serialized. They know where every can is on every base."

"Then how does someone go about, you know, trying to acquire them?"

Noah smiled. "Other countries are not as careful as the U.S. A few dollars here, and a few dollars there, they can be acquired, with the right connections."

Troy flipped his hair over his back. "There are other ways too. The bad guys have them. Some of the big drug cartels, some of the Taliban. If a good guy decides to beat the crap out of a bad guy, you know—for humanitarian purposes—he might find himself in possession of spoils."

Noah added. "They're worth a lot of money, too much money for most company clerks to resist."

Jake figured that was all he was going to get, so he changed the subject. "Well, I'm glad we had them. It made this an entirely different battle."

Jake had heard the standard line for all those years about how the citizens had no reason to own an assault weapon or a hi-capacity magazine. The whole discussion was centered on lunatics who shot up schools and universities. Jake had once believed in those arguments. He had actually thought the NRA was a little over the top in fighting against all gun regulations. But now, he saw it from a whole other perspective. The real reason for the second amendment wasn't for hunters, or even self-defense. It was this, right here. It was for the citizens of America to be able to keep their government in check. Was it fair for the government to have full-autos and the citizens not? No way. Was it fair for the government to have grenades and explosives, but not the people? Hell no! Which led to another question.

"Why didn't they use grenades on us?" Jake asked. "We were packed together like sardines. They have 'em, right?"

Troy and Noah looked at each other.

Noah shrugged. "The cops don't have high explosive grenades like I just used. They have smokers and flash bombs but not killers." He pointed at the barricade. "The G.I. Joes do, but they probably got sent here with a defensive mentality. They thought they could turn us back easier. The thought of putting a high explosive grenade into a crowd of Americans was probably beyond their thinking."

Jake pointed at the barricade. "Well, now that we used ours," he pointed at Noah's launcher, "won't they smarten up? Could they use them on us later?"

Troy and Noah looked at each other again, as if this thought had not occurred to them.

Jake pointed at the barrier. "Any chance there are more grenades over there in those army vehicles?"

Both men answered by walking quickly toward the second barrier.

When they reached the barrier, they found a much more gruesome scene than the last time. The grenades had done a number on the police and military. They weren't just dead; many were missing parts. Jake finally took Mario's advice to not look at the fallen. Even trying not to, he couldn't help but notice many wore wedding bands. They were Americans, with families. What a sickening waste.

It had always amazed him, when death toll numbers were talked about for wars, that the Civil War had almost as many fatalities as all the other American wars combined. How could that be? When Jake pictured a bad war day for America, he thought about D-Day in World War II and landing on the beaches of Normandy, or the endless killing in Vietnam. Yet the Civil War had been twice as bad. It was incomprehensible. And yet here they were again, Americans killing Americans. And for what?

This war was about how big the government was allowed to grow. It was about whether a single president could make his own laws and kill everyone who got in his way. As Jake looked around at the fallen Americans, it made him sick. But what was the alternative? An all-powerful government led by a murderer? That was definitely worse, wasn't it?

Jake realized he was lost in a zone, staring at nothing. Troy and Noah were gone. Crowds of rebels moved past him. Jake didn't know a soul. He looked around. His friends would likely be at the military vehicles searching for supplies or weapons they might find useful. He looked between the Humvees on the front line, and the troop carriers behind. He decided the Humvees had probably already been looted, so he headed for the larger vehicles.

"Jake!"

Jake turned and saw Mario and Clive. He felt a wave of relief.

"You need to stay with me!" Mario said impatiently.

Jake pointed at the troop carrier. "Sorry, I lost sight of everybody but Troy. I followed him."

"He'll get you killed," Mario said. "The guy's a lunatic."

"At least he's okay," Clive said. "What about Noah?"

Jake pointed that the troop carriers again. "He's with Troy." He motioned for them to follow as he walked toward the large green truck.

When they reached the first troop carrier, they looked in the rear and saw it had been completely stripped. The second looked no different. They spotted Troy and Noah talking to some other men near the second truck. The men handed a large green ammunition box to Noah, then shook hands. The ammo box was twice the size of Jake's. The other guys walked away.

"They didn't know what they were," Troy said as he saw them approaching.

"What are they?" Mario asked

Noah responded, "What we wanted."

"Will they work in your launcher?" Clive asked.

Noah shrugged. "Sure."

"How many of yours did you have left?" Troy asked.

Noah looked distrustfully at the others. "I put two in the barrier, and wasted one, so I had six more."

Mario said the obvious. "Then these are gonna help."

Clive pointed back to where they had seen the side-by-side. "Let's go tell the general about these. He should know.

Noah didn't look like he was too keen on anyone knowing anything about his grenades, even the general.

CHAPTER 18

The general was busy interrogating the captured men, but when he was done, he was happy to talk to Clive. The four others stood aside in the grass and waited. Gunfire, sometimes heavy, could still be heard blocks away. Jake found it very difficult to relax with the sounds so near, which was probably a good thing. While they waited, Mario pulled an energy bar from his pack and started eating it.

Mario pointed at Jake. "Eat now, while you got time."

Jake decided it was good advice and followed suit. They both chased the snacks with water.

When Clive returned, it was so crowded on Constitution that he steered them south, away from the barrier into the center of the mall, to the other side of the Constitution Garden Pool, along the Reflecting Pool toward the World War II Memorial. The memorial was fairly new, Jake guessed less than ten years old. It wasn't here when he'd visited Washington as a kid. It was a large open oval water fountain, not a building. They gazed at it as they walked by. Jake thought of the men that were just killed in the grass behind him and wondered if there would someday be a memorial in the mall for them, for ousting Singleton and taking back America. Of course, that would depend on the outcome. After all, the winners always got to write the history books. If they failed, Singleton would get the memorial, and they would be labeled as traitors and forgotten.

On the other side of the memorial were the open fields around the 555-foot obelisk of the Washington Monument. As they walked into the open, they gazed left. The White House was somewhere out there in the trees, but they couldn't see it yet.

On the open grass, they merged with tens of thousands of other rebels, thousands from the south, from the southern bridges, thousands from the Capitol building east of them, and thousands from the west, including the contingency from Pittsburgh. In all directions, the rebels just kept marching into the mall, as if there was no end to them. Jake remembered the map Clive had shown him with the rings around Washington D.C., and how long it would take them to arrive. He wondered where these newcomers were from. Cincinnati? Detroit? Could they have made it here already?

The large mass swarmed in the same direction, north to the White House. Some of the volunteers ran, some jogged. Jake's group walked. He was grateful for the pace. He felt like the adrenaline expended at the two barriers had taken something out of him. And he was still carrying the box of ammo, even though it was noticeably lighter now and easier to carry due to the rounds they had already used. Although it was easier, he wished he still had those bullets, because he was betting the battle had just begun.

When they crossed Constitution Avenue, they briefly passed through more trees into a huge circle of grass. Finally, Jake could see the White House up ahead, about a half mile away. He felt exhilaration at the sight, some reverence, but also lots of disgust and anger at the man inside.

"There she is!" Mario yelled. "Let's go get her."

Troy pointed at the huge circle of grass "What is this?"

Clive said, "It's the Ellipse."

"What's it for?" Troy pressed.

Noah answered, "It's for nothing. It's just another park."

Mario pointed ahead to the far side. "See that tree, that's the White House Christmas tree. Haven't you ever watched the president light it?"

Troy shrugged. "No. I got better things to watch than that."

Clive motioned around the huge grass field. "This field used to be stables. They kept the horses here, back when—"

"Before the president got helicopters, and Air Force One," Mario finished.

"Yeah," Clive agreed.

Jake ignored the chatter about the Ellipse and instead focused on the White House. Sure, he'd seen it when they first walked through the trees onto the grass, but the trees on the South Lawn concealed

211

most of the structure. Now as they approached, he could see better, and there was something different, wrong. Were those tubes? And then he recognized them. Tanks!

He pointed. "They've got the whole place surrounded!"

On cue, one of the tanks fired in a bright explosion. Jake saw two-dozen men on his right blown to smithereens. One minute they were walking, the next, they were down and mangled, or just gone. A loud boom reached them a fraction of a second later.

"Down!" Mario yelled.

Mario's yell was mixed with other men all over the Ellipse yelling the same thing. Jake was already on his way to the ground. On his way down, he saw another fireball erupt and more rebels, farther to the right, go down.

"Cover!" Mario yelled, and this time he climbed into a crouch and sprinted to the left toward the trees.

Jake wasn't sure if that was such a bright idea, but he saw the others from the Suburban follow in a running crouch. Troy's hair flew behind him as he ran. Jake hesitated. Suddenly, another shot exploded and took out a swath between Jake and his team. If he would have followed, just behind them . . .

He waited another few heartbeats, then got up and ran as fast as he could. It wasn't much of a crouch. Screw that! It was speed he was after. He considered dropping the damn ammo box. The Ellipse was huge, and the trees were so far away. But ahead he saw Mario reach the tree line, then the others. He was way behind. He glanced toward the White House, at the damn tanks. He heard another boom, then another. They must have been firing behind him, because he didn't see any more soldiers mowed down in front of him. The others were waving, motioning him to hurry. If he could just close the gap and be enveloped by the protection of leaves. Time was slowing down now. There was too much time for them to fire again. The next shot would take him out like a racecar through a crowd of spectators. He was only a few feet away. If only he could get there in time. Another boom.

Then he was there, and the others were grabbing him and pulling him deeper under the trees. He fell onto the shady grass. He was panting from the run. The loud explosions continued. He heard gunfire now. Rebels out on the Ellipse were firing at the tanks.

"How come you didn't follow?' Mario asked angrily, standing above him.

"If I had, I'd be dead!"

"Not if you were faster!" Mario snapped his fingers twice. "When I tell you to do something, you don't think, don't question, don't consider, just do it. Immediately! Maybe you'll live through this thing." He turned away. More booms out on the grass. More gun fire.

Clive knelt down next to him and grabbed his shoulder. "I thought we lost you. I saw those guys go down behind us, while we were running, and I thought you were one of 'em." He put his head down. "I'd never forgive myself if I let anything happen to you."

Jake thought about Monica at home, his wife. What the hell was he doing here? They were right; he didn't have a clue what he was doing. He would get himself killed, and maybe somebody else. The shots continued.

"That's why Mario was yelling at you. He thought we lost you back there." Then Clive smiled. "I think he's starting to like you."

Jake looked at Mario, who was standing away from them, puffing urgently on a cigarette. How could any of these guys like him? They hated him. They thought he was an idiot. He was just extra baggage, and they were afraid he was going to screw up and get them all killed. They were probably right. But another thing occurred to him, maybe they weren't only thinking about him endangering them, maybe Clive was right, maybe they liked him enough to not want him to get killed.

And then Mario threw the remains of his cigarette in the grass and walked back to them. "Get up. It's time to move."

CHAPTER 19

The area under the trees was crowded with rebels. The remaining rebels out on the grass Ellipse were either dead, severely wounded, or mourning over their fallen comrades. The tanks had stopped, but who knew for how long. As the five men weaved their way toward the White House through the maze of men, they heard pieces of a million conversations.

"How'd they get them in there? There must be a couple thousand troops in there. Did we bring any anti-tank weapons? We might as well go home. How can those soldiers fire on Americans like that? How come nobody knew? They probably just killed a couple hundred men. We can get past the troops, but how do we get past tanks? Who's in charge? Is the president even in there?"

Mario brought them to the edge of the trees. Ahead, they saw a huge mass of rebels packed like sardines up to the fence bordering the south lawn of the White House. They filled the street and packed into the first hundred feet or so of the Ellipse. Thousands of volunteers could also be seen on the left, crowded along the west side of the White House, pouring out of all the streets from cities farther north like Baltimore and Philadelphia. It meant the White House was completely surrounded now.

The only place Jake could see that wasn't packed with people was the area directly south of the White House, where the tanks had been firing. Even that was filling in though, as the rebels had no place else to go. The sun was way above the horizon now, and Jake shielded his eyes as he took in the South Lawn. He counted five tanks just past the fountain, but there could have been more hidden behind the

214

trees. Behind the tanks were thousands of troops. Between the tanks and the troops there was some sort of waist-high white wall, probably concrete barriers. Obviously, the president had been busy as they had driven in from Pittsburgh the night before.

Jake felt vulnerable. Although the tanks had not fired in their direction toward the trees yet, there was nothing stopping them. All they would have to do is rotate the turrets right a few degrees, and wham, mass casualties. He looked behind him to see if there were some building or monument they were afraid to hit, but the foliage blocked his view, and he had no intention of moving out in the open just to satisfy his curiosity.

"Why aren't they firing?" Mario asked.

Jake wondered the same. "Who knows?"

"We're all packed together," Mario said. "They could kill a hundred of us with every shot."

Jake agreed. If they just kept firing, the rebels would be decimated, tens of thousands dead after only a few hours. That would be a victory for the president, wouldn't it? The body count would be stacked against the rebels. Jake thought of the rebels losing confidence and running in the opposite direction. It would be a lopsided victory for President Singleton. He would be seen as powerful and ultimately unchallenged. Or would he?

"Maybe they're afraid of how that might look." Jake said.

"What are you talking about?" Mario asked.

Jake pointed at the White House. "Think about it on the news. Firing on foot soldiers with tanks. Death count in the tens of thousands. What would the press say about that?"

Clive was nodding.

"Who cares?" Mario said.

"He's right," Clive said. "Even Americans who oppose guns are going to have a hard time watching the government kill 75,000 rednecks who opposed him."

"He'd just say we were committing treason," Troy said.

Mario said, "Yeah, and if the reporters didn't print it the way he wanted, he could murder the reporters. He's done it before."

Clive looked like he disagreed, but he didn't argue.

Jake stared at the tanks, and a thought occurred to him. "What if they got cold feet?" Jake pointed at the tanks. "Maybe the soldiers in those tanks are reconsidering. Maybe their commanders are too."

The men looked at the tanks for a moment.

Mario had a skeptical look on his face.

Jake continued, "How do you think it feels to look through your spotting scope and see a hundred fellow Americans mowed down with a single shot? How does it feel to look out over the Ellipse and see a thousand dead, or dismembered and dying?"

Mario joined in. "How does it feel when your sergeant stands behind you shouting, 'Keep killing 'em!'"

Clive seemed awed by the question. "So you think it's possible they're over there having a discussion on the White House lawn about whether or not to follow orders?"

They all looked at Jake.

Jake thought about the men they had captured at the barriers. They had expressed what? He pointed at the tanks "Think about it. They're Americans too. They were probably called in yesterday to come and fight. Next thing they know, they're firing on their neighbors with tanks, massacreing them."

"They had no idea they'd be killing other Americans," Noah said, joining the conversation.

"They were just following orders," Jake said. "Doing their jobs."

"So they just stopped?" Clive asked.

Jake wondered what would it take to tip the scales? What would it take for them to throw their weapons down and walk away? There was a lot of pressure to do what you're told, especially for soldiers. But today's soldiers go through a lot of humanitarian training too, don't they? They're indoctrinated to look out for the underdog and save the old women and babies from the terrorists, aren't they?

Jake pointed at Mario. "You guys are soldiers. What happens when your platoon leader tells you to kill a village of women and children?"

"That never happened to me," Mario said.

"Sometimes the platoon leader gets an accidental bullet in the head," Troy said.

They stared at the big man for a minute.

Jake knew that it probably happened both ways. Sometimes the soldiers did as they were told and killed the innocents, and sometimes they refused. The statistics of how often it happened, either way, were buried under a ton of paperwork and bureaucracy, or were never whispered to anyone under oaths of secrecy between soldiers.

Clive broke the silence. "So the question is, were they told to stand down, or did they just stop?"

Jake asked, "What do you think is going on up there, right now?"

Mario said. "Who cares? If we rush 'em, we can take 'em." He pointed behind him at the growing mass. "There's plenty of us."

"I agree," Troy said.

Jake thought about that. He imagined the masses running over the fences, storming over the fountains and up the lawn. The tanks and the machine guns would kill the population of a medium-sized city. But there were so many rebels, some would ultimately get through. It would be a blood bath, but it was winnable. Jake didn't have the stomach for it right now, though.

Mario said, "We should attack now, while they're figuring out what to do."

"I agree," Troy said again.

Jake shook his head. "What if they are arguing with themselves? What if they're not sure—"

Mario cut him off. "All the better! We get a small measure of surprise. We attack before they can think about how they're going to stop us."

Clive put his hand on Mario's shoulder. "Hang on. I want to hear Jake's theory."

Jake pointed at the White House. "We can always storm the grounds, and we may have to. But our advantage for storming gets better the longer we wait."

"How do you figure?" Mario retorted.

Jake pointed behind, back at the huge obelisk of the Washington Monument. "Look at them come." They all looked at the people flowing through the trees. "By noon, we'll have over a million people here. Time is on our side. If we have to sacrifice thousands of bodies to the tanks and soldiers, it's to our advantage to wait." He pointed up at the White House. "They can't get any more tanks or soldiers in there."

Mario argued, "Yeah, but just waiting . . ."

Clive said, "Jake, what about what you said," he pointed to the White House, "about what they're talking about up there, right now?"

Jake shrugged. "I don't know, obviously. But they stopped firing, didn't they? After proving to themselves that they could kill us as fast

217

as they wanted." Jake looked around at the others. Why would they listen to him? "If I were sitting in a tank right now and had just killed a thousand Americans, mowed them down like they did, I wouldn't feel that well. I would feel sick inside. Maybe a little guilty."

"I might puke on my feet in the tank," Noah offered.

Jake smiled at him. "Yeah. Maybe they're thinking about what they did. Maybe their officers are thinking the same thing. Or maybe they're not. Maybe they're arguing with the gunners to keep shooting. I don't know."

"What if they are?" Clive asked.

Jake shrugged. "Then we let them. We let them argue. We let them discuss the ins and outs of killing their friends and neighbors. We let them pontificate as long as they want to."

"Pontificate?" Mario asked. "What the hell is that?"

Jake waved at the air dismissively. "Discuss, trade ideas, ponder, lecture, argue. Who cares?" Jake held out his open palms. "We can only hope that some of them, a few, start questioning what they're doing, and how much appetite they have for killing Americans to defend this president, a president who many believe is an egomaniac."

"All presidents are egomaniacs," Mario argued.

"Yeah, but how many have killed other politicians to increase their power? Or killed reporters to look better?" Jake asked. He looked to see if any of the others were going to argue with him. "Look, we all know Singleton is different." He pointed toward the tanks, and troops. "And they know it too."

Clive continued. "So, you're saying, let 'em talk, as long as they want. The more they discuss it, the more hearts might be softened, and the more likely they are to refuse."

Jake nodded. "Look, I have no idea if that's why they stopped fighting. Maybe they're taking a coffee break. I could be completely wrong. But time is on our side. Our numbers are growing. The longer we wait, the more they get to think about what they are doing . . ."

". . . and the more soldiers who cross to our side, or miss on purpose," Noah finished.

Jake looked at the grenade-launching soldier. Just when you thought you were starting to get to know someone. "Yeah," Jake said.

Clive looked around. He picked up his radio. "I'd like to discuss this with the general, if I can find him."

* * *

An hour later, there had been no action from either side. Everyone was obviously waiting for the other side to move first. Jake and the others were sitting Indian style on the grass. Luckily, they had a shady spot in the trees surrounding the Ellipse. Many others were not as fortunate. With no place else to go, the herds of new recruits arriving were filling the grass on the Ellipse. Gunfire, even in the distance, had all but ceased. The word passed around was, "Only fire, if fired upon." All barriers in streets around the White House had been defeated, and now the rebels choked all streets, parks, ingresses, or any other breathing space around the White House. Basically, there was standing room only in all directions surrounding the eighteen-acre White House lot for a mile in every direction. Streets were completely clogged. A person flying over would not even be able to see the asphalt.

In fact, there had been some flyovers, mostly by helicopters, some of them news helicopters, which was strange, since Jake had always thought there was a no-fly zone over the Capital, and he reasoned the restriction would be even more critical now. It made him wonder if Singleton himself had lifted the ban, thinking the publicity would help his cause.

One helicopter came very close, with a tethered cameraman hanging out each side of the rig. It had a huge logo "FOX 5" painted on the side. Many of the rebels waved at it. Many others held up their guns. Some pointed their weapons at it. But nobody fired. It was all fairly jovial. People liked to be on camera.

Jake thought it was a very similar atmosphere to the million-man marches often held in Washington, to protest this or that, or to show solidarity, except for all the guns, of course, and the dead and wounded from this morning's skirmishes. No, probably not the same atmosphere, but there was no question the mood had lightened since the shooting had stopped. There was a general feeling that something big was going to happen, but the crowd was more than happy to wait for it. In the meantime, the rebels kept arriving.

Later a big military gunship passed over them. There were soldiers aiming chain guns down at them. Rifles came up all around. The crowd watched them pass over quietly. Not quite as jovial as the news chopper.

They had not seen Clive since his departure to meet with the general. Jake wondered if all eight of the generals were together now, in one place. Probably not – too risky. He wondered if they had all survived their skirmishes. Was there an overall commander? He didn't know. He had no way of knowing whether Clive had convinced the others to wait, or whether someone else had already come to the same conclusion. All they knew was that the voice on the radio had said to sit tight for a while and let things play out. Jake had heard another radio in the area besides theirs. The message was definitely being disseminated effectively even though not everyone had a radio, which was working better than anyone could have predicted.

They had been ordered not to use their cell phones, but Jake saw many others disregarding the rule. He pulled his out and considered. What would Clive say? Jake decided he didn't care. Monica was probably on needles.

He texted, "Hi, wife. Doing fine. Don't worry."

He received a response almost immediately, although not from Monica. "All circuits busy."

He cursed and put the phone back in his pocket.

* * *

By early afternoon they were going stir crazy. They had now been sitting around for over three and a half hours. Noah and Troy were sleeping. Mario had been asleep for a while, but was now awake smoking another cigarette. Noah's head was propped against the newly acquired box of grenades. Troy was lying sideways with his head on his backpack. Both held their rifles in their hands.

While they were waiting, time had passed incredibly slowly. At times Jake wondered if his watch had stopped. During the lull, they had heard approximately a dozen gunshots around them, but they were all isolated, and Jake attributed them to accidents, or boneheads firing into the air, or an occasional pot shot at the White House. He guessed that should be expected when you packed a million random people with guns into a small space like they had. Every time the sound was heard, everyone jerked awake with their guns in the air. It always took a few minutes for everyone to settle back down and re-engage the safeties on their weapons.

After an hour of sitting around, Troy, Noah, and Mario had started cleaning their guns. Jake had followed their example. When he began cleaning the M16, the others gave him advice and pointers. Since they all were very familiar with the M16 from their military experience, they knew the gun inside and out. Each had tricks. When Jake had the bolt out, Troy completely disassembled it and inspected each piece. He declared the weapon in very good condition with only minor wear for a full-auto. In fact, he thought some of the wear could have been done that morning as they ran almost ten magazines, three hundred rounds, through it. They showed him how to use a shell casing to pump oil down into the extractor and how to flick the bolt before reinserting it into the upper assembly. Jake was impressed at their suggestions, and he felt better about the gun when it was reassembled. Shooting that many rounds through it, so fast, had made him wonder if it would start to jam soon. Now he felt the M16 was better than new.

Mario stuck his cigarette into the grass to extinguish it. "The reverend is back."

Jake looked up to see Monica's father sidestepping around seated rebels as he weaved through the throngs toward them. He was constantly smiling, nodding his head, excusing himself, and patting strangers on the back, or shaking hands. He was a master at making all around him feel welcome and appreciated. When he arrived, he scanned the group. Noah and Troy had awakened from their naps and sat up.

"That took longer than expected." He motioned in the direction he had just come. "This place is packed." He pointed at the ground where Noah and Troy had been lying. "You guys have more space than most."

"What'd the general say?" Mario asked. "Are all the generals together?"

"They're not all together, but they're in contact. There were two other generals with General Bowen. They liked Jake's theory. They had wondered about the same thing, whether the soldiers had lost their stomach."

"So, what's the plan?" Mario asked.

Clive glanced toward the White House. "Well, in a few minutes, a couple of us are going to approach the fence over there, holding a white flag."

"We're going to surrender?" Mario said, with distaste.

Clive shook his head. "No, no, just a conference. We just want to talk to them for a few minutes. We want to get a better feel about who and what we're up against."

Jake thought that was a good idea. It might help with generating compassion from the other side.

"Who's gonna talk to them," Noah asked, "the generals?"

"Not all of them," Clive responded. "General Bowen will be the mouth. General Jolley, from Raleigh, will be there. But the other generals will stay back. I'll be there—and Jake."

Jake's mouth fell open. He was floored. Why would they include him? From a million soldiers, why him?

Clive looked at him. "General Bowen liked your theory – about what they were thinking up there. He said you sounded like a discerning fellow. Your role is to listen only. After we're done, General Bowen wants you to tell him what you think."

Jake began shaking his head. General Bowen had obviously lost his mind. Jake was just a construction guy, divorced. Hell, to that point, if he had any discernment, why hadn't he been able to foretell about his ex-wife and the doctor?

"How do we know I'm not completely wrong about everything? Those thoughts just popped in my head. I'm terrible about reading people."

But that hadn't always been true, had it? Sure, he had missed on his ex-wife, but the signs had been there. He had just chosen to ignore them. Actually, Jake did sometimes feel like he could tell how other people felt. It was one of the reasons he believed others liked him. But interpreting the enemy's intentions from a negotiation session—that was way over his head.

Clive countered, "You have no choice. It's an order." He smiled at Jake. "You won't be the only one there listening. I'm supposed to do the same, and one other guy with General Jolley. When we're done, we'll all share our thoughts. The generals will listen. Maybe, they'll take us seriously, maybe not."

"When?" Jake said.

"Now. We need to work our way over there."

Jake retrieved his M16.

Clive pointed at it. "You won't need that. Let Mario keep it."

"No guns?" Noah asked.

"No guns," Clive responded, "Just us. Our eyes and our ears." He tapped the side of his forehead.

Jake reluctantly handed the M16 to Mario. He now felt naked without it. He began to detach his holster and the Browning, but Clive shook him off.

"You can keep that."

"You said no guns."

"I didn't mean that one."

Mario held his fingers out as an imaginary pistol, then aimed at his own head and let his thumb come forward like the hammer of a gun. "If you get the chance, Jake, execute a few of them traitors."

Clive smiled at Mario. "I don't think anybody is going to be executing anyone, Mario. Just a quick conference, a chance to talk to the other side."

Mario made the signal repeatedly with his finger gun, firing three rounds. "Be ready Jake, just in case. Make us proud."

CHAPTER 20

Jake felt strange as he followed Clive through the dense crowd. Clive led the way, excusing himself to the people he was moving past. The going was slow. Many resisted, trying to protect their position like a mass of teenagers crowding the stage at a rock concert. But Clive kept explaining they were on a mission from the general and needed to meet someone for strategic reasons. He gave no indication of the imminent meeting with the enemy, which Jake attributed to not wanting to entice anyone to follow them.

"There they are!" Clive pointed. Jake saw the green camouflage uniform of General Bowen in a tight group of men twenty yards away. The general was only ten yards from the gate around the South Lawn. Jake had that eerie feeling again about the tanks, since they were directly ahead, and he was standing directly in their firing path.

General Bowen and a few others were pushing forward to the gate. Clive positioned himself behind the general, and he and Jake followed in their wake.

The general announced himself to the men in front of him, "Please make way. General Bowen and General Jolley. Official business. Please make way."

Finally, they were at the gate, after they displaced some disappointed men who had to relinquish their front row seats along the fence. Jake looked over the tall, gray-haired man standing next to General Bowen. He was rugged looking, with an angular jaw, and was dressed in black assault-team garb. He wore wire-framed pilot sunglasses. He was probably in his late fifties. He had to be General Jolley.

224

A man next to General Jolley extended a telescoping silver pole with a huge white silky flag into the air. He kept telescoping it up until it was ten feet over their heads. Remarkably, a small breeze caught the flag, and it flapped lazily sideways in perfect view of the White House. General Bowen raised a bullhorn and spoke into it.

"Hello!"

The sound was very loud, and it quieted the rumbling crowd.

The general continued. "This is General Bowen and General Jolley. We are requesting a peaceful conference. Please send some delegates. We promise your safety." He looked back over the crowd as if to assess whether he had promised more than he could deliver.

Jake looked up the South Lawn at the White House and the army between the tanks. They were roughly a football field away from each other. He saw helmeted heads turn at the announcement as the soldiers discussed with each other the ramifications of the announcement they had just heard.

"This is General Bowen. We are requesting a brief discussion about options. Please send a group of negotiators forward. We promise to stay our weapons."

Jake heard a rumble from the soldiers and, behind him, from the rebels. Obviously, this action was a surprise to both sides.

The general put down the bullhorn.

"What now?" General Jolley asked.

"Let 'em think about it." General Bowen said. "They need time to decide who in their bureaucracy they should send. They might need to discuss it with their lawyers."

Jake realized the general had just made a joke.

They waited for a few minutes. Jake wondered if the soldiers might decide to put the crosshairs on the two generals and pop them instead. He was fairly sure there were sniper rifles aimed at them right now. From only a hundred yards, they were probably debating whether to aim for the left or right eye of each man. Jake wondered about the tanks, too. This would be a great time to fire and watch the rebels scatter in all directions. Screw a peaceful conference when you could wipe out a thousand traitors with just a few shots.

"Give us a few minutes." The sound was loud, sent from a very powerful PA system from one of the vehicles, or maybe even from the White House itself. They probably had some sort of audio system for parties on the South Lawn.

Jake held on to the rungs of the metal gate as he waited. The generals waited patiently as if they expected this to take a while. General Bowen looked calm, like a grandfather waiting for his wife to get ready for a party. He had a soft, friendly demeanor. General Jolley, on the other hand, looked stone-faced, like he might bite your head off if you even hinted you might say something. The man holding the flag looked like a businessman in his forties. The black assault uniform didn't look right on him. He looked like he would be more comfortable in a suit. Standing next to Jake, Clive gazed up at the White House in wonder. Jake had strong feelings for this man he had just met only two weeks before, and he hoped they both lived through this. Clive was now Jake's father in-law, and he knew they would become better friends over the years if they just got the chance.

Up by the White House, some men climbed over the concrete barrier on the side of the left tank. There were half-dozen of them. Jake's stomach tightened at what happened next. A soldier handed them a pole with an American flag on it. One of the six took it, and the group started walking toward them carrying the stars and stripes. The fact that they wanted to be seen holding the flag while they met with these rebels was a statement, an advertisement.

They waited as they watched the men march toward them. It took forever. The small group rounded the left side of the fountain and then steered toward their position and the white flag. When the group arrived within ten feet of the fence, they stopped. The two groups inspected each other.

The soldier on the left was holding a black assault weapon. Not an M16, something more modern with all kinds of lasers and scopes mounted on it. The gun was aimed straight up in a non-threatening way. Jake guessed the soldier was in his twenties. He wore no wedding ring, and his face was unreadable.

Next was a seasoned soldier, probably an officer, although none of them had any bars or insignias. Jake guessed he was in his late thirties or early forties. He curiously scanned the faces of the rebels. He made eye contact for a moment with Jake, and Jake felt like the man had looked right through him. He was sharp, that was for sure, but Jake didn't sense any anger or animosity, just a shrewd character.

Next was their leader. This man was almost fifty. He had the same angular jaw and demeanor as General Jolley; he was just a little shorter. He had the air of command, and looked like he was used to being deferred to. He didn't even glance at Jake, focusing instead on the two generals. He was probably a general himself.

The guy next to him was his assistant. That was obvious. He had glasses and deferred to the man. He didn't have a clipboard, but he looked as if he would feel more comfortable with one. He glanced at Jake, and they caught eyes for a moment. Jake saw he did have a wedding ring.

The next guy over was another young soldier with another modern assault rifle. This guy was huge and black. His biceps bulged from inside the uniform. He could've been a linebacker for the Redskins. His eyes stared straight forward and focused on nothing. The last was the soldier carrying the flag. He looked like a young soldier, probably recruited for the flag duty at the last second. He was nervous, and his eyes were darting all over. He looked at Jake a few times but always looked away when Jake looked at him. His feet were moving as well, and he kept adjusting his hands on the flagpole.

"I'm General Bowen, and this is General Jolley." General Bowen motioned to his partner.

Their leader said, "Neither of you is a general, and both of you will definitely hang for leading this treasonous mob against the United States of America."

General Bowen acted as if he not heard the slant. He smiled and asked. "And who might you be?"

The man responded indignantly, "General Landry, U.S. Army."

"I thought that was you, Bill," General Bowen said. "We were in Germany together, back in the nineties, weren't we? You weren't a general back then though. Colonel, right?"

Landry sneered back. "What happened to you, Bowen? You miss the Army so bad you decided to start your own? Does your doctor know you stopped taking your lithium?"

Again, General Bowen took it in stride without rising to the challenge. "General Landry, it was good of you to respond to our invitation. Thank you for walking down here to discuss our options."

"The only option for you is to go home, or be exterminated by our superior weaponry, position, and troops," Landry said.

"There are many other options," Bowen said. "Like remembering you're an American citizen and helping take back your country from a murdering fool—restore America to what it once was."

"Oh, please. You really expect us to buy into that traitor hogwash? You created a militia, declared yourselves sovereign, and decided you didn't want to pay taxes anymore. People been doing that for hundreds of years. That dog won't hunt, Bowen."

"Bill, we've had bad presidents before. And we deserved them for being dumb enough to elect them in the first place. But we've never had one this bad. We've never had them murdering congressmen before. Or declaring martial law and killing thousands trying while disarming them. After all your training as a soldier, do you really think a president has the right to bypass Congress, make his own laws, and come into your house and take your guns away? Is that what you're defending?"

Jake thought General Bowen had struck a nerve with that one.

Landry took a moment before responding. "If he's dirty, Bowen, then our Constitution has a process—it's called impeachment. First they investigate, then the Congressmen you elected votes, and then Singleton is on the unemployment lines. That's how it's supposed to work. Not like this." He pointed out over the Ellipse and the tens of thousands. "You just can't start shooting muskets whenever the wrong fella gets elected."

"I wish it were that simple, Bill. Tell that to the Germans that served under Hitler. Just wait it out. Good will prevail. Unfortunately, there are guys like you, Bill, who will kill others to defend a murderer you know is guilty. Cause you're just doing your job. Just doing what you're told and protecting your pension. You've been saluting bureaucrats so long, you lost your ability to—"

Landry lost it. He pointed at Bowen in anger. "Don't talk to me like that. Once you might have been a general, but now you're just a crazy old man. You lost it. This isn't Germany, and Singleton isn't Hitler."

"Don't be so sure, Bill. The president has a lot of power, and once he starts using it to increase his influence—"

"I said there's a way!" Landry screamed. "It's on Congress. They need to do it. They need to investigate."

Bowen responded softly, "They can't, Bill, because you and your soldiers are defending the murderer who is killing them one by one. If you want the government to operate as it should, lock Singleton up so the Congressmen can investigate. Give them a chance."

"Stop calling me Bill!" Landry yelled. "I'm a general of the United States Army. You should understand the respect. You were one."

"I'll show you the respect you deserve as soon as you start leading in a way that deserves respect, instead of carrying out the orders of an evil emperor."

Jake saw that the eyes of the other soldiers were wandering more now than at the beginning. The guy on the left with the rifle was now glancing sideways at his general. The general's aide, with the glasses, looked like he was going to wet his pants. The officer on the left of the general glanced into Jake's eyes.

"What options did you bring us down here to discuss?" Landry asked, bringing his temper back down.

General Bowen said, "We would first like to start by inviting any of you six," he gestured forward "to step forward and join us as we restore the government of the United States of America to the people, to the citizens."

Landry scoffed. "You're kidding."

"That applies to you too, Bill. Join us, and sleep well tonight. You don't want to be like those German generals we hunted down after we got Hitler, do you? Don't you want to be on the right side?"

Jake saw that all eyes on the other side were darting around.

Bowen motioned them forward. "Any of you? Now's your chance. You don't need to die knowing you killed innocent Americans to protect a modern-day Hitler. Join us."

Landry's response was even, but forceful. "They know they'd be hanged as traitors like you. They're not stupid."

Jake couldn't believe Landry had just said that. He had actually threatened his people not to defect. Was he panicked enough that he thought he needed to do that? Jake smiled slightly.

The officer next to Jake caught his eye again, but when Jake looked at him, his eyes darted away.

Bowen continued in his inviting manner. "If any of you change your minds later, and want to stop killing Americans and instead save the country, just run across the lawn toward us, waving your hat over your head. We'll pass the word. They won't shoot at you."

Landry erupted again. "Nobody is going to surrender to a bunch of rednecks when they're supposed to be defending the White House. Who do you think you are? Do you have anything else to discuss before this ridiculous meeting is over?"

Bowen ignored the general, and spoke to the other five. "You go back and tell your buddies that my offer is open indefinitely. You don't need to die defending Singleton. If you think he's a scoundrel, join us."

Landry motioned for his men to follow. "This is over." But after taking two steps, he turned back to get the last word. "Bowen, Jolley, this is your last chance. Disassemble these idiots, or a bunch of them are going to die. This doesn't need to happen." He turned, and they began walking away.

General Bowen called out to them. "Any time fellas. Wave your hat and join us!"

When Landry's team reached the fountain, Bowen called out to them again with the bullhorn, so all the soldiers could hear. "Our offer stands, wave your hat in the air as you run toward us, and we won't shoot. You don't need to kill Americans for a dictator if you don't want to."

* * *

After the meeting, General Bowen led them through the crowd, under the trees on the west side of the Ellipse, then south, almost to the Washington Monument. He led them to a green camouflage shade canopy with six folding chairs underneath. Men sat in a circle talking. When General Bowen and General Jolley arrived, three men scrambled out of their chairs, relinquishing them to the generals. The generals sat in two of the seats, and joined three other men who had remained seated. Clive was motioned to take the last seat.

General Bowen pulled his chair back to make more space and motioned on the grass next to them. "Bart? Jake?"

Jake guessed the man who held the white flag up was named Bart, because he sat down on the grass where the general had pointed. Jake sat next to him. Jake leaned back against a cooler.

One of the men who had remained sitting when they arrived spoke first.

"Well?"

General Bowen motioned to General Jolley. "I did all the talking down there, so I'll let Dexter give you the rundown."

General Jolley gave a summary of the conference.

"So he got mad?" General Toolson asked, raising his eyebrows.

"Oh yeah, a couple times. He was yelling to the point that his guys got a little nervous."

Toolson sat up. "What do you mean, nervous?"

"You know, their eyes started darting around, shuffling their feet, looking down."

Toolson looked around, even to Jake and Bart on the grass. "Any of you guys have anything to add? Observations?"

Jake thought General Jolley was doing just fine, and he really didn't want to say anything.

Clive spoke up. "They glanced at General Landry a few times like they were afraid Landry was going to blow up. I think they could all tell General Bowen was playing him, and frankly, I think they were surprised to be watching it—a little afraid of how he might react."

This seemed to satisfy Toolson, so Jolley continued the description.

"So, Landry starts pressing for what specific military tactics we wanted to discuss and Sherm invites them," he smiled at Bowen, "to join our cause, like we discussed."

"And?"

Jolley smiled. "It was better than we hoped. Sherm knocked it out of the park."

"But none of them did? None of them took you up on it?"

Jolley responded. "No, but they wanted to."

"How can you tell?"

Jolley grimaced. "Hard to explain. Nobody took a step forward or anything, but you could just feel it." He looked around at the others for help, including Bart and Jake.

General Bowen sat up and pointed to the two men on the grass. "Do you agree with General Jolley?"

Jake and Bart looked at each other.

Bart spoke first. "Yes, I agree."

"Why?" Toolson prompted.

Bart looked at Jolley for affirmation. "It's like the general said. It was more like a feeling."

"Jake?" General Bowen prompted.

Jake shrugged. "I agree, too," he said sheepishly.

Toolson leaned toward Jake. "How do you know you didn't misread it? Maybe they were just done talking, or maybe they needed to go the bathroom? What leads you to that conclusion?"

Jake was overwhelmed. Why was Toolson focusing on him? He was just a construction guy, a hack with a hammer. He looked up at Clive, and Clive gave him a subtle nod. Jake tried to remember how it had gone down, when General Bowen had invited them. He remembered how Landry had flinched at the comparison to Hitler.

"Well, Landry was scared, enough to threaten them." Jake looked at Clive for support. "He made a point of saying anybody who joined us would hang with us, or something like that."

Toolson pressed. "So, you think they were actually considering?"

Jake looked around for support, but noticed they were all waiting for him to talk. "Yeah. I do."

"How many, of the six?"

"All of them," Jake answered.

"All of them, but General Landry?" Toolson clarified.

"No, all of them," Jake said. "Including the general."

Jolley sat up. "You think Landry was considering joining us?" he said skeptically.

Jake nodded. "Yes, I do. It was the reference to Hitler, about whether Landry would fight to the end for Hitler, just because it was his job. That got to him. He was backpedaling like crazy then. He knew he was on the wrong side. He kept lecturing us that there were other ways, but he didn't believe it."

Toolson pressed, "But you said he was considering defecting."

Jake thought about that. "Maybe he wasn't. But if there was a magic door where those guys could just duck in, without anyone actually seeing them cross sides, I think all of them would go through."

General Bowen nodded. "I think Jake hit it on the head. They all wanted out of their situation, if not wanting to actually join our side, even Landry. But there was too much pressure; it was too big of a decision to cross right then."

"So, what's the net effect of our little conference? Did it do any good?" Toolson asked.

Jolley's head went down, then Bowen's.

Jake blurted out. "Absolutely!"

All eyes turned on him.

Jake tried to find his words. "It was like the general planted a seed. Actually, a virus is a better way of saying it. He put a lot of doubts in their heads. They're gonna talk. It'll spread. The whole unit is going to be talking about what happens when soldiers start running across the grass waving their hats. A lot of guys are going to hesitate. They're all going to wonder if they're defending a modern-day Hitler. There's gonna be intentional misses, slow re-loading, and re-checking orders, and all kinds of other conscious and subconscious inefficiencies. When the battle gets ugly, people will definitely be running across the grass waving their hats. For every guy that runs, there will be three others who wish they had the guts. You can guarantee it. The only problem is how to prevent them from getting shot in the back by their own guys. But if enough run, it won't matter, cause the whole thing is gonna collapse."

CHAPTER 21

Jake was happy to be back with the guys. He had spent close to an hour telling Mario, Noah, and Troy about the conference with the other side and the follow-up meeting with the generals. There had been many questions and many discussions about what it all would mean. Mario was optimistic that there would be defectors; Troy was pessimistic. Noah seemed not to care.

Clive had not returned with Jake to the team but had stayed with the generals for more strategy talk. Jake was glad to leave. He had shown that once his mouth was open, he had a hard time shutting it. Even though the generals had acted like they appreciated his input, it was obvious they were happy to see him go. Jake wondered whether Clive now regretted involving Jake in the two meetings. Maybe General Bowen's next assignment for Jake would be on the front lines during the next skirmish.

Troy sighed loudly, sat up, and aimed his rifle at a cloud in the sky. "What is it?" Mario asked.

Troy kept his eyes on his gun sights. "I'm going stir crazy here."

"Take a nap," Mario said.

"I took six naps already."

"Take another one. We need to be well rested."

"I am well rested, believe me. I could run a marathon right now. What are we waiting for?" He motioned back toward the Washington Monument. "We got our reinforcements. We got plenty of bodies. Everybody's here! I just talked to some guys from Wyoming."

The comment about Wyoming was in jest, and they all knew it. But Troy was right. So many reinforcements were arriving from other cities that now most of the newcomers couldn't even get close. They were stuck a half-mile or more from the White House. Looking south from their position, it looked like the lawn around the Washington Monument was as full as the Ellipse. And what did that mean for the men on the north of the White House, or west, or east? At least the south side had grass. The other spokes of the attack were stuck in city streets.

"I'm sure that's what the generals are talking about right now," Jake said.

"Well, I'd like to know what's planned, and when," Troy said. "Cause if we're not planning anything for a few hours, I might just sneak out and get a pizza."

"Yeah, and some beer," Mario said.

Jake thought it was amazing that they were only a hundred fifty yards from the enemy and their tanks, and that only that morning they had watched hundreds of men get shot, including one of their own, but with the slow hours ticking by, and with nothing to do, factoring in the confidence of infinite reinforcements arriving, there was a wave of casualness moving through the camp like a fog. Jake hoped the lack of concern wouldn't bite them too bad later.

A loud electronic chirp came from the White House, accompanied by low background static. The whole group sat up.

"This is General William Landry. I'm speaking to all of you who surround the White House."

The voice was clear where Jake's group was sitting. It came from the direction of the White House. It was very loud, obviously they had turned it up as high as it would go, because the general's voice was clipped and slightly distorted on some of the loudest syllables.

"We had a very friendly meeting with your leadership an hour ago. I met with a Mr. Bowen and a Mr. Jolley. Very nice men."

Jake knew that not acknowledging them as generals was intentional, done to demean their authority.

"As we discussed in that meeting, we have superior position, training, and firepower. We are in the right, defending the president. Please note, this is America, and we are all bound to obey the laws."

Jake heard a guy yell, "How come Singleton can murder then?"

Landry obviously didn't hear him, because he didn't even hesitate. "In America, we have a process to handle issues we disagree with. We call our congressmen."

"Mine's dead!" someone yelled.

"And Congress has the authority to investigate and correct, if necessary, any issues. So, from our meeting with your leadership, it was decided that you should return to your homes, and there will be no further deaths. Your concerns will be investigated and resolved as expediently as possible."

Jake heard the electronic static extinguish. A loud rumble of crowd noise erupted as a million rebels started as many simultaneous discussions. Jake saw heads turning across the whole expansion of the Ellipse. Many stood and looked around.

Jake heard three or four gunshots, none very close, and imagined a couple guys taking wild shots at the White House. But no response came from the Army. Which reminded Jake how precarious their position was. Just a random gunshot, and a quick response, could escalate in a fraction of a second to a full-blown battle. Obviously, Landry was wise to that possibility, and he had his team conditioned to not return fire unless commanded to do so. Otherwise, a million rebels would be firing right now.

Jake heard pieces of uncountable conversations. ". . . we going home? Why don't we just charge them? How did we agree to . . . never should have come. . . least I'm not going to die. Good, I was hungry. . . bluffing! . . .guy sounds like a jerk."

It was obvious the people around him needed leadership. Jake didn't feel like much of a leader, but he had attended the conference. He had met with the generals, and Landry was lying about them agreeing to go home.

Jake stood and cupped his hands around his mouth. "We never said that!" Jake yelled. "We never agreed to leave! He's lying."

A crowd of men surrounded him and barraged him with questions.

"Is it still a go?"

"What was said?"

"What did we agree to?"

"Are we supposed to stay or go?"

Jake held his hands out. "We never agreed to anything! We told them if they wanted to defect to our side, we would take them."

"Then, why did he say . . ."

"What is the plan?"

"Why aren't we hearing anything?"

Jake held out his hands, placating the crowd around him. "I expect word from the generals soon." He pointed at the White House. "Landry was bluffing." Jake pointed around at the crowd in chaos. "He wanted to cause exactly what you are seeing. He wanted to confuse us."

Jake turned as they heard more isolated gunshots. Again, there was no response from the soldiers.

He continued. "The generals will let us know the plan when we need it. We'll know soon."

Jake decided the only way this was going to end was if he gave them something to do, to distract them. "Pass the word, 'Wait for orders from the generals. Ignore the propaganda from the White House.'"

That did the trick. The men around him turned the other direction and passed the word. Jake heard the words, "generals" and "White House" propagate through the crowd.

Troy stood next to Jake. "You're good. That was good BS."

Mario and Noah stood next to them as they watched the crowd stabilize. Jake couldn't take credit for calming the crowd. He was sure there were many others that had said things. But the crowd did settle, and many sat back down. They still heard isolated gunshots though, including one that sounded like it was less than fifty feet from them.

* * *

At 6:50 p.m. Jake was eating some of the provisions from his bag. The sun was getting low in the western sky. The others around him were eating as well. Jake didn't know whether to eat his fill or save some for later. How long would they be out here, just tonight, or days?

Jake had wanted to try communicating with Monica again, but all the cell phones were showing "No Service." At first they had discussed that it might be the system being overwhelmed, but now the general consensus was that the towers had been shut down. The theory was that the White House didn't want the rebels to be able to strategize with each other or with rebels still arriving from other cities. Jakes' battery was almost gone anyway.

Also his water was getting low. About an hour before, Troy had taken a walk by himself. He returned a half hour later and told them about a storm drain on 17th street, in front of the Red Cross headquarters, which had been unofficially converted to a latrine. He said it smelled pretty rank. Most of them were just pissing in it, but a few had squatted right there and did their thing. "Oh the ravages of war," he said. Jake, Mario, and Noah had taken turns going over to the storm drain to add to the golden waterfalls.

They had heard more audio messages from Landry as well, about every half hour for a while. But they had not made nearly the same impact as the first. With each message, the yelling and cat calling from the crowd increased. Landry's broadcast around six o'clock had the whole crowd of rebels booing. It was so loud that Landry could not even be understood. He finally stopped talking. The crowd clapped and cheered. That had been Landry's last message.

After that, the crowd had relaxed. "Bored" was probably a better word. Many slept again in the late afternoon. Many of the unlucky ones without shade, which was the majority, had taken off their shirts and draped them over their heads to fight the sun. Jake felt very thankful for the tree they were under.

Clive had made a brief appearance, just after Landry's last call. He had just dropped by to check on them. He said there would be an announcement around seven. In fact, he had left his radio with Troy so they would hear it. They pressed him for a hint of what it might be, but he told them they would have to wait like everyone else.

After he left, the rumor about an announcement at seven had rippled through the crowd. They had heard it from others around them. It had galvanized the crowd. Finally, they had something to look forward to, even if it was only an update. Everyone knew they could endure that long.

After that, time had slowed even more. Men were constantly checking their wristwatches, and counting the minutes. Now, finally, they had only a few more minutes to wait. Jake wondered what they would say. Would it be a full frontal attack, storm the gates? Or maybe, they would tell all the forces to fire at the tanks. Unthinkably, maybe they would tell everyone to go home; although, Jake thought there was very little possibility of that.

Jake glanced at his watch and saw they still had three more minutes to wait.

CHAPTER 22

The radio in Troy's hand came to life. "Hello, visitors. We hope you've had a nice day touring our Nation's Capital."

It was the same casual upbeat voice they had heard in the morning.

"We're sorry to have to tell you this, but not everyone is being invited to the party at the White House this evening. If you are invited, you will be told. We would like to ask the rest of you to please not shoot off your firecrackers when the party starts. I promise you, that when the big party starts, you will all be invited, and will all get to shoot off your fireworks."

Jake knew it meant there was some sort of focused attack planned, and they were being asked to stand down while it happened. The radio had said the party would be in the evening. What did that mean?

"Regarding when the party will start," the radio said, answering Jake's question. "Do not show up early. Nobody likes an anxious guest. You'll all know when to arrive, I promise. Oh, and don't be surprised if there are some hectic preparations for the party. Don't confuse that with the party itself. Now, the rest of you kick back, and don't be jealous. Your time will come."

The radio went silent.

"Geez," Troy said, staring at the radio. "Where did they get that guy?"

Mario added. "And why do they need encrypted radios if they're always speaking in code?"

Jake glanced around and saw the crowd was mostly standing up now and glancing around as he was. When he looked west, the sun was in his eyes.

Then gunfire erupted not far from them, to the north. It seemed like it came from around the buildings just west of the White House. The gunfire was heavy for moments in one place, then another. Together, it sounded like short quick battles in multiple places at the same time. Jake heard a few explosions and saw smoke rise. Then more gunshots could be heard, some of these were muted, which he interpreted as being from inside the buildings. The gunshots tapered off, only occasionally being heard.

"Damn! I wish I was over there!" Troy said

"You'll get your chance," Jake reminded him.

"I'm tired of waiting," Troy said.

"Me too," Mario said.

They continued to hear gunfire, but it was sporadic and mostly muffled inside the buildings.

"Look, they're on the roof." A guy was pointing up at the huge French architecture building just west of the White House.

Jake and the others had to move out from under the trees through the crowd to see.

"Look at 'em all!" someone said.

"That's the Eisenhower Building," someone else said.

When Jake got a look, he saw men pouring onto the roof of the French building from multiple places. They were rebels, and they crowded over to the edge of the roof and aimed at the soldiers.

"Look at the tanks," someone yelled.

Jake looked and saw the turrets were turning to the west. He had to shield his eyes as he looked because the sun was almost down in the west. In the mean time, the men kept pouring onto the roof. Jake wondered if it might collapse.

They heard a muffled explosion, and a single flare was fired over the Ellipse toward the White House. It was red and left an arced trail of smoke in the air.

Immediately, to the northwest of Jake, gunfire erupted. Not just from the men on the roof of the French-looking building, or from the roof of other buildings across 17th, but from thousands of guns all along the streets west of the White House. It looked like a coordinated attack from all points west.

The Army responded, firing aggressively at the rooftops. He saw men get shot and fall off the roof.

Mario yelled into his ear. "The soldiers are firing into the sun."

Jake looked at the sunset and realized Mario was right. The attack had been planned at sunset intentionally, to blind the enemy with glare.

Jake saw more men fall from the roof. The soldiers were still having some success in spite of the glare. However, new rebels were pouring onto the roof. They could replace the fallen rebels faster than the troops could kill them.

Jake looked down at the troops and saw chaos. The men on the roof had a perfect downward angle on them, and were raining bullets down. Jake saw an explosion in the middle of the troops, causing bodies to fly in all directions. Looked like Noah wasn't the only rebel with a grenade launcher.

Two of the tanks fired at the top of the building. Showers of brick and debris exploded in all directions as the big holes were left in the roofline. But Jake saw more rebels climb immediately out of the holes, and within seconds every available space was covered with men again. From a distance, it looked like bees or ants. You could step on them and kill a few, but there were always more where they came from.

"Hats!" Mario yelled.

Jake looked back at the White House and saw five soldiers running across the South Lawn toward them, waving their hats. As Jake feared, they were fired upon from the rear, and two went down. The other three sprinted toward the south gate, and Jake was afraid they would also be tagged, but they weren't. It was hard to tell with the crowd standing in front of them, but it looked like somehow the rebels pushed down the gates and swarmed out onto the lawn to envelope the defectors.

The tanks continued firing at the roof of the French building until the roof nearest the White House was nothing but rubble, but the rebels kept climbing on top of the rubble and maintained their advantage. Jake saw two more explosions down in the troops with devastating results. Bodies were hurled in all directions. Another half-dozen soldiers defected, waving hats, and like before, they were fired upon. This time only one shot connected. The rest missed.

Jake felt a moment of pride. There were far too many misses to be random—some misses had to be on purpose. He wondered how much of the bad aim had been caused by General Bowen's virus, or had the soldiers themselves just grown a conscience about firing on their fellow soldiers? It didn't really matter, did it? As long as the misses were occurring. Jake wondered how many intentional misses had occurred shooting at the men on the roof.

"Why can't we fire?" Troy yelled over the sounds of the battle.

No one answered, but Jake felt the same compulsion, and could feel many in the crowd did, too. The turrets were pointed west into the sunset. The soldiers were focused west into the sunset. That left the south flank exposed.

Then rebels could be seen on the grounds. They must have pushed over the west gates and swarmed onto the lawn. They could be seen swinging their weapons at the soldiers. In the dimming light, Jake could see the flames from barrels as rebels and troops fired on each other from close quarters.

"Ahhhh!" Troy screamed. "Let's go!"

"We'll get our chance!" Mario called out.

The battle continued as the rebels kept coming and coming from the west side. Jake was sure there were huge casualties from both sides. Where were these guys from? Philadelphia? Baltimore? Maybe even other Pennsylvanians like Harrisburg or Hershey. Whoever they were, they were fearless.

And then a second flare was fired over the Ellipse. This one was green. And like a light switch flicking off, the rebels retreated. They stopped fighting and disappeared back into the trees west of the White House. All firing stopped from the rooftops, and the rebels disappeared, climbing back down in the building. The troops kept firing for a while, but the gunfire slowed and finally stopped as the soldiers realized the rebels had fallen back and were no longer a threat.

The air became shockingly quiet again at the cease-fire, like all the sound had been sucked out of the air. The sun was no longer visible, having set below the horizon. Jake wondered how long ago it had set. The battle had started just at sunset, while the sun was just above the buildings. But how long had it lasted? Time was all distorted. The battle was incredibly brutal, and watching it from so close, it seemed to go on for an hour. But that was unlikely. It wasn't fully dark yet, so the battle hadn't even taken a half hour.

Jake heard men screaming and knew there were terrible casualties on both sides. He imagined the scenes on the sidewalks west of the White House, up on the top floors of the French building, and up on the South Lawn in the midst of the troops. He imagined the blood, the dying, and the dead. He imagined the widows back home and the fatherless kids. Americans shooting Americans, was it worth it? For either side?

"Wow!" Mario said. "That was amazing."

"Why'd we stop?" Troy asked in frustration. "This could be over if they'd let us storm 'em."

Jake couldn't answer that. And no one else could either. They just stared at the South Lawn and let the question hang in the air.

CHAPTER 23

Fifteen minutes had passed since the battle ended, and in that time the sky had gone completely dark. The sounds of men screaming in pain had dissipated considerably, meaning they had either died, passed out, or been given some sort of medication or treatment to help with their misery. In the lull, it would be expected that the crowd would be seated again, but almost everyone remained standing. If they felt like Jake, they were too worked up, their adrenaline was still pumping, and their stomachs were too tight.

Out of nowhere, Clive appeared.

"Are you guys ready?" he asked.

Jake didn't know how to answer that. He had just witnessed the most brutal thing he had ever imagined. Could he do that? Yet, his adrenaline said go, and a huge part of him wanted to shove over the south fence and charge up the South Lawn bellowing like a warrior.

"Is it our turn?" Noah asked.

"In a while," Clive answered.

"What are we waiting for?" Troy asked.

"Another chit chat," Clive responded.

"When?" Mario said.

"Any minute now," Clive answered. He was staring at the fence.

They all joined Clive watching the fence. Jake knew from last time that it was crowded, and it would take, even for the general, to work his way through the crowd.

"Hello!" It was General Bowen's voice again from the bullhorn. The sound carried amazingly well in the night air. The crowd quieted noticeably.

"General Landry, can you hear me?"

The general and the crowd waited for an answer. They waited for a long time, an awkwardly long time, almost a full minute.

There was a chirp, then the background static from the audio system. "I can hear you," Landry responded.

"Glad to hear you're okay," Bowen said. "I was getting worried there for a second."

"I'm fine!" Landry spat. "It's you who needs to worry. You'll be hanged by morning for treason and for leading this bunch of traitors against the president. I warned you."

Bowen was unaffected by the anger or the threats. He spoke in his smooth, gentle voice, "I would like to invite anyone up there defending this rogue president to come down now and join us. Just walk away. Wave your hats—"

"Nobody is going to desert the Army for your thugs, Bowen."

Bowen continued, "You saw during the battle that a few honorable men came and joined us. They told us of your scare tactics. They're happy to be fighting for the right side now."

"They're traitors, and they will hang!" Landry barked.

Bowen said, "You just got a small taste of our resolve. We now invite all of you to drop your weapons and walk away—let us get what we came for. It will save thousands of lives and preserve thousands of American families if you do."

"If you think we're going to walk away and let you traitors loot the White House and murder our president, you're crazy."

"We promise no harm will come to Singleton, but he will answer for his crimes. It's time to restore America to the people, Bill. We can do this the hard way, or the easy. But I got a million patriots here that are not going to stand by and watch this president piss our country down the hole any longer."

The crowd erupted in cheers. It took a while to taper off enough for either general to speak again.

Bowen spoke first. "What's it gonna be, Bill?

"You address me as General Landry of the United States Army! And our answer is 'absolutely no!' You traitors can go to hell, and if you attack again, that's exactly where we're going to blow you!"

This time the crowd erupted with a long boo that lasted almost a minute.

When the sound dissipated, Bowen continued. "One other option, Bill. Send Singleton out here, and we'll take him into custody while a full investigation is launched on all his murders."

"That's not gonna happen."

"Okay, Bill. We gave you a chance. One last invitation to any soldiers—come on down."

"Nobody is coming!" Landry said.

Then the air was quiet again. Jake watched the South Lawn to see if any defectors would try to run across the lawn waving their hats, but he guessed they were afraid of getting a bullet in the back. Some of their soldiers would likely fight to the death, like Landry, not because it was right, but because that's what they were told to do. Some probably even believed Singleton was in the right. But he knew many were stuck in the middle, being told to kill people they didn't want to kill. Bowen had just uploaded more of the virus, and Jake guessed it was only a matter of time before the system crashed.

* * *

After it was over, they had tried to get Clive to give them some hints about what was planned, but he kept pointing to the radio he left with Troy, telling them to monitor it. Before he left, he did tell them one thing.

"If I wanted to be inside the White House for the final scene, I wouldn't want to be in the first wave; I might hang back and try to be in the second wave."

Then he left, most likely to accompany General Bowen back to the command center.

So they had waited. Then waited some more. It had been hours since Bowen's amplified argument with Landry. Troy finally handed the radio to Jake because he was tired of holding it expectantly. He stood and paced in the small space they had under the tree, his long hair swaying as he nervously walked back and forth.

Just after midnight, the radio finally came to life.

"Hello, tourists. I hope you've all enjoyed your vacation in the Capital. Don't go home early, because for the finale we have a special treat, a private tour of the White House. We pulled all the stops for this one. Unlike most tours, you will have full VIP access to everything, the west wing, the Oval Office, all the grand ballrooms, the fancy private meeting rooms and offices, and even the private family quarters of the Singletons. You should be happy, because no one gets a tour like this. Just a few tidbits, the White House is a national treasure, so don't break anything or steal the ashtrays. President Singleton will be coming home with us, but make sure he is unharmed. Everybody else, including the families and staff, should not be harmed or molested. Be compassionate. Unless they pull a gun on you." He laughed.

"Finally, because there are so many of us, we're going to do the tour in a couple shifts. The first red light means the guys on the north. The second red means the guys on the east. Then the final red means the guys on the south, and you guys on the west, who already attended a party, can join them if you still feel like partying. Just remember, we want the White House to be in great condition when the next family takes residence, so please conduct yourselves with respect. Oh, and when you see the green light, the tours are over. No loitering around. Go home and tell your families about your visit. Lastly, thank you for your courageous service. The country owes you a great debt."

The radio went silent.

"Damn!" Troy yelled. "I'm so sick of waiting."

"How long do you think," Jake asked, "before we'll go?"

"Who knows," Mario said. "It seems like all we do is wait."

Troy said. "And, if we're last, they'll already have him. We'll miss the whole thing."

Jake asked. "Do you really think they'll get in, the north and the east, before we even engage?"

"Absolutely!" Mario said. "You heard the general. We got a million people here. They could drop an atomic bomb on us, and we'd still get to him."

Jake laughed at the joke before asking his question. "Were you guys surprised about the order to take Singleton alive?"

Troy said, "Yeah. And I disagree with it. I think we should lynch him, hang him from the Grand Staircase."

Mario said, "What makes anybody think we can get him alive? It probably won't be possible."

Jake thought Mario had a point. With thousands of armed rebels shooting around corners and engaging with Secret Service, how possible was it to retrieve him unharmed? It seemed unlikely.

They were interrupted by a red flare arcing from the Ellipse to the White House. The sound of gunfire from the north side followed, but it was muffled by the White House itself. Since Jake's party could not see what was happening on the north side, it was frustrating. Jake heard the loud percussions of tanks, which confirmed a suspicion Jake had all day, that there were tanks on the north side as well. Unlike the south side though, the tanks on the north side would be firing directly into city buildings as the bulk of metropolitan Washington D.C. was north of the White House. As Jake heard the tanks fire over and over, he wondered if they were being commanded to fire low, or let 'er rip, and destroy the city and risk civilian casualties in order to protect Singleton.

After listening to the battle rage on, it became increasingly frustrating to not see what was happening. Who was winning? Had the rebels made any progress? Had they pushed over the fences and stormed the north lawn? Or were the troops annihilating them? Jake pictured the north streets, stuffed with rebels, swarming toward the north fence. But what if the tanks had them covered? What if the tanks were killing them as fast as they came? Maybe the rebels were hunkered down in the streets, out of sight of the tanks.

Jake started to feel sick that they were losing. What a loss of life this was turning out to be. How many people would have died in this mini civil war? A hundred thousand? A half million?

A second red flare was shot over the White House from the same place. It arced lazily through the sky, trailing smoke behind it. Guns erupted from the east side. The White House troops on the South Lawn responded. In the dark, the fire could be seen exploding out of the barrels of the guns with each shot. The turrets of the tanks swiveled to Jake's right, and they heard huge percussions as tanks began firing on the attackers.

"Get ready!" Troy yelled. "We're next!"

Jake lifted his M16 vertical, felt the magazine with his hand, and fingered the safety. He left the safety on for the moment. He saw Noah load a grenade into his launcher. Jake wasn't sure whether it was a gas grenade or a high impact. Troy and Mario both held their weapons ready. Jake reached down and lifted the box of ammunition, so he was ready to run.

The gunfire from both the north and east continued. Jake saw rebels running onto the South Lawn from the east. Obviously, they had broken down the fence. He saw a dozen small flames of fire arc though the air at the troops, then explode into fire where they landed. Two landed on the tanks and left fires burning on the turrets. Another volley of the fires came arcing in.

"They're throwing Molotov cocktails at 'em!" Mario yelled.

They watched as the fires kept flying through the air at the troops. The tanks fired over and over. Jake remembered that morning when each shot from the tanks mowed down huge swaths of men. He wondered how many were getting caught in each of those shots. Like the north, each eastward shot from the tanks would eventually impact city buildings, and Jake wondered what damage they were likely causing, architectural and civilian. He seemed to recall the Treasury Building was east of the White House.

In the midst of the battle, an Army defector came running down the South Lawn, waving his hat. Then came a dozen more. This time, Jake saw none shot down. After that, many more followed.

"Give us the damn red light!" Troy screamed.

Jake could see the silhouette of Troy's bayonet on the end of his gun.

CHAPTER 24

Finally, just when Jake thought his heart couldn't beat any faster, the final red flare was launched. The south crowd let out a shout and pushed forward. Troy and Noah disappeared. They were gone. It was just him and Mario.

He heard gunshots all around him and ducked. What the hell were they thinking? He crouched to avoid friendly fire. The mass of men pushed forward slowly. There were too many people in front clogging the area. Finally, up ahead, Jake saw shadows of men running up the South Lawn. They must have pushed over the south fence, because all of a sudden the area in front of Jake became wide open, and men started to run forward.

Jake remembered what Clive had said about the first wave, and let the more aggressive rebels push past him. He kept his eye on Mario next to him and jogged slowly forward, the M16 in one hand, the ammo box in the other. He stumbled and almost fell when he stepped off the curb onto the street. He recovered and kept jogging, letting men speed past him. Ahead he could see more silhouettes sprinting up the South Lawn. Several rebels in front of them tripped and fell, their guns hitting the ground. So, Jake carefully jumped from the street up onto the curb. A man hit something hard below his waist, and Jake remembered the waist-high poles to prevent cars from crashing through the fence. Jake dodged through them. The wrought-iron fence was down flat, pushed over by the sheer force of thousands of men. Jake and Mario ran over it. They were on the South Lawn.

He looked up just in time to see a tank turret, with fire burning on top of it, swivel to aim due south. It was aimed slightly to his right, so he kept moving. The tank's blast was staggeringly loud, and he knew hundreds of men had just been obliterated, but he didn't look. Machine gun fire dropped men just to Mario's left. Grass, dirt, and debris flew through the air. Jake and Mario dove for cover and landed behind some bushes behind the fountain. They were joined by others. More debris landed on them as they took gunfire. Jake ducked below the rock, or marble, or whatever it was.

The Army machine gun had blocked the whole section to the left side of the fountain. They were mowing down all the rebels trying to run up that portion of the lawn. There was literally a wall of bodies there, and Jake felt lucky to have been missed. Every time the rebels tried to move through that section, they were gunned down. Jake looked ahead to see where the gunner was and found him between two of the tanks. It was easy to identify the fire spitting from the barrel.

Jake knew that if he fired on the spot with the full-auto M16, he would draw attention to himself, but how could he not? The rebels were being annihilated. He lifted the gun slightly to indicate his intentions to Mario, then pointed for Mario to get down. Mario hunkered behind a marble pedestal and smiled to signal he was ready.

Jake moved the safety to FULL, positioned himself as prone as he could get behind the fountain, put the peep sight on the barrel of spitting fire, and pulled the trigger. He dumped all thirty rounds into the spot, then ducked.

Chips of marble and dust rained down on them as the troops responded, but so far the marble fountain gave them enough protection. He saw some of the rebels storm up the lawn, taking advantage of the distraction Jake had given them. Jake shucked his backpack and traded the spent magazine for a full one. Mario grabbed the other three loaded magazines and held them ready for Jake. Jake took aim again and unloaded the full thirty into the same place. He had no sooner ducked below the rock than the army's response came in a rain of marble chunks and dust.

Mario screamed. "Move, now!"

Jake didn't hesitate. His two volleys of bullets had made his spot a target. He obeyed his partner, and they began crawling over three or four guys on their right.

They were both thrown farther away from their original position by a huge impact. Chunks of marble were hurled past, barely missing them. Obviously one of the tanks had fired into the very spot they had occupied a moment before.

Jake took a second to get his bearings. He retrieved the M16 from the grass in front of him. His pack was underneath him. The box of ammo and the remaining loaded magazines? He had no idea. Then Mario held up the ammo and the magazines, smiling. Jake shook his head in amazement.

They raised their eyes above the fountain and assessed the situation. The rapid fire from the Army machine gun had resumed, and the lawn west of the fountain was clogged with bodies again. None of the tank turrets were aimed directly at them, so they had obviously moved on to richer targets.

They couldn't get up and run to the left, or they would be mowed down by machine gun fire like the others. They could go right, around the back of the fountain, and join the crowd storming up the lawn from that side. Or Jake could use the other three magazines in the M16 and try again for the machine gunner. Jake had already fired sixty rounds into the spot, without inflicting any damage. Maybe the Army had some sort of shield in front of the gun. Where was Noah with his grenades? Jake decided to fire at it again. This time he would move the barrel around a little, and maybe get some bullets a little higher or lower than they expected.

He replaced the empty magazine with one of the three from Mario, took aim, and pulled the trigger. Sparks flew from around his target as some of his bullets hit metal. Before he ducked below the fountain, he saw the machine gun still firing uninterrupted. Damn! What was it going to take?

Mario reached for the M16. He exchanged magazines and took a turn. But his luck was no better. Were they just wasting bullets? There was only one loaded magazine left, should they use it? Or save it? Maybe the last time would be different.

He replaced the empty magazine with his last full one. While he was still weighing his options, there was an explosion and a ball of fire right behind the gunner, and the machine gun finally stopped. He didn't know if it was Noah, but it was the same kind of impact as the grenade earlier that morning at the barriers.

Jake heard some yells from rebels on his left, and a pack of them took the long-awaited opportunity and charged toward the White House. Mario pointed, and Jake nodded.

He stuffed the empty magazines in his pack, shrugged it onto his shoulder, grabbed the ammo box, and headed after Mario. They had only gone twenty yards, before the gunner opened fire again. Half a dozen men went down on Jake and Mario's right. They dove left and hit the ground. They crawled forward and took position behind some fallen comrades. They were in a worse position than before.

Jake watched the continuous fire from the gun and thought that as soon as the smoke cleared from the explosion a moment before, someone else had probably run in to take his fallen friend's place. He watched the tanks fire over and over south into the Ellipse. So many dead. This battle was a killing zone, but nothing seemed to weaken Landry and his troops. Jake didn't see how it could change unless the army ran out of bullets. Even with a million rebels, how could they hope to make an impact against tanks and heavy machine guns?

He wondered about Noah and Troy. He had only known them for twenty-four hours, but they were a family now. They had been in front of him in the charge to the White House. There was almost no chance they were still alive. He assumed Clive was back with the generals, but who knew if they were safe, especially after all the tanks firing back into the Ellipse.

From their prone position in the grass, Jake watched the battle for a few seconds. His M16 was ready to fire, but where could he make an impact? Then he saw a tank turret rotate toward them. Could they know he was here, alive, with an M16, hiding? He tried to flatten himself into the grass. He and Mario were sitting ducks. But the turret rotated past them. It rotated clockwise until it was pointed at the White House. It aimed down slightly.

Mario held his hands up in a "What the hell?" motion.

Gunfire began ricocheting in sparks off the turret. Landry's guys were firing at their own tank. The tank bucked and fired into the first floor of the White House, leaving a gaping hole and a pile of debris.

It was as if the Army had forgotten about the millions of rebels, because they started firing on each other. The machine gun that had caused so much havoc with the rebels went quiet. Another tank swiveled, aimed at the rogue one, and fired. The rogue tank started smoking. A third tank swiveled and aimed at the one that shot the first, and fired. Smoke poured out of the second. Then Jake saw a large group of soldiers jump over the barriers, waving their hats.

Jake gripped Mario's arm and pointed to the White House. Mario nodded, and the two started sprinted toward the White House along with many others. They passed Army troops running the opposite way. They were almost to the line of tanks when he thought about the box of ammunition back on the grass. He grabbed Mario's arm, stopped, and looked back.

"What?" Mario yelled over the gunfire.

Jake motioned like he was holding the can by the handle.

Mario looked back at thousands of rebels running toward them, grimaced, and shook his head.

Jake nodded and the two men started running again.

As they ran, Jake switched the safety from FULL to FIRE, which meant from then on, when he pulled the trigger, he would get only one bullet, just like everyone else. When they arrived at the concrete barrier, bodies of fallen soldiers were stacked behind it. They had no choice but to step on them. The gunfire behind the barrier had almost ceased, and soldiers were pointing weapons at other soldiers with their hands in the air. Jake didn't know who was on whose side. He looked at the huge hole in the White House. It was on the left side of the first floor of the South Portico or round balcony. From a distance it had seemed to be on ground level, but up close, Jake saw a huge staircase on each side of the portico leading up to the first floor balcony. The left staircase was more crowded. Mario pointed right, and Jake nodded

When they reached the balcony, they climbed over the debris and joined the stream of rebels ducking into the hole in the wall of the White House.

CHAPTER 25

When Jake and Mario stepped inside, they found themselves in a large oval room with a very high ceiling. Dim wall lights were still on, with a blinking light over an exit door. Even through the dust and dim light, Jake saw the elegant room was decorated in blue. It had an expensive oval blue rug on the floor. Jake wondered briefly if this was the Oval Office, but when he looked around, there was no presidential desk, or any of the other decor he always saw on television in the Oval Office.

The tank's violent shot had dropped part of the left wall, exposing a square, red room next door. Both rooms seemed to be reception rooms, either for parties or formal meetings. There were two dead men with suits partially covered by the rubble. Both had earpieces and guns, obviously Secret Service standing in the wrong place at the wrong time.

They heard gunfire out in the hall, outside of the blinking light exit door where most of the rebels were headed. He brought the M16 up to his shoulder and prepared to follow them into the hall.

Mario tugged on his sleeve. "No. Follow them." He pointed at a smaller group going right into an adjacent room.

Jake followed. This room was decorated green, just another reception room. Continuing in the same direction, they entered a huge room that consumed the entire east end of the building. He'd seen this room on television, packed with people, used for entertaining heads of state and the like. The most prominent decoration was the de-facto portrait of George Washington, the one of him standing next to a small desk with his right hand extended in welcome. The painting was huge, six or seven feet tall. They heard more gunshots from other parts of the building.

"Where are we going?" Jake asked.

Mario pointed. "Follow them."

They followed the others out of the room and entered into a large corridor that stretched the length of the building. Here they were reunited with the main stream of rebels exiting the blue, oval room where they had started. The stream of men was all heading toward the north door, and Jake's group joined them. They passed through columns, past a grand piano and into the entry hall, where they could look out onto the North Portico where the tanks fired and the battle still raged. The north lawn was completely overrun by the rebels. There was no open grass or ground, just a mass of men and soldiers in hand-to-hand combat.

Some of the men that Jake followed exited the front door to join in the battle, but most of them headed for the stairs. Here the group split, with some of them heading upstairs and others down. Jake and Mario hesitated.

"Which way?" Mario asked.

Jake didn't know. He pointed up. "Family quarters are up."

"Is that where he would be?" Mario asked.

Jake didn't think so. He pictured the president surrounded by Secret Service. No wife or kids. Jake thought about the oval room he had first entered, and his surprise that it had not been the Oval Office. Maybe the president was in the real Oval Office. If so, where was it?

Jake asked a man hesitating at the stairs in a shooting vest, "Where's the Oval Office?"

The man looked at him like he was an idiot, "It's not even in the White House. It's in the West Wing."

Jake wasn't sure whether to believe the man or not. The Oval Office wasn't actually in the White House? He had always thought those windows from the Oval Office looked out the South Portico, under that round balcony. But Jake had definitely heard of the West Wing. They had a television show about it, although he had never watched it. It made some sense that the Oval Office was in the West Wing. To Jake, the West Wing seemed like the place all serious business would be done. It seemed like a likely place for the president to be holed up.

"Where is it?" Jake asked.

"Follow me," the man said and headed down the stairs.

As they descended, the gunfire became louder, and the stairway clogged up. Jake took that as a good sign that they were headed in the right direction, but a bad sign that he was more likely to get killed. He heard another full-auto weapon. But he couldn't see because the men in front of him had stopped on the stairs before they reached the bottom. Rebels lay dead on the fancy red carpet in the corridor below. He could tell, by the way people were hiding, that the gunfire was coming from the right, or west. Could that be where the West Wing was?

A group of men at the bottom of the stairs blindly pointed their weapons around the corner and fired west at the machine gun. Two rebels made a run for it to the room across the hall, but both were shot down in the corridor. As they watched, Jake heard a voice he recognized from behind.

"Make way." The huge guy with long black hair over a Polamalu Steelers jersey pushed past him.

Troy! He was alive.

Troy pulled a grenade out of his pocket and loaded it into Noah's gun. Troy no longer had his own weapon with the bayonet. Did that mean Noah was gone? Jake guessed so and felt sick. Troy held the grenade launcher in his left hand, pointed it around the corner, and fired. He saw Troy's arm propelled backwards from the recoil. Then Troy pulled the gun back out of the gunfire. Jake waited, then heard a loud explosion and felt the heat wave pass over them. His ears popped as well. Best of all, the full-auto went silent.

The men on the stairway started moving again, pouring off the stairs into the corridor. They split, some left, and some right. Jake and Mario went right. That's where the gunfire had come from. That's were Troy went. Right supposedly led to the West Wing.

As they jogged down the corridor, men peeled off to check the rooms on each side. Most of the doors were open, eliminating the need to break them down. Jake remembered the command on the radio to not trash the building. He saw a room on his left with a fancy rug and ornate decorations. Had all the rebels gotten the word?

At the end of the corridor, they stepped around five dead agents in combat gear, and a tripod-mounted gun lying on the ground. Jake followed the others through French doors with frames riddled with bullets. They had left the White House and were in some sort of foyer.

"Where are we?" Mario asked.

Jake looked around and saw double doors on the south and north, exiting the building. There was a door straight ahead, and double doors ahead left heading west.

"Palm room," a guy with a riot shotgun answered. He veered to the doors heading left. "This leads to the colonnade to the Oval Office."

The group split. Jake, Mario, and Troy followed the guy with the shotgun onto the colonnade. When they passed through the doors, they were outside again and engulfed by masses of rebels. Jake recognized the colonnade from pictures and TV, and realized it was the covered outside corridor that led to the West Wing. He'd seen pictures of Reagan and Clinton here. He'd seen pictures of one of the presidents with a dog out here.

The rebels were crowded along the colonnade, but not moving. It looked like they hadn't got inside the West Wing yet.

"Clear out! Make room!" The sound was amplified and came from behind. It was accompanied by the roar of a diesel engine.

Jake looked behind him and saw one of the tanks moving toward them. It was slowed by the mass of rebels.

"Move aside!" The amplified voice said. "We'll open it!"

Jake plastered himself against the wall next to his friends. He touched Troy's arm. "Troy?"

His long-haired friend looked down at him in shock, and then smiled. "Jake. I can't believe it."

Troy was covered in blood, which had been masked by the black jersey. Now Jake saw that the yellow and white numerals, and the yellow stripes on his shoulders, were stained red. Troy's face looked weary as well.

Jake pointed to the gun. "That's Noah's isn't it?"

Troy nodded and grimaced. "He was key to us breaking . . ."

They went quiet for a moment as the tank came past them. It smashed through a rose garden as it went. It could have moved faster, but there were too many rebels, and they had to part to make room.

Jake thought the tank was going to blast a hole in the West Wing like the other one had in the White House itself, but it didn't. It just crept forward until the barrel was in front of the double doors into the building, then it drove forward a little more until the heavy doors broke open.

The crowd didn't even wait for the tank to withdraw before swarming inside. Gunshots were fired, and a few rebels dropped. The men went in with guns blazing. Troy led Jake and Mario in as the tank withdrew. Inside, Jake saw cubicles, a corridor, and office space on his right, and rebels storming through them, but Troy yanked Jake down a hallway. Mario followed. The hall veered left; Troy followed it, and then went left again through a door. They were inside the Oval Office.

CHAPTER 26

The Oval Office was relatively empty, only Jake, Mario, Troy and a half-dozen rebels who had preceded them in. Jake looked up at the presidential seal molded into the ceiling. He looked down at the rug, which was audaciously bold with red, white, and blue stripes coming in like spokes to the presidential seal in the middle. White stars on a blue border formed the outer ring. Jake remembered the media commenting on the rug. It had gotten a lot of press when Singleton designed it during the transition. Although every president was allowed to decorate the Oval Office to his liking, and design a rug for the room, Singleton's design was louder and bolder than any other president in history. Jake wondered how any work could get done in here at all, with such a gaudy color scheme.

Troy and Mario were peering under the president's desk. Jake approached.

Troy stood up and grabbed the corner of the desk, and called out to the others standing around. "Help me with this!"

Jake grabbed a corner of the old desk, along with Mario and four or five other men. They lifted it, and moved it about six feet aside. It was heavy. Underneath the desk was a trap door. Jake was amazed. He had always thought the trap door under the desk was a myth.

"Where does that go?" Jake asked.

Mario lifted a panel, exposing a steep, narrow staircase. He looked up. "No idea."

A guy holding a huge stainless steel revolver standing next to them, said, "Nobody knows. It used to go down to the Secret Service Command Post, but they changed everything after 2010." He motioned around them. "They redesigned the whole underground shelter, and now nobody knows what's down there."

Mario was first down the stairs, everyone else in the room jockeyed to follow him. Troy was about five bodies behind, Jake behind Troy. The stairway was a long descent, longer than a single story.

Troy pulled the encrypted radio from his belt. "Clive, you out there?"

The radio responded. "I'm here. What do you need?"

Jake surged at the sound of Clive's voice. He was alive!

"We're inside the Oval Office. We're going down the trap door. What should we expect?"

Silence.

Troy stopped descending. "Hello?"

"We hear you, son. We don't know what's down there anymore. Call us after you look around."

"10-4," Troy said, and put the radio back on his belt.

As they descended, some bright lights clicked on automatically. When they arrived at the bottom, they found themselves in a perfectly round room with stainless steel walls. No doors. No windows. The presidential seal was painted on the concrete floor, and there were silver dollar sized presidential seals mounted on the steel walls. The room was large, at least twenty feet in diameter

"Now what?" Mario asked.

"I don't know," the man with the revolver said, waving it around. "There's no door knob or keypad or anything."

"Up there!" Troy pointed at the ceiling. "Cameras."

Jake looked up. The whole ceiling seemed to be some sort of see-through material, glass or Plexiglas. Above the glass was the source of the bright lights, modern LED spotlights, very bright and efficient. Above the glass, dispersed around the ceiling, were cameras. They were being watched.

"We can't get through if they don't let us through," Mario said.

"What about explosives?" the guy with the revolver asked.

"You got any?" Troy asked.

"Somebody go get some!" the guy with the revolver said.

In the mean time, the room was becoming crowded as an endless supply of rebels descended the stairs.

The guy with the revolver halted them. "Stop! We can't fit any more people. Go find some explosives!"

Jake considered the room. Obviously, in an emergency, the president descended the stairs, waved to the cameras, and they let him through. But through where? No doors. The men in the room had begun exploring the walls. Jake felt the metal wall, very smooth. He pushed against it, solid, probably metal over concrete. He looked up at the cameras. They were probably watching him right now. What if he were the president? They push a button, and what? Jake scanned all around him. The round room was not constructed as a single tube; it was many pieces, or sections. There were vertical seams every six feet or so.

"One of these has to open," Jake said.

Mario started feeling around next to Jake. "You think?"

Jake looked up at the cameras again. What if the president was under attack, and there was no power? "There's gotta be some sort of latch," Jake said. "Some mechanical release mechanism."

"It's probably on the other side." Mario pointed up at the cameras. "They need to open it when they see him."

"Maybe," Jake said. "But what if the cameras are down?"

"They got backups," Mario responded. "Redundancies."

Jake nodded. "What if there was a nuclear attack, or electromagnetic pulse? What if a huge power surge fried all the electronics? This bunker was designed for all kinds of emergencies, right?"

Mario nodded skeptically.

"What if everyone on the other side was dead, or something went wrong, or they decided not to open the door? If you were the president, wouldn't you want a fail-safe method to gain entry?"

"Okay," Mario said, still not looking convinced.

Jake started running his hands around on the wall. His fingers felt nothing but flat metal. No buttons. No levers. Only the small presidential seal on each metal panel. He moved to his right and moved his hands up and down the vertical seam. Nothing.

Troy came over. "What are you doing?"

Jake looked at his friend. "I'm looking for something to release the door."

Troy pointed at the cameras above. "Don't they need to open it?"

Jake bent down and ran his fingers along the seam between the floor and the wall. "Maybe." He scooted to his left and let his fingers follow the seam all the way to the next panel. "But if I'm right, there's another way."

Troy bent down next to him and started feeling around. "What are we looking for?"

Jake ran his hand up the seam on his left. "Anything."

Mario stood. "Everybody, start feeling around for something—a button, or a lever."

Some of the men looked puzzled, but others started feeling around on the wall, like Jake. Many knelt down and started feeling around on the floor.

Troy tried the radio. "Clive?"

Static.

"Clive?"

No answer.

Troy said, "I'm going back up the stairs to report what's happening."

The guy with the revolver pointed it at the ceiling. "What about the other entrances?"

"What do you mean?" Troy asked.

"I mean not everybody comes down here by crawling through Singleton's legs. This is for emergencies. There's gotta be another way in, probably someplace else in the West Wing. Maybe even a secret passage from the White House."

Troy held up the radio. "I'll ask."

The guys standing on the stairs moved back up to make way.

Jake continued feeling around. He felt around on the concrete floor near the wall. Nothing. Just smooth concrete with paint on it.

"What about these medallions?" Mario said.

All the men looked over at him. He was feeling around one of the presidential seals on the wall. Each panel had its own, so Jake stood up and inspected his. They were mounted just below eye level, right on the face of the metal wall. Or were they? Jake looked at the edge of his and after closer inspection, discovered the medallion, or seal, or whatever it was, seemed to protrude out of the wall. It wasn't mounted on it. It was like the wall had been drilled and the medallion mounted inside. Maybe it wasn't a flat medallion at all, but the face of a column. Maybe it actuated something behind it. Jake pressed his, to see if it would move. Nothing.

263

Jake alerted the others. "This one isn't on the surface, it looks like it goes back through a hole into the wall."

A couple guys poked their noses near Jake, and he pointed at what he had discovered.

"Mine too," the guy with the revolver said.

Soon all the men in the room were spread out inspecting and probing the medallions.

"What if you pull it?" Mario asked.

Jake tried to pull his, but the medallion didn't protrude enough to get a good grip.

"Let me try," a guy standing next to him said.

Jake stepped back and let the man pull, push, and fiddle with it. He made no better progress than Jake, and finally he stepped back and shrugged.

Jake reached back up and tinkered some more, and even tried to rotate, or twist it. The guy standing next to Jake saw what he was doing and relayed it to the others, "Try twisting."

Nothing. Jake stood back and let others try. He looked around the room. This was taking way too long. When they had attacked the White House and overrun the Army troops, there was a feeling of being close. Storming the White House had ratcheted up the tension. Using the tank to break into the West Wing had brought them even closer. When they invaded the Oval Office and descending the stairs, they were hot on his trail. Now this. It seemed like everything had screeched to a halt. Jake looked up at the cameras and wondered who was watching. Secret Service? They were probably laughing. He pictured President Singleton with a bag of popcorn, pointing at the security screens, making jokes about the rebel's inability to get any farther.

When the underground tunnels and bunker were remodeled in 2010, they had obviously made huge improvements. This room was likely one of them. What chance would a bunch of rednecks have, really, to bring down the president of the United States? They had over a million men out there, but what good was it? They were battling against a government with infinite resources at its disposal.

Troy came clomping down the stairs. "They found the other entrance. There's another way down into the bunker from the West Wing."

The men in the room looked up, excited.

Mario pointed at the walls. "Can they open the doors for us?"

Troy shook his head. "It leads down to a room just like this one. They haven't got through yet, either."

Jake felt a pit in his stomach. The others were no closer to getting through than this team of misfits. He looked at the guy with the revolver, and the guy with the bushy mustache. He looked at Troy and Mario, and considered himself. What they really needed down here was some of those PhD puzzle masters from TV, or maybe a few mechanical engineers who could reverse engineer how this room was designed.

Jake saw several men feeling around on the stairs and moved over to see what they were doing. They were sliding their hands around the stairs and rail looking for anything that might open the doors, but Jake had little hope they were going to find anything.

He looked at the presidential seal painted on the floor. He had seen more of these in the last half hour than he had seen in his entire life. They were plastered all over the place in the White House and the West Wing. The two most noticeable were the ones in the Oval Office; the one molded into the ceiling, and the one in the center of Singleton's overly bright rug on the floor. Jake noted the talons of the eagle's feet sticking out from under where the stairs ended. One of the talons held arrows; the other held some sort of flower or plant. It was the same design as on the back of some coins he remembered. Those items in the eagle's talons meant something significant. The arrows had something to do with war. He had no idea what the flower meant, probably peace or something.

Unlike all the other seals he'd seen, this one was cheaper, just painted on the floor. All the others had been fancy, embroidered in carpet, molded, or cast. He looked at the silver medallions protruding from the walls surrounding him. They looked expensive. The eagle on the floor was just paint. And, right now, all these guys were trampling all over it. Jake could see where the paint had been scratched off, near the stairs. Someone probably had to come down here and touch it up every now and then. The scratches came off the side of the stairs in an arc. Jake glanced up the stairs. Did they rotate, or slide? How else would the scratches occur?

He felt his chest tighten. "Clear the stairs!" he yelled.

The men in the room looked at him expectantly.

Jake reached over to the handrail and pushed against it. But there were too many men standing on the stairs, and even more waiting to descend.

"Get off! Too much weight. I think they'll move."

Everyone clamored to get off the stairs. When the stairs were clear, Jake pushed on the handrail to try and rotate it away from him. The stairs rocked. They were definitely not fixed at the floor, but they didn't rotate away. He tried pulling. The stairway moved! It felt like it was on wheels. Men jumped in to push from the other side, but it wasn't necessary. It rotated easily, easy enough for one man to do it.

"There's something down here!" Mario was looking down at the floor now exposed by moving the stairs.

Jake moved to where he could see. It was a round concrete pedestal, about two inches in diameter that extended about an inch above the floor, right out of the eagle's stomach. Everybody in the room knew what it was for. Mario stepped on it, and everyone in the room heard a click.

"Are they open?" Troy asked.

Men started pressing on the walls. Nothing opened.

"Hold it down while we try to open 'em!" somebody yelled.

Mario stepped on it again, but this time Jake did not hear the clicking sound. The men pushed on the walls, but nothing moved. Men leaned into the walls pushing as hard as they could. Jake knew it wouldn't require that much effort once they found the trigger. Jake saw a man reach up and press on the metal medallion on the wall on his side of the room. They all heard a click.

"Hey, something happened!" the man called. "I pressed this, and it moved. It didn't move before when I pressed it."

Men started pushing on the walls near the guy, but nothing opened. Jake stepped over to the wall near him, and pressed the medallion. Nothing. Others pressed medallions around the room. Nothing happened. No clicks.

"Push yours again," the man with the revolver said to the guy whose medallion moved.

He pressed, but nothing moved or clicked.

Mario stepped on the floor button again, and they heard the click.

"Press it again," the revolver guy said.

From behind the stairs, a man called out, "Mine moved and made a clicking sound."

Men pushed on the walls, but nothing opened.

Jake remembered that after Mario stepped on the floor button the first time, it clicked. But it didn't click again until after the button on the wall clicked. It was like the button on the wall had reset the button on the floor. Now another button in the back had clicked.

"Mario, step on it again," Jake said, pointing at the floor.

Mario did, and it clicked. Before Jake could press his medallion, a guy on his right got a click from his.

"Mine clicked!" he called out.

Men leaned into the walls, but still nothing moved.

"Step on that thing again," someone called.

Mario stepped again, and they heard the click.

The first guy called out, "Mine clicked again!"

Jake waved his arms. "Stop. We need to take turns. Let's try them one at time. Okay, step."

They heard a click.

Jake pointed to a guy standing directly in front of the stairwell. "Okay, you."

They heard a click, but men pushing on the wall made no impact.

Jake pointed to the guy just to the right of the last. "Okay, one o'clock."

Same result.

"Two o'clock."

Same result.

Jake was three, but he also had no success.

They worked all the way around the room, one at a time, until the last one, just to the left of straight ahead. When the guy hit his button, they heard another click, but the wall moved. Just an inch. It rotated in on the right side, and out on the left, like it was pivoting in the middle.

The men near the wall wasted no time. They rotated the panel all the way open and began running through. Gunfire erupted and Jake saw men fall into the opening. Guns came up and returned fire. Jake had a bad angle, and couldn't see through the door, so he stayed back, hugging the wall. More rebels rushed down the stairs, and many were shot near the bottom from the open wall.

The Secret Service, or whoever was shooting at them from the other side, had planned the attack well, and the rebels were taking great losses. But there was an infinite supply of rebels coming down the stairs to replace the fallen, and Jake was seeing more and more rebels jump through the opening to the other side.

Then the gunfire stopped coming through the open panel completely. The rebels had them on the run. Jake and his two friends moved toward the opening before Jake remembered the other door.

"Troy?"

The big man stopped. He had been ready to join the fray pouring through the open panel.

"You need to go back up." He pointed to the radio. "You need to tell them how to get through the door. We need them down here."

Troy grimaced, but he had no argument. He was obviously put out to not be able to be on the front lines for the pursuit. Jake watched him hold the radio up, so the guys charging down the stairs could see it.

"I need to go up and pass the word," he yelled.

Jake knew it would take a minute to get the guys off the stairs so Troy could go back up them. Jake didn't wait. He ducked into the line of men passing through the panel.

CHAPTER 27

On the other side of the round room was a wide corridor. There were dead guys on the floor, both rebels and men in suits. Jake and Mario jogged after the others, while gazing at the dead men on the floor.

Jake knew that when Troy relayed the necessary information, rebels would be filtering down from another entrance as well. The underground complex should be swarming with rebels soon.

They rounded a bend, and Jake saw a command center behind glass windows. However, it was completely empty. They had likely abandoned it as soon as the round room was breached. Some of the rebels stormed the room anyway, but Jake and Mario stayed with the main fray.

At the end of the hall, there was a large intersection; straight-ahead were two large elevators, to the left, another wide corridor. Jake wondered if the left corridor led to the other entrance, and a group of secret servicemen guarding it. Maybe they could ambush them from behind. Others must have thought the same, because many men peeled off and took the left corridor. But also at the intersection, on the right, a wide staircase descended below, farther into the underground shelter. Jake, Mario, and most of the others took the stairs. The president of the United States was down there somewhere.

The stairs were wide, at least ten feet across, obviously built to accommodate lots of people descending very quickly. They descended a story to a landing, turned ninety degrees left, then descended again. On the second leg, they heard gunfire from above and guessed the main entrance had been breached and the rebels were engaging the Secret Service. They continued descending until Jake lost track of his directions and how many stories they had descended.

And then the stairs ended. They ended in a huge concrete space with a twenty-foot ceiling. The room was big, as large as the formal entertaining room on the east side of the White House. Straight ahead of the stairs was the door. He had never seen anything like it in real life, only on TV. It was fifteen feet tall and at least that wide, with huge metal cylinders locked into cavities above, below, and on both sides. Jake guessed the door weighed tons, and was closed and opened with hydraulics or powerful motors. Unlike the round room above, he had no expectations of pressing a few hidden buttons to open this door.

Mario reared back in frustration. "Now what?"

Jake felt his energy deflate. He said nothing. He just stared and shook his head. This door was meant to protect the president from all kinds of threats, including a nuclear weapon. They had come this far for nothing.

Footsteps could be heard on the stairs causing Jake and Mario to turn and look back upstairs, and they saw Troy descending with a crowd of rebels. Jake and Mario moved past other men toward their long-haired friend.

"We need to go back up," Jake pointed up, "and tell them."

Troy held the radio to his mouth. "Can you hear me?"

Jake pointed up. "If they couldn't hear you from the round room, they can't hear you from here."

The radio responded. "We can hear you. What do you see?"

Troy answered Jake's unasked question. "They put guys down the hole with radios, to relay the messages through."

Troy responded to the radio. "We got a huge metal shelter door like you said. It's a big one."

The radio responded "10-4. I'll relay the message."

Jake then heard the guy on the other end of the radio repeat Troy's description of the metal door. Then they waited.

"We expected a door like this?" Mario asked.

Troy nodded. "Absolutely. The data on this new shelter was sketchy. But somewhere, someplace, they knew we would end up at a door like this."

Jake hardly dared to hope. "So, we can open it?"

Troy shrugged. "I hope so. I don't know how. But I think they have a plan." He motioned above him with his thumb. "I know they talked about it. We'll have to wait and see."

Jake, Mario, and Troy waited. Rebels kept descending the stairs until no more could fit. Mario motioned over by the wall where the stairs ended, and Jake and Troy followed him.

Soon Troy's radio blared, "Clear the room! They're bringing the explosives down now."

Jake looked at the room packed with rebels and wondered how they were expected to accomplish that task. He told Troy, "Tell them not to send any more down here."

Troy relayed the message.

Jake and his friends began passing the word that everyone needed to start hiking back up the stairs because of the explosives. There was a lot of grumbling, but the crowd began retreating up the stairs. Somebody discovered the two huge elevators worked, so many of the men ascended in them. After several trips, the doors of the elevators opened and Jake saw a demolition team. There were at least a dozen of them, and they hefted at least that many heavy boxes off the elevator. Their leader was a small skinny man, dressed in coveralls with a ratty goatee and thick glasses.

He looked over at Troy. "You Troy?"

Troy walked toward him. "How'd you know?"

"You're the only big guy with hair and a Steelers jersey that I see."

Troy smiled. "What do you guys need?"

They shook hands. "I'm Bruce. We'll need everybody out of here." He looked around. "We'll set the charges. It'll take us a while."

Jake asked. "How far do we need to go? Will it be a big explosion?" He wondered if they would need to exit the shelter completely, back up into the West Wing.

Bruce looked at him over the thick glasses. "It's not really an explosion per se. These are cutting charges. They're used to cut metal, like for ship demolition. When we detonate, the charges will basically melt right through that door in a few seconds."

Mario asked, "What about the heat? How far do we need to be away from that?"

Bruce nodded, and looked up the stairs. "A couple stories ought to do it."

Jake asked. "How long before you detonate?"

Bruce glanced at his team, who were inspecting the door as they waited for his instructions. "Geez. They're waiting for me. I gotta go." He turned and walked away from them.

Jake watched as they started unpacking the boxes. The men were forming what looked like gray putty in strips around the perimeter of the door. Bruce pointed instructions to them.

The elevator dinged, and when the doors opened, Jake saw Clive walk out with Generals Bowen and Toolson. Clive's face stretched into a wide smile when he saw Jake. Jake took a few steps toward the man and reached out his hand to shake. But Clive hugged him again.

"I can't believe you're down here. When I promised Monica I'd look after you, I pictured you behind me. I never dreamed you'd be. . ." He motioned at the blast door, ". . . on the front lines." He stepped back and appraised Jake. "Are you okay?"

Jake thought about all the close calls he'd had. He thought about men getting shot who were standing right next to him. He thought about the tank firing on him and Mario when they were hiding behind the fountain, and the marble raining down on them. "No. I'm okay. I've been lucky."

Clive nodded his head. "Yeah! I'd say you've had a guardian angel looking over you."

"That would be me," Mario said.

Clive pointed at him and laughed. "I believe it."

"How long is this supposed to take?" General Toolson asked, pointing at the demolition team.

Troy shrugged. "Jake asked the skinny one over there in charge," he pointed, "but he didn't really give us an answer."

Toolson seemed to consider that. "Well, we should probably just let them do what they need to do."

* * *

The demolition team finished by sticking detonators into the plastic explosives they had formed around the door. Jake noticed that Bruce's team had put the putty on the cylinders as well, the ones that locked the door into the wall. The demolition team finally finished, and they started retreating up the stairs.

"That's our cue to go," Clive said.

"I wish I could watch," Mario said.

"You'd be blind if you did," Troy said.

Clive, Troy, Mario, Jake, and General Bowen began the hike back up. General Toolson had taken the elevator back up. They had decided a few minutes before that he should be farther away from the blast just in case the heat radiated higher up the stairs than projected.

They hiked up and up, and with each step Jake realized that it must be well after midnight. He was starting to feel the fatigue of the night before in the Suburban, the morning of barrier battles, an afternoon in the hot sun, then a night of heavy battle.

After what seemed like at least three stories of ascent, Bruce stopped them.

"That should be enough."

He took out the remote detonator, inserted a key, which illuminated a light and sounded a buzzer, then pressed a button. A moment later, they heard loud cracking sounds, like a terrible impact of two huge metal objects, then a pounding impact of something heavy falling. Jake guessed the door was down.

A hot wind passed over them that made Jake panic, like he would be roasted, but the heat gradually dissipated.

Rebels with more energy than Jake charged past him down the stairs. Jake and his friends followed. The farther they descended, the hotter the air became, until it was almost as hot as the wave. When the stairs neared the bottom, the air was filled with smoke and concrete dust. Mario led them into the large room, and they hugged the right wall where it seemed slightly cooler. Gunshots erupted as rebels engaged Secret Service on the other side of the door. Through the smoke, Jake could see the door had fallen outward, and he could see light from inside the bunker. Jake saw a rebel try to climb over the door, but he fell back screaming and clutching his leg.

"The door's still hot!" Mario yelled over the gunshots.

Jake realized it had just been melted less than a minute before. As if in answer to his thoughts, they were all doused in a spray of cold water. Either the temperature or the smoke had tripped some kind of fire alarm and turned on ceiling sprinklers. Steam rose from the hot blast door in a hiss as the spray of cold water cooled the hot metal. The cold water was a lifesaver, as Jake had reached the point of not tolerating the heat any longer. Gunfire stopped, and Jake guessed the Secret Service had retreated to another room.

They waited with water running down their faces and watched other rebels test the door's temperature. It wasn't long before someone jumped up on the door, and the final invasion began. Jake and Troy followed them. Just inside on the left was another command center, with computer screens and desks. It was empty, as was the first, and Jake didn't think the computer geeks would be happy with the water damage from the sprinklers. Jake was just behind his friends running down the hallway when he stumbled over a body on the floor. He stopped and looked down at a man in a suit, Secret Service. It looked like he had taken a bullet in the gut. Jake tried to move on, but the man clamped his hand hard on Jake's ankle.

Jake jerked in surprise and tried to pull his leg free, but the man had a death grip on him. His eyes were wide and his teeth were clenched. He blinked the water from his eyes.

Jake reached down with his right hand to his holster and pulled out the Hi-Power.

"No choice! So sorry." the man whispered in agony.

Jake realized the man meant no harm, and holstered his weapon.

His words were hard to understand. "Sworn to protect . . . even if . . . scumbag."

Jake waited. This guy obviously had regrets. The agent's face contorted in pain. His eyes rolled up, and Jake thought he was passing out, and then he recovered and refocused on Jake. Jake felt his grip clench even tighter.

"Where are they?" Jake asked. "How do we get him?"

The man looked at Jake, confused. He looked as if he had lost his train of thought in mid-sentence.

Jake leaned down and touched his face. "Where's Singleton?"

The man gasped a single-word answer. The answer shocked Jake. He never would have guessed it in a million years. He looked up at the rebels running past him into the bunker. They didn't even suspect. He had to tell them.

He looked back down at the Secret Service agent. His eyes were glassy now, and the grip had slackened. Jake removed the man's hand, and placed it on his stomach. He took a last look at the man, middle-aged, short hair, handsome face, and a wedding band. "Sworn to protect, even the scumbags," the agent had said.

Jake stood, checked the safety on his M16, and joined the other men jogging into the bunker. He hurried to rejoin his friends.

CHAPTER 28

After Jake passed the command center and the Secret Service agent with the death grip, he exited the sprinklers. Maybe they were isolated to the bunker entryway. The bunker was a strange combination of a fancy home mixed with an office building. There were large conference rooms, offices, and cubicles on one side, and a kitchen, dining rooms, TV rooms, a library, and a computer center on the other.

A dozen cooks and other staff held their hands up in surrender in the kitchen, and some rebels moved to cover them. Moving farther into the space, there were bedrooms, including a wing of rooms much fancier, probably for the president's family. There was a huge stockroom with shelves full of food and supplies. Jake heard the rebels yelling just ahead.

"Hands up!"

Everyone stopped. In the back of the shelter, there were two large rooms. On the right, a large situation room with a huge conference table, and on the left a perfect replica of the Oval Office. Both rooms were stuffed with people. Secret Service agents formed human shields in front of all the politicians and their families. The agents had their hands in the air. Jake guessed they were smart enough to know that they were cornered, and returning fire would mean too many casualties, including, possibly, the president himself.

Jake saw the face of Singleton, standing behind the desk in the Oval Office. He had at least forty men in front of him. Also, in the back of the pack were a few of the president's staff, including his chief of staff, Secretary of Defense, Attorney General, and Secretary of State. No vice president. Jake scanned the people in the room on the right in the situation room. He saw several women in the back, although they were shorter and harder to see behind the agents. He guessed most of these were families of the politicians or the president.

Jake jostled through the rebels until he was next to Mario.

"They want me." Singleton called out, and he walked forward with his hands up. "I'll surrender now if you promise not to harm the others."

The Secret Service parted, and let him through.

"If I go with you, will you retreat peacefully, and let Washington recover from this shameful episode?"

Jake looked at the man, turning himself over honorably to a bunch of rebels. Sacrificing himself for the good of his country. Putting the good of his country above himself. It didn't feel right. He felt uneasy as he watched this display of bravery from a man he knew to be so self-serving.

Jake let his eyes wander through the crowd. He looked at the women and children, all terrified. He looked at the Secret Service Agents, all angry. He looked at the politicians, some scared, some disgusted. How did they feel about letting their president fall on the sword for them? Some of the women looked grateful.

"We need all the Secret Service to throw down your weapons, and lay prone on the ground with your hands over your head." It was General Bowen's voice.

"Why, General?" Singleton said. "I'm who you want. Just take me and leave. There's no need for any more positioning. You came for me, and I'm letting you have me."

General Bowen hesitated. He seemed to be thinking about what to do.

Jake scanned the audience again. He looked at the faces of the Secret Service. There were men with blond hair, black hair, and no hair. They were of all sizes. A few wore sunglasses, even in the bunker, which was curious. He looked them over closely. He looked at the women in the back. There were a few taller ones. One had a rough face, and too much makeup.

"General, why make this more complicated than it needs to be? You can take me and withdraw, and we can avoid endangering any of these innocent people." He motioned to the women in the situation room.

General Bowen said, "All right, come forward. Over here."

The Secret Service let the president go. They didn't budge. They just let him walk past them and right up to General Bowen. Jake heard handcuffs click onto the Singleton's wrists. Jake now knew the agent that had gripped his leg was right. He'd told Jake with his last breath. And it was true. It was the only possible answer. Letting the president surrender was completely against everything the agents stood for. That alone made Jake know it was all a scam. There was no way a hundred Secret Service agents would stand down while the president turned himself over to a lynch mob.

"Don't do it!" Jake called out.

General Bowen looked over his shoulder to see who had said the words. The Secret Service had come to high alert. No guns came up, but that was only a moment away.

"What's wrong, Jake?" It was Clive's voice.

Jake pointed at the president. "He's a fake, a decoy!"

Now the guns did come up, on both sides. No one fired, but a hundred guns were aimed in both directions with itchy trigger fingers all around.

"That's crazy!" The president said, "Are you nuts? You're gonna believe that idiot?" He pointed at Jake.

"Jake?" Clive asked.

Jake didn't look at Clive or the fake Singleton. He was scanning the crowd through the sight of the M16. He moved the barrel from one person to another, looking for anyone that looked like Singleton. He could have his hair dyed, or makeup. He could be dressed as a woman or who knows what else.

"Don't you recognize me?" Singleton argued.

Jake saw motion down at the feet of the agents in the situation room. Was that just someone's feet, or was someone down there?

He aimed the M16 where he had seen movement. "Over there! Under the table."

The president's voice got louder. "That's ridiculous! There's nobody down there. Take me."

His voice had changed as he tried harder to convince them. It was higher, and less commanding. It was more desperate. It sounded less like the real Singleton.

The Secret Service in the Situation Room huddled closer together in front of the table where Jake's gun was pointing.

"Stand aside," General Bowen said. "So we can see what's down there." He motioned the Secret Service to part.

"Can't do that," one of the agents said. And he pointed his weapon at the general.

The fake Singleton called, "What difference does it make? I'm here, and I'm volunteering."

But everyone in the room on both sides now knew the man was a fake. The Secret Service's actions left no doubt. They'd stood aside as the decoy surrendered, but they had drawn guns and went to high alert to protect whoever was under the table.

Bowen stayed calm, even with guns pointed at his head. "Agent, I respect what you're trying to do." He motioned behind him at the mass of rebels. "But we have the numbers now, and resisting is just going to get more people killed. The decoy was right. Now, please stand aside."

The fake president's voice rose until it didn't resemble Singleton at all. "I'm him. What do you care who's under the table?"

"Shut up!" one of the rebels shouted. "Shut the hell up!" He motioned like he was going to club the fake with his rifle.

The fake cowered, and his shoulders slumped in defeat.

"Now lower your weapons," General Bowen coaxed. "You're not going to save anyone if this gets ugly, including Singleton."

A few of the agents lowered their guns.

"That's it. You're in a dilemma here," Bowen said gently. "You're sworn to protect, but you're grossly outnumbered and outgunned. The best way to assure the president isn't harmed, and these civilians aren't hurt, is to turn him over. Doesn't seem logical, but it is."

A few more guns were lowered.

The general spoke down to whoever was under the table. "Now stand up, so we can get a look at you."

The real Singleton's voice came from under the table. "Shoot them! You all took an oath. Now pull the trigger!"

Jake saw the conflict in many of the agents' eyes. A few guns came back up.

General Bowen held out his hands. "Please don't. He's not thinking straight. He's not thinking of the final—"

"Kill them, Carlo. What the hell am I paying you for?"

A man standing in the back stepped forward. He lifted a pistol and started firing. The first shot took down General Bowen. He got off about three more before a volley of bullets cut him down, including one from Jake's M16. The women scattered away from him, screaming.

The Secret Service, miraculously, did not start firing, so when the man named Carlo went down, the firing stopped. The room went quiet except for the women sobbing.

Jake had the M16 sighted on the agent who had said earlier he couldn't step aside, but the agent didn't look ready to pull his trigger. Clive stepped forward from behind and knelt down by the general. Jake glanced down, but the general had a hole in his forehead. He was dead. Jake's eyes returned to the Secret Service agent, via the M16's peep sight.

Clive stood up. "Okay, you all got a taste of Singleton and his hit men. His guy killed the general on his order. You saw it with your own eyes. He's killed others. Are you still willing to take a bullet for this slime ball?"

More guns came down. Only about ten agents still had weapons aimed at the rebels.

Clive looked at the remaining agents. "It's just you guys now. Everyone else has figured it out. We could gun you down right now. We got plenty of firepower. But I don't want to. The plan here is to get this criminal out of our government and try to get the country back on its wheels. Unfortunately, the congressmen we all elected didn't have the guts, or the ethics, to do it the right way. So, we had to do it. We haven't given up on the Constitution, or the laws of the land. But we had to remove someone who did. We hope and pray that this episode will wake up Americans, and hopefully, they'll think twice about who they send to Washington, and what kind of shenanigans they tolerate." Clive hesitated. "So, I'm asking you, as fellow Americans, please step aside and let us take this man peacefully. We've got a lot of work to do, together."

The agents' guns came down slowly. Jake saw tears in the eyes of one of the agents, just before he lowered his weapon.

"What are you doing? You're supposed to be protecting me!" Singleton screamed.

Jake saw the agent with tears turn his head, so he didn't have to look at the president. As the other agents parted, they saw Singleton, on his hands and knees on the floor. His eyes were blazing. Jake lowered the M16, engaged the safety, and joined a few others as they reached under the table and grabbed the president of the United States.

EPILOGUE

Two months had passed since the Second Revolution. Jake and Monica had moved into his small row house. It was very different than Jake's first marriage. He couldn't wait to get home from work every night to see her. She seemed to feel the same way about him. They had trouble keeping their hands off each other. Some of Jake's friends had been surprised that Jake had married a woman so suddenly, after only knowing her for a couple weeks. But they all liked her.

The country had gone through some major turmoil. Over ten thousand Americans had died in the Second Revolution, more than Iraq and Afghanistan combined. The stock market crashed the day after. Rioting had continued around the country. Some riots were aimed at retrieving more confiscated guns, but there were also some raids of police stations and armories, with rebels stealing law enforcement weapons. In California, a dozen state senators who called for more gun control had been tarred and feathered. In Chicago, rival gangs had declared war in the streets with over a hundred dead.

The country was divided. About half supported the removal of Singleton, and half thought it was a travesty. Vice President Jonas was sworn in as the new president of the United States, and he vowed to restore the country to stability as soon as possible. But some felt he was as corrupt as Singleton and were demanding his resignation.

Although the country was terribly divided on the necessity of the revolution, the whole country was united in wondering where

President Singleton was and what had happened to him. President Jonas and the Attorney General had warned the rebels that President Singleton should be surrendered immediately or whoever was holding him would be hanged.

The media, meanwhile, had completely turned on Singleton. Facts were emerging almost every day regarding corruption in his office. Carlo Rinaldi, the hit man who shot General Bowen, was found to have numerous ties to mob hits over the years, but no convictions. There were five additional ex-mobsters discovered in various White House staff positions. Two were missing, but the other three had been taken into custody by the FBI. One of the missing mobsters had been tied to another mobster in Atlanta who had rented a black sedan the night before the mayor's hit-and-run death. The rental car was never returned. The media called that a revelation of circumstantial evidence that Singleton had ordered the hit.

Additionally, an investigation had been launched in the death of President Swenson, the president that Singleton had replaced. Many were now speculating he had been poisoned. Investigators had found anomalies in the autopsy reports, leading some to think the reports had been falsified. There was talk about exhuming the remains to repeat the tests and search for indications of poisoning. However, there was much opposition to digging up an ex-president's body.

Two weeks before, after many calls for Singleton's return, a preacher in Washington D.C. stepped forward. He held a press conference and read the following statement over national news:

"My name is Reverend Paul Revere. Yes, the same name as the famous patriot. I have not physically seen the president since he was taken, nor do I know who is hiding him or where. But this morning, however, I participated in an Internet video call where I saw and talked to former President Singleton. In my judgment, he is unharmed, and is not suffering from any malnourishment, physical, or emotional abuse." He looked up at the cameras. "He wasn't happy, but he looked good. The people who are holding him refused to identify themselves, but they said they are pleased with how the investigations are progressing, and with the evidence-gathering taking place regarding the president's accused crimes, including the murders of the politicians and the reporter. They are also pleased that the death of former President Swenson is being investigated and are anxious to hear what is found."

He looked up at the cameras. "They said they'll return him when they feel enough critical evidence has been collected and other collaborators have been identified and captured so he can stand trial for murder and treason. They said it would be interesting for all Americans when, for the first time in the history of our country, a sitting president is executed.

They told me that they might use me to communicate occasionally, as long as the government allows that possibility and doesn't suffocate me to the point they aren't able to provide me updated messages. In that case, they will choose other spokesmen as necessary."

There had been a huge reaction after the reverend's statement. Some accused him of lying. Some accused him of being one of the kidnappers. He was investigated thoroughly by the FBI, including his Internet history, but they found he was contacted by an untraceable IP address that no longer existed. In the mean time, his congregation had mushroomed since the press conference.

The media, many politicians, and about a third of the population were flabbergasted that the president was being held captive. They demanded his immediate return and demanded gun militias nationwide be raided to find him. Another third of the population were disgusted with the latest findings on Singleton. They were more than happy he was being held someplace. Some hoped he was being tortured. The last third of the population seemed embarrassed by Singleton and wanted the problem to just go away. Some said they hoped Singleton was never heard from again.

Nationwide the re-elections and appointments for the murdered congressmen had been closely watched. The political awareness of the population seemed to have gone sky high. In Wisconsin, the citizens were threatening to impeach their governor for appointing a replacement for the murdered Senator Banister. Apparently the voters didn't like the replacement.

Aside from replacing the murdered politicians and investigating Singleton, there was yet another debate raging in Washington. The country had been legislating against guns and other weapons for years in spite of the Second Amendment. California and New York had almost completely prohibited any kind of weapon that could be used to fight against other people, including handguns, semi-automatic rifles, grenades, or full-auto weapons. The Second Revolution had shown the necessity for such weapons, and now some congressmen were recommending what they called "Pro-Assault Weapon Legislation," which was intended to restore national rights to own handguns, assault weapons, or any other weapon necessary for combat, and would prevent states or local governments from restricting them. Some were suggesting the legislation should include anti-tank weapons and bombs up to certain tonnages. Needless to say, the proposed legislation was highly controversial.

Additionally, there had been a surprisingly strong push for term limits for the House and Senate to rid the government of career politicians. The media was finally reporting that the population had overwhelmingly demanded term limits for years, but the politicians had ignored them. Retirement plans for politicians were also being questioned, as were preferred medical benefits. It seemed Americans didn't want their representatives being elected for life and then living the life of luxury after they retired. But statistics showed that incumbents almost always won elections, even after scandals. Something had to be done.

One thing Jake hadn't found time for since the revolution was to go shooting. In fact, after all the craziness and near-death experiences, he hadn't really had the desire. He still hadn't actually fired the Browning Hi-Power, and he had no idea whether he could hit anything with it. He had suggested they go to the range, but Monica had a better idea.

Clive had invited them to dinner at the club, so they had made the drive north from Pittsburgh after work. It was now late October and the leaves were turning bright yellows, reds, and oranges. As Jake drove the pickup down the small country road, he saw in his rear-view mirror the leaves moving in his wake. Ahead, the canopies of the trees had grown together over the road, making a colorful tunnel. Monica was tucked against him with her hand on his.

"It's that one," she said, pointing to the turnoff.

Like last time, Jake was hopelessly lost. But he recognized the lane after turning onto it. As before, he stopped at the security gate and keypad.

"Now that we're married, can you trust me with the code?"

She leaned across him, as she had done before, and punched in the code herself. When she was done, she held up two fingers. "I told you, two babies first."

"What if I want to come out here with the guys sometime? You know, when you're too busy changing diapers."

She gave him a look.

He drove through the open gate. "You don't expect me to drop everything, and just hang out with you and the baby, do ya? I gotta live a little."

She ignored him.

Jake marveled at the lodge again as they approached. He was glad they had come in the fall, as the colors made the log edifice seem even more luxurious. After they had parked, Jake got out of the truck and Monica slid out after him, exiting on his side.

She took his hand, and they walked up the stairs and over the large porch. Jake opened the door for her, and they went inside. Jake had forgotten how impressive the lodge was as they walked past the sitting area to the open eating area in the back. Jake again admired the floor to ceiling windows and rustic decorations. Clive waved them to a table by the window. Besides Clive, there were four other men at the table. Jake recognized one of them immediately. He was a big, muscular guy with long black hair. Troy!

As they walked closer, Jake recognized the other men. Two generals sat next to Clive, General Jolley, and General Toolson. The other man was Mario. Jake had seen none of these people since the revolution. Troy and Mario stood, and Jake embraced each of them in a long hug. Jake felt they now formed a special brotherhood, and he wasn't sure it would ever go away. But seeing them also reminded him of Noah, and Mason, who were killed in Washington. They were also included in his brotherhood feelings.

When Jake introduced Monica to his fellow rebels, Troy shook her hand, but Mario made a big production of kissing it.

Clive pointed to the two generals. "I'm sure you remember Generals Jolley and Toolson."

Jake nodded to both men, again being reminded of another hero who didn't make it, General Bowen. The two men nodded back at Jake.

Clive invited everyone to sit, but he remained standing. He looked at Jake. "This worked out well. The generals had already planned to visit the lodge tonight. And when I invited you," he pointed at Jake, "I asked Troy and Mario if they could join us."

He motioned to all three rebels. "We'd like to thank all of you for what you did for the United States of America. We still have major problems, but with the latest news coming out of Washington, the country is finally learning how bad it was. We're fairly sure that fifty years from now, historians will look back on the Second Revolution as a defining event in American history. When the dust settles you traitors might even be recognized as patriots."

Clive wiped his eye. "I never would have guessed, when our Suburban left Pittsburgh, that us seven men, from the millions of others, would play such an integral part in the victory."

He focused on Jake. "And to my son-in-law—I don't know what happened." He motioned to Troy and Mario. "These guys were soldiers. I had high expectations of them. But you, you were a kid, inexperienced, untrained. I didn't want you to go, but it must have been God's plan, because look what happened. You came. But not only that, you were indispensable. We couldn't have done it without you. Figuring out how to open the underground barrier was key. Recognizing the president had a decoy was brilliant. Not to mention your insight that helped us set the timing on attack day."

Jake thought about his impact and considered most of it luck, or help from above. He could take no personal credit for any of the contributions mentioned. He had never been good with puzzles, so he still didn't understand how he'd been able to figure out the triggers and buttons to open the door.

Clive continued, "But as I look at you now, married to my daughter, I'm amazed. If I try to add up the events, and factor in your accounts of people dying around you, I can't help but think you were part of God's plan. You were an instrument in his hands. I've talked to these two soldiers about you. Neither one considers himself that religious. But neither can deny that it was more than luck that carried you. There were too many coincidences."

Clive looked at the two generals as if he had been caught rambling, and then returned his gaze to the others. "Look, if you guys were soldiers in a real war, we would be handing out medals tonight, to all of you. Your country owes you a great debt. And I thank you, from the bottom of my heart."

Clive reached out, and first shook hands, then embraced Jake, Troy, and Mario. The generals also stood, and shook hands with all three.

"I hope we don't get hanged as traitors," Mario said jokingly.

As they finished with the congratulations, Clive spoke, "I hope you don't mind if we're joined for dinner by one other guest."

Jake shrugged. He saw similar gestures from Troy and Mario. He guessed it was someone else involved in the Second Revolution, but couldn't guess who. Maybe one of the other generals he hadn't met?

Clive waved at the staff, and they came over and set another place at the table, borrowing a chair from another. The new guest would be sitting between Jake and Troy.

"It looks like the food is ready," Clive announced.

They all sat as the staff brought out food on large serving platters. They were all given prime rib with a baked potato and steamed vegetables.

Jake was turning back the foil on his baked potato and inserting a few slices of butter, when the table went silent. Jake noticed Clive and the generals were staring directly behind him. Jake turned his head around to see if the other guest had arrived.

From a room near the kitchen, a dignified man approached their table flanked on each hip by escorts carrying AR-15s. It was a face Jake had seen on television multiple times. It was a face he had seen two months ago, up close—a face he had studied as he compared it to a decoy. Singleton!

The former president of the United States sat next to Jake just as a plate of prime rib was set in front of him. The two escorts stood behind him.

Singleton immediately cut into his steak and took a bite. He savored the taste, actually closing his eyes while he chewed. "About damn time you people served me steak."

Jake noticed the generals did not take their eyes off him.

The former president took a drink then glanced over at Jake, finally recognizing him. They locked eyes. Singleton's eyes opened wide, and he pointed his fork at Jake. "You're him!"

AUTHOR NOTES

Back when I lived in California, even before I finished my first book, Wet Desert, I had already been thinking about this story. It was a frustrating story, the story about someone victimized by violent crime, who wanted a gun to defend himself. I actually wrote a couple chapters. The working name of the book was Placid Avenue, as in violent things sometimes happen on seemingly peaceful streets. The book would cover the frustrations of the protagonist as he tried to navigate the crazy gun laws in California. I envisioned the protagonist using his gun to defend himself, resulting in the police coming after him, as if he were the criminal instead of the people he was defending himself from.

I didn't have any idea how it would end. I was kind of stuck. So, I concentrated on finishing my first book and getting it published. Placid Avenue was shelved. When my first book was done, everyone asked if there would be a sequel. My immediate answer was no, but I investigated other similar stories, and even wrote a few chapters of another book about terrorists.

During this period I had a job that drained me emotionally and left little creativity to write. I wondered if my first book would be my only book. Then in 2010, I was laid off on Friday the thirteenth. It was like a weight off my shoulders. I wasn't depressed at all, and I quickly began writing all day during my unemployed time. My neighbors and family were worried about my lack of a job, but I wasn't. By then I had a vision of how the story would end, and I realized it needed to take place in a city near Washington D.C. Being from the west, with little experience with cities in the east, I chose Pittsburgh because I had been a die-hard Steelers fan since mid-season 1972 when Franco was a rookie. I was only eleven years old when I watched the Immaculate Reception live on TV.

Since I had never been to Pittsburgh, I used frequent flyer miles and flew to da-Burgh for a few days in 2010. My goal was to blend in and get the feel of the place. The Steelers were out of town for a

Monday night game. But that was okay, because I couldn't afford a ticket anyway. Instead I cruised in and out of bars on Carson Street trying to blend in with Steelers Nation. I was hoping to see some old steel workers with hard hats, but they were gone and the crowd was young. I had a great time and tried to absorb the atmosphere.

I was unemployed for only three months before I was offered a great new job in late 2010. So, I was back at work with no energy left to write, and this book, with only about 75 pages written, was back on the shelf. I somewhat blamed my wife and told everyone she prayed me back to work before I could finish the book.

Then after the 2012 presidential election, the country panicked and bought over 30 million guns. I knew the timing was perfect for this book, and I tried to write in the mornings before work. Then, unthinkably, I lost my job again, which seems to be my lot in life. Again my neighbors thought I was crazy, but I rejoiced at the job loss and wrote. It was my chance to finish the Second Revolution. I set a goal to write ten pages a day. I didn't achieve that, but I knocked the whole first draft out in a little over two months.

When people read this, they are going to ask whether it was written about a specific president, and if I am personally recommending a revolution to throw him out. The answer is no. I do not believe things are bad enough in America for the revolution in my story, but I do believe that one is possible in our future. I think the government has grown into a bureaucratical nightmare, with too many lawyers creating an impenetrable maze of laws and regulations. I think it is ripe for a dirty president to take advantage. I think if America doesn't wise up, we are headed in that direction. Sorry for the gloom and doom.

Anyway, many helped with my story. The following individuals provided important insight. Four members of my Kaysville Critique group, Jenny Moore, Gaynell Parker, Susan Tejan, and Cindy Hogan reviewed the manuscript and suggested important changes in characters and plot. Spencer Watts and Brandt Gray were my eyes and ears in Pittsburgh. They read the manuscript and offered valuable suggestions. My agent, Erica, spotted a few glaring issues immediately, and gave me feedback. My copyeditor, Charity West, went above and beyond copyediting, recommending major surgery in a couple places, which I agreed with. My wife Becca and my mother Joan, both read it multiple times and found various problems that needed fixing. Bottom line: My writing relies heavily on the critical input of my friends.

Additionally, please remember that this book is a work of fiction. I'm sure it wouldn't be near as easy to storm the White House and capture the president as I have depicted here, and that's probably a good thing. Note: My research could take me only so far into White House security. Nobody was going to tell me how to extract the president from his bunker. So, once the story went down the stairs under the Oval Office, we entered fantasyland. All of that is fictional, as is the gun club north of Pittsburgh and the gun range in the old steel mill, and a bunch of other things. There are no real people in the story either. So, if you thought I was writing about you, you're wrong.

What will be the effect of this story? Hopefully it won't cause people to shoot at the police or politicians. But hopefully it makes Americans think about how bad it could get if we don't sit up and stop what's happening in both our federal and local governments. And hopefully, we don't send a president to Washington as corrupt as Singleton, who could turn our own government against us. Aggressive term limits for the House and Senate, along with the elimination of retirement plans, would go a long way toward ridding the government of career politicians.

By the way, I probably need to apologize to my readers. I've now written a novel about pro-gunners overthrowing the government, and one about an engineer chasing an eco-terrorist down the Colorado River. What do those books have in common with each other? Probably nothing, other than they both tickled my fancy at the time. Will my audience crossover? Unknown. Maybe, I should stick with one genre to keep my audience happy. Or, maybe not. What's next? Well, you know I used to be a SCUBA instructor. Maybe we'll go underwater for the next book.

Thanks for reading.

Gary Hansen
gary-hansen.com

P.S. If you liked The Second Revolution, please post a review online. New authors depend on reviews to get noticed.

Also from Gary Hansen

WET DESERT

Whitney Award Finalist - Best Novel by New Author

"It reminded me a great deal of reading a Tom Clancy novel, but it is faster paced and the device doesn't slow down the story. But like Clancy, the author welds together diverse story lines and characters into one highly suspenseful tale that has the reader reluctant to miss a word or to set the book down." -- Meridian Magazine

"Wet Desert was an exciting novel, I relished the entire book. It was a supremely engaging story with a lyrically drawn sense of place. This is a stellar debut." -- Once Upon a Crime, Minneapolis, MN.

"I could tell you this is a fast paced page turner. I could also suggest that through most of this book you will find yourself on the edge of your seat, but it would not do justice to this spine tingling thriller. I recommend one last trip down a Colorado River you have never before experienced." -- Sam Weller's Zion Bookstore

"Wet Desert is a fast paced book that takes place over a three day period. Descriptions of the collapsing dams and muddy, fast flowing water keep the reader involved and turning pages. The reader watches the damage happen while the long-term repercussions are discussed and illustrated. This book by a first time author is worth looking into." -- Mysterious Galaxy, San Diego, CA

"Wet Desert succeeds in creating gripping suspense while making readers realize that even a behemoth like Glen Canyon Dam cannot be taken for granted. The book keeps you in suspense throughout by using a local "sacred cow" to grab our attention and not let go." -- The Lake Powell Chronicle

"I was overwhelmed with the magnitude of the river and the force of the water. The damage to the dams down river, the towns, farms and the California aquifer are unbelievable, and Hansen makes you feel that you are right there." -- Southern Utah News